PRIMAL KILL

THE ORDER OF VAMPIRES
BOOK FIVE

LYDIA MICHAELS

For my beautiful cubby, Devyn.
#WolfPack

SOUNDTRACK
Enjoy the Music that Inspired Primal Kill
Click here to listen to the series playlist on
Spotify.

Black Magic Woman by VCTRYS
It's My Life by Bon Jovi
Go Your Own Way by Fleetwood Mac
Songbird by Eva Cassidy
Zombie by The Cranberries
Wings by Birdie
Kill of the Night by Gin Wigmore
Three Little Birds by Kacey Musgraves
Wolves Without Teeth by Of Monsters and Men
Love, Reign o'er Me by Pearl Jam
Can You See Me In The Dark by Halestorm & I
Prevail
No Light, No Light by Florence + The Machine
As It Was by Harry Styles
Hungry Like the Wolf by Duran Duran

PROLOGUE

Long After 1730...
    Time has lost all meaning...
    Life is only pain...
Death is the only relief...

CERBERUS MADDOX XI GROWLED, choking on dust and rubble, entombed by the crushing weight of clay-hardened earth that slowly compacted with time. Roots and gravel bound his mutilated body—enough to trap, paralyze, suffocate, and kill him again and again.

Unsure how long he'd been suffering or how many times he'd died only to return to this eternal torture, Cerberus clung to what was left of his decaying sanity, though his mind fragmented long ago. Immortality had no power here, and longevity had become a curse. With no blood to alleviate the endless pain or speed his recovery, existence was insufferable.

Sensory deprivation left Cerberus deaf, blind, and incapable of movement. He sometimes suffered the sweet relief of hallucinations where the fixed memories of his past also tortured him.

Those agonizing memories became his mirrored reality, his escape from the physical suffering that was his endless existence until he died once more.

Again.

And again.

And again, only to be brought back to this living hell.

Awareness came like baptism through fire. Sharp pain pulsed and surged through every wasted shred of him. The cycle never ended. It couldn't. And by the thousandth time he died, he was certain immortality was a curse and his desire for vengeance would live forever inside of him.

His body hummed in agony. Each throbbing beat of his heart radiated awareness as tortured nerves buzzed and burned.

Echoes of muscle memory faded. Wounds deliberately healed and the dead cells withered away. Rotting. He was rotting.

Gone were his arms. Gone were his legs. Torn flesh and muscle left him a fraction of the warrior he once was. All he had was breath and pain, but there was no air left to breathe, so the pain inevitably won.

Dampness chilled his bones, stiffening every torn joint and shredded muscle into a tough, ossified husk. His decaying body became a raw nerve with time, exposed and infected, tingling with haunting twitches as he decomposed into a living corpse—buried alive for a long, possibly eternal, restless repose.

The stench of his rotting arms and legs reached his nose. His tormentors left his severed limbs with him so he could suffer the slow decay of his own muscle and flesh.

This deep in the earth, sand dampened to mud and slowly solidified into cold clay. Fossilized in time, encased in agony with no limbs left to claw his way out, nothing existed beyond his tortured mind.

The odd sensation of wrigglers and beetles nibbling the decay became a constant torment and comfort. So long as the worms were with him, composting his body's organic matter, he was never truly alone.

Trapped in the nothing.

No space.

No time.

Only pain.

His agonizing existence repeated on a steady loop of suffering and death.

Suffering and death.

The ricochet of time was lost in the darkness.

His disoriented mind forgot what it was to walk and breathe without agony. After years of this relentless imprisonment, he struggled to recall the wholeness he celebrated before his limbs had been torn clean—amputated by force with the excruciating purpose of punishing him.

Punishing him for her. He inwardly snarled.

She was nothing! A whore, like her mother...

He should have let her die when he killed her the last time. He could have prevented her from coming back. She was immortal but utterly fragile compared to him. How dare they do this on her account?

Once again, he vowed to make her suffer tenfold. He relished the day he would finally escape this living tomb and show her the agony he'd survived. How long had it been since he looked up at the sky and breathed fresh air? Years? Decades? Centuries?

Too long.

She knew nothing of real pain. He ached to show her how truly dreadful he could be. His craving to repay her for the crime of quartering and entombing him alive obliterated all other desires.

I'm coming for you girl...

The debt she owed him would cost her dearly. One day, she would pay for leaving him this way, just as he made her mother pay in the blood of those she loved.

Vicious bitch.

It was no wonder Lilias's descendants were equally venomous. Wiping out her line would do the world a service.

Like a delicious poison, the temptation of his

memories puzzled together a vision of Lilias when they first met. She'd been fresh and frightened, with supple breasts and a wet little quim just beyond flowering.

He seethed, hating the memory as his body reflexively responded with an unwanted jolt of lust. Damn the conniving cunt for still holding power over him. He still dreamt of her, still fantasized that she might choose him, even after what he'd done to her children.

It was a piss poor way to mask the current pain he suffered, pain caused by her daughter, but those memories were his only escape from his reality. Until his mind walked him to the end of his memories, and he suffered her abandonment all over again.

Like his lust, his hatred for Lilias never waned. He craved to cut her open, ignore her cries for mercy as her blood and tears flowed into a river, from which he would fill his cup. He'd drain her of every falsehood she'd spoken.

She was a beautiful pit of lies. She only used him for blood, protection, and secrets. She was a poison that needed to be cut out. Cauterized from this earth. Destroyed once and for all.

Color flashed in a memory and he could still hear her laughter. The exquisite sound thrilled him despite knowing it was a lie. Even the exact green of her eyes was still so precise in his mind.

He'd do anything to escape his present pain as the earth crushed him inside this fossilized tomb, so he chased the vision, hunting it down and transforming her affection into a malleable pleasure it never was.

He let his mind play, recalling the reality and imagining what it might have been had she not betrayed him in the end—*poisonous witch.*

The phantom tingle of his missing hands balling into fists haunted his delirium. An unfulfilled twitch that started to itch where he could not reach—would not reach for several more years.

Ah, she's going to pay... And her daughter would pay. And her sons... well, they had already paid for the sins of their mother in life's blood and hopeless cries.

He should have slaughtered them all, including Lilias's self-righteous mate.

At least here, in the dark, she was still his. He had time to experience his Lilias in every way he could imagine.

Sometimes, he fantasized about choking her until her sobs silenced. Other times, he dreamt of slitting her throat again and again. But mostly, he envisioned the peaceful moment when she could have looked into his eyes and confessed her love.

In his mind, she could become anything he wanted, so why not make her the fantasy of his dreams? It was a cruel game because in those clawing final moments, when he was jerked back to the present and suffocated by the crushing earth once more, the dream ripped away, and the truth cleaved through him with ruthless precision.

It was his last thought before every death. His greatest failure. His eternal regret. And the one inescapable truth he could not erase.

She never loved him.

CHAPTER 1

Centuries Later...

BRANCHES TORE at Adriel's skin and clothes as she launched into the canopy of trees. Her heart beat frantically as her body slammed hard into the trunk, her claws embedded into the soft bark. Eyes wild, she scanned the area, but her senses stayed dull for her protection.

The moment she'd spent centuries dreading was finally here. How much time did she have before Cerberus caught her? Minutes? Maybe days if she was lucky? Her time had always been marked, but now it was up.

Her mate tracked her down and burned her out of her home, leaving her no choice but to run. Adriel knew he'd inevitably come for her, for his revenge. Just as the lion could not resist toying with the pitiful, helpless mouse, Cerberus, no doubt, relished the chase ahead of him.

For all of her worry, she was no more and no less prepared to face him.

He found her. Taunted her. Vowed to have his long-awaited vengeance as he burned her house down and forced her into the open. Without shelter, she was truly vulnerable and had no choice but to run. The Order could no longer protect her, and it was now her duty to protect those who saved her years ago. That meant luring Cerberus as far away from her friends as possible.

Her time was up.

Labored breath wheezed from her lungs as she raced through the woods. Heart pounding with the muffled chirp of nightcrawlers, she ran as fast as she could. With serpentine leaps, she raced from the trees to the forest floor, trying hard to disguise her scent.

Owls screeched, aware of a predator nearby. While she was far more fearsome than a night bird, she was nothing compared to her mate, Cerberus Maddox XI.

Shutting her eyes, she paused and focused on the ground below. He'd easily track her if she searched too closely for him, so she kept her touch feather-light as she scanned the dark forest. The tingle of his nearness sent chills knifing down her spine. Slamming her mind shut, she sucked in a sharp breath.

Her lungs burned from smoke inhalation. She

needed to feed, needed to heal. Her blistered body suffered terrible burns from the fire, but without more blood, her damaged cells would not repair. On the contrary, her energy was draining.

She could not afford to stop or hunt. She needed to keep moving.

Her attention snapped to the east as a twig cracked. Something was out there.

Small, possibly immortal, but not Cerberus. Not yet. Needing to keep her mind closed, she could only use her other senses.

Sniffing the air, Adriel growled and curled her lip, exposing a razor-sharp fang. The intruder was an unwelcome distraction, perhaps sent by Cerberus to slow her down.

Adriel crouched low, panting for breath as she scanned the shadows. Her claws extended, and her eyes dilated they retracted to pinpoints as she prepared to attack.

She tracked the sound of approaching footsteps, fanning her senses over the forest floor until she latched onto the encroaching threat. It was small but...otherworldly.

Immortal? Perhaps, but not quite. Something else. What, Adriel did not know.

Bare feet whispered over the soft vegetation, cushioned by fallen leaves and pine needles, as the intruder drew closer.

"Fuck!" A soft voice using such profanity was not of their Amish order.

Adriel drew back, hiding deeper in the shadows, her eyes watching with nocturnal precision.

Soft footsteps padded over the damp underbrush as the ripe scent of a female tinged the air. Her approach was far too light-footed to be male but also lacked the agility of an immortal.

What was it?

Adriel could feed. If the intruder was, in fact, immortal, she could use its blood to heal. But feeding would slow her down, and she needed to keep moving.

Her hand shook as she wiped the dirt, blood, and sweat from her singed face, eyes stinging from vigilance and acrid smoke. The fire had damaged her vision, and the nearby trees appeared blurry. She could not waste another second investigating the forest intruder. She needed to run.

Leaping into the trees to perch high in the safety of the branches, Adriel searched the ground below. Probing the black woods, unsure where she was heading, she pieced together a plan. There would be no going back.

Sharp heartache followed that petrifying thought. The worry of never seeing her son again crippled her with grief she could not afford. She was truly alone now. The Order could not protect her, and she needed to protect them from Cerberus.

Where would she go? Who would she become? Would she even get that far?

Swallowing a gasp, she choked on the over-whelming uncertainty. She had no choice but to leave. The farm was no longer a haven for her to call home.

The Order's stringent views had protected her for centuries. Safeguarded by privacy and shielded from modern society, their Amish life-style allowed masses of immortals to hide in plain sight.

She could not jeopardize the peaceful sanctuary the elders built. Cerberus would stop at nothing to burn The Order to the ground and expose whatever was left in the ash of his rage. She needed to protect them now the way they had once protected her.

The daunting thought of entering a world she did not know threatened to snap the thin thread of hope she held. As a female, she'd been indoctrinated through the Amish faith and taught to fear the outside world. Exposure terrified her, but Cerberus was far more frightening.

Her mate was ancient, and once he latched onto her mind, there would be no escaping him. He possessed powers far beyond Adriel's skills. She was a peaceful country mouse that angered a vicious dragon capable of horrific crimes.

The bishop was right. She had to run and keep moving until Cerberus was gone. But he would never be gone. He would never forgive what they did to him centuries ago, nor would he rest until he sought the vengeance he believed she deserved.

Pressing her brow against the trunk of the

evergreen, overcome with worry and dread. Apprehension swelled inside of her. It was hopeless. Perhaps she should surrender and end this life-long fight to escape her destiny. But Cerberus would not let it end after what they did to him. He was going to make her pay.

Crippling, daunting, horrifying visions attacked her mind as a jagged breath cut through her scorched lungs. He was going to torture her. She could not allow her panic room to grow, so she quickly smothered the fearful thoughts of her future.

Stiffening her shoulders, she forced her body to stand at full height. Moonlight cut through the branches, dappling the dark earth with silver-blue. Fixated on the scuttling sounds racing along the underbrush, she zeroed in on the approaching footsteps of a…animal?

No. The same familiar scent tickled her nose. Unwashed human hair and traces of sweat. But her pursuer was not mortal. A mortal would never be able to keep speed. So what followed her?

Listening for cues, she caught the swift breath of a feminine gasp as a branch cut into the pursuer's skin. The scent of fresh blood pulled a growl from Adriel's throat as weakness begged her to feed.

The creature's sharpness was animal-like, akin to that of small prey, reminding her of a fox or a coyote. Adriel's nose twitched at the sharp metallic scent of fresh blood—not immortal blood nor purely mortal.

Hunger carved her insides hollow as the gamy canine-like scent called to her. Her head jerked upward as the scent intensified. It was getting closer.

Releasing her grip from the tree, Adriel dropped off the branch, falling forty feet to the earth below and landing in an agile crouch. Her eyes dilated, and her fangs extended as the swift rush of footsteps raced toward her.

Low and alert, she growled and pounced as a twig snapped. Snarling hard and vicious, she collided with the soft body, plowing it into the dirt. A sharp scream pierced the forest, and lesser creatures scattered as Adriel slammed a hand over the girl's mouth, recognizing the escaped witch as The Order's prisoner.

"What are you doing here?" Drawing back her claws, she hissed, fully engaged as a predator prepared to defend her life to the death if need be.

"Don't hurt me!"

Adriel stilled as the witch cowered in fear, her arms protectively blocking her face. Grabbing her by the throat, she jacked her off the ground and shoved her hard into the narrow trunk of a tree.

"Why are you following me? How did you escape? And what do you want?"

The witch struggled to work her voice past Adriel's lethal grip. "Please," she choked. "Don't...

hurt…" She tried to pry away her hold, but Adriel's claws only lengthened, pressing harder into her narrow larynx.

She had no time for mercy or entrapments. Witches were not to be trusted. "How did you get out of your cell, and why are you following me?" She loosened her hold on the girl's slender neck just enough for her to answer.

She gasped and choked down a breath. "Dane let me out. The bishop knows I'm gone."

Eleazar permitted this? Why?

Out of habit, Adriel nearly reached for her shared mental link with her friend but quickly remembered that such communication could jeopardize her safety. She would need to rely on her intuition alone. Because she was utterly alone.

Her jaw hardened. Anything the plebe said could not be trusted. She jerked the girl by the throat. "How did you catch me?"

A witch as lacking as this plebe should not have been able to keep pace with an immortal as ancient as Adriel—injured or not.

"I…I don't know."

Adriel's eyes narrowed. Had she used magick? Had she gone in circles? Tightening her grip, Adriel bared her teeth and growled, "Stop fol-lowing me."

"I…" the witch croaked, her voice straining to escape. "I can help you."

Adriel released her and turned away. "I highly doubt that."

Brushing a hand over her shorn red hair, she scanned the sky for the north star, reorienting herself with the direction she needed to travel.

Gathering her skirts in hand, she glanced back at the witch with scathing promise. "Follow me again, and I'll kill you."

Knees bent, she crouched to spring into the trees—

"You're Amish!" the witch blurted.

Adriel staggered off balance and scowled at the girl. "I'm many things. Most of which you should have the common sense to fear. Are you so dense and depraved that you require physical proof of my nature? I *will* kill you, girl."

"Look…" The witch held up her palms in supplication, her filthy hands shaking like leaves. I know you're s-s-strong and immortal, and you could kill me with little effort, but—no offense—you're sheltered. You probably don't know anything about modern technology, and you seem to be running from something. Plus, aren't vampires really old?"

Adriel rolled her eyes. Age only amplified an immortal's powers. And despite her maturity, she didn't look a day over twenty-five. "Go away, child."

"I'm not a child! I can help you."

"I don't need your help."

"That farm is all you've ever known, am I right? You're ignorant of the ways the real world works. It can be dangerous out there—especially for women."

Her lip curled with annoyance, covering a tremor of fear. Adriel had survived thus far, and modernization should have made the world safer. Shouldn't it have?

The girl was getting in her head, so she growled, "I've seen dangers you couldn't imagine, and I assure you, I'm much stronger than I look."

"Probably, sure," the witch rushed out in a desperate attempt to plead her case. "But outwardly, you're just a doe-eyed, pale-skinned waif with a pixie cut, and that's what they'll see when they look at you. They'll see you as an easy target, and they'll take advantage of your ignorance."

"Who is *they*? Who do you speak of?"

"Criminals. Thieves. Predators. Bad men. It's not safe out there for women, especially women who spent their entire life sheltered on an Amish farm."

"Mortals are the least of my concerns."

"I can help you escape whoever you're running from." The plebe's gaze skittered to the blood-stained collar of Adriel's dress. "I saw what he did to your house—the fire. They didn't kill him. I saw him get away, and I imagine he'll catch up with you soon. I know you're scared. What does he want with you?"

Ice formed in Adriel's veins as a chill raced down her spine. The urge to flee caused her knees to tingle. She looked east, fanning out her senses as she tried to detect footsteps. There was nothing.

"I can help you," the witch urged. It's a big

world out there—nothing like what you're used to. I can drive a car, and I know how to talk to people and how to dress." She glanced at Adriel's long sleeves, grimacing at the primitive apron and Amish attire. "I can help you escape whoever you're running from—whoever *he* is."

Her eyes widened. No one could help her. This witch could never understand the heinous atrocities Cerberus was capable of. The girl lived in captivity for years, and now she was desperately trying to cling to any escape.

"You're hardly a woman of the world—"

"What does my age matter after the things I suffered? I haven't been a child in a long time." She pointed a sharp finger toward the distant sound of civilization. "Everything I know is out there. I may look young, but I'm an adult who can help you."

"Go home where it's safe," Adriel spat.

The witch snatched her arm. "I have no home! Your people saw to that when they murdered my aunts."

"Exactly why I would be a fool to trust you!" She jerked her arm free. "Witches and immortals are natural enemies. Touch me again, and I'll show you why."

"I have magick!"

Adriel ignored her and headed north, but the girl followed, struggling to keep up.

"Do you hear me?" She yelled. "I have powers!"

Adriel's blurry stare narrowed as she trudged

through the trees. "If you had powers, you would have escaped long before tonight."

"You saw how they kept me. Hands tied and mouth muzzled. Witches need to chant. When we lose our voices, our spells are hobbled."

Cerberus was still out there. Adriel could not mend broken birds if she wanted to save herself. "I do not have time for orphaned witches."

"Please. I have nowhere to go."

Adriel pivoted, prepared to unleash on her, but hesitated when the moonlight caught the witch's tattered smock. The dirty rag reeked of sweat, fear, and something unmistakably masculine.

Her gaze traveled from her mud-spattered calves to her long, unkempt hair. She'd suffered. Adriel could see it now, and empathy pulled at her heart.

"I'm sorry," she said, forcing the words out. "Perhaps you cannot return to where you once lived, but you cannot come with me."

The witch straightened her spine and lifted her chin. "I'm tougher than I look—"

"Enough! You're free now. Have the sense to save yourself."

"Can you?"

"Can I what?"

"Save yourself. I watched him take down several immortal men twice your size. You're small and hurt—"

"You know nothing of the atrocities I've survived or the horrors I've escaped. Size means little when one is cunning and determined."

"Exactly! So why would you dismiss me when I'm offering you help?"

"Because you'll only slow me down—"

As she dropped to a crouch, Adriel's words cut off with a gasp. A blast shook the forest floor, rattling the trees and propelling sleeping birds to flight.

"What is that?" Juniper gripped the trunk of a tree for balance as the earth quaked and roots rattled free of the soil, tipping trees into each other and sending creatures scurrying for shelter.

He was shaking her out. "*That* is what you claim you can protect me from." More trees fell as another boom shook the forest floor.

Adriel had no guarantee she could outrun Cerberus or even cause him to flinch in combat, but she was certain such an enemy was well beyond the plebe's abilities. The girl might be a witch, but she was young and untrained, still in the infancy of her shadow work. And while Adriel had never killed a living thing in her life, some primal part of her knew she would kill Cerberus if it came down to her survival or his.

"You will die if you stay with me," Adriel shouted over the quaking rumble.

"You will die if I leave!"

Trees crashed to the soil as branches rained like meteors. Adriel clung to a vibrating trunk as tremors rolled like waves under the earth's mantle.

"Juniper—that is your name, yes?" Adriel shouted, and the witch nodded. "It is not a matter of want. Do you see how powerful he is? No one can help me now. You must leave this place—"

They fell to their knees and gasped as another earthquake tore through the trees. A chasm ripped across the forest floor, loosening soil and sending them crawling for shelter, but nothing was stable.

Juniper grabbed Adriel's shoulders and instinctively pulled her closer for protection. Adriel flashed her fangs as the invisible threat roared closer.

Juniper screamed as another blast rolled through the black woods, making it impossible to rise from their knees. Soil danced at the earth's surface, then the ground cracked, and they scurried back from the opening.

Beetles rushed up from the coniferous debris. Branches whooshed and heavy trees collapsed into the earth forming a cage around them, the gnarled roots turning skyward as the force of the thunderous rattle left them clutching for unsteady balance.

Then everything stilled. No, not everything. Just the earth beneath them and the air around them, as if they were in a bubble of safety protecting them from the cataclysmic chaos assaulting the forest.

Breathless whispers hissed from Juniper's

lips. The foreign incantation seemed to still the ground at their feet while the world shook violently around them. The witch held her palms outward as her eyes stayed shut, and she cast some sort of protection spell that formed an invisible forcefield around them.

Adriel screamed when another tree fell, coming directly toward them. The trunk crashed into the invisible shelter overhead, deflecting the heavy branches and protecting them. Her shocked stare darted back to the witch.

"That is a great power, indeed."

The witch kept whispering words but met her gaze as if to say she was aware.

Adriel rose to her full height on unsteady legs, her knees locking and her footing solid as the forest shook around them. She bolted forward only to fall to her knees when she left the witch's proximity. Looking back, she found Juniper standing at her full height, balance perfectly intact despite the chaos ripping through the forest.

The witch's chin lifted, still bruised from where she'd worn the metal muzzle for so long. A smug grin curved her lips, the quakes no longer impacting her balance. "The protection spell stays with me." Her isolated tranquility displayed incredible influence over the elements. "As I said, I have powers that can protect you."

CHAPTER 2

The witch offered the only shelter that could protect Adriel at the moment. Weak from injuries and the effort of blocking her mind from Cerberus, she frantically tried to reason her way past this nightmare, but there was no escaping his powers or the opportunity for escape in front of her.

Desperation mingled with panic as she looked at Juniper. "Can I trust you?" It was a foolish question that would only broker a false sense of security.

"Let's not start on a lie. You don't trust anyone."

Directness was as close to honesty as they would come in a rush. A hurricane raged around them, lifting debris and whipping through the trees. The witch closed the distance, sheltering Adriel in the protection of her spell.

Something flashed in Juniper's deep violet

eyes. "Were you there, with the rest of the vampires, when they were torturing me?"

Adriel recalled many horrific days when the witch's muffled screams penetrated the walls of Council Hall. She'd hoped to dull her pain, but interfering in council business was forbidden—especially for females. To this day, Adriel's empathy for the witch haunted her with regret. No one deserved what The Order did to her.

But regrets never saved anyone. "I'm not a vampire," she clarified. Vampires were lost souls, and Adriel had survived hell and back to save hers. "The correct term is immortal. And I was nearby but not a firsthand witness to the interrogations."

"Immortal then," Juniper corrected, rolling her eyes as if it were an insignificant detail. "Are you like them?"

"I can be cruel when crossed," she confessed honestly. Witches were cunning creatures that distorted the laws of nature. They were not to be trusted, and therefore, Adriel needed to maintain some sense of upper hand.

"I won't cross you as long as you don't cross me. Let's start there. I can escort you where you need to go and hold the protection spell as we travel."

Adriel looked back at the rumbling woods, a fallen graveyard of trees layering the forest floor. Did she have a choice?

"Look, I'd rather not have a coven of vampires after me. Maybe we can protect each other."

"They're not vampires."

"Immortals. Whatever. They're still pissed and scary as fuck. If one can find you, one can find me, so my goal is to ensure that never happens." The branches overhead rattled and shook as the earth moaned and the wind howled through the trees. "He's about to send another earthquake. We don't have much time."

She tugged at Adriel's apron, plucking free the straight pins and tossing them onto the forest floor.

"What are you doing?"

"Getting rid of this." The witch yanked her apron off and tossed it to the ground. "You'll need modern clothes."

"As we're both empty-handed, I'd assume the time to undress is later."

The trees creaked as another wave of earthquakes shook the world around them, but Adriel's footing remained stable. "The apron will hold your scent. We'll leave it here to throw him off." She stepped back and grimaced. "You still look like you escaped the set of *Little House on the Prairie*, but whatever. We have to go. Do you have a safe place in mind?"

"I have nothing."

In a wave of self-pity, she sensed the witch's weariness. "How long can you hold the protection spell?"

"A while, but it will slow me down."

"I'm afraid haste is a necessity." Adriel bit into her wrist.

Juniper bolted back. "What the fuck are you doing?"

"You need to keep pace and keep your magick intact." She stepped forward.

Juniper drew back. "No. Absolutely not. I'm not drinking your blood!"

"It will not change you. It will only make you stronger." It would also help Adriel track her if they separated.

"I said no."

Adriel's arms crossed at her stubbornness. "Then you cannot come with me."

The girl didn't argue. But when her face pinched tight and she turned her head, Adriel caught the collar of her smock.

"Hey! Get off!"

"Those barbaric hypocrites." Adriel released her, seeing all she needed to see in the shadows of a puncture wound on her neck. "Did they feed from you?"

Juniper's jaw trembled, as did the forcefield around them. Cerberus was getting closer, and the witch's foolish pride could cost them their lives.

"Do you want to die? If you're coming with me, then open your mouth. The blood will give you strength and speed, which we need to make it out of here alive." Adriel snatched her by the hair when she still hesitated and forced her mouth to her open wrist. *"Zippel hex,* drink."

Juniper stiffened, and a sharp pain knifed

through Adriel's head. She released her immediately and gasped.

Glaring back at the witch, she snarled, "What are you?"

"I'm not someone who allows compulsion. Are we clear?"

"I was trying to help you!"

"Not without my consent." She closed the distance. "Are you all right?"

"Don't come any closer." Adriel rubbed her temples, unsure what the witch had done to reject her compulsion. "Perhaps you're stronger than I first assumed."

"Gosh, I should have said that." She rolled her eyes and glanced back at the fallen trees. "Can we go now? I should be able to keep the spell moving with us."

"Should?"

"Pardon me, but I've never been in this situation before. I was once normal, with a normal freaking life before vampires fucked everything up."

They were going to die. "Weren't you raised by witches?"

"Yes, but… We were sort of living in the broom closet. My aunt harnessed my energy at times so I could watch her practice, but I rarely did spells on my own. The protection spell is the first thing we learn."

They were doomed.

The trees creaked and bowed. "We'll head north as far as we can get on foot. If you drop the spell, he'll find us, and you'll be as good as dead, so let's hope this works."

"Wait." Juniper caught her arm. "I don't know your name."

She hesitated only a moment. "I'm Adriel Schrock, eldest of my line, matriarch of my family, and certain to suffer more cruelty than you can imagine if we do not leave this place now."

Her hand moved from her wrist to close tightly about her hand. "I won't let you die, Adriel. Let's go."

CHAPTER 3

Gracie's bare feet beat against the damp earth as she battled back a sob. It couldn't be true. He would never leave without saying goodbye. Yet, as she opened her mind, all traces of Dane were gone.

She rounded the schoolhouse. The children were still abed as the sun barely crested the horizon. The air still held the acrid scent of damp soot and burned wood from the fire last night.

Cutting the corner quickly, her feet slipped on a flat, moss-covered rock embedded in the mud. Before she hit the ground, her hand flung out to catch the post of the split rail fence that lined Dane's property.

Pausing to catch her breath, she looked at the barn, her heart pounding and her mind reaching, but he wasn't there. It was empty.

Dane?

Dane, are you there?

The absence of his noisy thoughts stirred a terrifying ache in her chest. The closer she came to the barn door, the heavier the truth became. In the silence of his missing thoughts, her heart roared like thunder.

He was gone. Dane was gone. After everything, he left. Though she always feared he would —even wished it occasionally—the reality of his disappearance burned like bitter medicine.

Her hand pressed to her woozy stomach as she stumbled up the path. Colby did not bark or rush out to greet her. In the dog's absence, ever-cheerful songbirds mocked her bewildered heart with their first morning refrains.

Her mind reached for his again. *Dane? Are you here?*

The gaping silence that answered chilled her to the bone. There was nothing but hollow, aching emptiness. No sign of his dreaming mind, no sound of his breathing, no lingering scent of lamp oil, sweat on his skin, or sunlight baked into his clothes.

Her vision blurred as her heart denied the quiet she found in the shadows of the barn. He could not be gone. He wouldn't just leave. He… He wouldn't.

The ghostly silence expanded past the shadows, and her stomach hollowed, a sharp ache knifing through her heart.

Dane…

Stillness saturated the lifeless shadows as she pushed open another door. A shiver chased under her gown as she gazed at the dark rafters above. She needn't go any further to see the cavity was empty of all but a cold bed and hay.

His absence pricked her skin with a tingling chill that lifted the hairs on her neck. Her arms closed protectively over her chest as she covered her mouth and swallowed back a sob.

He was truly gone.

Leaning into the wall, gravity pulled her to the ground. How could he just disappear without a goodbye? What about Cybil? What about her?

Only then did Gracie believe his hateful words from the other day. Until that moment, she thought he spoke out of frustration more than truth, but she'd been wrong. There was no love in his heart for her. Only hatred. He wished to be away from this place and her, and his wish had finally come true.

"Why?" she cried, murmuring to herself. He had to know this was not easy for her. He had to realize she… "How could you just leave me without…" She sniffled and wiped her eyes, but more tears fell. "We were at least friends—I thought."

Dane had always despised her faith, but now he scorned her for being faithful. If he wanted to hurt her, he'd succeeded.

The last time he lay with Magdalene, Gracie had lashed out, shattering the windows and screaming at him to leave her be. And so he had. Alone, with only the echo of their final words left to haunt her, she tried to understand how they had come to this.

Was this her fault?

Had she made a crucial mistake?

She honestly didn't know and couldn't think past the ache in her chest.

What did it matter? He was gone.

Biting into her fist to stifle another sob, she suffered sharp regret.

No matter how she tried, she couldn't control her tears. Bellowing at the injustice tearing her heart into two, she shoved his dresser to the floor. Drawers slid out of their compartments, spilling the contents onto the floor. A shirt, a pair of work gloves, a pocket knife, all items he'd left behind. Forgotten. Unimportant. Like her.

She pulled the shirt to her nose, closing her eyes to breathe in his scent, only to draw back with a hiss. Even now, in the emptiness of these wooden walls, Magdalene's stench perfumed the air, mingling with Dane's earthy musk. It corroded the fabric, overpowering and stealing the only lingering traces of Dane she had left.

Her upset stomach revolted, and knots twisted inside her. Denial would not bring him back any more than it would change her fate. She would never know the secret parts of him the way Magdalene had. And while her soul belonged to someone else, her heart would not listen to reason.

Tears tripped past her lashes. If he could leave without a farewell, he obviously never cared for her like she cared for him.

Had Magdalene earned the courtesy of a

goodbye? Was her body worth more than Gracie's friendship? More than her sentiment of…

No. She would not call it love. Love should be shared. Reciprocated. Love was too precious to abandon. If Dane loved her—truly loved her as he repeatedly claimed in his mind—then he would not have been able to leave her. The proof of his desertion rewrote her in ways she didn't recognize.

Her sorrow transcended into anger. Magdalene had stood in this place countless times. Laid in his loft, stared into his eyes. Jealousy poisoned Gracie's insides until a cold chill seeped into her blood. Ice formed a cage around her heart, and she once again closed off her mind. Without Dane's thoughts fluttering through her mind, it was nothing more than noise.

Inescapable, incessant noise broadcasted at her from every angle. When she was young, they called her telepathy a gift, but she soon discovered it was a curse. With age and practice, she'd learned to block the intrusive thoughts of others to keep them out of her mind, but Dane somehow always broke through her barriers.

She once wondered if his presence was a sign, but then he was identified as a half-breed, and all hope was lost. Soon after, he found comfort in Magdalene's arms—another half-breed—and her sense of betrayal was complete.

It was a known fact that half-breeds could not get called, as they lacked the predestined genealogy the rest of their species shared. Gracie could not fault Dane for seeking comfort. But, as she tried to navigate so many confusing emotions, he continued to subconsciously penetrate her mind with thoughts of another female.

Gracie could never entirely block him out, so she suffered countless memories of his hands on Magdalene's flesh, his body entering hers, the scent of her arousal mingling with his, and the taste of her blood on his tongue. All intimacies she would never personally know until she met her called mate.

Now he was gone, and she finally had the silence she asked for. It was for their own good, she supposed, but nothing about his absence felt right. She was alone and hollow, misguided and without her friend.

Gracie had no choice but to reaffirm her faith and continue a life of devotion as she waited for her calling to come. It was all she ever wanted. So why did it feel like he'd stolen something precious from her?

She wished to run or scream or break something. Anything to get the confusing pain out.

Gasping, she tried to make sense of her feelings. He was not her mate. Not her destiny. She'd told him they could never be more than friends and he'd abandoned her. So why did it hurt in places she could not name?

Dane was a momentary lapse of judgment, a smile that would eventually fade. This was a test —the cost of patience and the price of purity.

She vowed to save herself for her mate, and

that was not Dane. In the end, it would all be worth the discomfort.

Her hand settled over her pounding heart as she waited for her labored breath to slow. She wiped away a tear. A subtle calmness slowly swept in as she accepted that which her sorrow could not change. Dane was never going to be the other half of her soul.

Cold and heavy, like a glacier, the truth anchored her to this place in time. As a half-breed, he had no place in her future. There was a perfectly suited immortal male out there waiting for her. A true calling would not stir such confusion, and she looked forward to a life of peace.

She craved stability and family. She wanted simple dependability, not passionate kisses that tasted of sin and whispered of darker temptations meant to steer her off course. This was a test of faith, and she planned to honor her mate, not just once they were called, but now and forever.

Yes, Dane leaving was for the best.

The silence calmed her racing heart as she accepted her role, accepted that her body and soul belonged to another. And as the truth blanketed her, her emotions turned to ice.

Numb.

Still.

Perhaps quiet calm was best right now. It certainly softened the pain. But the coldness in her heart was as comforting as it was cruel. There would always live a memory of the warmth Dane stirred, and in that memory hid truths untold. They whispered through her in silence even when she prayed, and she wasn't sure those feelings would ever fully go away.

She loved him.

Tipping her head back in defeat, another tear escaped. She accepted this ache would take time to heal.

Would he ever come back?

Would she ever see him again?

These were questions she should not ask. There was so much she wanted him to know but could never say. It was best that those secrets remain unsaid.

What sweet mercy it would be to meet her mate soon, but there had been no symptoms of a calling, and some immortals waited centuries for that destined moment to arrive. She needed to mend her own heart. Time would help.

Her fingers delicately traced her lips, recalling the press of Dane's mouth and how his hands awoke her skin through her clothes. His touch had been possessive and fraught with desire. One look into his intense eyes and his heated stare burned through her body like the fire of a thousand suns.

For her own protection, she made him believe his feelings were unmatched, that he was alone in his desperate desires, but Dane had never been alone. She, too, had a storm of want and need raging inside her.

Perhaps he knew all along, so he'd left

without a goodbye. He wanted to hurt her, to punish her for being a liar. And so he had.

"One day, you will forgive me." Her head bowed under the weight of her shame.

Her stubborn denial might have angered him, but he had not witnessed the wretched outcome of unmated souls as she had. Her parents' love was not enough to prevent the heartache that came when her father was eventually called to his true mate. Her mother was still paying the price.

The consequence of loving a male not or-dained by God came with a dear cost Gracie feared. She resolutely committed her life to waiting for her true-called mate, never expecting such a promise of faith to cause such conflict in her heart.

Self-discipline did not negate the conse-quence, however. Denying her feelings for Dane had cost her—so much so that every encounter left her depleted and weak.

One day, her true mate would claim her, and there would be no resisting the call. She paid Dane a kindness by saving him from such pain. He never fully understood what he was asking. He wasn't just kissing her. He was asking her to betray not only her destiny but also her god. If he loved her, truly loved her, he would have never asked her to take such a risk.

Her gaze drifted across the floor as the morning light cleaved the darkness. His boots and Colby's water bowl were gone. Her heart plummeted, the gutting sense of loss expanding until it was all she could feel.

Why did her last words to him have to be in anger?

Falling forward, she sobbed at the injustice, giving herself this moment of unguarded truth to let the ugly resentment inside of her spill free. What if, when she eventually met her mate, she continuously measured him to a memory of Dane?

She needed to let him go. Truly release him from her thoughts once and for all.

A sad fury consumed her, and rather than reel it in like she usually did, she let it out. She could not be like the centurion females of The Order still waiting for their call. Did she have the fortitude to suffer this solitude for a hundred years?

Dane was not fully immortal. Therefore, he had limited time on this earth. He could have been a balm to her loneliness, but then what? No matter what, it all ended in loss.

Sobbing, she belted out her fury at such injustice. What sort of god would allow her these feelings when her soul was predestined for her mate?

Dane had been willing to love her *now*, willing to pass the time with her so she need not suffer in isolated wait. The few stolen kisses he took were all they would ever have. She should be content with knowing they at least shared those awkward firsts. First glances, first blushes. The first time her chest heaved with nervousness when his thoughts whispered through her mind. The first time he touched her in a way that left her insides clenching.

Those firsts would always belong to Dane.

It would never be more. She knew it. He knew it. Everyone understood why they couldn't be together, but her heart didn't. And while Dane might have finally accepted her decision, deep down, she knew he'd never respect her choice.

Would it always hurt like this? Perhaps some foolish part of her never truly expected him to give up.

But he had.

Now, he could move on. They both could.

Her head jerked to the shadows as soft footfalls approached. The scent of dewy grass kicked up as labored breath broke the silence. Someone was coming.

Grace abruptly wiped away her tears and staggered to her feet, alarmed to be discovered in such an inexplicable condition and place.

"Dane?" Magdalene bolted into the barn and staggered to a halt.

A low growl seeped from Grace's chest as her tender heart turned to stone. Rage blazed in her belly. She should rip out that obnoxious blonde curl that escaped Magdalene's *kapp* and choke her with it.

"Grace, you startled me." Magdalene pressed a hand to her brow, her arms sliding loosely to her side. "Is it true? Is he gone?"

Dane's horrible words came back to her. *I kiss*

her everywhere, Grace...She likes my hands on her... She likes touching me... And I like being inside of her...

Lips parted, Gracie bared her fangs, tempted to scrape her claws down Magdalene's fresh face until the flesh fell from the bone. "Get out," she snarled, unsure what she might do if the female came any closer.

"Grace, your eyes—"

She sprung, lunging forward as she slammed the female into the barn wall and fully bared her fangs. The girl was weak. It would take very little to maim her.

"Grace, stop!" The stark look of horror in Magdalene's eyes instantly set things in hierarchical order.

Grace possessed the strength and power to permanently end her, yet her faith and decency forbade such brute behavior.

Disgusted by her envy and shocked at how deeply it tormented her, she released the terrified female and fled the barn, running until she was miles away from the farm and lost deep in the woods. That was when she noticed the downed trees and destruction.

What had happened here? It was as if a tornado or earthquake had come through.

Scanning the forest for danger, she sensed nothing among the woodland creatures and birds. Then she spotted something white on the ground, the acrid stench of smoke mixing with the metallic scent of blood staining the fabric.

Leaves crunched underfoot as she bent to pick up the cloth.

An apron. But whose?

She sniffed fabric and instantly recognized Adriel Schrock's scent, intense and bitter with fear.

Grace searched the forest, fanning out her senses, but found no trace of anyone. She should alert the bishop that something was amiss.

Then she had a thought. Perhaps Dane had gone with her. What if they were in danger? What if Dane needed help?

Gracie's fist tightened around the apron as she ran toward home.

CHAPTER 4

"We have to stop."

Adriel slowed the moment she realized Juniper had paused to catch her breath. Startled to find her doubled over, gripping her knees as she panted, she asked, "What's wrong?"

"*What's wrong?* We've been running at full speed for over an hour. I don't have shoes. My feet are blistered and bleeding. I can't go any further."

They'd hardly traveled at half speed, but Adriel supposed the pace was a lot for Juniper. Her gaze darted to the distant woods in the direction they'd come. "We can't slow down."

"I need a break, Adriel! I'm not as fast as you."

They were hardly making headway. "No breaks . If we don't keep moving, he'll catch us."

The witch caught her arm the moment she pivoted. "You aren't listening. I *can't.* I'm not like you. My body hurts, and I'm hungry. I can't keep holding the protection spell and running like this."

Without the spell, Cerberus would track them. It was an infuriating limitation but the only thing allowing Adriel to escape at the moment. She was also in need of rest, so her thoughts were not as guarded as they should have been, but the protection spell made up for what she currently lacked.

Perhaps it would be wise for both of them to find a place to rest if their strength was mutually waning. With wide eyes, she scanned the woods. She didn't dare open her senses for fear of her mate slipping inside of her head, especially if Juniper's spell was weakening.

Despite her exhaustion, it still felt too dangerous to stop. "I could carry you. Could you do the spell then?"

Juniper looked up at her—slack-jawed with a fist wedged into her ribs. "We need a better plan."

"The plan is to keep moving." They needed to run and keep running. "If you can't keep up, then I need to leave you here."

"We're in the middle of nowhere!"

"I told you I would be running all night. I warned you."

"If this is the extent of your plan, you're going to be running for more than a night. Where are we even going?"

"North."

"North *where*? Do you even have a destination in mind? What happens when we cross a state line and then another? Eventually, we'll end up in Canada. How do you expect to get past border patrol?"

"I can use compulsion if necessary, and there are Amish sects over the border."

Juniper scowled at her, the pale moonlight catching her features. "They aren't *your* kind of Amish. We can't go to another order. It would put them in danger. Besides, I don't trust the fucking Amish any more than I trust vampires."

"Immortals."

"Whatever." She pushed her tangled hair behind her ears and rose to her full height. Beneath the thin material of her chemise, she was little more than skin and bone. "You're not like the Amish in Canada. And you have some insane psychopath chasing you. You'll lead him right to them, Adriel. Is that what you want? They're unarmed, mortal, and helpless pacifists."

Juniper's devotion to protecting the innocent surprised her. She'd assumed the witch would be more self-serving. But she was right. If they stopped at another sect, it would only lure Cerberus and put innocent souls in danger. Her mate would slaughter anyone who stood in the way of what he wanted, including Juniper.

Though their alliance was short-lived, Adriel was startled by such a realization. She did not want the young woman risking her life.

"This is wrong."

"What are you talking about? We don't even

have a destination, so going the wrong way is impossible."

"That's not what I meant." As much as Adriel appreciated the spell and the witch's help, doubt and guilt resurfaced. This mission was a death sentence. "You shouldn't come with me. It's dangerous—"

"Really? This again?" Juniper flung out her arms. "We've been through this. You're not ditching me in the middle of nowhere. You need me. And before you argue that you don't, let me point out a few things."

"I'm only trying to protect you, Juniper. You're young—"

"What does age matter? You're no bigger than me—"

"It's different. I'm immortal."

"So is the ex you're running from." She glanced back at the dark woods. "You said yourself that he'll hurt you if he finds you."

"He'll hurt me, but he'll kill you. Death is a mercy he'd never allow me to have."

"He doesn't own you, so he can't allow shit, Adriel."

"That's not how matings work. Once he finds me, he'll take control of everything. He'll make me suffer and think nothing of killing you."

"I don't care how it works. It comes down to what you want and how hard you're willing to fight to get it. Do you want to run forever?"

"No."

"Do you want him to catch you?"

"Of course not. That's why I need to keep moving."

"Look at yourself, Adriel. You're exhausted. Without me, you're as good as caught. He's, like... I don't know the words you guys use, so sorry if I say this wrong, but he's super old and strong, right?"

"Yes."

"Older and stronger than you?"

"Much."

"So eventually, he'll run you down. If he's stronger, faster, and crazy enough not to give up, then sooner or later, he'll catch you."

"What's your point?" Adriel snapped, not appreciating how her tension and fear rose with every accurate statement.

"My point is we need a better plan than running our feet bloody and brainwashing our way over the Canadian border. Your mate may be old and powerful, but you're female, and females are clever. If you had a halfway decent plan, you wouldn't have to exhaust yourself running for your life."

They were wasting time. "This is the plan I have! I don't have the luxury of pausing to think! Don't you get it? Every moment I waste debating if there is a better way, he gets closer to catching me!"

"You have no target! What's your end game? We need to move toward something, or this insanity will never end."

"The target is north!"

"That's too broad and too far! There has to be a closer destination. A hideout. Someplace safe. A hidden space I could spell and protect so we can rest. I can't keep actively using my magic if there's no end in sight, and you need my magic if you want to beat him."

"I don't know any place like that! I've lived on the farm for too long. That's all I know."

Adriel's voice trembled as her fear got the better of her. With such a sheltered existence, she knew nothing of the modern world. She only had the good sense to fear it.

"Well, I can assure you it's not safe here in the woods. We're wide open and unprotected. We need walls and a door."

"Again, I don't—"

"I get it." Juniper held up a hand. "Your home was on the farm. Blah, blah, blah. Adriel, if you want to evade this guy, you'll have to throw out your old rules and find some balls."

"What does that mean?"

"It means you're a freaking vampire. Act like it."

Her eyes widened in horror. "I am no such thing! I'm immortal—"

She waved away the technicality. "Tomato, *tow-mah-tow*. I'm not the only one with powers. Use yours so we can find a place to hide."

"What do you expect me to do?"

She pointed to her forehead. "Do that mind thing you guys do! I know you can bend people's wills and make them forget. We need a place to stay. Let's find a house. You can do your dazzle thing or glamour or whatever the term is to the owner. And then we can freaking rest and regroup."

"Are you suggesting we steal—"

"Borrow." She gathered up her straggly brown hair and twisted it into a knot on top of her head. "We need to find a house that looks safe. Something with some property, maybe some sensory lights, and a camera system with security would be sweet."

"I'm not familiar with such things."

"I am. I just need you to do a little mind voodoo to get this ball rolling."

"It's not voodoo."

"I don't care." Juniper glanced back at the woods. "Do you feel him? Is he close? It's been a while since the earth shook. How does he do that?"

"If I use my senses to find him, he'll be able to track us, so I have no way of knowing how far he is. And I don't know how he's able to shake the earth. We all have different disciplines. When in a temper, he'll pounce, and the impact is startling. Sometimes, the earth splits open, as you saw. He's also clever with fire."

The Cerberus she knew several centuries ago was terrifying. This one was somehow worse. Just as Juniper pointed out, he was also older, which made him stronger. And, after what they'd done to him, he was undoubtedly angrier.

Juniper swept away a dark strand that escaped the knot on the top of her head. "Then you're going to just have to trust my survival instincts. Which way is civilization?"

Adriel listened for vehicles and pointed east. "If we leave the shelter of the forest, we're more likely to be seen."

"We're also more likely to blend in and disappear. It's a big world out there, and the one thing I know about modern American culture is that no one gives a shit about anyone else, so it should be easy to hide." Juniper started eastward. "Come on. Step one is shelter. Step two is getting us some normal freaking clothes. Step three is food —and not your kind."

They walked for several miles before reaching the road. The noise and vibration of modern civilization interfered with Adriel's senses and left her on edge.

When they first emerged from the woods, homes were cluttered like broken teeth in a crowded mouth, and the air smelled of chemicals and decay. Already, the pulse and tempo of modern living had Adriel on edge.

Few animals explored this far into the mortal population, doubling her concerns. While immortals were said to be natural predators, modern civilization had a way of making her feel like prey.

"This is a bad area," Juniper explained as she scanned the houses. "We need something a little more upper-crust."

"Upper-crust?" Adriel tilted her head, frequently confused by the girl's English vernacular.

"Look!" Juniper pointed to a strip of shops in the distance.

Large, brightly colored signs marked the roads. The sun was up and the traffic had intensified over the last hour, but even under broad daylight, Adriel couldn't see whatever hope Juniper found.

"What is it?"

"That building over there, they rent cars. Come on."

Adriel hesitated.

"What's the problem, Ade?"

She looked down at her black dress. The dirt and blood were only slightly noticeable, but Juniper's pale, threadbare smock showed every soiled stain. "What about our clothes?"

Juniper briefly glanced down and grimaced. "I...I can't think about that right now. Shelter first, then we can worry about a wardrobe change."

It wasn't fashion that worried Adriel. It was the need to stay inconspicuous. Their filthy, blood-stained, smoke-ridden attire screamed for attention, and wasn't the point blending in?

Juniper seemed unconcerned. She crossed the parking lot, swiftly walking toward the store where several modern vehicles were parked.

"I'm not sure how the whole glamour thing works, but just follow my lead and step in when I give you the signal."

"What signal?"

"I'll look at you."

Juniper's plan didn't seem any better than Adriel's. "Won't they expect payment?"

"Not if you do your mind control thing."

"But that's dishonest."

The witch's rapid steps halted, and she pivoted. "Are you serious? Adriel, look at me. I'm in a smock. I'm barefoot. I've been living in a freaking underground dungeon for two years, suffering whatever the hell that deranged order of yours decided to do to me. I'm over your version of right and wrong. Fuck honesty. I'm done playing nice. We need a goddamn car, and you're going to make them give us one. Hang up whatever ethical issues you're having and get with the program!"

"But…"

"No buts." She walked quickly toward the store. Unsure how far her protective spell reached and unwilling to find out, Adriel hurried after her.

The glass door of the establishment magically parted and beeped as they entered. The hum of electricity buzzed to the overhead lights and strange devices on the counter. Adriel was unused to such technologies and wondered how mortals tolerated the constant beeps and buzzing.

Smooth tile turned to flat carpet underfoot, and a man stepped out of the back office, chewing something and wiping his mouth with a napkin.

"Can I help you?" When his glance finally took in their appearance, his eyes widened, and he looked around nervously. "Are you ladies actors or something?"

"We need a car. Something that gets good mileage."

His stare dragged over their dirt-stained clothes, lingering at the sight of dried blood crusted to Adriel's neck. She self-consciously covered her throat with her hand.

"Should I call the police?" He reached for the telephone.

"No," Juniper snapped, buying them a few seconds. She shot Adriel a sharp glance and whistled. "Now. Do it now."

"Oh." Adriel was shoved toward the counter to meet the man's gaze. Unsure what Juniper wanted her to achieve, she first focused on buying time. "You will not call anyone."

His hand retracted.

"Tell him we need a car," Juniper instructed, glancing out the window nervously.

Morally torn, she forced the words out. "We need a vehicle. Which one works best?"

He pointed toward the storefront window. "I have a decent hybrid Prius. It has a combustible engine and an electric motor—"

"We'll take it." Juniper jumped back from the window and was at the counter, her fingers tapping incessantly on the smooth surface. "Tell him to give us the keys."

"Find us the keys."

Without another word, he turned to a cabinet on the wall and removed a small black device.

Juniper snatched the device. "You have to erase his memory. And ask him if there are cameras."

"Are there cameras recording us?"

He nodded and pointed to the corner of the storeroom.

"Tell him to erase the feed."

"I want you to erase any recordings of us."

"I'm not supposed to mess with—"

"Do it," Juniper snapped at the man, then looked at Adriel. "I thought they couldn't object to compulsion? Isn't that how this works?"

Adriel wasn't used to compelling mortals to do her bidding, so she supposed she wasn't using a strong enough command. Lifting her chin, she pushed further into the man's mind. "What's your name?"

"Matt."

"Matt, you're going to destroy any traces of us being here. Then you'll forget that you saw us. You came to work, ate your breakfast in the back, and had a slow morning with no customers."

His eyes glazed over as he turned to the computer and pressed several keys. Juniper backed toward the door, and Adriel followed. As they crossed the threshold, the monitor beeped again, but Matt never looked up from his task.

"Come on." Juniper rushed out the door, jogging toward the cars in the lot. A horn chirped, and lights flashed on a small vehicle. "There's the car. Get in."

Adriel had never been inside a motor vehicle before. The upholstered seat was surprisingly comfortable, and her hearing was muffled when both doors shut. It was an airtight space, quite different from a carriage.

Juniper seemed to know exactly how to operate all the bells and whistles. She slid back her seat, adjusted the mirrors, then pressed a button and the car purred to life.

"You probably want to buckle up. I've only had about a hundred hours of driving."

"That's a hundred more than me."

Juniper's stare met hers for the briefest moment, and she chuckled. The sound was sweet and natural, utterly contradictory to the chaos surrounding them. Then the moment was gone, and they were backing out of the parking spot and whipping into traffic on the crowded interstate.

Adriel's claws extended, digging into the hard plastic surface in front of her. "Must you be so reckless?"

She slunk low in her seat and tugged at the belt by the door as her body leaned with every turn. Her stomach rolled, and she gasped, nauseated by the motion.

Tires screeched as they nearly collided with a larger truck. Her heart thumped hard in her chest as the car barely escaped a head-on collision.

"I told you, it's been a minute since I drove. I'm still finding my bearings." Cars blared their horns, and people shouted as Juniper wove her way through traffic and picked up speed.

"I'm not sure I believe you've ever driven before—*watch out!*"

Another oncoming vehicle nearly collided with theirs. "Get out of my way, ass-clown!"

They swerved around several cars, picking up speed. Every muscle in Adriel's body locked as she braced for impact, but Juniper wove fast enough through traffic that they were never hit.

"Music?"

"Pardon?" Adriel hadn't blinked since they got on the road.

"You can unclench, Ade. I've got this." Her hand flicked a dial on the control board, and a demonic sound filled the car. The screen above the buttons illuminated with the words, *It's My Life.* "Perfect." She twisted the dial and shouted with the voice wailing from the speakers, *"I ain't gonna live forever!"*

She was having some sort of fit. Adriel had never heard or seen anything like it. The melodic pounding that beat through her chest electrified the air like a bolt of lightning. She wasn't sure if she should cover her ears or roll out of the vehicle to escape the noise.

The music was utter chaos—rapid, aggressive shouting—yet Juniper seemed fully aware of the words. By her smile, she appeared to be enjoying the riotous sound. The tempo guided her speed as they wove through traffic, unimpeded by fear.

Adriel's breath quickened as she watched in enchanted horror. Juniper came alive as she sang, her eyes vibrant, and her voice an uncaged bird that morphed into a mighty lioness.

Her hands pounded the wheel that drove the car, and she danced like a woman set free. Free of all of it. The suppression, the subjugation, the endless, crippling indignities. How did she do it? It was as if a switch had been shut off the moment the music turned on. Rage mixed with joy in equal parts. She was happy yet full of fire and vengeance.

She had never witnessed a female behaving so freely. There was no shame, only vibrance. She was loud and alive. Without the hindrance of propriety, she appeared unapologetically stronger than any female Adriel had ever met. And for the briefest moment, that gave her hope.

Adriel's mouth curved into a smile. She might actually find her way out of this mess and survive. Perhaps it was right to trust this strange woman. Maybe they could be stronger together. A witch and an immortal, what a preposterous thought.

Laughter bubbled in her belly as a strange sense of assurance came over her amid the absolute chaos. Any belief that the female form was somehow vulgar and needed to be hidden suddenly seemed laughable in the witch's shameless presence. Women like Juniper clearly gave no thought to such claims, while every bit of Adriel's teachings since coming to the New World had been about *kapps* and coverings, modesty over comfort, virtue and duty before dreams or independence.

The Order demanded females hide any show of glory. Her life had been tied into a constricting moral corset for centuries, but the further away from The Order they drove, the easier and deeper Adriel was able to breathe.

This unmatched energy about the witch went beyond magick. Both captivating and stunning, she was radiant. Confident and wildly ungraceful yet beautiful in her recklessness, she was un-shackled and limitless. It was a magnificent show that stole Adriel's tension away. And, as she stared at the wild display, her mouth curved with a smile.

"I fucking missed music!" Juniper twisted the dial again, and the volume turned deafening. "Do you like Bon Jovi?" she yelled over the riotous noise. "What am I saying? You've probably never heard anything like this before."

This was not what their music resembled on the farm. Not at all. And Adriel had a hard time categorizing it as better or worse. The panoramic contrasts were too broad for her mind to mea-sure, so rather than judge it one way or another, she simply observed the effect it had on Juniper and laughed.

"You're possessed."

"Girl," she laughed. "I've never felt more free! Hold on tight." Gripping the wheel, the wild witch veered onto a ramp that led to a massive thoroughfare with multiple lanes.

Adriel's eyes widened as the dials rose with their speed.

"Nothing beats fast cars and the right song!" Juniper yelled, pressing a button to lower the glass.

Wind filled the car, and Juniper's tangled hair whipped toward Adriel as the witch laughed like a lunatic. The vehicle whizzed beyond the traffic, and they burst onto an open road, zipping past the trees. For a moment, it felt like they were flying.

How? How was the girl so happy when she had been a captive for years, lived in dark squalor, grieved the death of her entire family, and survived the countless inquisitions of the elders?

She recalled the marks she spotted on the witch's neck, confident whoever bit her did not have her consent. Their laws forbade them from feeding off the unwilling, and the bishop would never have permitted such a crime. Only in extreme emergencies were exceptions made.

Abusing a helpless, shackled witch who had been promised sanctuary in The Council's care was a moral crime. But was it sanctuary when the poor girl had been placed in bondage, tortured with fire, and held underwater? In the light of day such practices seemed excruciatingly cruel.

Shame filled Adriel as she tried to justify her silence. Females were not permitted to interfere with council business. She would have been disciplined if she tried to interfere or speak on the witch's behalf.

Juniper had committed crimes of her own, which was why she'd been placed in a cell. The Order justified her treatment by labeling it merciful because they spared her life. As accurate as all those pieces were, looking back on the whole picture provided a different view, one ripe with inhumane offenses and gross abuses of power.

The more removed Adriel became from The Order, the more extreme those events seemed. How had she just sat there? She should have intercepted and done something. But she'd done absolutely nothing, and guilt now clawed at her in a way that marked her partially responsible for those horrific crimes.

The woman was entitled to rage, yet she showed an inexplicable resilience Adriel could only admire. How did she compartmentalize her anger? It was there, but it also made room for other emotions. Was this how she survived the past few years? Most females would have broken, but the witch was solid—slightly cracked, perhaps—but somehow holding it together.

In the presence of Juniper's strong spirit, it was easy to contrast their differences. Beliefs that females should be gentle and obedient shifted the direction of Adriel's life long ago.

In exchange for The Order's protection, she and many other females allowed themselves to become less. The males held all the power.

After centuries of living such a sheltered life, fearful that her mate would one day find her, she became a shadow. Her potential was stunted like a rootbound plant in a small pot with nowhere to grow, and many of her natural disciplines were lost to disuse.

Was she truly only meant to be half of another's soul? She always sensed she was capable of more, yet without a male, so many saw her as nothing at all. There was even a time when the elders tried to assign her to a husband to keep her on the right path in her mate's absence. But she refused to be led and paid dearly for the little independence she gained.

Drawing back from such a dangerous thought, she frowned.

Centuries of indoctrination still filled her with nervous energy. Being outside of The Order placed her life in an unflattering light. Ashamed by her lack of independence, knowledge, and confidence, she considered how one might correct such inadequacies while Juniper displayed no such shortcomings.

The witch still wore the physical markings of her bondage, yet Adriel was the one shackled by oppression. The moment Juniper was free, she was free. Could Adriel say the same? Perhaps freedom was so unknown that it was part of her fear, and ignorance was her greatest prison.

Mortified, she wondered what ingrained compliance still limited her now. She was as helpless as a domestic bird forced into the wild— defenseless, useless.

Tightness cinched her lungs as the world rushed by. It suddenly seemed so calculated.

She stayed and obeyed because she knew no other way to live. Her fear of the outside world worked in their favor, spreading like a disease from one generation to the next. The standards for trust and obedience were so ingrained that even the slightest ripple of rebellion could feel like a tsunami of an uprising. All the more reason why The Order demanded conformity.

Adriel had been told more than once not to make waves. Some families even shunned her simply because she cut her hair, and they did not want their daughters to be influenced by her misguided actions.

She clutched her chest, thinking of all the decisions made for her and how unprepared she was to face a future in the real world. Domesticated as a bird clipped at the wings, her abilities had been bound by bonnets and Anabaptist faith.

The noose tightened around her neck as she struggled to breathe. She was immortal but so far from feral that death seemed inevitable.

How was she going to survive this place? Every sight and sound was foreign. The speed at which people carried on frightened her. She couldn't even catch her breath. It was all moving too fast. She was a helpless bird falling from the nest, plummeting to the earth with no plan or idea of how to survive out there on her own.

"Hey." The music lowered. "Are you okay?"

She couldn't do this. It was too much, and only a matter of time before Cerberus found her. She had centuries to sharpen her skills and hone her abilities, but she'd done nothing to prepare for this moment that she always knew would come.

"Adriel, look at me."

The command of Juniper's voice broke through her panic, and she glanced at her, tears of fear brimming in her eyes. How had they not broken her?

"Do you feel something? Is it him? Should I change directions?"

"No. No. Keep going."

"What is it? You're white as a ghost."

Gasping through shallow breaths, she swallowed back the lump in her throat. "I just...got scared."

Juniper's eyes flared. "Why? What happened?"

"I...realized how little I know and... I'm so ignorant. I have no idea how to do this."

"Ignorance isn't terminal. You can learn what you don't know. I'll help you." Juniper held out a hand.

Adriel hesitated but slowly took the offering. When the witch's fist tightened around her fingers, lending much-needed courage, she instantly calmed her.

"Thank you."

Juniper nodded, then returned her gaze to the road. "We've got this. As long as we stick together, we can do anything."

Adriel had grown so used to living alone and depending only on herself, she didn't know if she possessed such trust. The girl had lived a mere fraction of a lifetime, but there was something worldly and brave about her. Something trustworthy and good.

Protectiveness raced through her, and her hand tightened. She could not let Cerberus hurt her.

"We cannot underestimate his cruelty."

Juniper frowned. "We won't. Once we find a place to rest, we'll work on a plan."

Adriel already had a plan. Should Cerberus find her, she would make certain he could not hurt her, ending her life before he had the chance to punish her, thereby not giving him the opportunity to harm her friend.

She wasn't exactly sure what had shifted, but she could no longer look at Juniper as merely a liability. Without her, she never would have made it this far. In a way, she was starting to trust her. Yes, she was abrasive and somewhat more aggressive than Adriel was used to, but maybe that was a good thing.

Juniper might be the last person to see her

alive. If her days were numbered, perhaps she could teach her how to live.

Adriel's eyes tingled with the sharp sting of unanticipated tears. She'd wasted so much time hiding and being afraid. She didn't know how to be brave. But she wanted to try. She wanted to be more than the elders believed any female could be.

Not Cerberus's aimless mate or the troublesome female of The Order who rejected conformity, but rather a person with a purpose. Her life and story could not merely be a footnote to his. She wanted—desperately—to be remembered for something more.

She might not have much time left, but she was finally free to live her life as she chose. The last time she'd been free, she lived at home with her family, long before her calling and before she knew what suffering truly was. She'd forced her mind to forget that carefree life long ago—forget the parents who raised her and the brothers and sisters she'd lost when Cerberus went back to slaughter them.

As she tried to recall the shape of her mother's face or the shade of her father's hair, only blurred images filled her mind. Her heart could not bear to think of her parents and all the siblings she'd lost. Did her mother and father blame her? They should.

If not for her, Cerberus would have never hurt them. He would have never gone back and done those horrific things to punish her. But that was how he'd always been. Cruel. Calculating. Controlling through the most vile means necessary.

His viciousness cast a shadow over her entire life. She had been younger than Juniper when she was called, but that did nothing to gentle him. He stole her away, never allowing her the chance even to say goodbye. And that night, he rutted into her in the mud and rain. That primal wound was the first, but far from the last time he made her bleed.

Adriel tipped her head back, closing her eyes, pretending for a moment that she was safe in a place where neither history nor gravity could touch her. Wind teased the short strands of her uncovered hair as the present moment sank into her bones.

This was her life. Hers.

Freedom was a luxuriously terrifying privilege to wear, one she hadn't tried on since reaching adulthood. The idea, alone, fit awkwardly and flooded her with self-doubt.

What would her last hours look like? Would she show courage or fear?

A sense of urgency surged through her as the invisible shackles she'd worn for centuries fell away. Her choices were now her own. Her heart leapt with uncertainty as the extraordinary pressure to decide her future weighed her down like gravity. Her path ahead was genuinely unknown.

CHAPTER 5

The fragile nightingale chirped and trilled from the branch below, uttering the same cheerful refrain until Cerberus snatched it in his fist and snapped its neck. Eyes on the freeway, he bit into the small songbird, spit out the head, and guzzled its blood.

She got away. The bitch somehow evaded him.

It didn't make sense. She was weak and injured. Her fear alone should have left her lame, but she escaped.

Tossing the feathered carcass aside, he stared over the morning traffic, fanning out his senses for any trace of his mate. She was older now, so she would know how to block her thoughts, but she was no match for him. He'd been in her head before. He would get there again.

Kicking a small nest of fledglings from the branches, Cerberus settled into a comfortable crook and tipped his head back, closing his eyes as his other senses went on guard.

He'd rest for a while, then find her. His body exulted at the impending hunt, the thrill of gaining on her. He would torment her like a weak little mouse, alerting her as soon as he was near but never letting her gain the upper hand.

Licking his lips, he recalled how delicate her body was in his arms. How she cried and screamed. How she broke under his will. Those memories had been long overlooked until he caught a glimpse of her forgotten beauty.

However, her attractiveness did not titillate or excite him. On the contrary, it enraged him. After all of these years, after centuries of being apart, she still resembled her mother.

His eyes narrowed as he gazed about the forest, once more checking that he was alone. She might look like her mother, but she was no replacement for Lilias. She was merely a fee, taken as punishment for her mother's despicable deceit. But now, the girl had her own personal debt to pay.

Oh, what he planned to do to her once he had her...

Adriel... he taunted, reaching for her mind. *Girl...you can run, but I'll still find you...*

He closed his eyes again, recalling the years of pain he'd suffered underground because of her. For decades, his flesh hung loosely from the bone, and his muscles withered away while she escaped him.

His limbs still twitched with a phantom burn. The memory of dirt corroding every abscess, driving his mind to madness as he waited for his body to heal and his limbs to regenerate, still haunted him.

Those recollections were now seared into his soul far more profound than any bond they once shared. His desire to find her existed only to serve his need for vengeance.

The years of waiting, entombed underground without proper food or water, were excruciating. The tightness, the pull, the itch, and that unreachable, phantom ache that existed where his limbs had been ripped away…

She indeed had a debt to pay.

He'd spent lifetimes plotting his revenge. When the putrid stench of his decomposing body became the only thing he knew, he calculated a million ways to punish her.

She left him to rot and starve, buried underground for centuries. The girl knew nothing of pain compared to the hell he survived—a hell of her making—but he would gladly teach her all that she did not know.

He could still feel the prickling throb of his limbs regenerating at a glacial pace. Ten, twenty, fifty, more than one hundred years of starvation and suffering as he waited for his body to heal. He spent an eternity inventing endless ways to make her suffer.

Marbleized by time, he existed as a wasted bag of cold, blue flesh, condemned to an unknown sentence of suffering that he feared would never end. His lungs repetitively seized, and his heart continually ruptured, shutting down his mind for the briefest moment of peace only to awaken in agony once more in that encapsulating hell.

The ungodly pressure of the settling earth built with time and modernization, forcing his capillaries to harden and his organs to fail without access to proper nutrition, killing him over and over again. But as a *draugr*, a skull warrior, a Viking of the undead, he could not die.

Dragging his hand over the roped muscle of his arm, he recalled the fury that built inside him during that time. There was no space to open his mouth and scream. No clean air to blink his eyes in the compressing blackness. Only the deafening silence and the struggle to breathe.

Even now, recalling the lunacy of confinement that mingled with such physical agony caused him to inhale deeply, assuring himself that there was plenty of air to breathe.

His eyes darted over the rushing cars weaving through traffic as he rested in the trees. She was out there—living. He had no desire to kill her. No, he had other plans, lessons he longed to teach her.

Did she know how the lungs burned like fire and popped when no air was left to breathe? She would soon learn. She would know all the pain he'd suffered and more.

The foolish girl assumed having him

stretched and quartered and buried alive would defeat his rage, but it had only delayed and fueled it. Now, she was marked. And once marked, her life was as good as over. But he was cruel enough to ensure her life never ended—there would be no amusement in that.

Once he had her, reclaimed her as his, punished her for defying him, tortured her beyond her wildest fears, he would destroy all that she loved, torment her with endless terror and suffering, but never grant her the privilege or mercy of death.

His mouth curled in a slow, maniacal grin as the promise of such long-awaited satisfaction stretched within reach. Soon, he would reclaim what belonged to him, and, this time, she'd learn the full extent of his savage nature.

He'd show her true pain, the sort that went beyond the physical and lived in the purgatory of a dark mind with no escape. No hope. He'd use her up every way a female could be used, and then he'd carve open her chest, keeping her alive to watch as he slowly ate her ever-regenerating heart.

I'm coming for you, girl...

Let her run. He would eventually see to her misery. Fear had already shadowed her ephemeral happiness in this world, and he was far from finished with her. She would suffer the totality of her betrayal repeatedly until the debt was paid.

CHAPTER 6

Juniper followed signs for upstate New York. Exhaustion radiated from her as her grime-coated knuckles clenched the steering wheel.

Occasionally, she'd stretch and pop a muscle in her neck, exposing dark creases of dust marking her skin. Dirt caked under her finger-nails, and her dark hair appeared as if it hadn't been brushed in months. Such signs of neglect angered Adriel. The Council had a duty to see to her needs, yet it was very clear they had not.

"Did they bathe you?"

Juniper's sharp glance cut from the road to Adriel's face, a cold laugh puffing past her lips. "They gave me a pitcher of fresh water every day. I could drink it or wash with it." Her eyes nar-rowed on the road ahead. "Some days, I was too weak to do either. I'm sorry if I reek."

"There's no need to apologize. Immortals

scent emotion more than any superficial perfume or residue. While sweat might have an odor to you, I can only smell the compounds of the diaphoresis—the cause."

"You mean, you can tell the difference between sweat from exercise and sweat from fear?"

"Exactly. Or sweat from disease."

"Interesting. And probably a good thing because odors are coming off of me that I don't want to contemplate. I can't wait to take a shower." Her upturned nose scrunched as her alert eyes followed the road.

"If you had magick all this time, why didn't you use it to escape?"

Her plump lips flattened into a firm line. "My magick has limits. Once they had me tied and muzzled, I was pretty much helpless." She drew in a shaky breath. "My magick also wasn't that strong to begin with. I was just starting to learn before my aunts…"

Her words cut off, and grief became all Adriel could smell. She was glad Juniper escaped.

After overhearing the atrocious things the elders had done to draw out her magick, Juniper's resilience was all the more impressive. She gave them nothing. After months of tolerating their torture, she never buckled under the torment or betrayed the secrets of her kind.

"I think you're stronger than you realize."

Juniper's mouth curved, but the flash of a smile faltered. "I couldn't give in to them. Not because of any choice I made but because…

when I'm scared, my magic sort of dries up. I don't have control over it."

For a woman in her twenties, she'd survived quite a bit. Her strength was there, even in the absence of her courage, and it was admirable. Juniper was the type of female who was stronger than most, even in her weakest state.

"Your control over your gifts will improve with age."

She glanced at Adriel, her gaze unsure. "How old are you?"

Embarrassed by her longevity in the face of such youth, she said, "Much older than you."

"How much?"

She drew in a long breath and sighed. "I was born in the first half of the fifteen hundreds."

"Holy shit. For real?"

"Watch the road." Adriel glanced ahead as the girl gaped at her. "And yes. For real."

"So that makes you... Over five hundred years old?"

Another sigh. "Yes."

"You guys are like wine, though, right? You get better with age?"

"That's one way to look at it." While her bones were solid, her muscles strong, and her body functioned without aches or disease, there was still a weariness to her mind. She remained sharp but jaded by the things she'd seen. Half a millennia was a long time to live, even from a mostly sheltered standpoint. "Time hardens a person, especially if life isn't kind."

Juniper glanced at her again, taking a quick measure of her form. "Do they mistreat all women?"

"Females are cherished among our kind, but not all males are honorable."

"Ain't that the truth?" Her expression turned contemplative. "You must have seen so much in your lifetime."

"I'm old, but my experiences in this world are limited. I'm shamefully ignorant."

Juniper frowned. "I doubt that."

It was humiliating just how naive she could be. "I never would have considered taking a vehicle to travel. And if I had, I never would have known where to find one."

"Adriel, you would have eventually figured something out. Cars are everywhere, and no one can run forever—including immortals."

But even after Juniper suggested a motor vehicle, it had not occurred to Adriel to use compulsion to steal one. If she couldn't run forever and she wanted to evade a male as evil and conniving as her mate, she needed to start thinking like a lawless rogue.

"All of my adult life, I've been disciplined to obey the rules."

At that, Juniper smiled. "Rules are meant to be broken, Ade. There's no one here to discipline you now."

Wringing her hands in her lap, she sensed a tiny thrill at such a thought. "I've never lived outside of someone else's authority."

A dark, slender brow arched high on her brow, and she smirked. "Sometimes you just gotta say fuck it and do what feels right. Take charge of your own destiny."

Adriel swallowed, every instinct inside her tensing with reluctance. Regardless of a person's belief system, certain crimes came with great, unavoidable consequences. That was why they abandoned Europe in the 1700s. Order was sometimes a luxury, and living without it could lead to devastation and uncontrollable chaos. They craved a lawful society, and so they created one.

The Order had strict laws by design. Anyone who violated the fundamental principles faced The Council of Elders and was typically met with harsh punishment. Unfortunately, those laws were curated to maintain authority, which belonged solely to the males. Even her son, by age five, had more authority than she.

Females were not invited to debate their charges but were forced to silently endure the sentencing. Adriel had been publicly flogged many times for her strong-willed defiance. Having the bishop as a close friend did nothing to save her from such painful humiliation. Eleazar often begged her to reel in her stubborn campaign for equality because even he, her closest friend in this world and the most decisive authority within The Order, could not see past the imposed limits of her gender defined by their faith. And even the bishop could not overrule an edict of The Elder Council.

The religion the elders selected upon arriving in America required female obedience. As a female older than many elders, Adriel rejected such expectations and argued countless times for equality.

Not without penalty, of course.

Females were born with the same abilities as the males in their species. But, among The Order, time and Amish culture constricted female potential like an ever-tightening vice. The expectation was indeed meekness. Anything more was corrected, including the expression of personal identity, which was likely why she had no sense of who she was. Without her faith, without The Order, she seemed as lost as a fallen leaf drifting through its final bow.

She shook her head slowly and scoffed. "I'm not sure I believe in destiny anymore. I detached from my faith long ago. Why should I honor a God that would call me to the devil himself?"

Cerberus was pure malevolence. No decent God would sentence her to such an eternity.

"My aunts believed in the power of three," Juniper said, her voice quiet and reminiscent. "What is done will be repaid in kind. Good is rewarded with good, and evil is repaid in suffering. Man created society. The universe created natural order. Everything takes care of itself."

Was that true?

In the old days, Adriel's family's faith had

been steeped in the belief that evil deeds would be punished by an all-powerful god. Guilt and fear seemed all she ever knew.

"Your aunts' faith sounds…simple."

"I guess it is." She shrugged. "It's all based in nature—what is above is also below. People think witches worship the devil, but Satan is a Christian belief. Our practice demands respect for all earthly creatures. For the good of all and the harm of none."

"Yet, your family attacked Jonas Hartzler."

"And paid dearly."

Adriel would not debate right and wrong with her on the subject of Jonas. For whatever reason, the witches must have believed they had just cause to go against their faith. There were always exceptions to the rules, just as the elders found exceptions to her situation with Cerberus.

While the elders believed there was nothing more sacred than the divine calling of mates, they helped her escape hers—but not without great judgment.

They assumed his anger would wane with time and that she'd eventually repent and correct the errors of her past. This placed a great deal of accountability on her shoulders since the female is viewed as the peacekeeper of a home.

Repenting was never her plan, and no bonnet or prayer book would change her mind.

She dressed the part and abided by their laws but never stopped thinking for herself. Deep down, she believed females were just as entitled to rights as males—a belief that significantly contributed to her loneliness over the centuries.

Adriel cut her hair every week, determined to keep it short. There was no law against such an act, but the others saw it for what it was: a blatant show of disobedience beneath the prayer *kapp*.

The *kapp* was a symbol of submission—to God and husband—but Adriel would never willingly surrender her autonomy to any male ever again—that included the males of The Elders' Council as well as her son, who out-ranked her scant authority as a boy simply because he was male.

A pebble flung into the windshield, and Adriel gasped.

"Stupid truck." Juniper shifted lanes and appeared undisturbed by the tiny chip in the windshield, so Adriel forced her muscles to unclench.

Startled by a pebble. Pathetic.

"How come you were always sitting on that bench with Dane?"

The question caught Adriel off guard. "You knew I was there?"

"I could always sense Dane. He came to the cells every night, so I knew his voice and smell. Sometimes I heard you two whispering, so I asked him who you were. He told me a little about you."

"You two talked?"

"Occasionally. In the beginning, we had

nothing nice to say, but then, over time… He was the only person I trusted."

Dane was a familiar topic that comforted Adriel. He spent a lot of time in the basement of Council Hall visiting his sister, Cybil, so it made sense that Juniper would have learned of his good nature since her cell was close to his sister's.

"What did he say about me?"

She smiled, her gaze focused on the road. "He said you weren't like the others. That you were older and a bit of a badass. Whenever we talked about you, his voice filled with protective pride, the way a son might talk of his mother."

That made Adriel smile. "Dane is a good man."

"Yeah. But we both agreed your real son's a prick."

Dane's dislike for her son did not surprise her, but it did bother her. Her son was a good and honorable male who faced centuries of judgment for her choices.

"Christian is…softening now that he's found his mate." Her son had always been a concern. He was part of her but also part of Cerberus. "I'd like to blame Christian's father for his flaws, but I'm afraid he gets his hardheadedness from me."

Juniper chuckled. "You are stubborn."

Adriel frowned but then understood she was only teasing. Her defenses softened. "We sat on that bench because females are not permitted to enter Council Hall unless summoned by the elders."

"But Dane's a guy."

"He's not a purebred immortal, nor is he a true member of the faith."

"Neither are you."

She hesitated. Sometimes, the simplest assumptions required the most complicated explanations. "I abide by the basic principles of Amish life, but I confess, my faith crumbled long ago."

"Then why did you stay in a place that made you wait outside like a dog on a leash?"

"I was not waiting like a dog."

Juniper studied her briefly and snickered. "Dane's right. You've definitely got a little badass in you."

"I'm sure I don't know that term."

"It's a compliment."

She wasn't sure how comparing her to poorly trained livestock could double as praise, so she asked, "Did Dane help you?"

"He actually needed my help. He was trying to kill that...*thing* in the last cell."

"You mean Isaiah?" Adriel straightened in her seat. "Did he?"

Juniper laughed without humor. "No. It went ballistic the second he shot it, then it broke through the walls—like they weren't even holding him in. His sister came after me, and that's when I ran. She got hurt. Maybe killed, I don't know. That thing took her."

"Isaiah took Cybil?"

Juniper's brow pinched as the scent of regret filled the car. "I told Dane my magick was limited, but he didn't believe me."

Adriel laid a hand on her arm. "It's not your fault. Cybil is no longer meant for this world. She can't be saved."

"What about the other thing?"

"Isaiah is far beyond redemption. Both of them should have been put down long ago."

They were silent for a long moment until Adriel asked, "Was Dane the one who fed—"

"No."

When she said nothing more on the subject, Adriel instinctively reached into her mind—

Juniper jerked her body toward the door, and the car swerved. "Hey, back off!"

Adriel gasped, pressing her hand to her temple. "What was that?"

"What was what? You're the one who came at me."

"You deflected me."

"I didn't do anything."

But she had. There was some sort of barrier protecting her mind from trespassers, which meant that if someone abused her, they did so without the anesthetic of compulsion. That only left force.

Shaking off the ache in her head, Adriel asked, "You won't tell me who hurt you?"

"I can't. I never saw his face."

If an immortal had Juniper's blood in their

system, they would be able to track her. "Do you think they'll come after you?"

Silence stretched as the scent of regret shifted to pungent anger. Juniper's grip tightened on the wheel, the color bleaching from her knuckles.

"Let them. My hands aren't tied anymore. As soon as I get settled, I intend to figure some shit out. No one will ever get me in a cell again. I plan to make sure of it."

Adriel appreciated her honesty and believed Juniper would seek the protection she needed to feel safe again. "To relieve your guilt about Dane, Cybil is undead. She does not need to breathe consistently to live. Her lungs will pump again as long as her head and heart remain intact."

"That's how you do it?"

Adriel frowned. "Pardon?"

"Kill a vampire. You need to cut off their head or rip out their heart?"

While she wanted to once again argue the terminology, she was startled by her preoccupation with death. "Take my advice, Juniper. Knowing how to end an immortal life and possessing the capabilities to do so are two very different things."

She glanced at Adriel nervously. "Will you try to kill him, the one that's after you?"

The breath in her lungs turned heavy like a cold mist. "Cerberus is older and stronger than me. I will do whatever I need to do to survive him, but he is not easily destroyed." And if she couldn't accomplish that, she would find peace in leaving this world.

Juniper shifted lanes again. There seemed to be fewer vehicles on the road than earlier. "I'm glad Dane's sister is still alive."

"For Dane's sake?"

The witch nodded.

Adriel could not match her sentiment. Cybil was perhaps closer to being vampire than anything else. After her brutal transition, her soul was lost. Dane refused to accept that his little sister, the last of his mortal family, was gone, so he clung to the hope that he might one day save her.

"If Isaiah took her, I don't know how long she has."

Juniper frowned. "I don't know about that. The way that thing acted with Dane... It was like he was trying to protect her. He saw Dane as the threat. I don't think he wanted to hurt her."

"Isaiah has committed unspeakable atrocities. I assure you, he is not protecting that child—may God have mercy on her soul."

"I thought you didn't believe in God."

"I never said that. I said my faith had crumbled long ago. I believe in a God, but I don't necessarily believe He is good and always on our side."

"I can respect that." She shook her head, her brow scrunching as she watched the road. "I can't stop picturing it. He carried her off like a rag doll. Maybe it's best she doesn't know what's going on." Glancing at Adriel, she asked, "How long can you guys play dead?"

"I wouldn't categorize it as playing. There is pain and then...emptiness. Peace. It's disorienting when we come back, but... I think Cybil's mind's beyond the point of addling."

Adriel shut her eyes, recalling the many times she'd gasp back to life only to find herself still in the grip of her vicious mate.

The thought of Cerberus filled her with unease. He was still out there. Adriel wished she knew how far behind he was or if he had a handle on their location. She wasn't sure shelter would bring any real peace, but she was anxious to reach their next destination.

"How much longer do you expect we'll be traveling?"

"About an hour. Maybe two before we find a house for you to dazzle. Why?" Juniper glanced at Adriel. "Do you have to pee?"

"No. I, um, will need to feed."

Juniper's horrified expression preceded the wild thumping of her racing heart. "Don't look at me. I'm not on the menu."

"I meant we should stop, preferably somewhere with animals. Anything larger than a raccoon will suffice."

"Right. I'll, uh, just pull over at the first petting zoo we pass."

CHAPTER 7

Cerberus awoke with a jerk, every muscle contracting tightly as he braced for pain that did not come. Reflexively, a frantic panic pulsed through his veins as his body prepared for suffering. When no capillaries burst in his skull, the haunting memories of endless trauma eased, and a sense of safety settled in.

No explosion of chaos ripped through his chest.

His limbs were intact.

His clothing was clean, and not a speck of dirt covered his skin.

He could breathe.

He was not trapped underground.

Those telling moments upon waking always gave away how deeply his centuries entombed still disturbed him. He lived and died a million times, buried alive through that infinite loop of suffocation and agony. Trauma like that didn't fade upon escape, so his mind didn't easily differentiate those insufferable moments of waking up in a living tomb from waking up in a fucking tree.

Breathing a deep breath of fresh air, he savored how easily oxygen filled his lungs. Nothing like the stale, shallow gasps that killed him countless times before.

Glancing over the busy freeway, he monitored the traffic, calculating the time of day by the placement of the sun in the sky. It looked to be just after four.

Withdrawing his phone, he checked the clock and grinned at his impressive accuracy. Four o' six. Not long ago, he'd only had the rotting stench of his decaying limbs to track the passing time.

A tingle of excitement invigorated him as he stretched and refocused on his purpose.

I'm coming for you, girl...

He fanned out his senses but, once again, to his infinite fury, found no trace of her. He would eventually have her in his grip, and he couldn't wait to watch the life seep from her eyes as she begged for mercy—over and over and over again. He would show her the same mercy the cold earth showed him as he lay trapped in a deafened tomb of endless suffering.

During those centuries underground, his fractured mind became the only escape he had. Some days, he could not bear the gradual passing of time, so he distracted himself with thoughts of the past, forgetting the girl and thinking back to a time long before she ever existed.

He shamelessly found comfort in the hidden corners of his mind where his deepest secrets lived. Those tender emotions of his youth had been siphoned away by time and battle, but in his darkest moments of despair, he found great relief in the presence of such memories.

In the presence of *her*.

Lilias.

Beautiful, majestic, enchanting Lilias...

He had loved her selflessly and completely. To think, she saw the purest side of him, and it still wasn't enough to sway her. She ultimately left him for someone else.

During those wretched moments of his darkest despair, he did not think of her betrayal, only her beauty. He sometimes preferred the lie and found sanctuary in the memory of her artificial kindness. Those lies were the only comfort he could find in the cold, dark, silent earth.

Now, those delicate recollections crumbled under the heavy weight of his deep-seated resentment. Despite his ever-present, unrequited desire to have her, he sincerely wished he'd killed her. Stealing her first born and murdering her children was not nearly enough to punish her. Lilias was the catalyst behind his centuries of suffering.

No matter how many times he died or how many years passed, the pain of her abandonment remained the greatest injury of his life. He'd fought in hundreds of battles and died repetitively underground as he wasted away in his own dismembered despair, but nothing compared to the excruciating misery he'd discovered through love.

His foolish affection was his highest regret. Lilias was his first and his last. His only. And she paid dearly for her deceitful choices.

Today, he reveled not in the tender recollections of a love-sick boy but in the memory of the inescapable pain. The agony he'd suffered shaped him into a hardened male. When he was underground, he welcomed the madness. His mind became his only escape and he found hidden corners that were so dark a lesser immortal would have flinched and shied away.

But Cerberus welcomed the darkness inside of him.

Behind the mask of a modern businessman lived a monster. His duality served him well, and he'd adapted quickly to the ease of modern living, finding great comfort in wealth and luxury but never forgetting his purpose.

The polite grins and tiresome nods were all lies. Years of suffering had shredded any remnants of his moral fiber. He plainly saw what he was and accepted his true self without shame.

Human entanglements only confused the simplicity of his nature. Mortals were food. Unlike before, they served him now.

His lack of empathy and his innate hunger for living flesh and carnal pleasures lived at the base of his needs. He was a predator. He did not lower himself to consider the pitiful feelings of his prey the way he once had.

Accepting his dark nature unleashed the full extent of his potential. No longer bound by propriety or restricted by social expectations, Cerberus worried about one thing and one thing only—surviving long enough to have his revenge.

He chuckled. To think, the bitch had been hiding on an Amish farm living a life of self-imposed discipline when she could have done anything. Pathetic.

He rejected any suggestion that immortals required social order. The lion did not cower to the rabbit or the jackal, so why should immortals limit themselves by the laws of mortals?

As a *draugr*, he was top of the food chain, the son of a snake-shifter, and king of whatever he claimed. In all of his misery, he'd made peace with the unsavory parts of himself, and once he escaped the constraints of morality, he never pretended to be anything less than the rogue, vicious barbarian they created.

His time entombed only sharpened his need for revenge. Other times, he embraced the excruciating repetition of suffering and death with silent calm, surrendering to his lack of control and testing how composed he could remain in the face of fear.

His hatred anchored his mind in fury and gave him a place to bide his time. He blamed the girl, Adriel. He blamed her mother, Lilias. He blamed the males who put him into the ground and Lilias's mate, Lazarus, for taking her away. He even blamed King Charles, the sniveling weakling, for bringing her into his life and creating discontent where Cerberus had once been satisfied with next to nothing.

No matter what he felt over those long, torturous centuries, immortality always saved him in the end. The certainty that he would one day have his revenge comforted him through the darkest times. Very few knew how to finish a *draugr* and, be it a comfort or a curse, his true end would not happen buried in the earth.

It took decades for his limbs to regenerate without the aid of mortal blood and centuries to escape the ground. Time lost all meaning as his muscles wilted away and his sanity liquified. The unforgettable pain of new skin glacially regrowing over bone just as maggots rapidly ate it away was enough to drive the soundest immortal mad.

Shaking off the memory, not wanting to trigger old fears, he fanned out his senses again, pushing further than he had the last time.

Girl... Where are you, girl? You do not want to anger your mate... Answer me.

Leaping from one tree to the next, he continued to search for her but found nothing. He preferred to be outdoors after centuries of confinement and took pleasure in his hunt.

Looking out from the trees at the mortal chaos that filled the roads, he grinned. The meaningless lives and routines of mortals were about as entertaining as ants moving grains of sand. But their cars and technology fascinated him.

For ages, he'd wondered at the curious rumbles coming from above ground. Gentle vibrations of unrecognizable sounds changed over the years, from hoofbeats and wooden wheels to water-cooled car engines and the unknown.

Those endless rumblings were a welcomed disruption to the darkness. Curiosity could be a great distraction from pain. While trapped underground, he'd thought the noises above to be many things. Gods smiting the earth, floods, or even earthquakes. But in the end, the technology of motor vehicles went far beyond his limited imagination.

The shock of seeing motor vehicles rushing over roads once terrified him. Now, he owned several. But nothing beat the thrill of hunting by foot.

Dropping from the elevated branches to the earth, Cerberus landed in an agile crouch. He brushed a hand over his tailored pants and grimaced at the scent of smoke still clinging to his clothes.

Moving toward the rumbling road, he scanned the traffic for a victim to join him for this evening's meal. Cars swerved, and horns blared as he walked directly into rushing traffic. One quick mental command and an SUV pulled over.

He knocked on the glass window and pointed to the mechanism in the door. "Unlock it."

The small knob clicked upward, and the mortal female stared at him, her adrenaline pumping wildly through her veins as her body remained hypnotized but not anesthetized under his compulsion.

He preferred them frightened because nothing sweetened the blood of prey like the spike of adrenaline. The door closed as he slid into the passenger seat, buffeting the noise from the highway and stifling the air.

"Drive."

He lowered the window as she turned her attention to the road and eased back into traffic. The delicious pounding of her heart triggered his hunger, but he needed to get her somewhere isolated.

Seeing her purse on the ground, he lifted it to his lap and sifted through the contents. The cash went into his pocket while her phone and the rest of the useless junk went out the window.

"You won't need that anymore."

A tear rolled down her cheek as the color bleached from her fingers gripping the wheel. Her chaotic thoughts rushed into gibberish as her mouth remained locked shut. If she could talk, she'd be blabbering through negotiations that would not work, begging for him to spare her pathetic life and bargaining with things that did not interest him. He didn't care about her children, husband, or pets dependent on her, so he compelled her silence.

Her chin trembled, desperation fracturing her thoughts as she entertained silent ways to appeal to his compassionate side. People would do anything to escape their worst fears. How unfortunate for her that he became incapable of empathy long ago. Only hedonistic emotions associated with hunger and his unsatisfied need for revenge interested him now.

"Turn there into that parking lot. Pull around to the back."

She had no choice but to follow his command, and when she could drive no further, he ordered her to stop beneath the shade of the trees.

Pushing the gear shift to park, he unclipped her safety belt. "Get out of the car."

She waited by the door as he walked around the vehicle. Despite his compulsion, she trembled violently.

"Come." He led her into the woods, stopping when they were far from civilization.

Jerking her forward, he pushed her back against the trunk of a tree and tugged at her clothes. Her breathing accelerated, and more tears fell as he ripped open her blouse and clawed away her bra.

When she whimpered, he paused to study her out of sheer curiosity. The scent of her fear perfumed the air, and her rushing heartbeat called to him like a tribal drum lured the rain.

"Hush, now," he soothed, lowering his voice and tracing his elongated claw delicately over her cheek as her breath punched past her teeth in petrified puffs. "I'm not going to ravish you."

Nostrils flaring rapidly and breath skipping, she met his stare with terrified relief.

Cerberus grinned, exposing the full length of his viper-like fangs, which enhanced her fear even more. Humans were so stupid.

"I'm going to eat your heart."

A strangled gasp escaped her throat as his clawed fist punched through her chest, tearing through the flesh, piercing the muscle, and yanking the organ free from the surrounding capillaries and bone.

Her body dropped to the forest floor like a useless bag of flesh as he bit into the tender tissue, still warm from beating. Closing his eyes, he savored the delicious delicacy.

Unfortunately, not long ago, his diet consisted of much smaller game—millipedes, beetles, arachnids, and whatever other insects he could compel into his mouth. Those tiny night crawlers had been his only sustenance for centuries, sustaining his atrophied body as much as the effort to compel them depleted his withered strength.

He'd since become somewhat of a foodie, as the mortals would say. He went to great lengths to find the most organically fresh nutrition to maintain a proper diet that kept him at the peak of his strength.

Gnawing into the cooling heart, he licked at

the blood that trickled down his fingers to his wrist. He could have just fed from her vein. He could have even let her live. But why limit himself?

He was hungry, and she was a weak, nothing of a mortal. Just as simple humans thought nothing of the animals they slaughtered, he wasted no time considering the irrelevant feelings of his food.

CHAPTER 8

"*C*an I get you another beer?"

Dane stared at the cute bartender, debating if he should find a place to crash or just keep drinking. Pushing his empty bottle forward, he motioned for a refill.

He hadn't slept, had barely stopped running, his mind was going a mile a minute, and he was no closer to forming a plan. What the hell was he going to do? He had no place to go, no family, no home, a dog tied out front, and a meager amount of money in his pocket for food.

The television on the other end of the bar re-played a clip of politicians rambling about the upcoming election. It had been so long since he thought of this world or those who governed it, he didn't recognize any of the names or faces on the screen.

His life had narrowed to the scope of a primi-tive peephole where secrets were protected by laws, and faith was a pillar of judgment. Now, that life was gone.

"Here you go." The petite brunette bartender slid another beer forward.

This was his first time drinking in such an establishment. Aware of every cotton T-shirt, hoody, and the fact that he was the only man not wearing jeans, he aimed to stay as unnoticed as possible, observing the others and mimicking their behavior to blend in.

He should consider getting some new clothes, but his money would be better spent on shelter and food. Honestly, he shouldn't even be drinking this piss when he had other needs to meet, but the beer was keeping him from completely losing his mind.

Trying to welcome the old, familiar sight of ordinary people, he waited for a sense of belonging to return. It didn't.

He'd grown up in the modern world, but it no longer felt right. Everything was loud and chaotic, very different from his life on an Amish farm over the past several years. Despite being a refuge of sorts, he'd accepted that strange place as his home. The homesickness he currently suffered could only be the result of some twisted mind-fuck refugees knew. That, or Stockholm Syndrome survivors.

They were not like him. These people were not like him. He was completely and utterly on his own. Figuring out where to go next wasn't a simple thing.

Having immortal bloodlines came with some perks, but nothing that would help him survive. Unlike the full-bred immortals on the farm, he couldn't compel others, and he could only read the thoughts of children or adults who thought in the purest form. A lot of good that would do him.

He wasn't Dane the teenager anymore. Nor was he Amish or like the immortals who lived on the farm.

Aside from the erotic jolt of energy blood-drinking brought, he saw no gains to his half-bred existence. He might be part-blood-sucker, but that part of him only added to his lonesome status as the outcast.

He had no clue who he was supposed to be anymore.

After learning his parents weren't even his real parents, he lost any pre-determined factors about his genetics. His biological father was a psychotic immortal, and a deranged vampire murdered his adoptive mother. Not something he could easily share in a grief circle or with his old friends.

Since learning immortals existed, he saw unthinkable things. Death, resurrection, insanity, violence, abductions, blood lust, and more. But worst of all, he saw the limitless power of a cult that flourished under centuries of indoctrination. The sheltered existence of The Order was perhaps the scariest truth of all.

Immortals were hiding in plain sight, but

their blanketed crimes hid beneath the laws of their faith. To think religion could hold more power than instinct.

Such illusions of peaceful domestication didn't fool him. They were still dangerous when it served them. They merely had to pretty up their actions by proclaiming their behavior was sanctioned by God. Such ideology had been ingrained in them since birth, propagated by older generations, and anyone who questioned their Amish ways or opposed The Council was shunned, like him.

Dane peeled back the damp label of his beer. His thoughts once again returned to Grace. She could have come with him. He would have asked her if he thought she might say yes, but she'd made it clear she would not abandon her faith.

Amish life was all Gracie had ever known. She feared the outside world, but he could have protected her and helped her acclimate. If she had just trusted him, they could have lived a normal life together. He could have shown her that the modern world she feared was not as scary as it seemed, but her innocence left her imagination limited. And it was such innocence that made him fall in love with her.

Gracie loved him, too. Or so he thought.

It no longer mattered. She would never be his. She would never set aside her beliefs and choose him over the so-called destiny her faith promised.

Grace...

Even now, his heart called to her despite the endless ache. Would that ache ever go away?

He turned his beer, wondering how he would go on, never knowing how her day was or if she was safe and happy. How would he make it more than a few hours without thinking of an excuse to see her?

He should have said goodbye. But then it would have been impossible to leave, and he simply couldn't stay, not when the bishop himself had exiled him for breaking their laws.

Dane's jaw locked, his hand balling into a fist tight enough to make his knuckles pop. Fuck the bishop and fuck The Order.

None of this would have happened if they would have killed Isaiah. The monster not only murdered his mother, the fucker now had his sister, Cybil.

Yet he was the one sent away.

That was what Gracie chose over him—an order that refused to see justice and masked atrocities by labeling them ordained acts of God.

Maybe she deserved them.

He gripped the bottle, chugging down the beer as he breathed through his bottomless rage. He wanted to break something. He wanted to watch that sadistic fucker bleed out until its eyes glazed and the life left its lungs once and for all. How could he have let that fucking beast get away with his sister?

His mind shied away from assumptions and images of what Isaiah might do to Cybil. He had no idea where she was or how to save her. It was over. He needed to let her go and accept that he'd lost—both his sister and Grace.

He'd lost everything.

"Hey buddy, you think you can move down a seat so I can sit next to my girl?"

Dane's head shot up, his thoughts scattering as he moved his beer and napkin aside, giving the man to his left plenty of room.

"Sure."

He'd lost track of time since sitting down. With no natural light shining into the pub, it was hard to determine if it was evening, but by the flood of new patrons coming in, he assumed it was after five.

The television set changed channels, and a game came on. He blinked at the bright, flat screen, his eyes no longer accustomed to watching such things. How long had it been since he enjoyed a show, a movie, or even played a video game? Those foreign concepts now felt like an utter waste of time.

An advertisement replaced the game as another cycle of commercials started. The actors moved about a fake set of a home as if detergent was enough to brighten their day. Had commercials always looked this artificial?

Frowning at the screen, he struggled to grasp the staged humor. Perhaps he was just too tired, or was he that out of touch?

The next three commercials were for medication. He'd forgotten how delicate regular people were. As a half-breed, he'd always healed quickly, but living on a farm full of immortals who never got sick really made one forget the tiresome necessity of maintaining good health.

Thoughts of disease brought about sad memories of his grandmother. Unlike Cybil, she could have been saved. She'd been one of the chosen ones. But she chose to die anyway. Perhaps that was the wisest choice.

The pub's noise and lights grated on him, so he returned his focus to his beer. The patrons were either talking or lost in their phones. Were people always this addicted to screens? It now looked utterly strange to him, like everyone was brainwashed and hypnotized.

Hairstyles had also changed. His once trendy style had grown out over the years, and he wore it neatly tied back, as was the fashion on the farm, but no one here had such a cut.

A few people stared at him, much like he stared at them. His face heated as he dropped his gaze to the counter. No one else was wearing suspenders. He definitely needed to get some jeans and regular clothes.

Straightening his spine, he tucked a long strand of hair behind his ear and swallowed, looking back at the TV so as not to stare at others. The technology simply couldn't hold his attention.

The bartender, a short woman with brown wavy hair, hustled to fill everyone's orders. She was pretty, taller than Gracie. Her eyes were brown rather than the stunning silver-blue he was used to.

Realizing he was measuring her against Gracie, he quickly cut off his thoughts. Could he think of nothing else?

A man at the other end of the bar pounded on the side of a machine.

"Hey! Don't hit the machine," the bartender snapped, returning to the taps to fill a beer order.

The pounding stopped, but Dane sensed the man's frustration. As terrifying as immortals could be, he learned to live comfortably in their presence. Now, mortals made him uneasy. He'd been away from ordinary society for so long that regular people now seemed unpredictable and volatile.

"This damn thing owes me a token." The man whacked the side of the machine again.

The woman behind the bar shoved a tray of glasses onto the counter and marched over to the disgruntled customer. She only stood up to his shoulder, but her glare stopped him in his tracks.

"Hit my machine again, and you're going to wind up with a repair bill." She rotated the device so the game screen faced her and pressed some buttons on the glass. A small receipt spit out and she tore it off, handing it to the man. "There. Now you can collect your three dollars." As she returned to her drink orders, she muttered under her breath, "Idiot."

When the man left and the after-work crowd got settled, things slowed down. The little bartender was constantly moving, but the rush wasn't anything she couldn't handle. She worked her way around the crowd and eventually replaced Dane's beer with another.

He awkwardly smiled. "It's pretty busy here, huh?"

"Yup." She always seemed to be doing three things at once between pouring drinks, ringing up customers, and rushing into the back to throw together food orders.

As a steaming tray of mozzarella sticks went by, Dane's stomach growled. He needed to watch his spending, but he also needed to eat. He wondered how much an order of fries would cost. Surely, he could afford some fries.

He was about to ask for a menu but the bartender rushed off, disappearing through a discreet door he hadn't seen her use before. When she returned a moment later, she was lugging a large tank for the taps.

He sprung off his stool and lifted it from her. "Let me give you a hand with that."

Startled by his offer, she hesitated and then agreed. "Uh, okay. It goes back there."

He dragged it behind the counter to where she pointed. Dane watched as she rigged the valves, disconnecting them from the old tank and reconnecting the tubes to the new one.

"Can I take that one away for you?"

"That's okay. They're light when they're empty."

"Hey, Gabby, when can I expect that drink order?" a patron shouted.

"Relax, Steve." She irritably flung a strand of hair away from her face. "I'm working on it."

Dane lifted the empty tank. "Where's it go?"

She sighed as more patrons formed a line at the bar. "Through the door and down the steps. Thanks."

He took the empty tank to a cellar where several other bottles and cans filled the industrial shelves. The thought of possibly stealing some food crossed his mind, but he resisted the temptation. Instead, he carried a large sack of potatoes upstairs for her.

He'd overheard her telling a customer the kitchen was running low on fries, so he figured this would help her out.

"Did you want these in the kitchen?"

She frowned at the sight of the large sack on his shoulder. "Oh… um…sure. Thanks."

He'd watched Grace fry potatoes a hundred times, so he had an idea of how it was done. Sometimes, he helped her dig up the potatoes in the garden. Her fair skin always glistened in the sunlight and he loved the way she smelled of sunshine and earth by the end of each day.

A familiar, sharp ache of longing drilled through him. He glanced at the exit, fighting the urge to return to the farm, back to her.

Every part of him wanted to return to Grace and demand she admit her feelings. But she never would. Nor could he go back now that the bishop, himself, had exiled him.

It wasn't Eleazar's fault. As the bishop, he needed to uphold the laws of The Order and answer to the other elders on The Council. Dane had violated their laws and that meant he was no longer welcome there.

The bishop could have acted harsher. He could have had him punished or worse. But he only wished Dane well. Then he stuffed his pockets full of cash and sent him on his way. It wasn't much, but it was more than anyone else had offered, so Dane couldn't resent the guy.

"Hey, what the hell are you doing back here?"

He stared stupidly at the bartender. What was her name? Gabby?

He glanced down at his hands where he held a potato under the rushing water of the faucet. "I, uh, figured you'd want these washed so you could use them."

Her scowl deepened. "What's your deal?"

He shrugged. "I wanted fries, and you said you were almost out."

"Do you usually just help yourself to other people's kitchens?"

He glanced around the small, industrial setup. Very different from any other kitchen he'd ever been in. "No."

"Gabby, can I get a refill?" a customer called, and she huffed, clearly overwhelmed by the crowd.

Taking pity on her, he said, "I can give you a hand."

She hesitated until another customer called her name. Then she pointed to the wall behind a metal counter. "The peeler's there. Once they're peeled and cleaned, drop them into that water cooler to soak."

The corner of Dane's mouth kicked up. "You got it."

When she returned to the bar, he filled a bowl with water and snuck out the back door. Colby sprung to his feet when he saw him, his orange tail wagging happily.

"Hey, boy. Got you some water." He'd see about saving some burger scraps too if any dishes came through the kitchen.

He nuzzled Colby one last time then left him to drink the water. When he returned inside, he sat on a flipped bucket, peeling and dropping potatoes into a cooler until the sack was empty and every spud was clean. He appreciated busy work, as it kept his mind off other things.

"So, what's your story?" Gabby asked, leaning in the kitchen doorway once the bar crowd dissipated. "Are you Amish?"

"I… I guess you could say I have Amish family."

"You guess?"

He shut the cooler lid. "My real family's gone. I was living on an Amish farm for a while."

"Guess that's why you only look partially Amish."

"Partially?"

She tapped her chin. "No beard."

No one in The Order had facial hair. Once immortals reached their prime, their bodies sort of regulated that stuff. Dane didn't want to stick out, so he made a habit of shaving.

"I'm guessing you're looking for money."

Her directness caught him off guard. "I…You just looked busy, so I figured I'd help."

"Well, I am busy. My chef quit without notice, and my waitress has a sick kid at home, so it's been a little crazy trying to keep up with everything."

His brow creased. "You own the bar?"

"My dad does, but he can't run it anymore. Dementia."

"I'm sorry."

She pointed to another cooler. "The potatoes in that one have been soaking, so they're ready to cut. We only slice a few at a time, or they get mushy and brown. They're pretty much made to order."

He looked at the other cooler. "Did you want me to slice them?"

"You've been sitting out there all day. You're hungry, right?"

He nodded.

"Then help yourself. The press is there. Drop them in the basket, and try not to burn your hands. Four minutes for regular. Six minutes for crispy." She looked back at the bar and cursed as more patrons arrived. "There's warm cheese in that pump."

When she left, he scanned the appliances. This was very different from Gracie's kitchen or his grandmother's, but he understood what everything did and could quickly figure out how the fryer worked.

Wedging the pre-soaked potatoes through the press was easy and he liked the sizzle the oil made when he dropped the basket into the deep-fryer. Rolling up his sleeves, he anxiously awaited the timer as the oil bubbled and the scent of food wafted through the air. He was starving and couldn't remember the last thing he ate.

Too impatient to wait for crispy, he gathered a plastic basket and lined it with paper. He pulled the fries and dumped them onto the platter. Glistening and still sizzling, he popped one into his mouth and cursed as it burned his tongue.

"Don't!"

Covering his mouth, he spun and found Gabby watching him again.

"They're too hot. You have to give them a minute."

The burn in his mouth was already healing, thanks to the blood in his system. But she was right. They were way too hot to eat.

"Here." She angled a fresh beer toward him, and he gladly took it.

Once he cooled his mouth with a sip, he plucked another fry from the basket and popped it into his mouth. He was ravenous, so he didn't waste time on things like table manners as he stuffed his face.

Gabby carried a bin of dishes and trash to the counter. "Why did you leave the Amish people?"

He swallowed. "I didn't have a choice. I broke the rules."

"What'd you do, use a lightbulb?" She laughed.

"Something like that." Except it was more along the lines of blowing a six-inch hole through a vampire's chest, but that was a lot to explain so he just kept eating.

"Do you have a place to stay?" She handed him a shaker of salt.

He shook his head and doused the fries in seasoning. "I haven't figured that out yet."

"Look, the last thing I need is a stray cat to feed, but you seem pretty honest—I don't know, maybe it's the Amish garb, or maybe I'm just exhausted, and it's making me stupid, but if you're willing to give me a hand, you can crash here for a few nights. I could use the extra help and pay you minimum wage plus a cut of the tips, which are decent."

"Really?" He hadn't expected her to offer him a job, let alone a place to stay.

She glanced at his exposed forearms. "Really. Plus, I hate lugging things up the stairs. You seem…capable."

He glanced down at the ropes of muscle covering his arms. Years of manual labor with primitive tools did that to a man. He never thought much of it since everyone on the farm was in impeccable health and had prime physiques.

"Thank you. I'm grateful for the offer."

"Good. You can show your gratitude by filling these orders." She handed him a slip of paper.

He read over the list. "How do I…?"

"First, you need to cover your hair." She plucked a hairnet from a box, then snagged a laminated sheet from the door of the steel fridge. "Everything's written out here. Clean up when you're done, and don't get hurt. I gotta get back to the bar."

As soon as she left, he sifted through the dishes, salvaging any dog-safe scraps for Colby. Once he had a plate made up for him, he ran it outside and then returned to the kitchen.

Over the next few hours, Dane had a crash course in culinary arts with minimal instruction. He couldn't taste-test the customers' orders as he went, so he had no clue if he was doing a good job. As long as the meat was fully cooked and no one complained, he supposed he was doing all right.

As the evening went on, he got the hang of the griddle and created a system for prepping things like onions and lettuce. When the orders stopped coming, he gave the kitchen a deep clean.

"Holy crap."

Holding the mop handle, he looked guiltily at Gabby. "Too much?"

"Too much? I don't think this kitchen's ever been this clean."

He grinned, relieved. "I wasn't sure when the grill closed."

"Ten o'clock." She glanced at the large clock on the wall. "You're good. I just cashed out the last customer so I should be locking up as soon as I get things straightened up out there." She pointed to the far wall where a tall metal rack housed large pots and pans. "There's a cot in the corner. I'll see what I can find for blankets after I divvy up the tips."

"Thank you, Gabby."

She hesitated as if his gratitude made her nervous. "I'm just going to point out that there are cameras all over the bar."

He nodded at her warning. "Understood."

She looked him up and down, sighed, then returned to the front.

He continued mopping the floor. When he finished, he dumped the brown water in the large basin sink. His motions halted as a loud clatter echoed through the bar.

He went to the door, but stilled before opening it. His senses sharpened, and his heart quickened as he registered the sound of Gabby's racing thoughts.

Fuck, fuck, fuck, fuck, fuck!

"Fill the bag," a hostile male voice ordered.

Dane darted from the kitchen into the bar, his movements fluid and silent. Gabby stood frozen at the register as a man held a gun in her face. Her gaze shot to Dane.

He shook his head, pressing a finger to his lips and warning her not to look at him.

"Let's go! Open the fucking register!" the man with the gun barked.

Gabby quickly did as she was told, her motions jerky and her breathing unsteady.

"Get that tip jar too."

Dane crouched so his reflection didn't show in the mirror behind the bar. The flash of a baseball bat filled his mind as he sensed Gabby's plan. He wished he had the ability to tell her not to challenge this man, but his telepathy was limited.

Dane had no choice but to move before she did something foolish and got herself shot. Her heart pounded as she reached for the baseball bat hidden under the counter, her mind racing with adrenaline-fueled thoughts.

"Hey—"

Dane sprung, tackling the man into the bar. A shot went off, the ear-splitting blast smashing through the stillness and throwing everything into chaos. Glass shattered, and Gabby screamed.

Dane dragged the man to the ground and banged his hand against the foot rail of the bar until the gun skittered across the floor. Stools fell as punches pounded into Dane's head. They wrestled and rolled across the tile.

The flash of a blade caught his eye and Gabby shouted, "He has a knife!"

Instinct took over. With a snap of his jaw, Dane bit into the man's throat. Panic spiked the blood, adding a sharpness Dane had never tasted, one not easily declined.

The knife clattered to the floor as his body bucked. Something dark and instinctual took hold of him. In that moment, he didn't care if he bled the man dry.

"Stop! What are you doing? Stop!"

Something solid and heavy cracked into his back, and he collapsed, gasping and choking as the gunman scrambled to his feet, choking and holding his throat.

"Get the fuck out of here!" Gabby screamed, now holding the gun and the bat.

The man bolted out the door.

Dane rolled to his aching back and groaned. The hot taste of adrenaline-spiked blood coated his lips and tongue.

"You get out, too! Now!"

Her horrified expression pinned Dane in place more than the angle of the gun pointed at him. "Gabby, he shot at you."

"You *bit* him!"

He covered his mouth, wiping away the evidence. "I was protecting you."

Her thoughts were jumbled, but he didn't need to see into her mind to realize she was terrified. "Are you some kind of cannibal?"

"What? No! Gabby, I—"

"Get out."

"But you said—"

"I don't care what I said, you sick fuck! Get out of my bar!"

He scrambled off the floor, glancing at the cash that spilled from the tip jar. He would not be paid for his work. Nor would he have a place to stay.

Shit.

Blood darkened his sleeve, and he examined the small tear in the fabric. His skin burned. It looked like a bullet might have grazed him. That was going to cause some problems. "Look, if I could just use the sink to wash up—"

"Get. The fuck. Out of here."

He thought of The Order and its laws about exposure. He couldn't leave her like this. He needed to protect not only himself but the others. If their kind were discovered, they would be hunted. His mind went to Gracie, his heart forever set on protecting her.

But he didn't possess the ability to alter a person's memory, so he didn't have a clue what to do.

The tension in the air crackled, and Gabby screamed, *"Get the fuck out of my bar!"*

He quickly fabricated a lie. "I didn't bite him. He punched me in the nose. This…this is my blood. A bullet clipped me—"

"I know what I saw!"

He shook his head. "It's just a scratch and nosebleed, Gabby."

Her jaw trembled, but she held her stance. "I already hit the alarm. The cops are on their way."

Fuck. He had no choice but to go. At least she gave him that option. He'd have to come back later tonight to destroy the camera footage.

He held up his hands in a calming gesture. "You're safe. I'm leaving. I won't hurt you."

Once he reached the door, she said, "Don't ever come back here."

As soon as his boots hit the pavement, the bolt on the inside of the door locked. Colby, sensing danger, strained against his leash to reach him.

"Hey, boy." Dane crouched, assuring him that he was okay. Colby sniffed the blood on his face and whimpered. Dane scratched his head and glanced at the plate on the ground. "At least you ate like a king tonight, eh? Alpha of the pack."

He pressed his head to the dog's and sighed. Life was pretty sad when the comfort from a pet felt like the only thing keeping him sane. Untying his leash from the pole, he led him toward a nearby park he'd spotted a few blocks away.

"Looks like we're sleeping under the stars tonight."

That evening, after returning to the bar and ripping the wires free from the cameras, he realized the days of video-recorded footage were over. Now, digital files went straight to people's phones, and he wasn't sure how to stop her from reviewing the footage.

He hated the idea that he might have exposed

those he still wanted to protect, but there was nothing he could do about it now. At least the few swallows of blood he'd stolen would help heal his injuries quickly and give him some additional endurance for the days ahead.

CHAPTER 9

$\mathcal{A}$driel had rested for most of the drive in hopes of tamping down her hunger. When they reached upstate New York, her ears adjusted to the high altitudes. As they ascended the narrow, winding streets, she took in the raw beauty of the waterfalls, fascinated by the natural canyons, caves, and gaping ravines.

Creeks carved through mountains, forming deep hidden valleys and gorges. Rapids lapped at the rocks in the basins below, where ancient rocks frothed with mist.

"That waterfall was once a brook," she remarked quietly, staring out the car window.

How could just a slow trickle transform mountains into such a masterpiece? To think it was accomplished by moving one granule at a time. These once gentle waters were now brimming with power, but even in its gentlest state, water possessed the strength to saw mammoth rocks in half.

"Can you believe what running water can accomplish?"

"That's great, Ade, but I really have to pee, so let's not focus on the water right now. Besides, you're supposed to be using your Spidey sense to find us a house."

Adriel glanced at the rooftops in the distance, but her attention returned to the cliffs. The subtle scent of methane gas further proved that these rocks had formed millions of years ago. She smiled. Very few wonders could make an immortal feel young.

"There's something powerful protecting this place. Don't you feel it?" The mist pushed into the air the way a thousand whispered secrets formed a scream.

"The only thing I feel is the need to pee. Do you sense any empty houses?"

Adriel sensed the ephemeral passing of creatures that no longer walked the earth, creatures that existed long before the invention of cars.

"I believe the mountains hold secrets. They're incredibly ancient. Doesn't it impress you? That water once belonged to glaciers in the sea."

"I'm much more interested in indoor plumbing at the moment. My bladder is literally about to explode, and you're still talking about water. Enough about the rocks."

"There's power here, Juniper. I can feel it. As a witch, that should interest you."

She growled and pulled down a narrow street on a steep hill. "Sorry, I need to stop."

Once parked, they both got out of the car. It felt good to stretch their legs. Perhaps Adriel could feed while Juniper conducted her business in the nearby woods.

She gave her privacy and hiked in the opposite direction. A glade of mud formed a path where rain eroded the earth. Sediment and moss gathered in every crevice. Adriel closed her eyes and took a few minutes to breathe in the majestic sense of peace.

"Ready?" Juniper opened the car door, and an incessant bell chimed, the modern technology disrupting the tranquility.

Adriel didn't move, unable to pull herself away from the rushing water.

"Whoa." Juniper approached her side, finally able to see what Adriel saw.

They stared over the hypnotic ravine, breathing in the damp air and absorbing the energy of the elements. "Do you feel it now?"

"I feel…something. Time… Power…"

"There is strength here, Juniper. Perhaps it can help you. There has to be a way for you to harness its natural energy to better channel your magick."

"Maybe. But we should keep moving. I'm exhausted, and I need to rest, or I'll be useless."

Adriel broke her stare with the distant chasm. "Yes, we should find a place to rest. Near the falls would be best, I think."

They drove a while longer, weaving in and out of the narrow, steep streets until they found a brick home that looked sturdy and well-maintained despite being several centuries old.

Juniper pulled over at the foot of the pebbled driveway. "I see lights on. Someone's in there."

Adriel scanned the house from the dormers to the cellar floor. "One person. An older female. She's mortal."

Juniper looked at her with an impressed expression. "You can tell her age?"

"I can feel her pain. She's arthritic. She's also partially deaf in one ear. She wears a device but only when she's watching her shows."

"Damn. That's pretty impressive. Anything else?"

"There's a cat in the yard, but that could be a stray."

She laughed and shut off the car. "Cool. Witches dig cats. You ready to do this?"

Adriel had never done anything like this before, so she hesitated. "I don't want to hurt anyone."

"Then don't fuck it up." She left the vehicle and Adriel scanned the house one more time to be sure the woman was alone.

"Don't fuck it up," she repeated, then followed Juniper toward the old home.

Pots of withered tomato plants lined the back steps, showing a lack of water—again, proof that the woman lived alone. The chipped iron railing showed an absence of maintenance.

Despite the house appearing well-kept at first glance, the scent of dust, cat dander, and time tickled her nose the closer they came to the back door.

Juniper pressed the button on a small electrical box.

"What is that?"

"Doorbell." She looked up at the windows. "Do you hear anything?"

Placing a hand on the bricks, Adriel closed her eyes. The scent of talc and rose tickled her nose as a soft shuffle approached.

"She walks with a cane. We must be patient."

The door opened, and a small woman appeared. "Hello." Her deep-set eyes appeared almost crystal against the translucent creases of her pale skin. "May I help you?"

Juniper stepped back, nudging Adriel forward. "You're up."

Adriel easily entered the woman's mind. "Hello, ma'am. I'm Adriel, and this is Juniper," she greeted with a kind smile. "May we come inside?"

The woman cocked her head. "Do I know you?"

"Well, no, but we were wondering if we might—"

"What are you doing?" Juniper snapped. "Don't explain yourself. Just make it happen."

"Don't pressure me," Adriel snapped back, overwhelmed by the trusting innocence that radiated from the woman. "This feels wrong."

The woman stepped back. "Are you solicitors?"

"No, ma'am. We're not selling anything. We're looking for a place to stay."

"Oh, I'm sorry, but this isn't a hotel."

Juniper caught Adriel's arm and hissed, "Do you want to die, Adriel? Did you forget why we came here? He's coming for you. I'm exhausted, and I can't hold this spell much longer. We have no money. If we want to rest, this is our only option, so set aside your moral hang-ups and do your thing."

She looked up at the brick walls, certain they couldn't save her from Cerberus. What if she was just putting one more person in danger?

Glancing back at the little old woman, she dropped her gaze. "I can't."

"*What?* Why the hell not?" Juniper's words trembled with desperation. "You have to. We came all this way. I helped you get this far. You can't just give up."

"I'm not giving up. I've been defeated. He'll find me. There's nothing I can do to stop that. But that doesn't mean I have to involve or endanger others."

"I'm already involved."

"I told you that was a bad idea, but you at least made the choice for yourself." She looked back at the confused woman. "She isn't choosing this."

"Please." Juniper grabbed her hands, her eyes pleading.

Heat rushed up Adriel's arms like a bolt of electricity. It had been so long since anyone touched her the contact startled her, but then a wave of protectiveness washed over her as Juniper's desperation overwhelmed her with empathy. It could only be magick. She didn't typically have such a strong response to others.

"I have nowhere else to go, Adriel. My home is a pile of ash. My aunts are dead. We made a deal. Don't make me regret trusting you. Please do this. I swear, nothing will happen to her. We can help her." She looked back at the little old lady. "Wouldn't you like that? We can sit with you and keep you company."

"Oh, I do enjoy having visitors."

"See," Juniper argued. "We'd be doing her a favor."

Adriel looked regretfully at the sweet woman and sighed. "Invite us in, please."

Any reluctance drifted away as she stepped back and opened the door. "Please, come in."

"See, that wasn't so bad." Juniper passed the woman and immediately started inspecting the dated kitchen's interior. "Yikes. Look at this place."

Maroon laminate tile, mustard yellow countertops, and brunette wooden cabinets darkened the space. There was only one small window over the sink and a buzzing light that hung like a pendant over the chrome-trimmed table and vinyl chairs.

Adriel looked apologetically at the wrinkled

woman. "No one is going to hurt you. We're friends."

Juniper locked the deadbolt. "Tell her not to answer the phone or door. Convince her that we're her distant relatives from out of state—her nieces—and we're staying here for a while."

Adriel looked into the woman's eyes and repeated back everything Juniper said.

"You must be Agatha's girls."

When she looked back at Juniper, the witch shrugged. "Sure."

The woman wrung her hands, the delicate bones of her knotted knuckles pressing against her crepe-like skin. "Did I know you were visiting?"

Gently resting a hand on the woman's frail shoulder, Adriel reassured her. "Yes, you were expecting us."

"Oh, dear, that's right." Capturing Adriel's hand between her cool, withered fingers, she softly squeezed. "I'll show you the guest rooms so you can get settled."

Adriel glanced over her shoulder and scowled. "Juniper!"

"Go on. I'll be right behind you." The witch hushed her and shooed her off as she continued digging through drawers.

Following the fragile mortal up the stairs, Adriel noted with concern the sharp blades of brittle bones that protruded beneath the woman's clothing.

"Do you live alone?"

"Oh, yes. That's why I've been so looking forward to your visit." She pressed open the door to a large bedroom. By the scent of dust in the air, Adriel knew it had been unused for several decades.

A large canopy bed dominated the far wall. "Do you have children?"

"I lost my daughter a long time ago and my husband shortly after. Danny checks on me from time to time, but other than him, it's just me."

Just as she was about to ask who Danny was, Juniper screamed, "Adriel! Get down here—quick!"

She caught the woman's fragile hand and looked into her eyes. "Don't leave this room."

Racing down the stairs, she burst into the kitchen, where Juniper pointed a wooden spoon at a middle-aged man.

"You must be Danny."

"Where's Ruth?" His gaze snapped to Juniper. "Who are you, and why are you going through her drawers?"

"We're none of your business."

He scoffed. "We'll see about that. I'm calling the cops."

Adriel quickly tried to defuse the situation as he pulled out what she assumed was a mobile telephone. "We're Ruth's nieces, Juniper and Adriel. She's been expecting us—"

"Ruth doesn't have nieces."

Juniper looked at her, and Adriel knew what she had to do. Leveling the man with a stare, she pushed into his mind and explained, "Ruth does have nieces—two of them." She pointed to herself and then to Juniper. "We're visiting on a private family matter. You will not call the police or tell anyone that we're here."

"He has a key," Juniper pointed to his hand. "He let himself in."

"So, what do you want me to do?"

"Take it from him."

"Give me your key to the house." He frowned as he dropped it into her hand.

"Find out what his connection is to the old lady."

Adriel pressed her lips tight, uncomfortable with this level of pretense. "What is your relationship with Ruth?"

"I take care of the property. She makes me lunch, and we talk."

Adriel sensed something else. She grabbed his arm, and deceit flooded her. "You're harboring dishonest motives."

"Of course he is. Did you see how shitty the plants out back look? His yard game is crap."

"Enough." She turned back to the man. "Tell me what you want from Ruth."

His eyes glazed. "The house. She's got no one to leave it to."

As an immortal, she never considered what happens to mortal assets when their owners die. "Do you care for her?"

He shook his head. "I just want the house."

"He preys on old people," Juniper said with

disgust. "I watched a documentary about scumbags like him. They're total con artists."

"Is that true?" She looked into his eyes with stern disapproval. "You only come here because you want the house?"

"She's got money in the bank too."

"Gross." Juniper grabbed a small blue ledger from the drawer she'd been rummaging through. "Check this out."

Various amounts of money were recorded. Payments to a Mr. Danny Hutchinson.

"Why does she give you money?"

He shrugged. "I visit, she helps me out."

This man had no honor. "But you lie to her about your intentions."

"She's a lonely old lady with no husband or kids. What does it matter what the truth is? I'm all she's got."

Adriel was also a lonely old lady without a husband. A snarl built in her throat. "A woman's older age and lack of husband does not justify such treatment. You should be ashamed of yourself."

"Look, lady, I'm just trying to live."

"So am I." She lunged, slamming his body into the door and sinking her fangs into his throat.

Juniper screamed.

Hot, life-giving blood flooded Adriel's mouth, and she moaned, locking her fists in his hair as she pinned him in place.

"Adriel, no!" Juniper yanked on her shoulders, and Adriel's jaw opened wider as she turned and hissed at the witch. She ducked and held up her hands in defense. *"Are you crazy?"*

Seeing how appalled she appeared, Adriel covered her mouth. " I wasn't hurting him. I was feeding. He'll be fine, just a little lethargic and dizzy. "

"He's bleeding!"

Adriel looked back at Danny. "Oops." She yanked him forward and quickly licked the wound. "All fixed."

Danny drooped against the door, eyes glazed and confused.

Juniper cowered in the far corner of the kitchen, her eyes lit with a mixture of fear and disgust.

"You're the one who suggested I change my thinking. I needed to feed. He's food."

Her face twisted in horror. "That's way different than glamouring someone for a place to sleep."

Adriel's jaw locked. She'd endured centuries of censorship and was finally free to choose for herself. "You were fully aware of what I was when you asked to come with me."

The potent human blood flooded her system —so much more intoxicating than that of a small woodland creature. She felt drunk on a mixture of elation and freedom. Such newfound autonomy flooded her like a drug.

What did it matter how she fed? She hadn't killed anyone. With only days, maybe hours left, it seemed fair that she at least enjoyed a decent meal.

After losing everything, she had nothing left to lose. Her home, her community, her family, and her friends—they were all gone, left behind in a place she could never return. There was no reason she should also have to starve.

Looking into Danny's eyes, she ordered, "Come back tomorrow."

"Are you insane?" Juniper rounded the counter. "He's a complication."

"No, he's a solution. I have to keep my strength up. Leaving the house opens us up to danger. Unless you plan on offering your vein, we need him."

Juniper scoffed. "I'm not a fucking blood bag."

"Which is exactly why you should be grateful we have Danny." Adriel returned her gaze to Danny. "Tomorrow. Same time. Tell no one of our presence, and don't be late." She opened the door and nudged him across the threshold. "Go home and contemplate the ways you've wronged others." She shut the door and sighed. "Don't look at me like that. I was hungry, and he deserved it."

"No one deserves *that*."

Adriel scoffed at such hypocrisy. "How do you act so high and mighty when you personally played a part in the near murder of Jonas Hartzler?"

"We were never going to kill him."

"And I was never going to kill Danny. Who do you think is better off, him or Jonas?"

"Jonas burned down my house and murdered my aunt!"

Adriel frowned. "I heard it was Grace Hartzler who killed her."

"That bitch killed my other aunt, Venus. Aunt Mabel died in the fire Jonas purposely started because she wouldn't help him."

"Is that true?"

"Why would I lie?"

"You could have told The Council—"

"Fuck The Council." The scent of her grief filled the kitchen. But there was also the delicate fragrance of truth and innocence behind her words.

Realizing there was much Adriel did not know about Juniper's story, she abandoned her point for the sake of their friendship. "I'm sorry, Juniper. I didn't mean to upset you."

The room silenced.

"Please don't look at me like I'm some sort of a monster. I also lost my home, and I may never see my son again." Adriel looked away as the truth became impossible to bear once she said it out loud. "He's all I've ever had, and I may never have the chance to tell him how much I love him again."

"I knew a different side of your son. That *council* was cruel."

Adriel instinctively defended her son. "Christian never ordered the things they did to you. I'm sure of it. I was listening."

"Well, he also never did anything to stop them or save me." Tension charged the air as Juniper's eyes shimmered with unshed tears. "Why do you protect them?"

She wanted to argue that The Council was made up only of honorable males, but Juniper knew that wasn't true, and Adriel would not minimize her pain or discredit her suffering by speaking lies. One of the elders had done despicable things to her, she could tell by the bruises on her neck and the faint scent of male sweat on her skin.

"My son was not the dishonorable male who hurt you. You cannot blame an entire population for one individual's crimes. Despite what happened to you, there is still good in The Order. If you told the bishop what was happening, he would have—"

"Seriously?" She flung out her hands. "What does it take for you to stop defending them, Adriel? If they're so great, why aren't they helping you?"

"They did help me! Without them, I never would have escaped the first time."

"Well, times sure have changed. Look around. They abandoned you. You're all alone. I'm all you've got. So please don't preach to me about their honor. Your son might not have hurt me but he also never protected me. They're only honorable when it suits them. You know what they're capable of. You knew they wouldn't risk their peace to protect you from your psycho ex, that's why you ran away."

She was right. They wouldn't have interfered because, in their eyes, Cerberus was still her mate.

"You have to understand, the life I had on the farm, it was all I've ever known. Before that, there was only pain. I can't remember my childhood or what it felt like not to live in fear. The Order made me feel safe."

"You were only safe if you lived according to their terms."

Adriel tried to picture what it must have been like for her, sentenced to a small, dark cell, muzzled and bound because they feared her magick. They tortured the witch with fire and water in hopes of breaking the spell on Jonas. But it was not just captivity and inquisitions she'd suffered.

Someone fed from her.

Someone took her blood without consent.

What else did they take?

Adriel lowered her gaze. "There's a lot we both don't know about each other, but I believe we both know more than any female deserves to know about suffering."

"So why defend them? I'm sick and tired of relying on others for scraps. There's more to life than fear or pain, Adriel. And I'm going for it." She turned her back and faced the window. "I refuse to accept that this struggle is all there will ever be."

"I am not them, Juniper. Feeding does not make me evil." She placed a gentle hand on her shoulder, and the girl flinched at the slight contact, her withered smock hardly disguising how emaciated she'd become. "Please know, I would never hurt you."

She nodded and sniffed, the salty scent of her tears tinging the air. "I know. I mean, I believe that. And I know that guy was a prick. It's just hard for me… I wasn't prepared…"

"I'm sorry. Next time, I'll warn you before it happens."

Again, she nodded. "That's fair."

"Are we okay?"

Her hand closed over hers, the gentle squeeze a testament of trust and forgiveness. "We have to be. We're all we've got."

Adriel's mouth formed a sad smile. "Then let's be good to each other, just as friends should."

"Deal."

CHAPTER 10

*J*uniper stared at the mirror, hardly recognizing the reflection of her naked body. Fading bruises marked her wrists and jaw. Her concave stomach pulled her flesh tight against her ribs, making her breasts appear larger than she remembered them being.

She was a mixture of femininity and utter neglect. No longer the body of a teenager—nor the mind—but a woman who had seen far too much for a young adult.

She was breakable but not broken.

Not yet, anyway.

Recollections scraped through her mind, wearing her down like the grind of brittle bone over a raw nerve. She'd blindly endured every insufferable moment in that cell and could still feel her fear whenever she closed her eyes.

The fear was the worst of it. At least when it was happening, she knew what she was getting.

When they tortured her, when he rutted into her and bit into her flesh, she at least knew it would soon be over. Those physical pains were somehow easier than the mental waiting game of wondering what horrible thing she'd suffer next.

She wanted her revenge. Not just on him. On all of them.

These emotional scars would never heal.

They were monsters.

The life she'd lived before vampires came into her life shimmered like a forgotten delusion in her mind, too thin to fully picture and too foreign to find. Her sanity started to crumble after only a few months in that dungeon, and once her mind started playing tricks on her, she lost track of what was real and what was not.

Weeks of darkness. Days on end of having her arms tied. During those silent hours with no end in sight, she existed only in her terrified mind, meeting parts of herself she didn't know, parts that scared her. But she found comfort in the fury.

They forced her to face the truth.

She was no one special.

Nothing. Not his. Not anyone's. And that awareness killed the fear until there was nothing left.

Just Juniper.

Who?

Her head twitched as she tried to recognize the girl in the mirror. This was who she was now.

Nothing but a vessel of secrets, a cluster of riddles even she couldn't fully understand.

She owned no part of herself in that hell. But she could reclaim herself now. She was finally free. Far, far away, and able to start over.

Was there enough left to somehow be reborn? Facing the actuality of all she'd survived made it harder to believe she possessed the strength to go on. She'd been a kid when they caught her, but now she was a woman. She knew firsthand all the horrors women didn't say, the things they shoved down in polite society and cried about in private.

Those memories were only air. They could not break her, not as long as she forced them to serve her in some way. She would use that pain and anger to make herself whole again. She had to, because the only other option was giving up.

Her fingers traced her collarbone, where a bruise marred the skin. Shadows of a puncture wound lingered just above her pulse. One blink, and she could feel him on her. One blink was all she could afford.

Forcing herself to look at her body and see what she'd become, she counted every rib. She was still in there. Ten fingers. Ten toes. One mouth. Two eyes.

She touched her lips and turned her cheek to see the bruise from where the bridle had cut into her jaw. Scratches and knicks ticked across her skin like little tallies—of what crime, she couldn't be sure. There had been too many to count.

After dozens of visits and countless inquisitions, she'd lost all hope of ever seeing the light of day again. As her optimism deteriorated in that cell, her sanity frayed.

She shivered as the memory of his voice teased through her mind. Though he rarely spoke, when he did say something, it had the effect of snakes on her skin. She'd been helpless, forced to let his words crawl over her as he helped himself to her body.

On the rare evenings when he wouldn't visit, her fragile sanity shattered. Those quiet nights were somehow worse. The waiting in fear burned her out, so much so that she was sometimes relieved to hear him unlocking her cell. At least then she knew it would soon be over and she could sleep.

Looking down at her dirty skin, she wondered how long it might take to actually feel clean again. After such an ordeal, could any woman truly live long enough to truly find out?

Some filth lasted longer than tattoos.

The faucet squeaked as water rushed into the tub. Steam billowed upward. She let the hot water wash over her dirty nails as she rinsed away the dust coating the tub.

Scabs formed where the ropes had cut into her wrists. Recalling the chill of blindly washing her tied hands in the basin they delivered each morning, she let the hot water rush over her arms, welcoming the slight burn.

Steam swirled like a plume of smoke, and she

reminded herself that was normal. She couldn't recall the last time she showered. The last time she felt safe or normal or clean.

Years. It had been fucking years of blind sponge baths and cold, dirty water in the dark. She doubted such filthiness would ever fully disappear.

Juniper adjusted the faucet and turned on the shower. Her legs were tired from running in the woods, and her feet needed serious care.

Moving under the spray of hot water, a gasp jerked against her ribs, sharp and painful, as too many emotions loosened.

Don't you fucking cry. Don't you dare shed a single tear.

All her tough talk did no good as another jagged gasp ripped through her. Her strength crumbled like a landslide, rolling into a harrowing sob.

Taking the hard bar of soap in hand, she gently labored over her tender muscles, lathering up her skin as she tried to wash the filth away. But the worst of it was inside her.

Closing her eyes, she whaled into her forearm as sharp notes of bergamot and citrus anchored her to this seemingly safe place, far, far away from the cell they'd put her in.

"I'm okay. I'm okay." Sobs punched out of her. "It's over. It's done."

Memories tickled like spiders crawling on her skin. She wished she could wash away the stench of the musty, underground dirt floors that still swamped her mind.

She missed her aunts. She missed her boring life, her shitty high school, and her aimless friends. She wanted to be a kid again. She wanted to go back to when she knew nothing about true evil.

More sobs built in her belly, constricted by the cage of her ribs as she gasped to get them out. She couldn't breathe. Was this what hyperventilating felt like? Was she having a panic attack?

Afraid she might black out, she lowered herself to the ground and let the water rain over her. Sliding the hard bar of soap between her legs, she tried to wash her shame away.

The emaciated jut of her hips angered her, and she punched the tile, splitting her knuckle open. She punched again, letting the pain anchor her to the present.

She could still feel him breathing over her, his crushing weight sinking onto her.

Her lungs tightened and the soap fell from her hands, sliding to the drain.

She was a vessel of pain. Nothing beyond a threat. Sometimes a treat. But always a parasite, even when he used her for pleasure.

I won't hurt you, he'd say, as if trust could live between them amongst such a vicious lie.

It always hurt. Every part of it. Her body. Her chest. Her heart. Her mind.

The cold press of his hands as they rode up her thighs.

It was never painless because it was never her choice, no matter how still she stayed for him. She fucking hated him with every single cell of her being. But her endless hatred had no target. He was a man without a face. A man who had no name. Her bottomless rage had no cure.

He was a monster. A monster who relished the fact that she couldn't even scream.

But she could now.

Drawing in a painful breath of air, she let her fury break free. The wail that bellowed out of her came from the darkest depths of her soul, where her rage burned the hottest. The deafening crescendo built into a blaring cry, and the mirror popped, glass webbing beneath the steam. She panted and stared at the broken glass, undisturbed by the damage, as she struggled to breathe this suffocating air.

"Juniper?"

Adriel's voice reminded her where she was, but she could only gasp and stare.

She pounded on the door. "Are you all right?" The knob shook. "Juniper, answer me!"

She stared at the door, numb and unblinking. What if she closed her eyes and woke up in that cell again? What if Adriel changed her mind, broke her promise, and turned on her? Was she a fool for trusting a vampire?

"Juniper, say something!" The knob rattled again, and the old door burst open. "Good Lord." Adriel rushed forward and shut off the water. "What happened? You're shivering." She bundled her in a towel, buffing away the drops that clung to her chilled skin.

What happened?

Three years ago, she was just a dumb kid about to graduate, stealing her aunt's weed and flunking math. After that…

A whimper escaped.

"It's okay. You don't have to say anything."

She needed sleep. She needed help.

Adriel wrapped the towel around her, holding her as if she might shatter. Perhaps she already did.

"You don't have to say anything, but if you want to talk about it, I'm here," Adriel whispered, gently rocking her.

It felt good to be held.

Safe.

Familiar.

Her emotions calmed, ebbing back into the shadows far enough that she could breathe again.

"That's it. Deep breaths." Adriel dragged a hand over her damp hair. "You're safe now. I've got you."

She closed her eyes, sinking into the comfort of her touch and resting her head on her shoulder. She smelled of sugar and mist beneath the traces of wilderness and smoke. Her touch was gentle, like an afternoon storm on a warm August day, but also strong. Capable. Possibly even fierce.

There was no pressure to talk or explain. And in that unspoken silence, they shared some sort of mysterious understanding. Without having to ask, she could tell that Adriel knew what it was like. She knew the fear and discomfort as well as Juniper. Perhaps more so.

The thought made her question how a strong immortal could also be weak. Perhaps the culprit wasn't weakness any more than being female was to blame. What if they were merely victims because monsters were masquerading as men?

Looking at Adriel now, she wondered how anyone could hurt her. She had the delicate bone structure of a pixie and skin as translucent as porcelain. "I'm crushing you."

Adriel stilled her when she tried to stand. "You're fine. Just breathe."

It had been so long since someone held her. How long had it been for Adriel?

Wanting to reciprocate the support she offered, Juniper tightened her arms around her waist. Adriel hummed softly and rested her head against Juniper's. Maybe they both just really needed a hug.

A sense of déjà vu washed over her, and she frowned. She must have been remembering a dream. It triggered the memorable scent of smoke in the air. She recalled the sight of stars in the sky. The vision was as vapor thin but weighed heavily on her memory as if it had actually happened. But how could that be? What she pictured in her mind made absolutely no sense at all.

· · ·

She'd been running—not on bare feet, but four padded paws. The world lacked color, and everything was tinged in pastels of blue and yellow. She was more animal than woman, dog-minded, with feline dexterity.

Then she was in a field, naked under a plume of black smoke.

Why had she been naked? What happened to her?

Fury returned, snuffing out her confusion, and she seized the opportunity before her. She was free and finally able to seek revenge. Supernatural energy charged the air as the raging fire licked the sky.

She gasped. "I saw the fire."

"What?" Adriel drew back to look at her, their faces close enough that she could see the sprinkle of cinnamon freckles scatted across her upturned nose.

"Last night. I was there."

"At my house?"

"I guess."

Juniper had siphoned the fire's power into her body and let it blast out of her. She remembered her aura glowing like a white-hot poker as her rage spilled free in a violent burst of light. She channeled the energy, and, one by one, the vampires had fallen to their knees. At that moment, she had full command of her magick. She could have killed them all and probably would have if the females hadn't screamed for mercy.

She knew that guttural sound of grief all too well. They were somehow experiencing the pain she'd inflicted on the males. How? Were they somehow connected? She couldn't justify hurting innocent people to simply cleanse the wicked. She didn't have that level of cruelty in her, and that tiny realization fractured her powers with doubt and left her vulnerable.

How foolish of her to feel sorry for them. The moment they sensed a tremor of weakness, they attacked.

She shivered, recalling the burn of claws slicing through her skin the moment the spell broke. "I saw him."

"Who?"

"Cerber—"

"Shh." Soft fingers covered her lips. "Do not speak his name. Tell me what you know."

"He was there. Last night. The house was on fire. I could tell him apart from the others." She frowned, wondering what gave him away. "He wasn't dressed in Amish clothes."

"You're just remembering this now?"

"I…something happened to me. I don't know. I was running, and then… I was on the ground. There was a woman. She was hurt."

"You're not making sense."

"I know." She shook her head. "It doesn't make sense to me either. Maybe I blacked out. I was panicking, you know?"

"What do you remember?"

She remembered unleashing her magick and then… She twisted out of Adriel's arms.

"What is it?" Adriel stood, her eyes pinched with concern.

Juniper's hand went to her back, searching for an open wound or torn flesh, but she found nothing. Had it been a dream? It seemed too real and detailed to merely be a figment of her imagination.

"Juniper?"

"It's…nothing."

The vision of Adriel ripping into that man's throat was still fresh in her mind. She might look young with her pixie red hair, youthful ivory skin, and those big, green, innocent eyes, but she was centuries old and could be as vicious as the rest of them.

"Did you give me blood?"

"No."

"You swear?"

"Juniper, you were there. I tried, and you refused."

"Maybe you used compulsion—"

"I didn't. I wouldn't do that when you so adamantly said no. Besides, you blocked me, remember?"

Juniper inspected her reflection in the mirror. Her bruises were fading fast. And where were the claw marks on her back?

"Juniper, what aren't you telling me?"

She was like them—half witch, half… Her eyes closed, refusing to admit the truth. She had questions, questions maybe Adriel could answer, but she suddenly wasn't sure if she could trust her.

Tightening the towel around her body, she faced Adriel. "I'm better now. Sorry about… scaring you. Sometimes you just gotta scream, you know?"

Adriel frowned.

She was a witch. But she was also half-immortal. How the hell did that add up to some small, four-footed, catlike creature with claws? Maybe she hallucinated that part.

"Juniper, you're white as a ghost."

Aunt Venus warned her that she would experience "growing pains" once she reached adulthood. Was that what this was? She met Adriel's stare but didn't know where to begin, so she lied, "I think I'm just cold. I need to find clothes and get dressed."

Adriel studied her for a long moment, then nodded. "All right. But if you want to talk about what's bothering you, I'm here."

CHAPTER 11

"The visions are making me insane!" Darius paced about the cavernous room lit only by the flames of the crackling fire and candles scattered throughout. Lumira's lithe body, ensconced in snowy silks, stretched across the chaise as she watched him.

"Darling, stop prowling. You're worrying for nothing. If she's immortal, you'll have plenty of time to claim her." The Luna trailed an inviting hand over the ancient furs that draped to the floor. "Come sit with me. Let me distract you from your doubts."

Darius studied the beloved Luna, her beauty as familiar and comforting as her scent. Her nurturing nature called to him but was not enough to distract him from more pressing preoccupations like finding his mate.

The visions had him confused and restless, crawling out of his skin with a sense of urgency, while an order from his infuriating brother demanded he stay put. Lumira, understanding more than anyone how bullheaded their Alpha could be, desired to put Darius at ease, but he didn't want distractions. He wanted to find his mate and claim her so his life could get back to normal.

"Darius, darling, your frustration comes at an unnecessary cost. Come here."

Lumira was not simply a female of the pack. She was also the mate of his eldest brother, Evander. As mate to the Alpha, she served as Evander's equal. There could only be one alpha and only one luna.

Despite his body's urges, his mind was divided, torn between the desire to please the Luna and the need to claim his mate. Drawn by her enchanting invitation, he drifted closer to the chaise. Her white blonde hair draped over the fur temptingly, and his fingers itched to wrap the silken weight around his hands.

Lumira lifted an arm, her dainty nails delicately curling through the air as she beckoned him closer. "Sit with me. I'll tell you a story, and you can comfort me while your brother's away on the hunt."

He should have gone with his pack brothers, but he was too angry to bear Evander's arrogance. Their infuriating stubbornness had sentenced him to yet another winter without his mate.

"My mate is out there and she's upset. I sense

her fear and worry, but I can't reach her. She's distraught, and for what purpose? I'm here and prepared to go to her. If she's in danger, I could protect her. But the others—"

"Hush." She pulled back the silk draped over her legs, revealing a long expanse of lush, ivory flesh. "You're worked up, and that helps nothing."

He lowered to the chaise and dragged his hands through his black hair, groaning in frustration. "They should be relieved to have another female."

"Darius, your brothers are creatures of habit." Her sharp nails teased the exposed skin around his collar. "They hunt and mate. Right now, with the way things have been, feeding is harder than ever. Technology limits us, and we must make due. We cannot risk others discovering our secrets. You must trust your Alpha and heed his call for patience. Evander knows what is best."

All of his life, Darius believed that was true. He trusted his family and dutifully followed Evander wherever he led, as did his other brothers, Atticus and Emmerich. But this time was different.

Instinct pulled him in another direction while his loyalty held him here. His inability to stray from the pack left him aching for his mate. Without their approval, he could only endure the agony of knowing she was also suffering. His divided loyalties were tearing him in two.

"If he'd at least let me answer her." His head pounded.

"You know that's not how this works." She raked her fingers through his hair, pulling him closer to rest on her full breasts.

She was softening, her milk no longer as fragrant as it had been a week ago. Last spring, when she'd given birth to a small litter, she'd been radiant and full of life. Now, the whelps were able to sleep on their own, and Evander insisted she no longer coddle the pups. Darius sensed she mourned the loss of their constant presence and needed comfort.

She pulled his hand to her chest to cup her breast. He massaged gently through the layers of silk as she combed her fingers through his thick hair. A soft moan slipped past her lips, affirming his touch was a means of calming her discomfort rather than a means to satisfy his carnal needs.

"Winter will come early this year," she said, voice soft and husky as her warm breath teased. "You can hear the cold approaching when the westward winds whine through the trees, and we can see it in the leaves. Perhaps your mate will be easier to find in the spring."

"Perhaps." He hoped that was the case. "When Evander was called to you, did you sense him trying to find you?"

She slouched lower and parted her thighs, lacing her fingers with his and pressing his hand against her apex. "Not at first, but over time we found our mental link. From there our connection only grew. By the time your brother came to me, we were already in love."

"So, there was no hesitation on your part?" He harbored fears that his mate would reject him.

"There is no force stronger than a wolf's imprint. It's greater than gravity and consumes us until there is no other loyalty besides that to our mate."

Gravity was a good comparison. But while gravity pushed them into the earth, an imprint pulled him toward his mate. "It's definitely stronger than gravity."

"The fact that you're able to resist the pull tells me it's still early. Over time, the call will grow until it's all you can feel. I was anxious for Evander's claim. Anxious to meet all of you. But he was beyond reason when he finally found me. Ravenous and resolute, as if he held the pressure of all the planets on his shoulders and would not be right until our bodies aligned."

Darius dutifully lowered to the floor when she nudged him, kneeling at her feet and opening her knees. Aware of what she wanted, he pressed a kiss on her soft flesh and traced his tongue higher.

Lumira's fingers tightened in his hair, drawing his mouth to her honeyed lips. "Do you know the story of the raven's red leaf?" She eased back and moaned when he licked inside of her.

"Yes." He rasped, nuzzling closer. He took his time savoring her rich flavor as he swirled his tongue through her delicate folds.

Stretching her arms overhead, she sighed. "Perhaps you need to hear it again."

He moaned in agreement, his focus now on her pleasure.

"You see, when the Norse gods grew tired of man's wars, they left a gift." She stroked said gift down his arm. "The pelts were fit for heroes. The gods wanted to end the wars of man. But when the pelts were discovered, it was by a corrupt father and his trusting son, not the brave warriors the gods had hoped for."

She gasped, rolling her hips, as he closed his lips around her sensitive pearl.

Her legs delicately quivered as she continued the story in a breathy rasp, "The father and son donned the pelts and transformed into wolves. A killing spree ensued. The father, easily intoxicated by power, led the rampage until there seemed no one left. Such greed for power corrupted his mind, and the father eventually attacked the son—his only heir—out of fear that the boy might usurp him as pack leader. But the son got away. Nevertheless, the father's behavior angered the gods."

She shuddered through a delicate release. Once the tremors subsided, she guided him from the floor and directed him to the chaise, loosening his belt so she could fist his length. Her slender fingers closed around him, firmly stroking, and he sucked in a deep breath, holding his arms at his side.

"The lethal wound should have killed the son, but the gods took pity on the boy as he lay bleeding on the forest floor, fur matted and whimpering in pain. Desperately, he howled at the heavens for mercy. Unlike the father, the gods saw goodness in his eyes and cause for redemption in his heart."

Straddling his hips, she lifted and slowly teased his engorged length against her sex. When he reached for her, she caught his wrist in an unbreakable grip, a stern warning flashing in her eyes. He sank back into the chaise, surrendering his control and balling his fists at his side so she might use his body as she pleased.

The Luna belonged to all of them, but their touch must be invited. They must never assume what was in her heart.

"The gods sent a kind raven with a gift," she said, releasing his muscled arms.

Darius sucked in a sharp breath as she took his length inside of her to the hilt. Slick heat dragged along his shaft, squeezing him like a glove as the tension in his back loosened.

Lumira rode him at a leisurely canter, her hypnotic beauty mesmerizing. No matter how often he saw her this way, her devotion to her personal pleasure always left him in awe. She was a stunning creature, unapologetically confident and graceful in every move.

"When the raven found the boy, it gave him the crimson leaf spelled with the highest powers. The magical leaf could save him, but if he wanted to use the spelled leaf, he first needed to kill his father and undo the gods' mistake."

Her lashes lowered as she moaned, her long

fingers trailing over her breasts. Folds of silk shifted in an entrancing tease as his gaze fixed on her chest. The peaks of her usually pale, peach nipple flashed engorged and dark, like the inner petals of a rose.

"The son wanted to survive and, therefore, promised whatever the raven asked of him."

Her self-exploring touch trailed to the long column of her throat. Darius's vision narrowed on her breasts as his lashes lowered. He ached to hold her hips but would not violate her command unless invited to touch her body.

"The boy was young and naive and didn't fully understand the laws of nature. The red leaf was made of blood magic, the darkest, most powerful black sorcery drawn from the dead and dying. Blood magick is sewn by the hands of mages and comes at an inescapable cost—only death can pay for life."

She leaned forward, riding him faster. Her claws extended, slashing through his leather shirt as she gasped in pleasure. Her pale blonde hair formed a curtain that blocked the glow of firelight, and their breath mingled. His fists remained locked at his sides despite the agonizing temptation to steal control from her.

"There was great pain," she said, exposing his chest and pressing the sharp point of her claw over his heart. "The bird used its beak to pack the wound with the magick red leaf, but the boy screamed and shivered, a great fever taking hold of his senses. When the wound was sealed with a mixture of wine and mud, his bones started to pop and break. Fur became flesh once more, and the son's body was transformed back into that of a man."

Darius understood the son's consequences all too well. The raven's spell had lasted generations, carried through their lineage, and gifted them with great power and an even greater responsibility.

She ripped the opening of his shirt wider, exposing the smooth flesh of his hard chest and digging her claw into the muscle, exactly where the raven had scored the boy. Darius grunted and gritted his teeth but permitted the pain as she dragged her claw over his flesh, firm enough to raise the skin and leave a mark.

"We are of the *magick*, Darius. We are the chosen. But we are not the gods. We live and breathe because of their mercy, eternally indebted to them for our lives." She shouldered out of her gowns. Firelight illuminated the lily-white flesh of her full breasts. "There remains a price for our salvation that must be paid, or we risk angering the gods."

Her head tipped back, her elongated neck flexing as she bared her fangs. Silver hair shifted behind her shoulders as her human ears transformed into points, softening at the tips with snowy white fur.

Lips parted, she gazed down at him, her tiny fangs poking past the fullness of her lush mouth. "What is the price, Darius?"

He flexed his hips, shoving his length as deep as possible into her clenched heat. These tedious lessons irritated him. Just once he'd like to have control and take her as he wanted.

Her palm planted firmly on his muscled chest as she gripped his jaw, angling his face so he looked her in the eye. "Answer me."

His molars locked. "Blood."

"Yes," she panted, riding him faster now. "Blood." Her nail slashed over his chest, opening his flesh exactly where the boy from the story had suffered the lethal wound.

Warmth seeped down his chest and torso, spreading to where their bodies met, trickling onto the sacred furs where ancients' blood had spilled before.

"Lumira…" His seed rose, and his veins tightened as he pumped his hips harder. He spoke the ritual words she needed to hear, "Will you accept my gift?"

"Yes, Darius," she moaned his name, rolling her hips as her hands dragged through his blood. "I accept your gift."

Their bodies arched and tensed. His seed rushed forward, pumping into her sacred womb. She rode out his release, taking the pleasure to a point of torture, never slowing until she milked him dry. Then she leaned forward, drenching her robes as she licked at the blood she'd spilled.

Every point of contact brought a twisted form of ecstasy. His body was hers. He was there to serve her, as were his brothers so that she could produce another litter and replenish their dying line.

The recent cubs had been a blessing. The pups had Evander's dark hair and piercing white eyes. But they needed another litter to diversify the breed. He was duty-bound to serve her and did so faithfully, yet deep in his heart, Darius knew the next litter would not be of his loins.

The door opened, and Lumira lifted her head, her long silver hair wet at the tips from his blood, her body still anchored to Darius's as his brother—the Alpha—stepped into the room.

"Darling," she purred, her welcoming stare set on Evander as his hulking body filled the door. "I've missed you."

Darius's cock twitched possessively, deep inside her heat. Dogs were loyal, but they were also known to stray, so no shock registered in the Alpha's face when he found them this way.

No matter how many times Darius or the other brothers of the pack mated with the Luna, the Alpha's territorial claim on her would not be undone. On the contrary, the intimate moments Darius shared with Lumira only emphasized how much he wanted a mate of his own—but his claim on his mate would never be uniquely his because that was not how the curse worked.

Their line was endangered, and they were duty-bound to share. It was the cost of their survival, the price the father's son bartered with the raven to maintain the gift bestowed by the gods.

Lumira slid off of Darius's body, and he

sucked in a breath at the sharp sense of detachment. It often ended this way. The Luna took from all of them, as was her duty, but her heart only belonged to Evander.

Darius tucked himself away and righted his clothes, discretely watching the exchange of affection at the door. Lumira pressed her body to Evander's and kissed him deeply.

The scent of blood and mud clung to his brother's skin, still fresh from the hunt. Evander's focus shifted into a narrow glare, pinning Darius in place.

Darius dropped his gaze, unsure if that hard stare was a challenge or a threat or merely his brother's lingering displeasure over their earlier disagreement.

"You should not indulge him when he avoids his duties," the Alpha told the Luna, tightening his fist in the tempting hair Darius was never permitted to touch.

She merely purred and nuzzled against her mate. "Be patient with your brother, Evander."

Although they used the term brothers, their lines were not as closely wound. They each came from different fathers. Their brotherhood was merely the result of belonging to the same pack, a pack that Evander ran.

Releasing Lumira, the Alpha crossed the room to warm his legs by the fire. "This is why you missed the hunt?"

Every instinct told Darius not to snap, though

that was exactly what he felt like doing. "I needed time to think."

"You mean mope."

"Be gentle with him, Evander. He's hurting for his mate." As Lumira lay a delicate hand on the Alpha's thickly muscled arm, he noticeably calmed. Tucking a silver strand of hair behind her angular ears, he paused to examine the blood that still dampened the tips. "Did you feed?"

"I did." He brushed a thumb under her lip, and she playfully bit at his finger. "But I'm far from satisfied, my love. Come. Finish what Darius started."

It had been several days since Darius voiced his concerns for his mate when Evander minimized any sense of urgency and postponed his plans of finding and claiming her. After that explosive confrontation, Darius entertained the idea of breaking from the pack, a thought that earned him the thrashing of a lifetime when his brothers discovered his intentions.

They were one. As such, their thoughts, as well as other things, were often shared regardless of intention. The weight of their broken trust shrouded them now, and Evander watched him with a shrewd, distrustful glare.

"You will have your mate when the time is right, Darius. I look forward to taking my time with her as she learns the ways of our pack."

Darius inwardly seethed. The intended threat left him panting with territorial rage, but he could not challenge the Alpha.

Yes, his mate would essentially belong to all of them. His brothers would know her intimately. It was their way. More than a custom. Deeper than tradition. Their magick, which traced back to the first gods, relied on keeping their endangered line alive. But he was experiencing difficulty accepting such traditions when he had yet to have her.

She was, after all, his.

"It's not a threat," Evander said, easily reading his displeasure. "It's a promise—one made to the gods, one you will uphold."

Evander's forefathers' ascension had been stolen from the powerful ancestors of the first boy, the son maimed by his father and saved by the spelled red leaf brought by the raven. The sacred pelts, divined of the strongest sorcery, still existed today and were the pack's greatest treasure. They were duty-bound to the *magick*, for it was the root of all their power, and without it, their line would die.

Those who challenged the pack in prior generations lost their lives for such treason. Evander's ancient line could be traced back to 800 AD, to a time when feudalism reigned and upheaval was greatly monitored by the emerging role of the church. But his family was not the first to rule. Authority had come to their pack through force, but power was a boon he would never voluntarily surrender. Therefore, obedience was required when it came to tradition, and Evander would never see it otherwise.

The first boy's rule lasted nearly two thousand years and was then passed down to his heirs for several generations. His line ruled long before the coming of Christ, the patriarch of Abraham, or the birth of the Buddha. And while power had shifted hands, those sacred vows could never be undone—not without great consequence.

Only during the blood moon could the spell be lifted enough for power to exchange lines, and only at the exact moment when the Earth passed directly between the sun and the moon, causing a brief but total lunar eclipse. In those passing moments, when the blood moon falls under the planet's darkest shadow and celestial bodies align, astronomical power is at its strongest.

An eclipse was coming. Darius sensed Evander's grip tightening on the reigns as a precaution to hold onto his power. These were dangerous thoughts Darius should not entertain, no matter how true.

While their rich and detailed history was important, obsession over such matters often triggered suspicions of power shifts. Which was why there could be no secrets among the pack. Evander ensured he understood that last week when he beat him for the mere thought of disobedience.

There was no separating. Survival of their line depended on tribalism that went far deeper than brotherhood. Their power required symbiotic harmony and disunity would not be tolerated.

Just as the Luna was required to take each of Evander's brothers into her bed, Darius's mate would be expected to do the same. Such pack loyalty could not be broken. The blood moon was the only way a brother could separate from the clan—but it was more likely for the pack to thin by death.

Should Evander suspect straying or treason, he would not hesitate to end Darius's life to ensure his reign was secure. Therefore, if Darius wanted to find his mate, he needed Evander's approval, which was not forthcoming.

"You may go now, Darius. But do not go far."

Lumira stripped Evander of his leather and weapons, then lowered to her knees, seeing to the Alpha's pleasure. Unlike the rest of them, Evander was permitted to touch the Luna however he pleased. Her body belonged to him, whereas the rest of the pack was duty-bound to serve the Luna.

Adherence to the Alpha's command wasn't necessarily a choice or matter of will. The link of brothers was wound tight at birth. It grew with them, the way tree roots interlocked into one co-dependent system underground.

Darius's obedience was written into his bones, his soul sewn to the one and only Alpha.

Only when the shadow passed, and he could clearly see his way to his mate, would he be able to go to her. He needed his brothers' tracking skills to find her, which was why they needed to move in harmony, together, as a pack, regardless of his impatience to leave without them.

Evander cocked his head, and the Luna stilled, her attention shifting from her duties as she looked back at Darius in fear. His unconscious thoughts were going to get him beat again.

"I don't trust you," Evander admitted, his sharp gaze penetrating deep into his mind.

Darius couldn't challenge the Alpha's intuition because, at the moment, he was having a hard time trusting himself. Rather than respond with empty reassurance, Darius stole one last glimpse of Lumira. "Goodnight, sweet Luna."

"Goodnight, Darius." Her gaze softened as she turned her attention back to the alpha.

As he left the cavernous bedroom, the wind whistled against the stone walls. Ancient ironwork sealed every cut window pane in the gaping hall, but this high up in the Scandinavian Alps, the cold could be vicious. The metallic bite in the air promised they would see snow soon.

Winters in the north were treacherous. Those long, cold months were often passed in the castle once the doors became buried by snow and the hinges encased by ice.

The locals knew the folklore, and while some assumed what they were, very few believed the truth. To most, they were a wealthy band of brothers with eccentric tastes for old-world charm.

Their reclusive way of life was a matter of

survival. Privacy was paramount to their species. Their kind could live more than two thousand years, which was why they rarely interacted with the townsfolk, only went out at night, and often changed form for hunts.

Darius traveled down the stone stairwell, taking the solid steps two at a time. The booming voices of his other brothers echoed from the great room, and he figured he should check in with them since he missed the hunt.

"Well, well, well, look who decided to join the party," Emmerich greeted. "You missed a great hunt." He tossed a warm shank of freshly roasted meat still on the bone at him.

Darius caught it against his blood-stained chest. "Thanks."

Starved, he took a bite and settled onto the bench seat beside Atticus. A large fire blazed in the cavernous hearth as more meat roasted over the flame.

Emmerich sniffed the air. "I guess it wasn't a wasted night after all. You smell like the Luna."

It didn't surprise him that his brothers could smell Lumira on his skin. Average wolves could scent objects from two thousand paces away and hear up to six miles, but shadow-wolves weren't average. Their senses went much further, and their possessive nature often got the better of them.

Of course, they recognized the scent of the Luna. The desire to get closer to her was a shared curse the entire pack suffered, and any attention from Lumira was an enviable gift. She was the great light to their shadowed existence.

"Did you get a lecture, little brother," Emmerich teased. "It smells like it was a good one."

Atticus chuckled. "She does love to talk."

Aside from her subservient role with Evander, Darius wasn't sure what sort of dynamic the Luna shared with the others. He'd only ever witnessed her intimacy with his brothers on the nights of the blood moon, a night when they all shared her at once with the single goal of getting her pregnant.

It was no accident that such a celebration took place on the night the Alpha was most vulnerable. The Luna was an irresistible temptation to all of them. Evander knew this and used her charms to his advantage—the wild, bacchanalian tradition was how his family maintained power for so long.

Darius reached for a dinner roll. "It doesn't matter. She's with Evander now."

"You sound jealous," Emmerich teased, guzzling back a dark blend of port.

"Not at all. He has every right."

His brother's pale eyebrow arched over one eye as he smirked. "You sure about that?"

"Leave him alone, Rick."

"How 'bout you shut the fuck up, Atticus." He turned his shrewd gaze back to Darius. "Lately, you've been harboring some dark thoughts. Maybe you need another thrashing to remember your place."

"Enough." Atticus stood and collected his plate, piling it with napkins and bones. "The winds have turned. There will be snow by the end of the month. It's too dangerous to go look for your mate now, but I'll go with you as soon as the weather breaks."

"There's still time to get out," Darius argued.

"Out, maybe, but you'll never make it back in time. You still don't know where she is."

Emmerich tossed a cleaned bone onto the pile. "Sounds to me like she doesn't want to be found."

"You don't know that," Darius challenged, despite his own fears that his brother may be right.

Atticus, the ever-present voice of calm and reason, clamped a staying hand on his shoulder. "Tradition requires the pack to meet her within the first moon phase of your mating. Without us, the imprinting won't be as strong. Trust that it's in your best interest—and hers—to wait until we can all be present."

Because they all intended to claim their rights. "I know what tradition requires."

"Then you know why we have to wait. Lumira needs more time to recover from the last litter before she can travel. You'll want her there to answer your female's questions in case anything goes wrong."

The females kept them alive during the long winters. Their blood carried healing powers that slowed time, but after giving birth, their offerings were limited.

"If we found my mate, we wouldn't need to survive on Lumira's blood alone."

"Had some human blood tonight." Emmerich licked his fingers. "She was a fighter."

"You're disgusting," Atticus remarked. "Darius is right. We need to find his mate soon, whoever she is. She belongs with us. We're indebted to the gods to hunt and protect her so that our line can survive."

"So fucking dramatic." Emmerich stood, leaving his pile of bones scattered across the thick slab of granite. "While you two are up all night braiding each other's hair, I'll be sleeping soundly in my bed, thinking of how I made that brunette scream."

As soon as Emmerich left the great hall, Atticus muttered, "He's an animal."

"We all are."

CHAPTER 12

The bedroom Juniper selected was on the third floor and removed from the rest of the house. The narrow staircase, hidden behind a small door in the second-floor hall, wound upward to another door. Something about the space's oddness filled her with a sense of protection. The air wasn't cold like a cellar, nor did it carry the faint musk of damp earth. She liked the additional security of a latched second door but also the smallness of the attic room, dwarfed by rafters, lit by dormer windows and jutting peaks where she could oversee the distant outside world for miles.

She would be safe here.

A soft laugh hummed through her throat as she found deep satisfaction with the view. Letting the sun-bleached curtain close, she scanned the room once more. Everything that wasn't painted putrid mint green was wallpapered in olive and jade floral hues. But she liked it.

She liked the sunlight that spilled through the windows and the sense that she wouldn't get lost in the space. Most of all, she liked the secret servant's passage she found in the paneled wall that led to a hidden stairwell and opened into the kitchen pantry.

A half inch of dust covered the bedding and furniture, but everything she needed was there. The dresser was full of handmade sweaters and scarves. Ruth was quite the crocheter.

A foot chest nestled against the dormer wall, brimming with clothing that smelled decades old. When she lifted a pair of stiff denim bellbottoms from the chest, a small metal disk clattered to the wood floor—a campaign button. The sharp point of the pin had rusted, and when she flipped it over, she grinned. The front read KENNEDY FOR PRESIDENT.

As she rummaged through the trunk, she found countless handmade items. The stitching was neatly done but not professionally made. Ruth kept everything. She had fringe vests, macramé halters, jeans, jumpers, bags, and even atrophied shoes.

Juniper stole a pair of bellbottom blue jeans and a pink cherry blossom top that tied at the neck. There was no salvaging the stiff, dry-rotted shoes.

Her hand hesitated as she reached for an

emerald green acrylic hairbrush. Was it wrong for her to use such personal things?

Her mind drifted to Adriel, confused by the humiliating way she'd held Juniper in the bathroom only minutes ago. Why had she done that? They barely knew each other, and up until then, she wasn't sure if the vampire even liked her.

Immortal, Juniper mentally corrected.

Despite looking close in age, she needed no reminder that the woman was centuries older. Seniority seeped from Adriel's aura in a way that told of innate confidence, the unobtrusive kind women often hid but rarely boasted about. Yet, there was also a strange innocence about her.

When Adriel gathered Juniper in her arms a momentary sense of safety cocooned her, like when Aunt Mabel used to read bedtime stories and tuck her in at night after a bad dream. But then, there was something else. Something not at all familial.

Juniper couldn't think of Aunt Mabel now. Her emotions were already in tatters, and she was holding on by a thread. Instead, her mind went back to Adriel.

Would she stay in that hideous Amish garb? Probably not. Yet she seemed in no rush to strip away the proof of patriarchal chauvinism misogyny that clothed her. Or did she not see their superiority as a slight to her own identity? Could she possibly feel a sense of safety from those who filled Juniper with such a deep sense of peril and fear?

Juniper had heard whispers of revered females in The Order, but everything she witnessed of the species warned the opposite. Was there a certain criteria for such reverence? Clearly, a calling came with no grantees if Adriel was terrified of her own mate.

She had questions that needed answers. She wanted to know why there seemed to be so many exceptions to the rules. Were all vampires so devoted to the same idea of destiny? Were they all Amish? Did they have to worry about more than Adriel's ex coming after them? How many were out there? Were they an endangered species or just hiding really well? Did Adriel know others? Would she have ways of helping Juniper find her mother? What kind of powers did she have?

Honestly, her questions were endless, which only further proved there was something wrong with her. After years at the mercy of the so-called "good ones," only an idiot would voluntarily hang out with an immortal. Yet here she was.

Maybe she should leave. What if teaming up with Adriel was a terrible mistake?

Uncertainty played like a tennis match in her head, each little consideration amplifying her trust issues. Three problems kept her here—fear, poverty, and utter exhaustion. Also, she didn't want to abandon Adriel because part of her was starting to really like her, aside from the whole vampire thing. But who was she to throw stones at glass coffins?

Once she rested, she'd think more clearly.

Then, she could figure out a plan to make some money. She was never going to feel safe until she found her own independence and her own place to stay, a place free of bloodsuckers and far removed from the drama that now consumed her life.

Was such an existence even possible anymore? She needed to learn as much as she could about vampires while she had access to one—damn it! Immortals! Why couldn't she get that straight?

Setting the brush on the dresser, she gasped and spun, certain she saw something move, but nothing was there. Her eyes played tricks on her as trees cast shadows on the windows reflected in the mirror. It was enough to chase her out of the attic for a while.

She found Adriel and Ruth on the first floor in the front room with the wide bow window. Ruth's chair sat alone on a braided rug facing an old television. The wood floors had three deep grooves where a grand piano might have once stood.

Juniper stepped into the den but lingered by the door, measuring the room's energy. It felt safe and oddly warm, as if they were actually welcomed here. That glamour trick had some horsepower.

Adriel turned from the window and silently studied her for a moment. "Are you feeling better?"

Juniper hated that she had witnessed such a

weak moment. She nodded. "What are you looking at?"

"Nothing of importance." Adriel moved to the chair beside Ruth's, but her gaze never drifted to the television. Juniper supposed such modern technologies would be foreign to someone who spent centuries living on an Amish farm.

She glanced at the older woman. "Is she okay?"

"She's comfortable. You can talk to her."

Juniper looked at Ruth but said nothing. It had been so long since she'd interacted with anyone normally. She forgot how to make small talk, so she formed a fake smile and turned her attention back to Adriel.

"You should rest."

Were immortals nocturnal? Did they sleep? Despite how cozy they seemed, Juniper didn't like the idea of leaving her here alone with Ruth.

"I wouldn't be able to sleep if I tried. But you should rest."

She was exhausted, but sleep would leave her vulnerable. "We both should. We don't know what will happen next, and we need to be ready for anything. That means rested and strong—both of us."

Adriel touched Ruth's hand and whispered something to the woman. The little old lady's eyes glazed.

Adriel stood. "My head has a strange ache."

"You mean a headache?"

"Immortals do not suffer such things. But it

does pound." She glanced at the plaster wall where a dated electrical switch hung. "I'm not used to this buzzing. My senses are overwhelmed, and I feel…drained." Her head cocked. "Are those Ruth's clothes?"

"I guess. I found some stuff in the attic." Juniper leaned into the thick wooden molding. "Pretty vintage, huh?"

"Vintage?"

"Yeah, you know…old." Recalling Adriel's age, she cleared her throat and clarified, "*Classic.*"

"I wouldn't know."

Juniper frowned. "I guess you Amish don't follow fashion the way the rest of the world does."

"No."

When the silence stretched between them, Juniper gestured to Ruth. "Can she hear us?"

"She's not listening."

"Then maybe this is a good time for us to talk. I need to know everything you can tell me about who we're running from and why."

Discomfort clouded Adriel's expression as she paced to the window, ensuring that the drapes were drawn and no one could see in. "*We* are not running from anyone. I'm running. You're welcome to leave at any time."

Back to this. Juniper was glad not to be a prisoner, but she needed some time to find her bearings. "You're always trying to get rid of me. I can help you—"

"This isn't about your value to me, Juniper."

Adriel studied her for a long moment and frowned. "You're young. It's not too late to start over. You can do whatever you want now."

"Not without a place to live or money. Regular people don't know how to live off the land and build barns in a day."

"Don't you want to move on and find happiness?"

"Happiness?" She laughed at such a notion. "How am I supposed to move on when I have absolutely nothing?"

"You just do."

"Right. And what about you? Will you move on?"

"Circumstances are different for me. I'm still in danger. You're free to go your own way—"

"This isn't as simple as a Fleetwood Mac song, Adriel. I have no money. No family."

She frowned in confusion. "What is a Fleetwood Mac?"

"Fleetwood Mac. You know, Stevie Nicks. Anyway, that's not the point."

"What is the point, Juniper?"

"We...need each other." At least right now, they did.

Exhaustion pulled at Adriel's eyes as she looked away, appearing frail and frightened. Juniper remembered how she'd comforted her upstairs but had no clue how to reciprocate.

"I can sit with Ruth for a while so you can wash up and change out of those dirty clothes."

As if only then considering that her attire

might need freshening, she glanced down at her smock-like dress and frowned. "I suppose that's a good idea. Were there dresses?"

"A few, but not the kind you'd like."

Soon after Adriel went upstairs, the pipes rattled with rushing water. Juniper smirked, wondering how a hot shower must feel to someone who lived on a primitive farm since the days of colonization and copper coins.

Once Ruth dozed off, Juniper lowered the television volume and wandered the house. The air smelled of paper and dust. Antique furniture filled every room. Gray particles gathered in the intricate eyelet designs of doilies. Even the candy jars wore a sprinkle of time.

Spotting a black spool of thread on a sewing table, Juniper pried open the narrow drawer and dug out a blue bobbin for protection. Snapping small strands of thread from the spool, she draped tiny pieces over latches and locks throughout the house.

She scanned the parlor, wondering what they would do if someone got past her flimsy security system. Would they choke an intruder with a lamp cord? Or maybe throw a paperweight. As far as weapons went, they were fucked.

The water shut off, and she glanced at the ceiling, reminded of the lethal weapon wandering around upstairs. Did Adriel even realize how strong she was?

Juniper tracked her footsteps. The old floorboards betrayed her every step with creaks and moans—another welcome security measure.

After checking on Ruth again, she quietly drifted upstairs, curious if she could sneak up on Adriel. When her hand reached for the knob, the door flung open.

"Why are you skulking around?"

"I wasn't skulking."

"You were."

Juniper glanced down at Adriel's clothes and smiled. "You found a dress."

"More like an undergarment." She turned away from the door, leaving an unspoken invitation at the entrance.

The room lacked the putrid green charm of the attic bedroom but made up for it in Pepto-Bismol pink ruffles that lined every chair, pillow, curtain, and coverlet. Juniper sat on the bed.

Adriel fussed with her hair, her fingers fluffing the short, copper spikes as she frowned at her reflection in the vanity mirror.

"What's wrong?"

"I feel bare without my things. I never thought I'd miss wearing a *kapp,* but, without it, I feel...incomplete."

"You look normal."

She turned. "You're sure?"

Juniper shrugged. "You look nice."

Adriel glanced down at her dress, tugging at the pink material barely brushing her knees. "I'm used to more modest attire."

"Isn't vanity, like, a sin?"

Her sharp green stare cut to Juniper. "I'm not acting vain."

"Sure you are. I'm not judging. That's what girls do."

"Well, I do not."

How did she bounce from a fresh-faced innocence to a lethal predator so seamlessly? Perhaps it was a gift, a survival tactic from living within a stringent patriarchy. Was the innocence an act or genuinely part of her character? Such questions made her wonder how self-serving Adriel might be if this ex of hers found them.

"Why didn't you help me?"

"I beg your pardon?" A cold chill rushed through the air.

She hadn't meant the outburst to sound so accusatory, but she needed to understand her part in all of this. "You were there, outside of that room, whenever they held those meetings. You could have helped me."

"I couldn't—"

"Bullshit. You're small, but you're far from helpless. I watched you attack that man an hour ago."

"I did not attack him. He was sedated. And that's different. He was mortal—"

"So am I."

Adriel's frown deepened. "You're not. You're something...*other*. I can scent it in your blood, and your body heals without the aid of intentional magick."

Apparently, they had both been studying each

other. "Well, I'm at least *half* mortal." That was the half she liked.

"And the other half? There's more than sorcery in your blood." When she remained silent, Adriel sighed. "Had I helped you, there would have been severe consequences. The elders forbid us from interceding in council business."

So, despite injustice, she put her own safety first—just like the others. Good to know.

"Juniper, if I could have done something, I would have—"

"Do you know what they did to me?"

Her lips pressed tight, but she did not look away. "From the hall, where I sat, I could hear most of the inquisitions."

Juniper's jaw locked as memories of torture flooded her mind. She wanted Adriel to admit she'd been complicit. How could anyone have simply sat through such awful treatment?

What if, on some level, she believed Juniper deserved their cruelty?

"Hearing isn't the same as living through it." She couldn't hide the anger in her voice. "First, they removed all of my clothes. Could you hear that?"

Adriel lifted her chin but didn't respond.

"I had to stand there, in front of a hundred immortal men, as they searched my body for markings. Could you hear my tears falling? Probably not because of that filthy blindfold they forced me to wear. Had I not been gagged like a bridled horse, you might have even heard me cry."

"If I'd had a choice, I would have helped."

"You *did* have a choice. You chose to sit there and do nothing."

She didn't deny it. She just held her stare, not looking remorseful or self-righteous. Just… there.

"Could you hear me when they brought in a basin and held me underwater?"

"Please stop—"

"Yes, that's what I screamed against the muzzle. But no one heard me."

Her gaze dropped. "They would have punished me for interfering. Females are not permitted inside of council meetings unless summoned by an elder."

Juniper's jaw trembled as she lifted her chin. "Would they beat you? Burn you? Try to drown you? Touch you without consent? Because that's what they were doing to me—for months—while all of you just sat there like I didn't matter. And maybe I didn't. I'm not one of you. You couldn't feel—"

"We do feel. More than you realize."

"Really? Did you feel what I did to them last night? Could you hear their screams?"

"What are you talking about?"

"When I escaped, they were all gathered around a burning building. The fire had them preoccupied. They didn't see me coming."

"Juniper, what did you do?"

"I showed them what pain is."

Adriel looked away, her brow pinched and her mouth a firm line. "My son was there."

"I earned a right to revenge."

"You make these blanket assumptions about my kind as if we're all cruel when we're not. Christian would never—"

"Your son wanted me dead."

"That's enough."

"I said that too. Begged, actually, but they didn't care."

She covered her ears. "I don't know what you want from me."

Juniper yanked her hands away from her head. "I want to believe you're prepared to fight. I'm laying my neck on the line for you. When shit hits the fan, are you going to fight? Because the days of meekly sitting on a bench are over, Adriel. There can be no hesitation. Do you understand? I need you to unlock whatever closed-off part of yourself you're hiding in there. Fuck propriety. Fuck the rules. This is life or death, and I didn't come all this way to die."

"Then why did you come with me?"

"Because we're stronger together! But I have to truly believe we're in this together. We're the only two people who matter now. I protect you, and you protect me. That's where our loyalty has to lie. Not with your son. Not with the elders. And not with other immortals. I'm the one here with you."

She nodded her understanding. "You're right.

We were taught to be pacifists, especially the females."

"Well, fuck that. You're tougher than you realize, and you don't need a man's permission to survive. You do whatever is necessary. From here on out, we only answer to each other. Got it?" She held out a hand.

Adriel stared at it. "What do you want?"

"I want you to shake it. It means you agree."

Their hands locked and Juniper exhaled a sigh of relief. "Good." She released her grip. "Now, tell me about Dane."

"Dane? What about him?"

"He's different, but I don't understand how."

She bit her lower lip. "Dane's mother was a mortal."

"And his father?"

"Was not."

"Like…" *Me,* she almost announced. "How old is he?"

"Young. Perhaps twenty. He and his sister arrived on the farm after Isaiah killed their adoptive mother."

"Adoptive mother? Was she like you?"

"No, she was mortal."

"Does he know who his real parents are?"

Adriel's gaze dropped. "His mother left behind journals. At first, we weren't sure, but after some tests we found a link in his blood that connected him to Christian."

"Christian, your son?"

Her mouth pursed and she nodded. "It turns out…they have the same father."

"Oh, shit. You mean your psycho ex?"

"I'm afraid so. It's how I knew Cerberus was free."

"What do you mean *free*?"

Her brow pinched, and she noticeably swallowed. "In order to escape him, we needed to detain him. Cer has always possessed extraordinary strength, so I needed help. Many of the males who later formed the elder's council came to my aid."

"If he was so terrible, why didn't they just kill him when they had the chance?"

"He was my mate. They did what they thought was best. Had I been able to speak at the time, I would have told them to finish him, but I could not. I was pregnant and badly injured."

"But you got away?"

She nodded solemnly. "They dismembered him and buried him deep in the earth, sentenced to wait out the healing process without blood or water. Dane's existence warned me of Cer's return, but we can assume he was trapped in the earth for more than a century."

"Are you telling me you buried him alive, and he was rotting in the ground for over a hundred years?"

"I imagine the slow passage of time was an intolerable sentence, but without his limbs, he'd have no way to escape. The elders believed it would give him time to think and repent."

"The elders are fucking idiots." She blew out a breath and plopped down on the bed. "No wonder this guy wants to hurt you. Fuck, Adriel." Juniper rubbed her head. "I really need to expand my skillset if this guy's as strong as you claim."

"He's terrifying. I'm not sure we can—"

"Stop right there. He might be terrifying, but we have to keep an optimistic attitude. We just need to think up a brilliant plan."

Should she tell her about her father? Perhaps there was some special key to unlocking whatever half-breed powers she possessed. "You helped Dane when you discovered he was part immortal?"

"I offered some guidance and always answered his questions as truthfully as possible."

"Was that because he's related to your ex?"

"No, it's because I consider Dane a friend."

So did Juniper, but she wasn't sure if Dane saw her the same. She did know that he trusted Adriel, however.

"Do you see me as a friend, Adriel?"

She studied her for a long moment. "Yes."

Then maybe she could help her the way she helped Dane. "Then I have to tell you something."

Adriel lowered to the vanity chair. "Go ahead."

"My father was immortal."

Her posture noticeably tightened. "Who was he?"

Juniper shrugged. "I don't know. He lives in Europe, and his name's Niro. He and my mother abandoned me when I was still a baby. That's why my aunts raised me."

"And now your aunts are both gone."

She nodded. "Along with any information about my lineage."

Adriel frowned. "That's why you were asking about Dane?"

"I figured if you helped him, you might be able to help me."

"But you're nothing like Dane."

"Why? We both have immortal fathers."

"Juniper, when two forms of supernatural blood blend, they veer into the unknown and create a sub-species. Dane had a mortal mother. You did not. Your mother was a witch."

"So what the hell does that mean? Am I, like, some supernatural freak?"

Adriel laughed. "Not at all. It means you're far more powerful than you probably realize."

CHAPTER 13

The following days were spent resting, researching, and putting out fires— literally.

"Try it now," Adriel yelled from the foot of the stairs.

Juniper released the pendant necklace over a sketched blueprint that crudely depicted the floorplan of Ruth's house and concentrated, holding the chain in her fingers several inches above the paper. The pendant swung chaotically at first but then settled into a rhythm that pulled toward the drawing of the kitchen.

"It's somewhere in the kitchen," she yelled.

"Where? You have to be more specific."

Juniper shuffled through her drawings, locating the one that included a layout of the counters and appliances. They had been practicing locator spells all morning.

Juniper had a hunch Dane left the farm,

which would have been smart, but Adriel had concerns. Apparently, Dane and Juniper's similarities didn't stop at being half-breeds. He also had no family, money, or place to call home.

As soon as Juniper learned this, she insisted they find him. If he was still at the farm, they would leave him be. But if he wasn't, he might need help.

Stationed on the second floor, utterly blind to what Adriel did below, Juniper had only her instincts to guide her through the spell. They spent the morning making a game of the practice. Somewhere in the house, Adriel hid a tiny crystal bird that belonged to Ruth, and then Juniper had to use her instincts to find it.

The pendant pulled toward the corner of the blueprint where the oven was drawn. Then it veered left. "It's in the refrigerator!"

"Where in the refrigerator?"

This was the tricky part. Juniper shut her eyes and visualized the crystal bird. She recalled the weight of it in her hands and the smoothness of the glass. Various distracting thoughts tried to intrude, but she pushed them all away, allowing only intuition to guide her.

"The butter dish!" she yelled, jumping up from the floor to run to the steps in the hall. "It's next to the butter dish!"

Adriel's laughter validated her accuracy.

Racing footsteps moved swiftly through the house as Adriel bolted onto the second floor with immortal speed. She triumphantly held the crystal bird in her hand and smiled. "That was incredible! Your accuracy has improved greatly!"

Lowering back onto the hardwood floor with her legs crossed and her feet tucked under her knees, Juniper smiled. "The visions are coming easier now. I hardly had to put any effort into it that time."

"Should we try something bigger?"

"Like what?"

Adriel chewed her lower lip, something Juniper often caught her doing when she had to make a decision. "What about me?"

It made sense to practice on a person since they were essentially trying to locate Dane. "Okay. But this time, I'm not using the pendant."

"Are you sure?"

"Totally. I think I know you well enough to trace your presence." She studied Adriel one last time to be sure, memorizing every feature from her delicate elfin bone structure to the feathered cowlick of her short copper hair. "I'm ready."

Closing her eyes, she concentrated on the soft scent of her skin and the way her voice shifted from throaty to dulcet when she laughed and ran out of the room.

Juniper whispered the location spell, her brow pinched in concentration and her mind's eye fully visualizing Adriel.

After finding a small bookshop selling occult books in town, she at least understood how these things worked. The texts were nowhere near as intense as the grimoire her aunts had owned—

there was a lot of pop-culture nonsense—but Juniper knew enough to piece some spells together.

So far, so good. Confidence, she realized, played a large part in her success, so every time a spell worked, her power seemed to amplify.

But what they really needed was a computer. Ruth wasn't wired for the internet, and Adriel generally viewed technology as unnecessary because, as an Amish female, she couldn't fully grasp its abilities. Juniper was working on it.

"…ninety-eight, ninety-nine, one-hundred, ready or not, here I come!" Juniper channeled all of her energy toward Adriel and a sharp but painless zap of awareness buzzed through her.

She smiled, sensing Adriel smothering a laugh as she hid somewhere dark and cramped. The odorous hydrocarbon odor of mothballs blended with the woody scent of cedar when she closed her eyes. Where would she find mothballs and cedar?

"A closet!" But which one?

She sprung to her feet and rushed out the door. In her mind, she saw loose hangers and a wool coat. She had an idea and paused in the hall, which was essentially the center of the house. *Veni ad me suaviter.*

A muffled clatter came from the den, followed by a startled shriek.

"Gotchya!" Juniper rushed down the steps, past Ruth, and wrenched open the closet. "I did it!"

"You cheated. The hat box fell on my head."

Adriel held out a pillbox hat that could have belonged to Jackie Onassis herself.

Juniper snatched the vintage accessory and perched it on Adriel's head. "Lovely."

She rolled her eyes. "Do I look ridiculous?"

"No. You look like you should wear hats more often. I can't believe I made the box move."

"I'm grateful it wasn't a bowling bag."

She pulled her out of the closet and glanced over her shoulder. "A few hours ago, you didn't even know what a bowling ball was."

"We're both learning so much."

They took a break to help Ruth make turkey sandwiches and decided to eat out back while the autumn weather held out. Adriel was incredibly kind and patient with the older woman, always asking if she needed anything or was warm enough.

Juniper liked Ruth but lacked Adriel's nurturing instincts. Perhaps she was that way because she was also older, or maybe it came from being a mother.

While the two women discussed the weather, Juniper thought of convincing arguments that might help her get online. If she had a phone or a computer—anything that gave her access to the Internet—she could find more witches and enhance her skills.

A trustworthy coven could teach her some basic skills. But it wasn't like witches were broadcasting their existence for the world to see. Most still lived in the broom closet.

The following day, when Danny stopped by, Adriel sent him home without feeding. Juniper looked up from the newest book she studied and raised a brow. "Not hungry?"

Adriel shrugged. "It didn't feel necessary."

Juniper had reached a point of acceptance with Danny acting as a blood donor, but she was nowhere near the point of encouraging the act, so she didn't mind when Adriel skipped a meal. But Adriel appeared withdrawn and pre-occupied.

"This waiting game can get annoying. Not that I want him to find us. We're far from ready. But some days, it feels like we're just wasting time."

Adriel turned her attention to the window, but Juniper kept talking. She'd been reading for days, and sometimes her brain needed a break. But no matter what she said, Adriel had little response.

"I guess that's where the saying sitting ducks comes from. While we have this time, we need to use it wisely. I need to get online. There's a store in town that sells phones. We would just need Ruth's ID and some cash to set it up." Still no response. "Or I could take a dune buggy to the moon, bang a few astronauts, and have a shopping spree on Mars."

"It won't be much longer."

"Ade, are you listening to me?"

"I'm sorry. What?" She turned away from the window.

"I said we could probably get a smartphone under Ruth's name so our data use would be more discrete. That way the IP address wouldn't be linked to the house."

"I told you I don't understand such things, June. What's wrong with a library?"

"Libraries are limited, and there's the risk of exposure. If we buy a smartphone, we'll have everything we need at our fingertips."

"What is everything?"

"Every book ever written, forums, community groups, search engines, videos, social media. The internet is an unfathomable web of information right in the palm of your hand."

"A whole book?" she asked, voice full of skepticism.

"Not just a book. All of them. Millions."

"That doesn't seem possible."

"Trust me, it is."

Adriel chewed her plump lower lip. "I don't know. I'm not comfortable taking money from Ruth."

Juniper glanced over at Ruth, who slept silently in her chair. "I'll never understand how you immortals pick and choose your ethics. We aren't taking advantage of her if she offers. We could just ask her for the money and see that she got it back eventually."

Adriel's stare returned to the dark window.

"Hey, what's going on with you?"

Her brows pulled together. "I don't know. Maybe I'm just hungry."

"So, get Danny back here."

Her lips twisted and pursed. "No. I think I'm just nervous."

She understood how anxiety was sometimes comforted with snacking. "What about a snack? Maybe something sweet or salty?"

Her green eyes turned upward. "I love tomatoes."

She scrunched her nose. "Tomatoes? Not chips or chocolate or a cookie?"

"Well, I wouldn't turn away a cookie, but I really love fresh tomatoes. I had an entire garden of them at home. I love the earthy way my fingers smell when I prune them. Maybe I'm just homesick."

"I'll add tomatoes to the grocery list."

"The store-bought ones taste like pesticides."

"You're picky."

"Maybe, but only because I've had better and see no reason to settle for less."

Juniper smirked, liking when Adriel flashed that sort of queen energy. "It's a shame all Ruth's potted plants are dead."

Glancing out the window, she sighed, her animated expression fading. "As good as a tomato sounds, I don't think that's what I want."

"So, call Danny."

She shook her head. "Last time I drank from him he…"

Juniper waited for her to finish. "He…?"

Adriel waved a hand. "You know. He…" She gestured toward her lap.

"Ohh! Ew! Seriously?*"* Juniper gagged. "Is that normal?"

"Feeding can be quite erotic for males."

"What about for the females?"

"I've never found it to equal the male experience."

"So much for my theories that God's a woman."

"I'd argue she is not."

Juniper curled her lip. "So, you guys just feel nothing while they…finish?"

"It's not that we feel *nothing*. It's complicated. And they don't necessarily *finish*. But the urge is there. The males can get…rowdy."

"Gross."

Adriel's soft laugh cleared the air. "Is the thought so repulsive to you?"

"I can handle blood. But the thought of drinking it…" She stuck out her tongue. "And something about letting some random dude grind into you while you feed—No, thank you."

"You might be surprised by how much you enjoy it if you stop thinking of it like a mortal. Dane was a half-breed, and he developed quite the taste for it."

"Dane's a guy."

"Most females love it as much as the males."

"Do you?"

She looked away. "Not the way most do."

"Well, maybe we're alike in that department. I doubt I'm that sort of female."

"You should lean more into your supernatural

side. You might discover more than a taste for blood once you start feeding properly."

"Don't judge me." Juniper rolled her eyes. "You've never even had a taco. How does someone live five hundred years without tacos? They're little corn envelopes of heaven."

She sighed. "Every time we have conversations like this, I become more aware of how sheltered I was on the farm."

Juniper turned to a blank page in her notebook. "I'm going to keep a list of all the things you need to try. All the pleasant *firsts* you missed. Tacos are at the top."

Adriel half smiled and turned her attention back to the window. Her despondency was starting to worry her. It was like watching a wild animal struggle to survive after too many years in captivity.

"Ade, talk to me."

She sighed. "The sensory overload of this place is draining. The traffic never stops, and the constant drilling and hammering of construction wears on my nerves."

Juniper frowned, hardly able to hear anything beyond the chirrup of the night bugs and the wind in the trees. She could only hear the soft chatter from the TV. They were basically in the country. "You must have really good hearing."

"I'm not used to all this noise and stimulation. It's making me feel…separated."

"Separated from what?"

"I don't know. My faith, maybe."

"Oh." She struggled to understand how something so oppressive could be missed. "Maybe you just need sleep."

"Perhaps."

After the nightly news, Ruth went to bed, and Adriel followed. Left alone with her books, Juniper made a cup of tea and took advantage of the quiet time to study. She'd finished the first book on occult practices sometime after midnight and moved on to the thick book full of herbalist spells next. The subject matter was so interesting that she couldn't put it down, and soon, the sun was peeking through the curtains again.

"Did you sleep?"

Juniper's head lifted at Adriel's voice, a guilty sense of embarrassment rushing through her as she noted the sun had come up. "Maybe?"

"Juniper, your body needs rest."

"I know, but I got really into this book. Check this out." She spun the book and turned the page. "Remember how you said there was magick in the gorges?"

"Yes."

"You're totally right. This explains how magick is basically divided into three groups—fundamental craft, intermediate alchemy, and high sorcery, which deal in both dark and light magick. Each sector is divided by the elements and then split into branches. For instance, high-air sorcery can manipulate the air through auras, gas, molecules, and weather energy. High-earth sorcery uses the strength of gravity and the earth's magnetic pull to lock structures into place. Water, however, is a thief of minerals and carries power from all over the globe. It's a huge energy source, and I'm not talking about the kind we get from the electric company."

Adriel blinked at her. "My brain hasn't awakened enough for this conversation."

Manic excitement had Juniper urgently explaining why this realization was so important. "It's like kinetic energy, the kind you guys probably used for milling on the farm, but this is actual magick. Think about ice, snow, vapor, brine, poison, blood, steam—they all contain water. It's an incredible carrier agent! And if I manipulate with water, I could probably manipulate blood."

Adriel frowned. "I'm not following."

Keeping in mind that most Amish women receive minimal formal education, she broke it down to the simplest terms. "Human blood is made of something like eighty percent water. I imagine an immortal's blood is similar."

"*Human* blood and immortal blood functions very differently."

"But you guys live off the stuff. Are you going to tell me there's no water in your blood? We humans are hydrated by vegetables that absorb water from the earth. Our food is responsible for a lot of the water in our system. And if we're your food source…" She held out her hands. "Do you get where I'm going with this?"

"You need to stop categorizing yourself as

mortal. We don't fully know what's in your blood. And I wouldn't know what's in mine."

"I'm not talking about me. I'm talking about immortals who drink blood. Adriel, they're full of water and water is a powerful agent of magick. There are spells for controlling water. If I learn them, I can apply them to more than lakes and puddles. I can use that sort of magick on asshole exes who are basically flesh sacks of water, organs, and blood."

"You can't underestimate his power, Juniper. You're far from a mage—"

"I can do this. I know I can. I just need to do more research and understand the science. Remember how you sensed the energy of the gorges? That's because, over time, the water charges with passing energy like a conductor of magick. It gathers sediment in the minerals, and minerals are full of power. The mist coming from those waterfalls could date back to the Paleozoic era. Dinosaurs, Adriel! Do you know what kind of power I could pull from something so ancient?"

"I don't."

She lifted the heavy text she'd been reading and shook the book at her. "Neither do I, but according to this, it's a fucking lot."

"I think you need sleep."

"I think I need more books. I'm almost finished with this one, and I only have two small ones left to read. We need better resources." She stacked the texts in a haphazard pile with her scattered notes. "I'm taking Ruth to town today so we can get a cell phone—"

"June, we agreed—"

"Amish time is over, Adriel. We need to look toward the future, and the future has Wi-Fi."

"Juniper, consider how you got here. You're young. Your magic is still developing. Think of what happened when you tried to cast a spell on Jonas."

"That was different. I had no idea what I was doing. My aunt harnessed my power." Which was why she had no clue how to reverse the spell on Jonas. "Water is a major element. My power can't compare. If I learn to harness the energy of the gorges, I can practice my craft in ways my aunts never imagined. It's an unlimited power source." She could still sense her skepticism. "I'll show you."

Juniper removed a drinking glass from the cabinet and filled it with water. Setting it on the table, she opened her palms over it and whispered, *"Celeriter cum sole per hanc aquam Mater Terrae opus est."*

Adriel stared at the cup, unimpressed. "And?"

"Come with me." She led Adriel to the back porch where dried-up flower pots sat full of parched dirt and dead, shriveled vines. She dumped the water into a pot. "Now, we wait."

"Wait for what?"

"You'll see. It shouldn't be long."

Adriel rolled her eyes. "You need sleep."

"Maybe. But I'm still right."

Adriel moved back inside and filled the kettle with water. In the time it took for the water to boil and the tea to steep, Juniper recorded more notes. Adriel gathered the trash from the bin and tied the bag.

"I suppose I'm the only one around here who knows how to empty the rubbish."

"Huh?" Juniper hardly looked up from her notes as Adriel took out the trash.

The door snapped shut then quickly opened. "Juniper!"

Her head jerked up and, seeing the look on Adriel's face, she rushed to the porch. A wide smile spreading across her face as she spotted the tiny, green sprout pushing through the soil.

"How did you do that? The plants were dead."

"I told you!" Juniper laughed triumphantly. "Water magick is amazing!"

Adriel's lips parted as she moved closer. "Impossible."

"Not impossible. Magick."

"It can work that quickly?"

"Faster even. This is why I need the internet. If I can find a seasoned witch, I can figure out the stuff not printed in books. We lost my aunt's grimoire in the fire, but hers wasn't the only one in existence." She smiled and pointed at the planter. "Look."

The sprout was now several inches tall and had slender green leaves. Adriel gasped and softly brushed her fingers over the delicate leaves, bringing them to her nose. Breathing in the strong, unique scent of the vine, she smiled. "It smells just like my gardens at home."

"I told you I'd get you some tomatoes."

Adriel looked at her with amused shock and laughed. "You are a witch."

Juniper nodded. "Yeah, I fucking am."

CHAPTER 14

"That one." Cerberus pointed to the willowy creature with ivory skin and long dark hair.

"Nicole," the club owner called, and the woman stepped forward. The other dancers drifted back to the shadowed part of the stage where heavy curtains hung.

She wasn't perfect, but she'd do. Reaching into his pocket, Cerberus removed a wad of crisply folded bills. Mortals were so economical. So disposable.

The club owner stepped in front of the girl. "Now, I know we agreed on five hundred, but if you want to keep her a little longer than two hours, I could cut you a deal."

Cerberus stared down at the beady-eyed urchin. "Are you altering the terms of our agreement?"

"Not at all. I'm just saying, for a thousand, you could have her all night."

He intended to keep her for the entire night regardless of what he paid. And come morning, there would be little left. At this point, the mortal urchin was negotiating his own fate. He despised weaselly little snakes, as he'd survived on a diet of slithery creatures for far too long. "We agreed five hundred."

"Then five hundred it is. Just make sure she's back before the end of her shift."

He tossed the cash at the man and caught the girl's arm, dragging her toward the door.

"You in town on business—"

"No talking."

He'd had a productive few days and managed to commandeer a vehicle and some new clothes. There had been no sign of his mate, but Cerberus was used to biding his time. He'd find her eventually, and when he did, he'd make her pay for any delays.

The girl sat in the passenger seat silently as he drove. Her questions visibly built, but under his compulsion, she was unable to verbalize a single moan.

She had Lilias's pale skin, but her hair lacked the sienna hues that lived in his memory. Ritual was important. Cerberus valued attention to detail.

Pulling into the parking lot of a corner apothecary, he shut off the car. She looked at him with worry in her eyes. The phantom scent of her anxiousness gave the air a bite. Pungent with metallic nuances similar to a sharp-scented onion cooking into a sweet broth. Like a good *béchamel*, the longer she simmered, the richer her flavor would be in the end.

Lifting a strand of hair from her shoulder he stilled and scowled. "What is this?"

Compelled to stay silent, she couldn't answer, so he tugged the synthetic strand, yanking it free from her scalp.

"Artifice." He threw the plastic strands on the floor.

Her brows pinched as her jaw trembled.

Jerking her over the center console, he sifted through her hair, finding several tracks stapled close to her skull. Fury built at the sense of being deceived, and he shoved her hard into the door.

"Take them out before I get back. Do not leave this car."

The bright artificial lights of the pharmacy irritated his eyes. After centuries underground, one developed a deep appreciation for darkness, so he often donned sunglasses regardless of the time of day.

Finding the proper color of hair dye was a simple task with today's conveniences. Nothing like it used to be for women with all the lead, ochre, and horse piss. Once he paid for his goods, he returned to the vehicle. The woman sat where he left her, now holding a nest of fake black hair on her lap.

Cerberus drove to the hotel. As soon as they

were alone, he stripped her of her clothing and gave her the box of hair dye.

She looked up at him with concern.

"Follow the directions. Then bathe. Come to me when you're finished."

He shut her inside the bathroom and stretched out on the large bed, folding his hands behind his neck, his mind retracing those familiar recollections of the one female that still haunted him to this day.

Lilias...

The mere mention of her name hit like a sweet opiate, and he calmed. Sometimes he hated her. Sometimes he loved her. But he never lost the urge to punish her.

She was always with him, tucked deep in the secret corners of his mind. His psyche had more fractures than the soldiers who lay dead at the Battle of Assandun, so perhaps he'd rewritten the truth over time and misremembered minor details, but her face and beauty were forever branded on his black soul.

Whether thinking of her fondly or enraged by the memories, his heart—to his annoyance—obsessed over what he could not have. Indulging in his fantasies never delivered the satisfaction of reality, but he did what he needed to do whenever he felt the urge to get her out of his head.

She was a spring flower on the coldest winter days. Her potent scent of ripe innocence enchanted him. But she had not been for him. She'd been a gift for the king.

As the King's most trusted guard, Cerberus had been privy to the immoral and often perverse happenings at court. He not only served King Charles as a loyal guard, but he also protected His Majesty's secrets. As a guardian of so many precious things, it only made sense that Cerberus would be entrusted with protecting Lilias as well.

Stretching out on the hotel bed, he folded his hands behind his head. His mind went back to that time when life was fresh and promising. He had yet to experience the duplicity of females, so he had not expected Lilias to be such a conniving little cunt.

CHARLES SAT in the shadows of the opened wardrobe, his thin fingers prattling slowly over the gilded arm of his chair.

"You found her?" the King said by way of greeting, his thin lips curling about his blunt teeth with palpable anticipation.

"Yes, Your Majesty." Mud and blood still dripped from Cerberus's heavy boots, so he did not fully enter the king's private chambers.

"Did she put up a fight?" Born a weak and sickly child, the King maintained fragile health all his life and a deep respect for Cerberus's strength and immortality.

"Four guards were lost."

"You were the one to finally seize her?"

"I did as you asked."

"Good. Your loyalty to the Crown will be rewarded generously. Guard her with the attention and devotion you guard your King."

"Of course, Your Majesty."

A slow, wheezing breath filled the silence expressing the King's excitement. "I want to see her."

"She's been taken to her chamber to—"

"Now."

"Yes, Your Majesty."

Pivoting out of the private chambers, Cerberus marched through the corridors untethered by ceremony. As a draugr, death was no danger to him, so protection was unnecessary.

The trappings of his armor added to his bulk and announced his approach with the alarming clamor of steel. And while he didn't soundlessly glide like a ghost, he moved with inhuman agility for a male of his heft and strength.

Despite not knowing what he was, soldiers instinctively moved out of his path. When he passed by, women frequently fell into prayer. He towered over the masses and carried the cold essence of the underworld with him wherever he went.

He existed to serve the Crown and lived without fear of torture. He was the King's greatest weapon of torment. No one within the kingdom's walls had the stomach to do the things he could do, and when the King needed answers or someone to blame, Cerberus was the first to get the guilty talking.

He did not resemble the men at court. From their feeble physiques to their foppish attire, they were perhaps the weakest generation of this race he'd seen thus far. The females were equally unappealing, nothing but wasted flesh on fragile bones.

It wasn't his Viking height or the clamor of his armor that set them on edge, but the fire in his stare, shadowed by the hammered iron of the Viksø helmet that fit his skull. He could slaughter every last one of them before they realized their pathetic mortal lives were over.

They were weak. Even the royal army was preoccupied with belts and buttons fit for fanfare instead of war. Overthrowing the throne would be easy for any man willing to approach it logically. And while Cerberus served this king, he'd certainly live long enough to serve another.

His gaze marked every onlooker as he dutifully went to fetch the female. For now, because it suited him, his loyalty was to His Majesty. Cerberus was content to serve as a hound and guardian of the Crown, and the King valued his loyalty.

Death did not haunt Cerberus, and he never hesitated to take a life. He often reported back to Charles with blood still dripping from the horns of his helmet and the echoes of lesser mortals' screams still echoing in his ears. None of that mattered as long as victory had been won.

"Step aside," he ordered the guard at the tower chamber.

Cerberus rapped his split knuckles on the metal door and entered. Lilias's hard glare landed on him with the unflinching regality of a royal, but there was no trace of imperial blood in her body.

However, she possessed immortality in her veins, which was why His Majesty wanted her.

Cerberus barged into her chambers, and she stood, the material of her gown still damp from the rain and clinging to her form. Her breasts jutted against the ripples of silk, unconfined or adorned with the trappings of a corset like the females at court typically wore.

"You promised I wouldn't be a prisoner here." She was a commoner with the confidence of a queen.

"You are His Majesty's guest."

"If I am his guest, why has he not greeted me?"

"His Majesty has requested your presence in his private quarters."

Staggering back a small step, she studied him.

His gaze dropped to the slender column of her neck as she swallowed tightly. The slight ripple in her confident façade intrigued him. While immortals were the more advanced species, they were far outnumbered and could quickly be overrun or tortured through experimentation if ever truly exposed.

"Does he know about us?" she whispered too low for the other guards to hear.

Although she was also Norse and of a similar species, she was from a far more delicate race. His breed had been called everything from ghost walkers to skull warriors while her kind awaited maturity and signals from the gods.

Cerberus held her stare and nodded. It was not his preference to mistreat the King's guests unless ordered to do so. "Cooperate, and you will not be harmed."

Unlike other females, she did not drop her gaze in his presence. "Do I have your word?"

She was wise, hiding her powers beneath symptoms of poverty. Cerberus should have known then not to trust her. "You have my word."

"What does he want from me?"

"Only your blood." His gaze again dropped to the slope of her breasts and the swell of her hips. "For now."

Her head cocked, and a tumble of radiant copper curls fell over her bare shoulder. She looked up at him with eyes as green and glistening as a dewy pasture. "Is he dying?"

"All mortals are dying."

"Is it the plague? Why not offer him your blood."

"A female can comfort him in ways I cannot."

"There is no curing him?"

"No, but your blood can sustain him and gift him with vitality."

Her chest lifted, pressing her firm breasts against the worn material of her thin gown. A single tear rolled from her ruby lashes down her ivory cheek. "This is not my purpose in life."

"Tears cannot change your fate now, princess."

Her gaze snapped to his, sharp with censorship. "I am not a servant to this realm, and you know nothing about my fate."

The fire in her stare caused his insides to burn with an unfamiliar heat. He could punish her for taking such a sharp tone, but something inexplicable held him back.

"The gods cannot save you now—princess," he repeated the endearment simply to needle her.

"Is that it then? My purpose in this life is to remain in this tower, occasionally called upon by the king and used for my veins?"

Blood rushed to his cock. The desire to brush away that lonesome tear had his roughened fingers twitching, but he resisted the urge to touch her for fear of breaking her. Never before had he felt so compelled to protect a female.

"Obey your King, and there will be no pain."

Her head lifted, her ruby curls cascading down her back. "And if I disobey, will you deliver the pain?"

She accurately understood his role, so there was no point in deceiving her. "Yes."

The sharp angle of her elfin face lifted in challenge. "Neither you nor your King could conceive my threshold for pain." She eyed him up and down dismissively. "I will not be in this tower forever. My destiny is elsewhere, and nothing you do can change that."

"Perhaps. I'll allow you to decide if your stay will be pleasant or unpleasant."

Her green eyes narrowed. "You'll never hurt me."

How wrong she'd been.

THE SHOWER STARTED, and the scent of ammonia cut through the air, quickly replaced by the floral bouquet of fragrant soaps. He shut his eyes, his anticipation slowly building. These fanciful moments satisfied him as he hoped they would, but they eased the longing so he could focus on revenge.

"TELL ME, *walker, how does someone like you find themselves serving a weak, diseased mortal king?" Lilias's throaty voice pleased him more than music ever could, and he enjoyed their discussions whenever he escorted her to and from the tower.*

The cold hunk of muscle occupying his chest seemed to thaw in her presence and flutter out of rhythm. Only she could cause such a reaction, though he never dared to ask her why that was.

"I was gifted to His Majesty as a young boy."

"But you chose to stay as a man." She understood a Norse skull warrior could not be ordered or forced into obedience.

"Yes."

"Why?"

"The King values me."

"The King is a weakling."

"Careful, princess." He could justly snap her fragile neck for such a treasonous statement. It would take no effort to pulverize her delicate bones into dust, despite his reluctance to do so.

Her lips, dark and wet like the seeds of a pomegranate, quirked to one side. "You won't hurt me, Cerberus Maddox XI."

He was a loyal guard and gatekeeper of His Royal Majesty's guests, protector of the crown, yet she could disarm him by simply using his name. In a short time, she also mastered the King and adopted a regal radiance that enchanted even the eunuchs of the kingdom.

Charles had been delighted with his new possession. She was intended only to serve him with vitality, but Lilias quickly became a coveted object of His Majesty's affection. He was set on not only having Lilias's blood but also winning her heart. Every day the King attempted to speak to her, but she remained stoically silent in his presence, providing only her submission and her vein.

When she kneeled before His Majesty and offered her vein, Cerberus sometimes caught glimpses of her reflection in the polished vases around the King's chambers. Those visions haunted him more than he wanted to admit.

Cerberus dreamed of her kneeling at his feet, not to offer her vein but in an act of carnal loyalty, an act of love. Such fantasies plagued him during the day, especially on the days when the King's addiction to her blood left her too depleted to walk, and Cerberus had to carry her wilted body back to the tower. Seeing her in such a state tempted him to steal her away and keep her as a prize for himself.

"You should not let him take so much." He gently placed her in her bed and brushed back her faded curls.

Under the weight of His Majesty's greed, her radiance and youthful glow dulled. Her veins frequently collapsed at the cost of the ailing King's vitality, but her beauty somehow remained.

She turned her face into his calming touch. "If I asked you to let me go, Cerberus, would you?"

His heart jolted at the thought of never seeing her again. He could not protect her if she left this place alone. At that moment, he made a silent vow to conjure a plan of escape, at which point they could both leave.

"I will see to it that life becomes more bearable for you."

A tear rolled from the corner of her eye. "My soul is dying here."

"I will not let you die, Lilias. But you must rest so you can heal. You need your strength before circumstances can improve."

Her eyes closed, forming crescent shadows under her copper lashes. "My mate needs me."

Cerberus stiffened, his hand curling around the hilt of his sword. "What mate?"

She licked her dry lips. "I sense him trying to find me, but he can't get past the Royal Guard."

Cerberus drew back and fanned out his senses, scanning the palace walls and the surrounding woods for any trace of an immortal male. He sensed nothing nearby.

His fingers gently traced over her brow and she sighed. She'd become prone to fainting spells of late. Perhaps her weakness was causing visions.

"Take my blood, Lilias. It will restore your strength and clear your head."

THE SHOWER SHUT OFF, and his mind jolted to the present. The mortal woman moved about the bathroom clumsily. He could hear the rapid thrum of her heartbeat and the quick clip of her shallow breaths. In another hour, it would all be over.

The blow dryer clicked on and his mind returned to Lilias, recalling the sweet decadence of her mouth drawing from his vein.

THE DELICATE CARESS of her tongue teased his soul, tugging parts of him no female had touched before. "That's it, princess. My blood will make you strong again."

He cherished those moments when he could cradle her close, always keeping his body under control by a fraying thread, ignoring the hardening of his cock and the tremble in his chest.

He was a slave to her beauty and honor-bound to protect her. The thought of anyone else touching her so intimately threw him into a murderous rage. Even the weak King was wearing on his nerves.

He'd been such a fool to trust her...

HIS HANDS CURLED into fists as he eyed the bathroom door. When he lay in the earth, dying a million deaths as he waited for his body to heal, he suffered those intimate memories of her again and again, bitterly aware that her kindness had all been a lie.

.   .   .

"I'M GOING TO MARRY LILIAS," King Charles had announced one evening. Cerberus had not turned his attention from the window. There was no love between the King and Lilias. On the contrary, she despised him and often moaned over how grotesque she found his feeble appearance and cold touch.

"She would make a fine queen, don't you agree, Cer?"

"Will you force her to wed?"

"I'm the King. Women would betray their god to have my name."

Women, yes, but Lilias was an immortal female. Marriage was a mortal practice that paled in contrast to the bonds mated immortals shared.

Charles was set on seducing his future queen. He gifted Lilias with flowers, jewels, the finest silks, and the most luxurious furs until she resigned herself to marry the King.

The wedding was a grand affair celebrated throughout the realm—until a plague struck. Corpses mounted with little explanation as mortals splashed holy water and burned the dead.

Bodies were drained of blood before they hit the ground, and victims typically suffered twin puncture wounds, which were said to be the mark of death. But this was not like the telltale rash that preceded the deadly fever or the lumps incurred by prior plagues.

It was an infestation.

Immortals learned of the illustrious Queen and took her presence in the kingdom as an open invitation. Households were bled dry and left for dead. Villagers grew weak with anemia. Bloodletting became a *fashionable practice as the palace became overrun with vampires.*

Lilias waited for her mate, but Cerberus ensured no immortal males breached the kingdom walls and, over time, the light in her eyes dulled.

A songbird imprisoned in a gilded cage, will eventually lose the desire to sing, but Lilias never lost faith that her mate would come. She waited by her window every night for his rescue.

The King's fanatical need to please the Queen became an obscene obsession. If she wanted music, Charles sent the finest harpsichords, flutes, and fiddles with musicians ordered to play until their fingers bled. If she craved goose, he'd have the fattest one sent to her table and carved.

Lilias no longer resembled the peasant girl who had captured Cerberus's heart. Her gowns were no longer plain, and her hair no longer hung loose beneath her jeweled crown. Maids doted on her as much as they doted on the King, and when Charles wanted to feed, Lilias went to him without objection.

She was so convincing, so enchanting, but Cerberus could scent her deceit. Something was brewing beyond the castle walls, and he wanted to know what secrets she hid.

"Do not act like a wounded bird with me," he snarled one afternoon, walking her back to her chambers after an especially petulant display at court.

"Mind your tone, walker. Charles is my king. Only he has the right to speak to me as he pleases. You do not."

"You haven't been a victim since the day you ar-

rived, and he has never been your king," Cerberus growled mockingly.

"You overestimate your position. I could have you replaced with any guard of my choosing. I only need to say the word—"

She gasped as he caught her arm and hauled her into a dark alcove, caging her in with his body. "And I would break your neck long before such a request would reach your lips."

Fire flashed in her emerald stare as she bared her teeth. "Take your hands off me."

Rather than release her, he crowded her more. "You don't love him."

"Of course, I don't," she practically spat. "And he doesn't love me. I'm merely a possession he covets."

"Then why visit his bed when you and I both know it will bear no fruit."

"If you don't like my position, blame yourself. I'm here because of you. Do not fault me for having the wherewithal to improve my situation. Eventually, the feeble King will die and I will inherit all of this, and you and the rest of us will be better for it."

He saw it then, the greed for power in her eyes. She didn't want rubies and furs. She wanted far more. While Charles wasted away, coveting a female whose heart he would never possess, she plotted to unburden the King of all his power using nothing more than her female wiles.

If Cerberus could remove his jealousy from the equation, it seemed a small and wise sacrifice for her to make. "You don't plan to be wed for long."

A cold chuckle passed her dark lips. "It wouldn't

take much. I could easily taint my blood with poison. The healers would simply assume he passed of natural causes."

"They would never let an immortal rule."

With no royal blood or noble lineage, the bishops wouldn't allow her to sit on the throne for long. And after Charles' passing, Cerberus would likely be the one ordered to take her head, an act that would kill him as well.

"The King must stay alive," he decided.

"Do you think I fear treason?"

"I think you're the most fearless female alive. But you will never outmatch me, and I'm who they will send to collect your head."

"First, you would have to find me."

His hand closed around her throat, framing her jaw and applying pressure until her defiant gaze locked with his. "There is not a corner of this world where you could hide that I would not find you." His grip tightened. "I'm more than the King's guard, Lilias. I'm a draugen. Do not speak to me as if I'm some impressionable pup meant to bring your slippers. Cross me, and you will pay. On that, you have my word."

And pay she had.

THE BLOW DRYER SHUT OFF, and his gaze returned to the door. The little mortal's heartbeat frantically purred like the wing of a hummingbird.

Ah, there was nothing sweeter than the sharp tang of torment that flavored a difficult surrender. While her instincts urged her to run, his compulsion overruled any sense of free will.

He crossed the hotel room and opened the bathroom door. "You won't need a towel."

Leaving the door ajar, he returned to the bed, propping himself up to watch as she inwardly battled her instincts.

Her hair was finer than it appeared at the club, but the copper dye had gone a long way to making her look more like Lilias. Her employer implied she'd done this before, so her hesitance was strictly the result of her fear. Her instincts likely recognized him as a predator and she as his prey.

Mortals were foolish creatures. They could suffer anything for the right pay. How they weren't yet extinct was beyond him.

Slowly, her foot stepped onto the carpet, and she crossed the threshold. Her chest rose and fell with every labored breath. As she approached the bed, her body trembled like a leaf.

Reaching out a hand, he caressed the curve of her breast. The nipple reflexively tightened.

"Too light," he remarked, recalling the distinct ruby shade of Lilias's areolas. "They were the same red as her lips. Dark like pomegranate seeds. Sweet and tart."

He pinched the tip of her breast, and her shoulders curled inward, her face strained under the sharp pain.

Cerberus released her flesh with a sharp tug and smirked. "Kneel."

Tears rushed to her eyes—brown rather than green—but she did as he commanded.

How many times had he fantasized of having her like this—cowering at his feet, eyes wet with fear, willing to do whatever he asked?

"I think I might have you drink my blood, princess."

Her face paled as her breathing quickened. Humans had such pathetic tolerance for discomfort.

"You don't like that idea?"

She shook her head.

He rolled his eyes. "Then distract me."

She glanced about the room but quickly returned her attention to his body. Females of all species understood their role in nature when confronted by a beast. He missed the days when women knew their place. This one did.

She loosened his pants and quickly got to work. He cared little of her comfort and stuffed her mouth until her shoulders jerked.

"Stop trying to lead," he ordered, fisting her hair.

Some mortals were not naturally submissive, but he found most of them quite teachable. Pain could be a powerful motivator, so any sign of resistance only increased his force.

"Do you think you can escape me now, Lilias?"

She whimpered in confusion, but he did not permit her to answer.

"Did you think I would let you get away with it?"

The rich scent of her fear swirled about the room like an intoxicating perfume. He lived to taunt them.

"You're probably going to die tonight."

Her breath hitched.

He could at least use her up before he fed. "I want you to fuck me like your life depends on it."

She climbed on top of him, and tight heat sheathed his cock. She frantically rode him, her breathless performance unconvincing and annoying. If only every woman lied as well as Lilias.

"I'm losing interest," he warned, and she quickened her speed, tits bouncing as the scent of chemicals on her hair made his nose twitch.

When she leaned forward to kiss him, he caught her throat. "What do you think you're doing?"

Her brown eyes widened.

"Answer me."

"Kis-s-s-sing you?"

Fury exploded out of him and he snapped her neck with one sharp jerk. She fell to the floor in a heap of lifeless limbs, her eyes blindly staring up at him.

"Stupid cunt."

Growling, he turned his focus to the window. His mind returned to Lilias, but he no longer wanted to think of her. "Fuck!" He slammed his fists into the wall, cracking the plaster. Seething, he shoved the television off the dresser, hating how she eternally lived in his head even when he no longer welcomed her there.

STARING DOWN AT HER WIDE, emerald eyes, so trusting and seemingly innocent, she gently pulled at his vein. No matter how docile she appeared, he never underestimated her cunning sense of pride. Lilias would do anything to survive

"Your gown." It had draped open while she fed, and he reached to cover her exposed flesh.

She caught his wrist in a delicate grip. "Do you not like to look at me, Cerberus?"

She knew he did. But it was not something they spoke of.

Tugging at the laces of the chemise, she pulled the covering lower, exposing the ruby tips of her breast.

"Lilias—"

"Feeding does something to me. I know you feel it, too."

He swallowed. The sensation of her full mouth suckling from his vein was perhaps the greatest torture he knew, yet he fought the temptation to taste her for fear that he would not be able to stop once he started.

She reached for a small pot of liniment. Dipping her finger into the fruit-scented salve, she traced the pink gloss over her lips, darkening the color. He'd seen her use it before but only on her mouth. He could not look away as she applied a dab to her nipples, leaving the tips glossed in a tempting shade of red.

She slightly arched her back, lifting her chest. "Did you want to taste?"

His gaze jumped to her face. "I..." His words cut off as she gathered her skirts, exposing her lush thighs.

"Have you ever tasted a female, Cerberus?" Her fingers delved between her petals, and his fangs elongated as his breath hitched. "You have my permission." She eased back, opening her legs. "Go on. Use your tongue."

Insanity struck as he parted her thighs.

Her fingers swirled invitingly within the glistening pink folds, and the scent of the fruit gloss called to him. The first lap of his tongue had his mind whirling.

"That's it." She arched, pressing her soft folds closer to his mouth.

He speared his tongue deeper, drinking in her flavor as his cock hardened to steel. When he reached for the latch of his belt, she stilled him.

"First, you must kiss me here." She pointed to her nipples. "I'll show you how."

Climbing onto his lap, she ran her fingers through his hair. He could hardly breathe through his lust.

"Suckle gently, Cerberus." She pulled his head to her breast. "Don't stop until I'm satisfied."

"Yes, my queen."

The familiar taste of fruit coated his tongue as he latched on. She moaned and stroked his hair. When the flavor faded, she directed him to her other nipple.

"Very good, walker. Now kiss me here." She pointed to her mouth, but when he leaned forward, he lost his balance. His vision blurred as one Lilias became four.

"*Something is amiss...*"

"*Shh...*" *Her fingers fanned through his hair, sending a tingle of pleasure down his spine as she eased him onto the bed. "Lie back."*

He looked up at her, confused. The candlelight blurred, forming a halo behind her copper curls. The recognizable clink of armor had him slowly turning his head to the door.

"*Who...*" *Words became too difficult for his numb mouth to form. His body suddenly weighed a hundred stones.*

"*Is it working?*" *a male voice asked.*

Lilias rose from the bed. "See for yourself."

Rage ignited inside of him as the blurry figure of a man stepped beside her. Not a man, an immortal male. It was then he understood his mistake. "You... poisoned me?"

"*It's only temporary. You'll sleep for a few days, and then you'll be fine."*

"*We need to move,*" *the armed immortal warned, already leading her toward the door.*

"*I'll find you,*" *Cerberus growled, aggravated by how weak the threat sounded to his own ears as he lay paralyzed by the poison. "You have my blood—"*

She pressed a finger over his lips. "By tomorrow, I'll be bound to my mate, and his blood will be the only thing in my veins. It's time to let me go, Cerberus."

IMPOTENT FURY still simmered in the deepest part of Cerberus's hollow heart. Unlike ordinary immortals, ancient Nords could not be called. His kind was born of the sea and sky with salt in their bones and the dragon's fire in their blood. Lilias's species was of a different order, divined by the cosmos and ruled by the other half of her soul.

Cerberus had no soul.

Glancing dispassionately at the dead mortal on the floor, his lip curled. The corpse had already started to rot. He needed more durable toys.

Fanning out his senses, he scanned the surrounding areas for Adriel. Lilias had paid dearly for her betrayal, but now her daughter owed a debt of her own.

She was out there somewhere. Sooner or later, he would find her.

CHAPTER 15

"It's a church." Juniper frowned at the vaulted spires, certain they were in the wrong place.

"An awfully fancy church."

She glanced at Adriel. "Maybe I did the spell wrong." If Dane was here, he wasn't the sort of guy she thought he was. "He didn't strike me as a big churchgoer."

Adriel scanned the area and frowned. "Did we make a wrong turn?"

"It doesn't work that way." Juniper once again looked at the folded map. The Indian ink made of soot, wood oil, and mineral water from the gorges was supposed to lead them directly to Dane. She'd been certain she'd done everything correctly.

"Maybe you mispronounced a word."

"That's possible."

Spells were written using the Theban al-

249

phabet and spoken in a Latin-English hybrid tongue, but sometimes—because grimoires were passed down through generations—traces of Old Norse and Creole terms ended up transposed.

"I was a little anxious when we started."

It was the first time they really left Ithaca. Juniper didn't feel ready to face whatever was hunting Adriel. She wanted to brush up on her basic magick and learn more because the last time things got scary, her magick froze inside of her.

Dropping to her knee, she dug through the backpack and pulled out the big book. For all she knew, they were scammed by the good folks on eBay and sold a replica of crap inspired by the movie *Hocus Pocus*, but she really hoped that wasn't the case.

A chill raced down her spine as her fingers brushed the soft leather cover, and her fears abated. There was tangible magick in this book, a presence that lingered in the carbon of the pages and the glue and thread that tethered each handwritten spell to the spine.

She opened the entry for the locator spell and dragged her finger over every scribbled word, whispering them silently to herself, enunciating the final verse aloud. "*Invenire unum cupio.*" Her hand rushed to her throat.

"June?"

It hit her like the wind of a hurricane, not quite solid but complete. She shut the book and slipped it back into the bag, hooking it over her shoulder as she stood. "He's here."

"Are you sure?"

"Well, no, I'm not sure. I've never done anything like this before, and we bought our spell book from an online auction. But this feels… right. Sort of." She just couldn't understand why he would be in a Boston cathedral. "Was Dane religious?"

"I don't recall seeing him at our prayer meetings."

Juniper opened the door and hesitated. "Crap." She looked at Adriel.

"Is something wrong?"

She shrugged. "It feels weird, right? A vampire and a witch walking into a church? There's a punchline there somewhere. Or am I thinking about the joke where the pope walks into a bar?"

"What are you talking about?"

"Nothing. I babble when I'm nervous."

"What do you think is going to happen?"

"Wait—" Too late. Adriel rolled her eyes and stepped across the threshold.

Juniper looked up nervously the moment she stepped inside. No bolt of lightning. No fire and brimstone. Not even a swarm of locusts or toads.

Adriel sniffed the air as Juniper shut her eyes and held out her hands, concentrating.

"What's that smell?"

"Shh. It's frankincense."

"No, there's something else." Adriel sniffed again. "Something…ripe."

"I can't concentrate through your talking." Glancing curiously at the basin of holy water, Juniper kept her hands to herself and crossed the vestibule into the open nave of the church. "Are you sensing anyone here?"

"No, but my senses are turned down at the moment."

They agreed that was best since Juniper was working the locator spell and unable to maintain the protection spell as well.

"But there is a trace of mortal activity."

"It's Monday. They probably had service yesterday."

Long, wooden pews lined the church's body, and a detailed portrait of archangels adorned the cathedral ceiling. As a descendant of witches, Juniper hadn't spent much time in buildings like this. Her family was more into rituals that required them to dance naked under the full moon or set out garden offerings for the goddesses and gods.

"This feels a little like trespassing. Maybe we should leave."

Adriel drew in a long breath, fully sniffing the air. "He's here."

"You can smell him? You're sure it's Dane?"

Rather than answer, she disappeared, moving at immortal speeds too fast for Juniper's eyes to track.

"Uh, Ade?"

"Up here." Her voice echoed from the mezzanine balcony above.

Juniper followed the closed staircase to an open loft set for a choir but frowned when the energy shifted. Something was off. The energy here was cold and solemn. Bad things had happened in this place. Things that could never be undone.

The aura of the gallery was dark and thick, hinting at haunting crimes that happened right where Adriel stood. "I think we should leave. Dane's not—"

Adriel pressed a finger to her lips and pointed behind a mahogany wall that housed the keys of an enormous organ. "Which one of us is carrying him out of here?"

Disbelief flooded her as she rushed forward and sucked in a breath. Dane lay passed out on the floor, wrapped in a purple tablecloth, hugging a bottle of what looked like wine. "Oh, my God."

"He's pickled." Adriel poked his foot with the toe of her shoe. "Dane. Dane, wake up."

Juniper frowned at the wrappers and crumbs covering his chest. He looked like death and smelled worse. When Adriel jostled him again, and he still didn't move, she worried he might actually be dead.

"Is he breathing?"

"He's fine. I can hear his heartbeat."

Juniper flipped a switch on the organ, and it hummed to life with a low vibration. She struck a key, breaking the silence as the instrument's drone blasted through the eight-foot pipes and echoed off the cathedral walls.

Dane bolted upright, sputtering and wrestling his way out of the tablecloth as the wooly timber cut off. Crumbs drifted from the stubble of his jaw, and a glass bottle rolled into the pew.

He stilled and frowned. "Adriel?" His gaze shot left. "Juniper?" His confused stare bolted about the church. "What…? How…?"

Juniper laughed. The spell actually worked! Holy shit. "You smell like hot garbage."

"And look worse." Adriel bent to pick up the bottle, sniffed it, and drew back with a frown. "Did you steal this?"

"What are you guys doing here?"

"I'm a fucking sorcerous!" Juniper broke into a touchdown dance.

"Take it easy," Adriel warned, gathering the trash off the floor. "Did you rob the tabernacle, Dane?"

"I was hungry. How are you here?" He brushed off his shirt and shoved the tablecloth onto a bench. "I'm so confused. How are you two together? Why are you in Boston? And what the heck are you wearing?"

Adriel's fair skin darkened to a scorching red as she pulled at the hem of her knee-length dress. "There have been some changes."

Juniper scowled and protectively stepped in front of Adriel. "Don't mind how we're dressed. Did you go on a bender of Jesus crackers and booze?"

"I ran out of money."

"Why Boston?" Adriel asked.

Dane shrugged. "Why not?" Something sad flashed in his eyes. "Where else should I go? I have no one. I couldn't stay on the farm. I couldn't even keep my dog, so I gave him away to a family with twin boys."

"You gave Colby away?" Adriel said, voice rich with empathy. "Oh, Dane."

"I knew you needed help. I could sense it." Juniper stuffed the grimoire back in her bag and closed the flap. "We've been crashing with a little old lady named Ruth. You can come back with us. She won't mind. I don't know about the dog though. We have a stray cat. I call him Jasper."

"Colby's in a good home. It was the right choice. I can't take care of him the way he needs. But you really think I can come with you?" Relief showed in his voice and eyes.

Adriel nodded. "There's no reason for you to do this alone."

"I haven't been doing much of anything. A few random jobs here and there so I can eat, but nothing lasting."

"Well, we have plenty of food, but we must return before Juniper's energy runs out. Come along. We have a motor vehicle."

"You're driving a car?"

"No, Juniper is. Thankfully it has safety belts and handles to hold onto. She drives like a blind woman in a rush to fulfill a death wish."

Over the next few hours, while driving back

to upstate New York, they brought Dane up to speed. Though he looked and smelled like something dredged out of a sewer, his spirits were high.

"You actually found me with magic? That's pretty badass, Juniper."

"I know." She smiled, glancing back through the rearview mirror as she drove. "We found a decent book of spells online that's been super helpful. I think the creator was a mage. It's like I've opened up a portal inside of me. The more knowledge I consume, the more manageable my power becomes. It's a total high. Soon I'll be limitless!"

"We're all just grateful it hasn't gone to Juniper's head," Adriel teased.

Dane leaned forward, wedging his body between the front seats. "I barely recognize you, Adriel. In street clothes, you look so…young."

Juniper smothered a laugh. If he wasn't careful, he would find himself hitchhiking the rest of the way.

Adriel drew back and covered her nose. "Sweet heavens, Dane. When's the last time you bathed?"

He sat back. "It's been a little rough."

Beneath the shag of his overgrown hair, his eyes creased with lines of worry. Dirty, gaunt cheeks gave away his hunger. Reaching into the center console, Juniper pulled out a granola bar. "Here. You look hungry."

"Thanks." He took the bar but didn't open it.

Adriel looked back at him with concern. "When's the last time you fed?"

Juniper's head jerked, her stare snapping to Adriel's. Sometimes she spoke about things too casually.

"It's been a few weeks."

Juniper frowned.

"You should feed," Adriel said. "You both should."

At that, Dane's stare bolted to Juniper. "Wait, what?"

"Thanks, Adriel."

"Why is it a secret? If we're going to be living together, we need complete transparency. Dane, you need to feed. I can offer my vein, but you must block your thoughts at all times. Cerberus is still out there."

Dane frowned and looked back to Juniper. "You're a hybrid?"

She grimaced. "I'm something. Apparently, when you're also a witch your blood mutates into a whole new sub-species. I could wake up as a mogwai tomorrow. Don't get me wet or feed me after midnight."

Adriel frowned. "I don't understand that reference."

"*Gremlins.*" Dane chuckled. "I remember that movie."

"God, remember movies?" Juniper recalled nostalgically.

Unclipping her seat belt, Adriel twisted to

face Dane. "Enough talking." She rolled up her sleeve. "You must feed."

"Wait, now? In the car?"

Dane pulled her wrist to his mouth. "Thanks."

The car fell into an awkward silence, broken only by the soft sound of Dane suckling from Adriel's vein. Talk about feeling like a third wheel. Juniper focused on the road, never blinking and careful to avoid any glimpse of what was taking place ten inches to her right.

Dane moaned.

"Do you have to make those noises?" The metallic scent of Adriel's immortal blood became all she could smell. "I'm pretty sure this could have waited until we got home."

"It's so good," he groaned.

Juniper glanced at Adriel and they both flushed. Did she like what he was doing? She couldn't stop thinking about what Ade had said about men humping like dogs whenever they did a blood exchange. Was she getting some sort of pleasure from having Dane's mouth on her?

"Don't take too much," Juniper snapped, as if she had any clue how this stuff worked and what was considered adequate.

"He's fine," Adriel assured, her voice all too breathy for Juniper's liking. And why were her eyes so dilated?

Dane moaned again.

"Oh, come on! I get that you have needs, but I need you to tighten it up with the moans and groans. This isn't a porn set. How much could you possibly need?"

They both stilled and stared at her.

Juniper kept her hands on the wheel and her eyes on the road. "What?"

Dane licked his lips and wiped his mouth. "I've only ever had Magdalene's blood. Hers is…" He shook his head. "Incomparable—in a good way," he quickly assured Adriel. "Uh, do you want me to…?"

"It's fine." Adriel retracted her arm and licked the puncture closed.

She supposed vampires didn't need to worry about germs or catching colds because they swapped spit while feeding like it was as casual as a make-out session. Did it have to be so intimate?

Adriel folded her hands in her lap and lowered her chin to her chest, her shoulders hunched inward. She was strangely silent.

Dane leaned back, stretching his arm over the headrests as he blew out a breath. "It doesn't usually hit me this quickly." His comment was answered with awkward silence. "Uh, Juniper, wasn't that the Ithaca exit?"

Veering onto the shoulder of the road, she threw the car in reverse. If she hadn't been so distracted by Dane's erotic feast of Adriel, she wouldn't have missed it. "Hold on."

They all grabbed hold of their seatbelts as she sped backward and made a sharp turn home.

Dane wasn't buckled in, so he nearly slid out of his seat. "Jesus, Juniper. Slow down!"

He was one to talk.

CHAPTER 16

"*I* won't let you!"

"Try to stop me!"

Adriel rushed up the back steps, which were now covered with overgrown tomato vines, and bolted into the house. "What's going on?"

Dane and Juniper sparred off from opposite ends of the kitchen. Ruth sipped her tea at the table, exactly where Adriel left her. When her hearing aid wasn't in, the mortal woman hardly noticed their incessant bickering.

"Tell her," Dane barked accusingly.

Juniper's chin jutted out in defiance. "You had no right to go through my things!"

"Your things? Everything you're wearing, you stole from Ruth! All of those books were bought with her money!"

"Ruth, do you care that I borrowed your clothes?"

Realizing she was being addressed, Ruth set

down her tea cup and smiled. "What's that, dear? We've got crows?"

"*Clothes,*" she enunciated.

"Oh, my shows." She reached for her cane. "I had better put my hearing aid in then. Where did I leave that?"

"Nice," Dane remarked as Ruth shuffled out of the kitchen.

Juniper scoffed. "Like you haven't enjoyed having a roof over your head and real food in your stomach these last few days. Don't act so high and mighty. You robbed a church."

"All right, you two," Adriel chided.

"Churches like to help the needy."

"Yeah, I'm sure it's one of their commandments to give drifters all their sacramental wine. Could you be any more of a hypocrite?"

"Can someone please tell me what started this?"

"Nothing—"

"She's planning to kill Jonas!"

The room silenced, and Adriel looked at Juniper in shock. "Is that true?"

She crossed her arms over her chest, choosing not to answer.

"Juniper?"

"What?" she snapped defensively. "He's suffering. It would be the merciful thing to do."

"Mercy would be reversing the spell, not killing him!" Dane yelled.

"No one is killing anyone. You two are friends. Where is this hostility coming from?"

"Why do you even care, Dane? They threw you out like yesterday's garbage."

"The Hartzlers didn't have anything to do with me leaving. They gave me a home when I had none. You would be hurting his family, and they don't deserve that."

Juniper's eyes narrowed. "This is about that vampire chick, Grace, isn't it?"

Adriel pinched the bridge of her nose. "For the last time, Juniper, we're immortals, not vampires."

"That bitch is a vampire!"

"Hey!" Dane snapped. "Leave Gracie out of this!"

"Oh, now it's Gracie? How many immortals were you sleeping with on that farm."

His scowl darkened, and Adriel stepped between them. "That's enough, Juniper. Apologize."

"For what? Jonas killed my Aunt Mabel. His bloodsucking daughter killed my Aunt Venus." Her scowl turned on Dane. "When you wanted revenge on Isaiah, I helped you. You owe me."

"That may be true, but there's no way I'm letting you hurt Gracie."

"I regret ever bringing you here."

"All right!" Adriel blocked her view of Dane and cupped her face, looking directly into her eyes. "Take a breath."

"I don't need to breathe!"

"Juniper."

"What?"

"Look at me."

Her chin trembled as her eyes flooded with unshed tears. She breathed in and slowly exhaled.

"Good. Now tell me—*calmly*—why you would consider going back there to do this." She held up a finger before Dane could interrupt. "And we'll hear you out."

"As long as Jonas is sick, they'll hold me accountable."

"The only reason they would come after you now," Dane snapped, "is if you provoke them. Do not hurt Jonas."

"It could be painless."

"Not for you."

"Enough!" Adriel snapped. "I will not tolerate this bickering. You've been arguing since we got back. I don't understand this animosity between you. There is no need for the two of you to go to war when real danger is afoot."

"Give me your word that you won't hurt Jonas," Dane demanded.

Juniper held his stare, her grief palpable.

"That's it for now." Adriel pulled her into a protective hug. The poor girl shook like a leaf. "Dane, clean up those papers. I need to speak to Juniper alone."

He scoffed. "Clean them up yourself."

The back door slammed as he stormed out of the kitchen. That was fine. They needed a minute of privacy.

Adriel poured two cups of tea and straightened up the papers as it steeped. Once she had the room tidied, she waved her to the table so they could both sit.

"You know, Juniper, Dane's been through a lot, too."

A tear rolled down her cheek. "They accepted him. They gave him a home and freedom. That's nothing like how they treated me."

"Is that it then?"

"No." She blew out a breath. "I'm not trying to diminish his suffering, but how could he not understand what happened to me? If not for Jonas, my aunts would still be alive and I wouldn't be here."

Adriel squeezed her hand. "But this is where we are. And no amount of revenge can undo what's been done. Tragedy does not excuse us to treat others cruelly. The moment you give in to your anger, a bottomless sorrow opens inside you. Some days, that sorrow is enough to swallow you whole. We cannot lose ourselves in such a way. If we do, they win."

An aura formed around the kitchen table. Adriel looked at Juniper in confusion.

"For protection," Juniper explained. "You're thinking about him."

"Thank you. That's wise."

She sighed. "I wish I could get over this anger. It eats away at me. I just want to get it out and get my life back."

"Justice is a natural desire. But the moment we forgo decency, we become no better than the monsters. Ending a life does not necessarily end the pain."

"But there has to be some level of satisfaction, some sense of restored order."

"Retaliation can go on forever when you're dealing with immortals."

"Nothing is completely immortal."

Adriel sighed. "I suppose that's true enough."

"All I want is peace."

Adriel offered a sad grin. "Violence does not achieve that."

"Then why are we planning to kill your ex?"

"Cerberus cannot be killed. He's different. I know this, which is why…" Juniper deserved her honesty. "Sometimes when fated mates pass, their counterparts also die."

"Are you saying if we kill Cerberus, we might unintentionally kill you?"

"I'm saying it would not be unintentional. Cerberus is unlike any immortal I've ever come across. I will not give him the chance to hurt me again, or anyone else for that matter."

Juniper tugged her hand free. "What the fuck are you talking about, Adriel? Killing yourself?"

"I would rather die than suffer his revenge. I'm not a violent person. I've never killed a living thing. This is the only way I know to evade him."

"By taking your own life? That's not a fucking solution." She sprung to her feet and paced the kitchen. "What is with you underestimating your power?"

"You don't know him, Juniper. He's incredibly strong and beyond cruel. He's not coming to reconcile. He's coming to punish me. Ending my life removes that option. It also bears the possibility of him dying with me. Mates are said to suffer shared mortality. There's a physical link as much as there is a mental and emotional one."

"Yet he beat you."

"Like I said, Cerberus has an incredible tolerance for pain."

"Men do not beat those they love."

A sad smile curved her lips. "Even as a girl of only four and ten, I was never fanciful enough to believe he loved me. I was a possession to him. An object to use and abuse." Her finger traced a knot in the surface of the table. "They say a mortal marriage cannot compare to the bond mates share. But I disagree. Love—actual unconditional, selfless love—is the strongest bond of all. Neither marriage or mating guarantees such a thing."

Sympathy bloomed in her chest. Like Dane, she understood what it was to want something she would never have. Adriel had given up any hope of love a long time ago.

She reached for Juniper's hand. "We must be patient with Dane. He loves someone who refuses to love him back. And despite her rejection, he will continue to protect her, even when it costs him. Do not make him choose. We must learn to work through our trauma, search deep inside ourselves, and find forgiveness."

"Why does she refuse to love him?"

"Because Dane is a hybrid, and hybrids cannot be called. Grace is saving herself for her true mate."

"How long will she wait?"

Adriel shrugged. "It could be tomorrow, or it could be centuries from now."

"So, Dane might not even be alive when it happens?"

"We don't know how long hybrids live. Proper nutrition plays a role, but so does lifestyle. He's trying very hard to accept that Grace will never be his, but I fear he's on a destructive course. We need to be very gentle with him right now. He's lost everyone. The best way we can support him is to love him. We must show him he's still deserving of that."

"Fine." She sat back in her seat. "I'll make a deal with you, Adriel. I'll give up my vendetta with Jonas if you give up this idea about taking your own life."

The breath in her lungs chilled. "That's not fair."

"Why not? You're the only person I have left. Like Dane, I've lost everyone. I can't lose you too."

"This is my choice—"

"Make another one."

"There is no other. I've thought of every other option. I cannot go back to the way things were. I won't."

"Then we figure out a way to end him before it comes to you taking your own life. It has to happen. Cerberus has to die."

CHAPTER 17

$\mathcal{I}$t made no sense that Juniper was this messed up over a woman she barely knew. But there was something worth saving in Adriel. Despite her five hundred-year existence, she barely lived.

Juniper needed to hone her magic. She needed to access all the hidden power inside of her. That was the only way they were going to beat Cerberus. It was the only way to save her friend.

However, that would mean actually acknowledging her vampire roots and…

Juniper swallowed, her insides souring at the thought. There was only one foolproof way to access that side of her genetics, but she wasn't sure if she could stomach it—literally.

Ugh, the thought of drinking blood…

She couldn't. She just couldn't.

On top of feeling nauseous, her insides were

twisted up in knots. She didn't want to face that part of herself, but she also didn't want to lose Adriel.

But what if this Cerberus guy was really as scary as Adriel made him sound? She was his mate, and Dane was his son, but that didn't even matter. It took a special kind of sick fuck to be that cruel to family.

If they decided to go after him, they were all at risk. Juniper couldn't bear any more remorse.

That meant they had to beat him. They needed a strong plan. Plus magick. They would need lots of fucking magick.

She chucked a rotten tomato into the bushes for the rabbits to eat.

"Hey." Dane stood at the gate.

"H-hey."

"Is it safe to enter, or are you going to pummel me with tomatoes?"

She glanced at the insane vegetation crowding the steps. "There are enough for me to do real damage."

He dropped his gaze and softly laughed. Unlatching the gate, he approached the back steps. "I, uh…I'm sorry I flipped out. I don't even know what I said—"

"It's cool."

"No, it's not. I know more than anyone what it's like to want revenge. My mom…"

"I know. Adriel told me." She pushed the basket aside and brushed away the dead leaves and dirt so she could sit on the step. "She also explained the, um, Gracie thing."

He frowned. "What did she say?"

Juniper shrugged. "That you care about her."

Hands buried in his pockets, he shuffled closer and sat beside her on the step. "Yeah."

"I'm sorry that didn't work out."

"Which part?"

"All of it. Your mom, your sister, not being able to help you with Isaiah."

"You tried."

She had tried, but she knew very little about magick, and she'd been weak and depleted. She wished she could have done more. Maybe then his sister wouldn't be gone, too.

"I'm free because of you, Dane. It's not my goal to upset you."

"I know." He plucked a ripe tomato off the vine and sniffed it. "I get the Jonas thing."

"I'm not gonna do anything. Truthfully, I wouldn't even know where to start. And I'm never going back there."

He nodded. "I know it doesn't lessen your grief, but if it's any consolation, Grace wasn't okay after what she did to your aunt. She's not a violent person, and she deeply regrets her actions."

"If only that brought my aunt back."

"At the time, she was only acting on instinct. Gracie didn't know what her father had done to you. If she could take back her actions, she would."

"She told you that?"

"She, uh…didn't have to."

Juniper frowned. "What do you mean?"

He pointed to his head. "I can sometimes glean impressions from others. I'm really not that good at it compared to the immortals, but Gracie has always been an easy read for me, which further proves her goodness."

"You can read minds?"

"Mostly just children. The more innocent a person's mind, the easier it is for me to sense what they're thinking. Gracie has a lot of regret about that day."

"If you feel all that for her, why were you with that Magdalen chick?"

"Maggie's like me—like us. She's a half-breed. She taught me how to feed, and we kept each other company. It passed the time."

She shivered, recalling how time never seemed to move in that place. "You were lonely."

"Yes." He set the tomato aside. "What I feel for Grace is different."

It was clear he loved her very much. "How do they know half-breeds can't get called?"

He shrugged. "The elders said so."

"And they know everything?"

He shrugged again.

She hated the elders. "I don't think they're as all-knowing as everyone makes them out to be. If they were, they wouldn't have been so afraid of little old me." That was why they kept her muzzled and tied, why they did not let her look at them. "Or maybe they know more about me than I know about myself."

"Aren't you curious? Feeding can be incredible. It's like a switch going off in your brain. Every cell in your body comes alive, and you feel —limitless."

"No one's limitless." Juniper would eventually experience what he described, but she didn't want to think about it now. "What if Gracie gets called to someone she hates?"

"It doesn't work that way. I've seen it with Adam and Annalise, and Larissa and the Bishop. The bond between mates is unbreakable."

"Bullshit. If that were true, Adriel wouldn't be running from Cerberus."

"You shouldn't speak his name."

"I have the whole property spelled." She studied him for a moment. "Do you feel anything toward him, as your father?"

"Fuck no. I care about Adriel. He's nothing to me."

He was one more person Dane would lose. Not a terrible loss, but a loss all the same.

"I don't know my dad either," she confessed.

"Do you wish you did?"

She shrugged. "Not really. I only recently discovered he existed. My aunts didn't know much about the calling stuff, but I assume that's why my mother abandoned me."

"Wait, she was called?"

"Why else would she leave her newborn child?"

"But she was a witch. Only full-bred immortals can be called."

Juniper's insides turned to ice, and she stilled. "Well, that's just fucking great. I guess it really was just about Niro the Wonder Schlong."

Dane nudged her shoulder with his. "It's their loss."

"Thanks." The whole destined mates thing came with too many rules. Just when she thought she had it figured out, she learned something new. "I'm glad my future isn't tied to someone I've never met."

"Me too."

"What will you do if Gracie never gets called?"

"I hope that doesn't happen."

"But you love her. Are you saying you *want* her to be with someone else?"

"I want her to be happy."

Dane, once again, proved he was a good guy. She couldn't knowingly betray or hurt him because she respected him. "I promise I won't do anything that hurts her—emotionally or otherwise."

"Thank you." He sighed with relief and then glanced down at the basket of tomatoes by her feet. "Are you making something with them?"

They might as well eat some of the harvest before it rotted. "Pasta?"

"Can I help?"

"Sure, but you should know my cooking skills tap out at Ramen."

"Maybe you don't need cooking skills. When I was looking at your books, I read something about water magick. This could be a great opportunity to practice your craft. Think you could cook dinner without the gas?"

She smiled, encouraged by the challenge. "I can try."

Adriel was in the kitchen when they entered the house. She didn't appear surprised to see them together.

"We apologized."

"I heard."

Damn vampires and their supersensory hearing.

Needing a change of subject, Juniper hefted the basket of tomatoes onto the table. "Do you like spaghetti?"

Adriel's smile triggered something protective in Juniper. She needed to heighten her magick skills because she couldn't accept Adriel's plan of surrender. "Who doesn't? I'll get the flour."

"Oh, okay. We're doing this old school."

Adriel glanced over her shoulder, already rummaging through the cabinets. "That's the only school I know."

The next hour resembled a Disney montage with dark notes of Grimm and a shortage of fairy dust. Those little pixies in *Sleeping Beauty* made it look so easy. The reality was an underwhelming mess.

After Adriel mixed the flour and egg on the table, Dane rolled out the dough. Juniper washed the tomatoes and chopped them into chunks.

Once they were on the stove, she grabbed her notes.

It couldn't be that hard. She'd made fire before. Just never on a gas stove. Time to concentrate and not blow up the house.

"Maybe we should put Ruth outside."

Dane dug through the drawer for a knife. "Ruth's fine. You're not using the gas. You're using your mind. Just try."

Juniper stared at the burner where the pot for the tomatoes and a pot of water sat. Without gas or wood, she would have to hold the flame herself, all while maintaining the constant weight of the protection spell she'd been carrying since they left the woods.

"Maybe we should just use the stove."

"You've got this." Dane nudged her toward to range. "Just focus and say the right words."

She grimaced, her attention on the base of the empty pot. She held up her palms, embarrassed when they shook. The added pressure of having an audience made the chance of screwing this up all the more embarrassing.

With a trembling breath, she whispered, *"Insignia."*

Nothing happened. Not even a spark. She doubled her focus and tried again.

"Insignia. Damn it. It's not working. *Insignia!"* Frustrated, she dropped her hands and rose to her full height. "I don't know what I'm doing wrong."

Adriel and Dane came to the stove to look at

the boring sight. "Maybe you're missing something." Dane inspected the surface and pots. "On the farm, you had all the elements, remember?"

He was right. The tomatoes were of the earth, and there was water in the pasta pot, but they were still missing a few crucial ingredients. How had she overlooked something so simple? This was Magick 101. "I need an offering for air and fire."

"You're making the fire."

"Oh, right." She was not good at this. "Then a feather. Something to represent air. There has to be an offering."

"Wouldn't the air we're breathing be enough?" Adriel asked.

"I'm not sure."

They went outside to look for a feather. Dane searched the hedges while she and Adriel searched the driveway. "Can't you manifest something?"

"I can try." Juniper closed her eyes and stepped out of her shoes, pressing her bare feet into the grass. Once she felt grounded, she envisioned the universe providing what she needed.

"Will this work?" Adriel held up a long feather.

"Holy crap," Dane said, his shock mimicking Juniper's. "Did you do that?"

"I don't know."

"I'll braid it into your hair, so this element is always with you."

Juniper smiled and nodded, feeling not only

supported by the elements but also by her friends.

Adriel sectioned off a thin strand of hair and got to work. A shiver skipped down her spine when Adriel's breath teased her cheek. Juniper froze, remembering when an immortal had been that close and ripped into her.

"Did I hurt you?"

"N-no." Adriel would never hurt her. She truly believed that now.

When she tied the braid off, the feather secured and hanging over Juniper's shoulder, she stepped back and admired her work. "There. Now, you'll always have it with you." The braid and feather slid through her tapered fingers, and she smiled. "Pretty."

Juniper ducked her gaze and mumbled a thank you, unsure why her face was suddenly hot. "Let's try this again."

They crowded her as she faced the stove.

"I need a little space."

She took a deep breath and channeled *Aether,* the primordial god of light. "*Insignia.*"

Adriel gasped, and Dane laughed when a little flame came to life, but it quickly disappeared.

"Shit."

"It's okay. It's okay. Try again."

Juniper breathed deep and squared her shoulders, focusing hard on the base of the pot. "*Insignia!*"

They cheered as a small flame blazed but then

quickly flickered out as if frightened by their excitement.

"I don't know what I'm doing wrong." It was as if her magick wasn't holding. "When my aunts did big spells, they would sometimes put their magick in other objects or borrow energy from other witches."

"Where are we getting another witch?"

She looked over her shoulder at Dane. "We're not." She needed something she could charge, something that could sustain its shape while the fire burned. "I've got it!"

She rushed out the back door without explanation. Dropping to her knees, Juniper used a stick to dig a hole near the fence where no one walked. Navigating the earthworms and roots, she dug until the loose soot transformed into a damp clay.

She pried a collection of geodes from the earth and then banged them on the walkway.

"Juniper, what are you doing?"

"I need to break these open to see what's inside."

Adriel closed the distance. "You're going to smash your fingers. Let me help." She took a stone in both hands and tightened her grip. It snapped open as if she were cracking an egg.

"Holy crap."

Unfortunately, the insides were not what she needed. "Can you break open the rest of them?"

Adriel cracked open several more stones, but none of them had anything more than layers of useless matter inside. She needed something powerful.

"We have to find a crystal."

They dug until the sun faded behind the trees. It seemed like a useless effort until Adriel gasped. "How about this one?"

Minerals sparkled from inside the broken rock Adriel held, and Juniper scrambled to her feet. "That's perfect!"

Taking the crystal inside, she washed it off to reveal a mixture of calcite and grey amethyst in the crevices. She set the crystal in the divot of the burner.

"Let's hope this works because I'm out of ideas after this." Calcite was great for amplifying energy, and amethyst was known to open the chakra around the third eye. Taking a deep breath, she held up her hands and called upon Spirit. *"Insignia."*

A flame caught, flickering from the gemstone, and Juniper laughed. "Nobody move!" Dane and Adriel held back as Juniper blew a soft breath on the flame, and it doubled in size. "I did it!"

"I'll start crushing the tomatoes."

Juniper continued to focus on the stove. The books explained how water was made up of memory. It was transient in form, converting from ice to vapor and able to undergo extreme heat as it traveled through the earth and air. If she tapped into the water's memory, she should be able to heat it to a boil. It was basic alchemy and something she'd watched her Aunt Venus do many times before.

Placing her hands on the side of the cool pot, she shut her eyes and poured her energy into the water. "*Memóriám liquoris calefactus sum. Memóriám liquoris calefactus sum. Memóriám liquoris calefactus sum.*"

The motion around her stilled, and the kitchen silenced. Dane and Adriel were on the other side of the table.

"What is it?"

"Nothing." Juniper frowned. "I…felt something." She refocused on the pot and continued chanting. "*Memóriám liquoris calefactus sum—*There it is again!"

"What are you talking about?" Dane frowned.

"I feel something—or someone—touching me."

"Where?"

"On my hand. It's not a bad feeling. It's like… an energy. Like they're trying to help me."

"We've already got an immortal, a hybrid, and a witch," Dane said with a shrug. "Sure, why not bring ghosts into it?"

Was it a ghost? If it was, the spirit wasn't trying to hurt her. On the contrary, she felt it wanted to help her.

"It's offering me its energy." Juniper drew in a deep breath and exhaled, refocusing on the pot of water as she chanted once more. "*Memóriám liquoris calefactus sum.*"

Adriel and Dane chimed in, and they found a

rhythm. Harmonizing, as if singing, they chanted and started to dance, much like the indigenous people did when they called upon the rain.

Ruth was drawn into the kitchen by noise and energy. "Sing with us, Ruth," Adriel invited, and the older woman joined in.

Juniper laughed as the water's energy vibrated with the gentle bubbles that preceded a boil. "Keep going!"

They chanted louder and louder until she yanked her hands back, the metal now too hot to touch.

Could she do it without touching the metal? How powerful were these words?

The air buzzed around her, and the tiny hairs on the back of her neck stood up. A surge of power flowed through her veins and streamed from her fingertips.

"Do you feel it? It's everywhere!"

Her brain hummed, and her heart raced as vitality powered through her like a live wire, something electric shooting through every nerve of her body, moving through her veins and pumping into her heart faster than cocaine. A dome of power formed over the kitchen, siphoning more energy from outside.

Juniper became a great maestro of the elements, conducting an orchestra of energy that built to such a ringing crescendo she could no longer hear the others chanting—only the intense buzzing around her as the water trembled and the pot rattled on the stove.

The steady buzz rang in her ears as her pulse vibrated. Faster and harder, energy pumped through her veins. It pulled from the earth and traveled from the soles of her feet, where it pulsed into every muscle of her body. They generated so much power she seemed weightless as if she could float through gravity and time.

Steam billowed from the surface of the water as tiny bubbles raced to the top.

"June?"

The pull was magnetic and delightful. She couldn't look away.

"Uh, Juniper?"

The glass trembled in the window frames and the doors jerked at the hinges. Invisible hands— dozens—pressed into her, lending enough power to lift her hair off her shoulders. The water started to hiss.

"*Juniper!*" Dane and Adriel screamed as more lights flickered, and then something popped.

Glass shattered.

Dane tried to grab her, but the invisible hands pushed him away, lifting her higher. He shouted, his words pulled into a howling vortex of energy that she could no longer hear. Her heart sped up as sweat beaded on her skin. The buzzing changed to a screech, and suddenly, the pot of water ruptured like a geyser.

"Look out!"

A burst of white-hot light exploded with a sharp whistle, and all went black.

CHAPTER 18

*H*is limbs were nothing more than flesh and bone, too weak to do more than wiggle his fingers and toes, loosening and shifting the dirt one granule at a time. The tickle to his bare skin never stopped, nor did the tingle of new nerves forming in his regenerated cells.

Weak and emaciated, far below the earth's surface, he doubted he'd ever see the light of day again. Tiny, silken grains of soil shifted, but the weight of bone-crushing pressure remained.

He roared in frustration, the taste of soil on his tongue and the grit of gravel in his teeth.

Mortals. He could sense their minds nearby—the ambulatory temptation of food taunted him from above. This surely was hell.

He was forever trapped by the weight of the earth, sentenced to this endless eternity of miserable life quickened by death, only to return to his wretched existence once more. He was never getting free.

Then, one day, an earthquake struck.

A crash, like a cannon blast, cracked open the earth's mantle, and sweet, intoxicating air drenched his lungs. A wild stampede trampled far above. Cerberus rocked back and forth, punching his way through the earth, motivated by the scent of uproarious life nearby.

Voices! He could hear voices!

Desperate to escape the confined darkness and repetitive death, he released an all-encompassing roar and shoved his energy upward. The earth moaned and buckled overhead. Rock spilled downward, scraping and pummeling him, but he held his concentration.

Embedded in the earth for decades as he was, left him with a sense of connection to the planet. He was one with the soil. The roots that wove beneath the earth's surface had supported him for years, and he felt a part of the ground and trees.

Concentrating, he slammed his back into the ground and the sinkhole widened. More precious oxygen seeped into his lungs.

He gasped and coughed. Dirt and debris spewed past his lips, tasting of years of decay and bad blood. His chest spasmed as he clawed his way upward, using roots and stone to find purchase. An unnamable sound roared, and pain spiked inside of him with fear, but he refused to die.

He was too close. Too exposed. "H-h-hlph..." He tried to call, but his voice was ravaged from disuse.

The earth rumbled again and the screeching transcended to screams. There was too much dirt in his eyes to see. But he smelled it. The sweet musk of human blood.

Blaring, shrieking screams blurred into an ungodly roar as he followed that faint trickle of blood that perfumed the air. Through the grit clouding his lashes, sunlight pierced his vision. Crawling and clawing, he pulled himself upward and reached out with a weak hand. The world erupted in chaos as earthquakes shook the ground, but he had survived far worse.

A man yelled, but his words were muffled under the deafening beat of his pulse. Cerberus waved him closer, coughing and hacking up centuries of dirt.

"Senhor?"As soon as the man bent closer, Cerberus struck with the speed of a python, his words cutting off with a gurgle as life-giving blood bathed his insides, and his withered cells rapidly began to heal. Muscle thickened as tissue rejuvenated. Once drained, he threw the body aside. More. He needed more.

GASPING, Cerberus bolted upright.

He wasn't in *Portvgalliae*, on that fated day he finally escaped the ground. Instead, he was in America, but the stink of decay seemed to have followed him.

He searched the hotel room, his body strong and whole, his mind sharp. The corpse of the stripper had stunk up the room, but that wasn't what woke him.

He found her.

Seething, he grinned and latched onto the familiar trace of his mate's mind, sinking into her memories, spreading over her conscious thought like an oil stain that would not wash away. As her vision became his, his claws lengthened. Dark anticipation bubbled anxiously inside of him.

She was in a house. A man stood beside her as she stared at a sleeping woman. Cerberus only needed a marker, something to tell him where she was.

Panic welled inside of him, but it was not his own. Whoever the woman on the floor was, Adriel cared for her. As she scooped her into her arms and carried her through a house, he recorded every detail.

Hardwood floors and quality carpentry hinted that the home was older. A set of stairs promised it had more than two floors. She laid the girl on a bed dressed in green linens and anxiously paced to the window. Mountains and trees showed in the blurry distance.

"Where are you, girl?" he whispered, searching her view for clues.

Locked into the vision, he stayed silently with her, a passenger and undetected traveler.

The traitorous bitch pressed a damp cloth to the sleeping woman's forehead. Was she injured? The act of kindness angered him.

She'd sent him to a dark purgatory where he lost his sanity and life too many times to count, yet she dared to show kindness to others?

"Disloyal cunt."

He waited, focused on her vision as she

tended to the young woman. He only needed one detail, one single lead that told him where she—

His spine stiffened.

There, on the table beside the bed, sat a bag with writing printed on the front. BRITTEN BOOKS. Just below the large font were the words *Ithaca, New York.*

A reptilian smile curled about his lips as long fingers seemed to tickle his insides. "It won't be long now, girl." Laughter crawled out of him like hissing snakes. "And when I find you, I'll enjoy forcing you to watch as I eat the heart of your little friend."

$\mathcal{A}$driel placed a flat hand on her stomach as nerves twisted at her insides. Her heart hadn't stopped racing since Juniper collapsed. She couldn't stop replaying the incident in her mind, and the longer she remained unconscious, the more she feared her friend had pushed herself too far.

"June, please wake up." She dabbed the damp cloth over her pale face.

As an immortal, she rarely saw others taken down by illness. She knew nothing of medicine and felt inept at curing whatever ailed her.

Everything inside of her insisted she fix her friend, so it made no sense why she was suddenly standing at the window, daydreaming and taking in the view. She looked back at Juniper, taking a step then pausing. Once again lured to the view.

She had the strangest urge to walk outside and stare at the house.

"Adriel, what are you doing?"

Startled by Dane's return, she frowned. "I…I don't know." Her gaze dropped to the bottle of pills in his hand. "Did you find something?"

"Not really. All Ruth had were some baby aspirins and some medicine for her glaucoma and blood pressure."

"Is this normal?"

He laughed without humor. "None of this is normal, but I think it's clear, neither is Juniper. I think we need to just give her time. Her pulse is steady, and her breathing's even. She probably just over-exerted herself."

"We shouldn't have encouraged her."

He caught her arm. "Hey, she's strong. And she volunteered for this. We both did."

They both studied Juniper's still body for a long moment. "You too are risking too much."

Dane waved away her words. "You know what would probably help her?"

Adriel met his stare. "Not without her consent."

He shrugged. "I'm just saying…blood heals."

"I understand. But I still think we should wait a little longer. She will wake up on her own, and then she can choose."

"I'll go check on Ruth. Call me if you need anything."

Adriel paced between the bed and the window, equally drawn to both. She stared into the distance where the Finger Lakes divided the land, taking note of exactly which side of the water the house sat.

She frowned and glanced back to Juniper. What was she doing?

Returning to Juniper's side, she traced a cool finger down her face. A small divot formed between her brows, and she moaned, her lashes softly fluttering as she met Adriel's concerned stare.

She smiled, frowned, then asked groggily, "Did you eat the spaghetti without me?"

Relief flooded Adriel, and she let out a sigh of relief. "You're awake."

"What happened?"

"You fainted."

Juniper groaned and shut her eyes. "I suck at this."

"No, you don't. You channeled so much power, it just…was too much at once for you."

She frowned. "Where's Dane?"

"He's with Ruth."

She glanced at the nightstand. "How did I get up here?"

"I carried you. You've been out for some time."

"Oh."

"I can sense your weakness, Juniper, and I think it's time we had that talk we've been avoiding."

"I know what you're going to say."

"The spells are draining you."

She grimaced. "I know. You're right. I've been

thinking about it too. Blood might be the only way I'll be able to keep going at this pace. But does it have to be Danny's blood?"

Adriel stilled. The repugnant thought of Juniper's first feeding coming from that greasy male mortal's vein was unacceptable. It should be with someone she trusted. She supposed Dane could do it, but that also wasn't ideal. His blood was relatively mild compared to… "I will do it. My blood is strongest."

Juniper dropped her gaze, and uncertainty nipped at Adriel.

"If you would prefer a male—"

"No, it's not that. I'd rather it be you. I'm just, nervous, I guess. What if my body rejects it?"

"It won't. Even basic mortals can digest our blood with little issue."

"But what if I don't like it?"

"You have immortality in your veins, June. Chances are you'll like it."

She blushed. "What if I like it too much?"

Now, it was Adriel's turn to blush. "Juniper, there's no shame in meeting your natural needs. Your body has likely been starving for proper sustenance. If you enjoy it, that's probably why."

"My aunts warned me this day would come. It just feels…awkward."

"It's just us here. There's no reason to feel self-conscious. I'll help you." Adriel rolled up her sleeve and gave Juniper a nervous smile. Now, she was the one suddenly self-conscious. "Are you ready?"

Their gazes met, and an intense understanding passed between them. This would be Juniper's first time, a moment she might never forget. Adriel wanted to make sure nothing went wrong.

"I'll…open the vein for you, then all you need to do is drink. The rest will come naturally."

Juniper swallowed and gave a tight nod, shifting to sit up on the bed. "I'm ready."

Adriel's fangs elongated, but she hesitated. "Before we start, can you check the protection spell? Feeding tends to leave us a bit vulnerable."

"Oh." She frowned. "Sorry. It must have shifted when I lost consciousness. I fixed it."

"Thank you. Now, let's replenish your strength." She bit into her wrist, and a slow trickle seeped from the twin punctures. "Go ahead."

The bed shifted as Juniper leaned forward, her stare bouncing from Adriel's wrist to her face. The soft scent of vulnerability tinged the air as the braid adorned with the feather draped past Juniper's shoulder. When the downy tip grazed Adriel's skin, her breath caught.

At first, she assumed the scent of vulnerability came from Juniper, but she realized it was her own uncertainty she sensed. Light and sweet, she couldn't recall the last time anyone drew such a scent from her.

"I'm a bit nervous," she admitted, surprised by the response she was having to her nearness.

Juniper looked up at her, her eyes unsure. "Why? If you don't want to do this, Ade—"

"I want to." Perhaps she wanted to do this more than she'd admitted. "Go ahead."

Something unspoken passed between them. Adriel's gaze dropped to the racing pulse below her jaw. The sweet air darkened with a heady scent she didn't recognize as her insides warmed like hot honey.

The delicate, feminine scent of Juniper's hair perfumed the air between them as she leaned closer. Adriel's breath turned shallow and caught at the first touch of her mouth to her skin. She swallowed, unsure why her emotions were riding on a razor's edge of sensation.

The first sweep of her tongue might as well have been across her lips. The sensation of her mouth closing over her wrist was so sharp and erotic, Adriel started to panic. She nearly pulled away, but Juniper's grip tightened.

"Mmm," she softly moaned after stealing a tiny sip and licking her lips. "It's not at all what I expected." She pressed her fingers to her lips and smiled. "You taste so sweet but earthy, like cinnamon sugar and cloves."

Adriel tried to maintain a clinical tone but her voice quivered. "Y-you'll need more than one single lick."

Her gaze got lost in the dusting of freckles across Juniper's nose. Her full lips darkened around the edges, and the thick line of her lashes accentuated her deep-set eyes in a way that entranced Adriel. She had never noticed how gorgeous Juniper was, but now it seemed all she could see.

"Maybe if we…" Juniper glanced at the pillows. "Is it weird if we lay down?"

"Not at all." She cleared her throat, once again second-guessing herself. We can do it however you're most comfortable."

Juniper scooted to the center of the bed and turned to face the far wall, giving Adriel room at the edge to lay her body behind hers. "Like this?" She looked back with such trust in her eyes that it stole Adriel's breath away.

Throat suddenly tight, she nodded.

They rested on their sides, staring straight ahead, swallowed by the heavy silence. Adriel scooted closer, aligning her body with Juniper's. She slowly draped her arm over her and swallowed.

Juniper took her wrist and pulled it closer to her mouth. Her breath fanned across Adriel's skin, and chills chased across her chest. The bed creaked as she adjusted her position so they lay even closer. Juniper's heartbeat fluttered erratically. "Is this okay?"

Adriel stared over her shoulder, afraid to look anywhere else. "I offer my blood freely to you, Juniper. Please take all that you need."

Her delicate mouth closed over Adriel's vein, and she sucked in a sharp breath, this time somehow more excruciatingly poignant than the last.

"Did I hurt you?"

"No. It just felt…different than other times."

"Oh. Sorry." She nestled closer, a soft flush tinging her cheeks. "I'll try to be quick."

"No rush." Adriel breathed in the soft scent of her hair. With her belly pressed so close to her back, she worried she might feel how it fluttered and swooped with each gentle sip. Something warm twisted inside of her. She leaned closer and whispered, "You smell like the rain."

A soft moan answered as her lips pressed tighter to her flesh. Every pull of her warm mouth made a delicate kissing sound, awakening something inside Adriel.

What was happening?

She closed her eyes and breathed deeply, her free hand gently sifting through her hair. "You're doing very good."

She loved the scent of rain when it first hit the earth. Juniper had the same fresh scent, perhaps because she was soft and delicate, one with the elements.

She'd been so frightened when she collapsed in the kitchen. The thought of anything happening to her was too terrifying to entertain. Adriel shyly lay a hand over her and a wave of satisfaction washed through her.

"We need you at your strongest." Her fingers loosely twirled a strand of her hair. "You take as much as you need."

Adriel looked up at the headboard, but there was no making sense of the feelings rushing through her. She had no basis for comparison. Her body was hot and needy. She didn't trust herself to move.

Juniper released her wrist all too soon. She twisted, turning her body so they faced each other. Adriel searched her eyes, unsure why she was looking at her in such a way. It was like being caught in a secret where only the two of them existed.

Juniper smiled and slid a hand into her hair. "Is this too close?"

Her heart stilled, unsure of her intentions. Their breath mingled as Adriel shook her head. It was purely indecent, but she couldn't pull herself away. She needed to know what would happen next.

Her fingers laced together with hers. "I've never done this before," she whispered.

It seemed clear she wasn't speaking of feeding anymore. Perhaps this was a good time to point out their age difference and the fact that they were both female. But Adriel remained quiet, her heart now thumping wildly against her ribs.

"My heart is beating so fast," she whispered, unsure what else to say.

Juniper cocked her head and laughed. "I can hear it. Is that from the blood?"

"Feeding does have a way of heightening the senses." Her throat was parched but she was too nervous to swallow.

She hooked her ankle around Adriel's leg and

pulled her closer. "I get it now, what you were saying about feeding being intimate."

One of them needed to be sensible. "Juniper…"

She traced her eyebrow as she held her stare. "Is this too much?" She tightened her leg and trailed her finger down Adriel's cheek. "I can stop if you want me to."

Adriel did not want her to stop. The air tinged with a sultry spice the more she touched her. No one had ever caressed her so gently. When her finger traced over her lashes, she closed her eyes. Something similar to fear bounced inside of her.

"Juniper, what are we doing?"

She laughed, the sound soft and warm, not at all mocking. "I don't know, but I like it."

Adriel opened her eyes. Their mouths were a mere inch apart. Everything stilled when Juniper slowly leaned closer. Her lips brushed Adriel's, and she drew back, her fingers rushing to her mouth.

"Was that not okay?"

How could she explain that after all these years, she'd never been kissed before. Perhaps her mother and father had shown her affection when she was young, but she had no memory of such things. Cerberus certainly hadn't treated her with kisses.

Embarrassment swamped her. "I'm afraid I… don't have experience with this."

"Me neither. I've only ever kissed guys."

She looked down, ashamed. "I've never kissed anyone, save my son when he was young."

Juniper caught her chin. "Hey, don't hide." She smiled. "I wouldn't have kissed anyone on that farm either."

She laughed. "That isn't exactly why."

"Then why? You're beautiful. I'm sure plenty of people fantasized about kissing you."

"I don't think so."

"Hey." She nodded. "I see you, Adriel. You are, without a doubt, one of the most gorgeous women I've ever met."

She licked her lips, unsure where to turn her eyes. "You're making me blush."

"Good. You look pretty with a little color on your cheeks." She caressed her cheekbone with the backs of her fingers.

"I'm ignorant when it comes to such things."

"You're innocent. There's a difference."

"I'm not. I have experience—"

"With this? Has anyone ever simply touched you for the pleasure of it."

Her vision blurred as that painful realization twisted like a knife in her heart. "No. I've never known that kind of pleasure."

"Shut your eyes," she whispered, and Adriel did.

Her breath hitched when Juniper's fingers softly trailed over her cheek and down to her throat. Tears built in her eyes at such loving affection. Juniper slowly traced every feature and curve. When her fingertip trailed over her mouth, Adriel's lips parted.

"Can I kiss you again?"

Adriel barely nodded, afraid the slightest movement might spoil the moment.

Warm breath fanned across her lips, and then there was soft pressure. Her lips were full and slightly damp, but she liked the way it felt. Juniper leisurely opened and closed her mouth, showing Adriel what to do. She mimicked the motion, and a delicate, encouraging moan whispered from Juniper's mouth into hers.

The elusive tip of her tongue teased passed her lips. Playful and intentional. Juniper's mouth curved into a smile, laughing softly, the sound as gentle as delicate windchimes in the distance. Nibbling at her lower lip and coaxing her way inside.

Toes pointed, and calves flexed as their bodies entwined. Sensation rolled through her, warm and buttery, as her hands climbed over her hips and squeezed with promise.

An unsure whimper escaped Adriel's throat as her hand trailed along the hem of her clothing.

"You have the softest lips," Juniper whispered, drawing back to look into her eyes. She returned to place several small kisses on her mouth and jaw, her nose teasing close to her ears and her words sending chills down her arms. "How was that?"

A hundred words rushed through her head. Soft. Pretty. Loving. Gentle. Passionate. Awakening. Scary. Exhilarating. Heart racing, she tried to say just one out loud.

Her overheated body ached in a way she never experienced. She didn't want her to stop, but she also thought they should. Nothing should feel this nice. Nothing ever had.

"Did you not like it?" she asked, a tinge of insecurity intruding.

"No, I did. Very much," Adriel quickly assured.

Juniper smiled and searched her face. "Was it…okay?"

It went far beyond okay. "It was…" She thought of the right word. Delicious. Decadent. Thrilling. Lovely. But when she tried to choose one she panicked and said, "Wet." Her face burned, and laughter bubbled between them.

"There's a word for it." Juniper nuzzled her nose alongside hers, dragging her body in ways that made Adriel aware of the places she never gave much thought. Warm breath teased the shell of her ear as teeth tenderly pulled at the lobe of her ear. Quietly, she whispered, "Your kisses make me wet."

Adriel's breath caught. "June?"

"Hmm?" Her hands shifted over her clothes, slowly revealing sensitive patches of flesh as if by accident, but her evident desire sweetened the air like honeysuckle on a breeze.

"Are we allowed to do this?"

Warm fingers teased beneath the hem of her shirt. "Who's going to stop us?"

Excellent question.

Her hand stilled. "Unless… Do you want to stop?"

She wanted relief. "No."

"Good. Me neither."

Pressure built deep in Adriel's core as their legs casually scissored back and forth. Her body was suddenly scorching. Between the sultry kisses and how her limbs entwined perfectly with hers, her skin was ablaze. Every caress left a trail of shivers in its wake despite how her insides burned.

Clothing abraded her sensitized skin. There were too many layers between them. Ravenous need built into a throbbing pulse that pounded through her entire body. She wanted to rip their garments off and pull her closer—flesh to flesh— until Juniper was all she felt.

Her body quivered with such yearning. The torrid thoughts racing through her head explicitly depicted visions of ecstasy she had no experience doing. When she closed her eyes, bright colors flashed in her mind. Shivers and heat. Desire and surrender. Existence became an endless push and pull. She felt parts of her swell like the tide's ebb and flow. She wanted to give in and wash away.

Juniper devoured her with kisses, trailing needy pecks along her jaw then returning to her mouth in a way that took command. Adriel surrendered control, trusting her to know what felt best. Their lips fit together like a jigsaw puzzle cut from a masterpiece.

The fevered pulse inside of her grew, blooming into an untamable ache. She looked at her with smoldering need, her hands pressing lower where the pressure throbbed.

"Do you like this?"

Her heart raced so fast it trembled. She liked it too much and feared appearing too eager. Adriel gasped as Juniper's thumb dragged slowly over her shirt, drawing both their attention to the turgid press of her nipple beneath the fabric.

Her gaze dropped, and she grinned, a soft laugh vibrating from her throat. "I'll take that as a yes."

She shuddered, her grip tightening along her hip as she turned her fingers and gently pinched the tip. It was madness. How could one touch feel so incredible?

Her pulse raced as she clung to sanity. Her insides melted as her skin continued to burn. The ache bloomed and swelled until her entire body quivered with tremors she could not contain.

Juniper's hand slipped behind her neck, hauling her closer. She seized her mouth with an unmistakable desire that consumed her. The slow burn building inside of Adriel ignited into something far more potent as she reveled in the pleasure-pain of wanting things only Juniper seemed capable of delivering.

The way she possessively cupped her breast

did not bother her. It was different in every way. What they were doing was wicked. There could be no other word for it.

Her thumb dragged over the sharp tip of her breast and Adriel arched closer, pressing her body firmly into her caress. Juniper fit her knee between her legs, and the building pressure reveled in the pressure, her body naturally seeking friction.

She clutched her shoulder as shallow breaths collected in her lungs. So overwhelmed with pleasure, she forgot how to breathe.

"You can make noise," June whispered, rubbing and caressing as she embraced her in an ever-moving grip. "Don't feel like you have to hold it in."

Her eyes closed as her lips parted on a shy moan. Soft hands combed down her sides and gently encircled her hips, but they didn't linger long. Her velvety skin brushed hers where their clothing had shifted and something electric bolted through her.

Lush, silken kisses left her dizzy. It was too much and also not enough. She gripped her shirt, moaning into her mouth. The unquenchable thirst for more grew, and grew.

Her body was supple and soft. Her touch fervent and skilled. Primal awareness kicked in and she yanked her closer. She wanted all of her, in every possible way.

Juniper's soft laughter whispered in the slight space between them where only heat and desire could survive. Insatiable greed grew inside of Adriel. The unyielding hunger to kiss, lick, taste, and bite her left her ravenous.

She was a raw nerve. Every touch was excruciating. Too much and never enough. She needed more. Urgent need overwhelmed her as their bodies rocked until the all-consuming need awoke the animal inside of her.

With a growl, she flipped Juniper to her back and pinned her arms at her sides. A flash of uncertainty blazed in her violet eyes.

"Did I hurt you?"

"No."

Adriel slowly lowered her head, delivering a kiss of her own. Her body dragged over Juniper's, pressing deliciously where she needed friction most. Their breasts collided as the urge for more built and built.

Fingers teased through her hair as Juniper held her close. The possessive way she touched her had her fangs elongated. Juniper yipped and Adriel quickly turned her face away, panting.

"I'm sorry."

"You don't have to apologize." She touched her lips, and when she pulled her fingertips away, she revealed a drop of blood.

Mortification stole through her, cold and alarming. "You're bleeding."

"I'm fine."

It wasn't. She shouldn't have done that. Juniper had legitimate fears and did not want to be bit.

"Hey." She cupped her face, forcing her to look down at her and meet her eyes. "I'm okay. We were having fun."

Fun... When was the last time Adriel considered anything fun? It had been too long to remember. "I didn't mean to bite you."

"I didn't mind. It's who you are."

She lowered her lashes, knowing full well Juniper hated what she was despite the immortality in her own blood. Then her heart stilled as Juniper's hand moved closer to her mouth, her thumb gliding lightly over the sharp tip of her fang.

"Will I get them?"

It was the first time she sensed any kind of acceptance from her. "I'd assume, but Dane would know best."

Her finger trailed to her throat. Adriel's pulse raced. She watched her curiosity shift as she slowly explored the throbbing vein in her throat, and then her stare met hers. "I want to feed you."

Fiery heat blazed inside of her. "That's not necessary—"

"I want to. I want to know what it feels like when..." Her gaze dropped to her lips. "...you to take it from me."

What if it wasn't? What if her bite triggered memories from whatever happened to her in that cell. Adriel could never forgive herself if she hurt her. "I don't think it's a good idea."

"You don't want to try?"

"It's not that." She ached with the desire to

taste her. "It might not have the effect you're expecting."

She recalled moments of her own fear and pain as Cerberus bit into her flesh and pulled so hard her veins collapsed. She remembered being too scared to make a sound as tears silently fell from her eyes. How she waited for it to be over, wondering why it was not as she'd expected.

She couldn't chance such feelings between her and Juniper.

Adriel turned her head, exposing her throat. "Take as much as you need."

"But—"

Her claw sliced open her vein. "I like the way your mouth feels, Juniper. There's no risk of you hurting me this way."

She sensed she wanted to argue but, instead, her breath turned labored and she cursed, "Fuck, why is the sight of you like this so hot?" Her mouth rushed to her throat, impatiently licking and sucking.

Adriel gasped, startled by her eagerness. The blunt, straight edge of her teeth scraped over her skin as her fingers forked through her hair. It was clear the licks were intentional, fueled by desire more than hunger.

Adriel moaned at the delicious pull of her kisses and thrilled at the teasing trace of her tongue. Her stomach clenched, and she slowly rocked into her.

Juniper sighed, whispered murmurs passing between them, each one sending a thrill of ecstasy to Adriel's core. Their spines undulating in a slow wave as their bodies rode the potent current of lust and desire. Need built into a searing wave of heat inside of her. She had no idea how to satisfy the burn or let it out, but the longer Juniper drew her blood, the hotter her body became.

She wanted it to go on forever, yet desperately sought the end. "Juniper, something's happening to me."

"It's okay," she rasped, licking and sucking at her neck. Her hand wedged between Adriel's thighs, pressing and rubbing, and the wave of heat burned hotter and bigger until it was more than she could contain.

A gasp of surprise tripped past her lips as Juniper's touch grazed her flesh. The barrier of her clothing was an inconsequential barricade, the fabric now damp with arousal and only adding decadent friction.

Short, shallow breaths panted past her lips. Wet and winded, something came over her. Juniper's mouth sucked harder as she rubbed her fingers against Adriel's core. Color exploded behind Adriel's eyes as she moaned and thrust her hips, grinding her body against hers. Nerves danced and sparked and then…peace.

It rumbled through her like thunder on a soft breeze, turning over parts of her that had never moved before. She gasped with startled joy. Who knew her body could feel that? Nothing had ever felt so good, as if she were falling into heaven.

"I've got you," Juniper whispered, pulling her closer. "Let it go." Her arms wrapped protectively around her, drawing her into a hug.

The pressure eased from her bones and her muscles clenched as kisses pressed to her hair. Only then did she understand. This was how it was supposed to be between lovers. Intimate. Safe. Mutual. Intoxicating. This was unlike anything she'd ever shared, and she was certain this was not what existed between mere friends.

CHAPTER 20

$\mathcal{J}$uniper paced back and forth in the crowded attic. It was late, but she found the evening hours the best time to practice her craft uninterrupted, and away from distractions—namely Adriel.

It had not been planned. At no time did she think, *oh, I should hook up with that fiery red-headed vampire*. Yet…it had been the easiest, most natural hookup of her life. Not to mention the hottest. And they only got as far as kissing and heavy petting.

It had to be the blood. That was the only explanation.

Now, things were awkward. Stolen glances and childish blushes. She couldn't think, and she needed to think because a psychopath was chasing them, and now, more than ever, Juniper felt compelled to protect Adriel.

Realizing she was once again lost in a tangent

of thoughts about her, Juniper growled. "Focus! You need to get this down. What kind of witch can't do simple fucking magick? No more thinking about her—at least not in that way."

A new shipment of auctioned books arrived that morning, and these were, by far, the most valuable collection yet, hand written and brimming with priceless knowledge, but often depicted in strange languages and symbols. She knew she hit the jackpot when several of the old texts were spelled shut. It only took a few tries to get the decaying pages to open and once they did, she found all the answers she needed.

What looked like gibberish to the untrained eye actually hid generational wisdom passed down through time. Witches started encoding spells the moment the patriarchy turned their hunt toward wise women with a deep understanding of herbs and cures.

Terminology was meant to confuse outsiders. It was the only way to protect magick from falling into the wrong hands. Ivy became lizard legs, and the eye of newt was nothing more than mustard seed. Gratitude for her aunts' teachings swelled inside of her as she recalled all these strange terms and remembered the exact translations.

For years, she hated being different. Her lessons never seemed more than a waste of time when she craved being like everyone else.

How wrong she'd been.

Juniper finally had reason to appreciate all

her grueling childhood lessons in reading runes. While other kids practiced cursive and print, she had been forced to trace ancient glyphs until she knew each one by heart.

The encoded pages filled her with nostalgia and made her feel somehow closer to her aunts. They would have loved to see her embrace her roots, and it made Juniper sad that they never got the chance.

She definitely had some regrets to work through, but again, those distractions could come later. Right now, she needed to learn as many spells as possible.

The books were more than inanimate objects. Energy radiated from the pages as if a spiritual guardian protected the spells. Every time Juniper opened a book, she thanked the creator for entrusting her with the knowledge, making sure they understood she would not abuse the power within.

Sometimes, her promise was met with skepticism. In those cases, she'd try another grimoire. But most times, the energy was positive and welcoming, even encouraging.

Like her, these spirits were descendants of the so-called heathens, healers, and hearth dwellers burned throughout the fifteenth century. Her once dispassionate interest in her ancestors' history was gone, replaced by an insatiable obsession to know who she was so that she could unleash her full potential. Witchcraft was more than a part of her heritage. It was in her blood.

Blood... Visions of Adriel's body writhing below hers filled her memory, drawing her focus away from the task at hand.

The surge of pleasure that came with feeding had certainly been downplayed. Never in her life had she expected it to be so...erotic. Was it merely the blood that had her so turned on, or was it an underlying attraction to Adriel? She couldn't be sure.

Blood was a drug, an easy addiction. Was there a side effect? She didn't think so. Her mind had been buzzing like a live wire since taking Adriel's vein. Her thoughts and ideas connected like the vines of a wild jungle until her brain felt overwhelmed by new growth.

The only thing distracting her from her studies was the thought of Adriel asleep in her bed one floor below. But she couldn't think about that. There were too many other things to consider.

But what would happen if she joined her? She bet her body was warm. Her voice would be soft and sleepy. Juniper could slowly wake her up and—

No. She had other things to do.

Channeling. She was working on her channeling.

She turned the page and scanned the runes, slowly dragging her finger down the faded paragraph of the entry, quietly reading the ancient wisdom aloud.

"The arts of channeling energy beith a potent and

revered practice. To harness the essence of life, one must attune their spirit to the elements. The adept practitioner draws upon these forces in ritual, merging their will with nature's power..." Her words faded as her stare drifted to the door, her attention once more stolen by the female below.

She threw her body back on the bed and groaned. This was taking forever. Why couldn't she concentrate? Maybe she had *too much* blood.

Giving in to her tempting thoughts, she sighed. Adriel was unlike anyone she'd ever known. She was strong yet delicate. Powerful yet beautifully humble. Touching her was like standing in the sun—warm and comforting, invigorating in ways she couldn't explain.

Her hand dragged slowly down her front as she stared at the peaked ceiling. Those sighs and lush thighs. Her lips were the softest shade of pink, and her eyes were green like moss. The delicate traces of floral in her hair.

Her eyes closed as her fingers slipped past the waistband of her jeans. Her knees bent and opened, as her hand delved lower. Lips parting, she sighed at the first caress. Her body was warm and wet—

A floorboard creaked and her hand jerked out of her pants as she bolted upright, scrambling for the book she'd set aside. She pretended to read, only to realize the writing was upside down.

Heavy footsteps climbed the steps and Dane's dark head emerged. "I figured you were awake."

"Don't you knock? I'm studying."

He cocked his head, suspicion narrowing his eyes.

"What?" she snapped.

He knew. He was a half-breed with an exceptional sense of smell. There was no way he couldn't scent her arousal in the air, which he clearly had when he cleared his throat and broke eye contact.

"Am I interrupting something?"

Obviously he was. She snapped the book shut. "You've already interrupted. What did you need."

He approached the vanity where several books sat open. "How do you read this crap? All I see is blank pages and ink blotches."

"It's far from crap." She defensively pulled the oldest book away from his view, holding it protectively against her chest. "They're loaded with ancient wisdom and power. They're more than books. They're grimoires, and they deserve our respect."

"Sorry. I didn't realize." He sat on the bed. "How long do you think it will take you to read through them?"

"Not too long. It would help if I didn't get distracted every two minutes."

"You've been up here for hours."

"And it's very distracting."

He frowned. "You okay?"

She groaned and scrubbed her hands down her face. "I'm fine. It's just so much information and I want to understand all of it."

"June, you're only human."

She arched a brow and they both laughed.

"Guess we can't say stuff like that anymore."

"Guess not." She sighed. "I wish we knew how close he was."

"We should be grateful we have the time we have. I don't think any of us are strong enough to face him yet."

What if they never were? Any mention of Cerberus brought a sharp twist of unease.

Dane moved to the window. "Do you want this window open—"

"Leave it. I'm channeling."

"Channeling what?"

"Magick pulls from nature. It's a constant give-and-take. It's easier to replenish my energy when the window's open."

He grinned. "Let's see what you've got." He set a pen on the bed next to her. "Can you move this."

"Yeah."

"Prove it."

With a deep breath, she closed her eyes, summoning the magick that lay dormant within her, focusing on everything she'd read and opening her third eye. The attic hummed with energy, but something was preventing her from retracting the power she needed to access.

"There's too much interference."

"What do you mean?"

She tried to explain it. "The walls. I can feel the energy vibrating off every structure. Even your presence creates a ripple."

"Would it be better to practice outside?"

"Probably." But she liked the privacy of her room. "I don't want to do too much too soon. I'm trying to build up my stamina. It's complicated."

"So, explain it to me."

She hesitated. These secrets were protected for a reason. "Can I trust you?"

"June, seriously?"

She still hesitated. "What? This is ancient wisdom. It's not meant for just anybody."

"Well, at least all this power isn't going to your head."

"Fine." She sighed. "It's not like you'll be able to use it."

"Gee, thanks. It's great to feel useless."

"That's not what I meant." She turned to face him. "You know how tomatoes are nightshade fruits, and they mostly bloom at night?"

"Yeah."

"Well, they're full of energy from the moon. Trees are a mixture of sun, air, and earth. Every living thing holds a sort of magical DNA. Trained witches can tap into the genetics to pull whatever power they need."

"You learned all of this from those books?"

"I've always known it was out there, but now I'm trying to master the skill. Think of it as knowing what Italian sounds like compared to being able to understand and speak it. I'm learning how to apply what I know."

"So, once you learn how to channel nature, you'll have more powers?"

"Sort of. The bigger the natural source, the greater the power when channeled. The ocean would be the strongest force, but we're hours from the Atlantic. However—"

"The gorges," he guessed before she could explain.

"Yes." Adriel had been right when she sensed the ancient energy of this place. "Once I know how to tap into all that power, I can pull it within."

"Is that dangerous?"

"We're already in danger. Me learning how to better control my magick only makes us safer."

"Are you saying we need a field trip?"

She grinned, anxious to stretch her powers outside of the house. "I think that's exactly what's needed."

CHAPTER 21

$\mathcal{T}$hey were lost.

Hiking in the dark woods sounded like a great idea until Juniper realized she was not quite as one with nature as her ancestors might have been.

A mosquito bit her neck, and she angrily slapped herself where it stung. "Damn it with these bugs! Are we sure this is the fastest path to the falls?"

Adriel seemed the only one with any sort of tracking skills, so they sent her ahead. In a flash, she doubled back, once again startling the crap out of Juniper.

"Damn it, Ade! I told you not to sneak up on me like that."

"I wasn't sneaking. You asked a question, and I was miles ahead. I didn't want to shout."

There wasn't enough blood in the world to

gift her or Dane with equal speed or super-human hearing to that of a purebred immortal.

Ade's eyes dropped to the mosquito bite on her neck. "You're bleeding."

"It's nothing."

Her stare met hers. That look was so much more than nothing. It screamed silent envy for the tiny creature that stole one drop of what they both knew she wanted. Juniper didn't under-stand why she hadn't taken her blood the other day. Her resistance made her want it all the more.

Adriel's stare cut away. "To answer your ques-tion, yes, this is the fastest route to the falls. If you open your senses, you can smell the minerals in the air coming off the mist."

The only thing Juniper could smell was the delicious scent of Adriel's skin. Her nearness was so distracting that it overpowered the energy of the gorges, which any witch worth her salt would be able to feel thrumming through the earth.

"I need some room to concentrate. I'm not grounded."

"I'll leave you to it then." Adriel rushed off, giving her more than enough space to focus.

"I can hear it," Dane said, pushing past her to take the lead.

Her hair lifted as Adriel abruptly returned, once again startling her. Juniper flinched, but then Adriel's knuckle casually grazed her hand as it hung by her side, and a wave of desire surged through her.

"Did something upset you?"

"No, I'm just having a hard time focusing." They had yet to actually discuss what happened the other night, and Juniper was starting to worry that Adriel had regrets.

"Me too." She tipped her face down and shyly watched her through her lashes. "I find myself unable to think through a single thought without also thinking of you."

Her words stirred some much-needed assurance. "Really?"

Adriel nodded, her green eyes especially bright in the moonlight. She leaned close and whispered, "I keep replaying the other night in my head, and all I want to do is…"

Juniper's breath held. "Say it."

The corner of her mouth twitched into a half smile, and she blushed. "This." The kiss was so fast it was over before Juniper realized it was happening.

"I wanted to tell you—"

"Guys, the falls are this way," Dane called. "What's taking you so long?"

Springing apart, Adriel rushed after him. Guess they were keeping it a secret then. Juniper didn't know if that was smart or dumb, but she could figure it out later.

Rushing after them, she navigated the muddy terrain and roots crowding the path, moving fast enough to avoid getting bit by more mosquitos.

It was fall. Shouldn't those little fuckers be dead by now?

When they reached the foot of the gorges, all other sounds muffled. Mist dampened the air, and the change in altitude messed with her ears.

"Do you feel that?" Adriel grinned.

Juniper nodded and set down her leather backpack. "I definitely feel it." She pulled the big book out and closed her eyes, taking a moment to ground.

Last night, she'd set all of her tools on the windowsill to charge. This morning, the books vibrated with energy as if not inanimate objects but something secretly alive.

Magick was merely the channeling of life from one source to another. It was all connected. Water and sunlight fed the grass that fed the animals, which then nourished the humans who supplied the immortals. In the end, everything from the earth to the ether was connected. Animals fertilizing the plants and freshened the air, which mixed with the solar system above. It was all magically connected in the cycle of life.

"You ready to do this?" Dane asked, rolling up his sleeves.

It had been his idea to practice on something bigger than pennies, rocks, and tomatoes, so he volunteered himself.

"Perhaps you should start with me, in case anything goes wrong," Adriel suggested. "No offense, Dane, but I'm less…breakable."

Dane rolled his eyes. "You're tiny. She needs to practice on something bigger."

"Ah, yes." Adriel rolled her eyes. "You Dane.

Dane big and strong." She thumped a fist on her chest then softened her voice. "Me little female, feeble and weak."

Juniper laughed. "Adriel has a point, Dane. I could screw up and hurt you."

"I think I can handle it." He stretched his legs and arms as if getting ready to run a marathon. "Besides, I fed an hour ago. I feel great."

Juniper did a double take. When had that happened? And whose blood did he drink? When Adriel flushed, she had her answer.

Juniper scowled, all jovialness leaving her at once. "Well then I guess we're ready."

"I really think you should practice on me, first, June—"

"Dane will be fine. He's a big, strong boy. I'm sure he can handle a few bruises." She looked upward at the cliffs. "Are you afraid of heights?"

Dane looked behind him. "I don't think so."

"Then up you go." Extending her arms overhead, she pulled energy from the earth and called it into her body.

Dane's laughter echoed off the stone walls as he lifted off the ground. The rushing spray of the falls snuffed out the sound.

She lowered her arms, which consequently lowered Dane back to the earth. Silence.

"What's wrong?"

Juniper frowned. "I thought I felt something."

"What kind of something?" Dane asked, now standing several feet away. "I felt nothing except lightness."

Adriel stepped forward. "Try it with me and see if you feel it again."

"Okay." Juniper turned her attention to Adriel's smaller form. Maybe it was like lifting weights and she needed to build up her strength for someone of Dane's size. "Ready?"

"Ready."

She concentrated, and up Adriel went. She was definitely lighter and easier to carry. Her laughter echoed much like Dane's until she was too far above the spray to hear. She deposited her at the top of the gorge, where a cliff protruded.

"There it is again." Juniper sucked in a sharp breath, unsure of what caused the chill. It was cold, like ice floating in the air. It slithered into her bones with a rheumatoid ache. "Ade?" Her eyes squinted as she listened closely for Adriel's voice.

"Do you hear anything?"

"Just water."

"Adriel?" She and Dane shouted, moving up the path toward the top of the cliff where she'd deposited Adriel. "Adriel, answer us!"

The air chilled again, and Juniper's worry doubled. Something wasn't right.

She rushed up the mud path, her heart pounding when they continued to call without a single answer from Adriel.

"Adriel!"

She lost her footing and slipped in a mire of leaves and sludge, falling hard and smashing her knee on a protruding root. "Shit!"

"Are you all right?" Dane pulled her up, his breath ragged from climbing the steep incline.

Her jeans had ripped and her knee was now bleeding. "Something's wrong." Anxiety spiked in her tight chest. The sky darkened and the dense tree coverage blocked the moonlight, making it hard to see the trail.

"Adriel!"

Thunder cracked, but no light webbed the sky. Blackness bled into the trees and a whisper of unease skated over her skin, snaking through the forest like a toxic gas until fear was all she could breathe.

"Why isn't she answering us?"

"This isn't right." The bitter taste of dark sorcery soured her tongue. That was not her magick or any kind of magick she recognized. The obscure sense of danger seeped from the shadows. "Something else is out there. We need to get to the—

A blood-curdling scream shattered her concentration.

"Shit!" Dane cursed as they bolted toward the sound of Adriel's cry.

The trees crowded them like silent sentinels, blocking their path and making it impossible to run as fast as she wanted. She thought the sound of Adriel's scream the worse sound in the world, until her cries stopped and silence was all they heard.

"Fuck! Come on!" She rushed forward, then

turned, confused which way led to the top of the gorges. "I'm all turned around."

"Me too. What the hell is going on?"

"I don't know. *Adriel!*"

"Wait, we both have her blood in our system. Can't we track her that way?"

"Do you know how?"

"No."

Panic welled inside of her. "We have to keep moving. *Adriel!*"

A loud bang had them suddenly crouching low as the ground convulsed violently. Shockwaves rippled through the rugged terrain, and a shudder raced up her spine. Dane slipped in a landslide of mud and leaves as Juniper clung to the wide trunk of a tree, now realizing what was wrong.

"It's him! He's here!"

She yanked Dane to his feet as a storm erupted from the earth under the clear black sky.

"Don't worry about me. Go find Adriel!"

Trees thrashed wildly, their branches lashing out like frenzied tendrils as the earth buckled and heaved beneath their feet. Juniper's palms slammed into the wet ground, her nails clawing into the mud for purchase.

The relentless force sent rocks tumbling. "Watch out!"

Boulders careened from the bluffs, pummeling the trees as if they were nothing more than pipe cleaners. "We have to get away from the cliffs!"

Dane caught her by the ribs as she lost her footing. "Hold onto me." Hands linked, they raced to the gorge's edge and looked down. Rapids slammed against the rocks.

"There's nowhere to go!"

A chasm parted the forest floor, and they jumped onto a moss-covered slab, sliding until they both went down. Dane caught the brunt of their weight, breaking their fall and landing hard on his back.

Juniper scrambled to her hands and knees, panting and searching for other options. There weren't any. The ground split open. Landslides crumbled the ancient stone walls, washing away years of vegetation.

"Watch out!" Dane yanked her back from the edge just as the earth gaped open.

She looked up at him in horror. He'd just saved her from falling to her death.

"This way!" he yelled, and they crawled to the nearest wall.

Amidst the chaos, the gulches opened into pits and sinkholes. The falls rushed faster and louder, flooding the banks and carving mudslides through the upturned trees. The mountain moaned, and water surged with newfound ferocity.

Dane lost his footing and slipped, his body sliding down too fast for Juniper to catch. *"Dane!"*

He grunted as he landed hard on his chest, his hand clinging to a slick vine. "Go! I'm right behind you!"

She couldn't leave him. "Don't move. I'll pull you up!"

She searched for another vine, but every root she grabbed was too slick to hold her weight.

"June, use your magick!"

Panic had made her forget her power, but the moment he said it, she tapped into the energy swirling around them. Her hands shook violently as heavy rocks fell around them, plummeting into the once-calm waters now raging below.

"I can't!" She was too scared of being crushed.

"Juniper, look at me."

Overwhelmed and unsure, her stare found Dane's as he clung to the vine. His grip was slipping, and his face pinched in pain. A nasty cut bled from his eye, and his clothes were drenched in mud. He strained to hold on.

"Listen to my voice and block everything else out. My left arm is hurt. I can't hold on much longer. You have to concentrate. You can do this. Don't let him scare you. That's what he wants."

He was right. Her fear was unprecedented. Cerberus was trying to block her the way she'd blocked him.

Squeezing her eyes shut, she called on the energy of her ancestors and forced the protection spell back in place. Calm encircled her and Dane, and her legs steadied. "I've got this," she whispered, holding out her palms and thrusting her arms into the air.

Dane propelled skyward just as the earth crumbled and the vine he'd been holding fell away. She lifted him with the ease of a balloon and set him on the ground beside her. As soon as he was safe, she lunged at him, hugging him tightly.

"I'm sorry. I don't know why it took me so long to figure that out—"

"There's no time for that. Come on. We have to get to Adriel!"

The earthquake could not touch them under such an acute protection spell, and the destruction left a trail of obstacles for them to climb. They were making progress until everything stilled. Not just the area she protected, but the ground beyond her spell.

"It stopped. Why did it stop?"

In the eerie stillness, the woods whispered secrets of their own, as if mourning the violence that had shattered their tranquility there. It wasn't just destruction. Death lingered in the air.

Holes and dens were buried. Nests had plummeted to the earth. And worst of all, Juniper knew he was far from finished.

"It's the calm before the storm."

Dane looked at the cliff above. "You have to send me up there. It's the only way!"

"Are you crazy?"

"He has Adriel! One of us needs to stop him before he goes too far."

"Fine!" She panicked. "But what if you can't?" She glanced at his injured arm as it hung limp at his side. "You're hurt—"

"Do it. And as soon as I'm up there, you climb

as fast as possible. I'll do whatever I can to slow him down."

It was an insane plan but the best option. "Fuck!" She raked her hands through her soaked hair.

"Now, Juniper! We can't wait any longer!"

With unsteady hands, she pushed him upward. Moonlight illuminated the landscape but once Dane disappeared over the bluff, she was blind and alone, clueless to what they faced above.

Breath punched out of her as she climbed over the upturned roots and navigated the ransacked woods in the pitch dark. Sinkholes pocked the soil, leaving it soft and unstable. She had to constantly keep her grip on the trees as she moved.

She tripped and fell into a tree, scraping her face on a branch. But a potent spark flooded her arm when her hand pressed into the bark. She gasped, reminded of the extreme power trapped in nature.

Her fear made sense, but her apprehension did not. Nature was a witch's most sacred place. This was her turf. She didn't understand where this crippling anxiety came from.

Then she realized. "He's fucking with me." She scowled upward, unsure how he was doing it.

"You motherfucker." Clamping her hands on the tree trunk, she siphoned all the power her body could hold and sent a jolt of don't-fuck-with-me energy outward. The force of the transfer, nearly ripped her open, but she was done being bullied by ancient blood-sucking fucks.

She gritted her teeth and pushed back when she felt resistance, refusing to let him win. "Get out of my head, you bastard!"

Like a dog shaking off an infestation of fleas, sharp resistance bit into her, but she somehow broke free of his hold. The moment she pushed him out of her head, her anxiety calmed, and she could think clearly again.

Her brain was bathed in a rush of solutions she couldn't see seconds ago, and she ran for the top of the gorge. Drawing an *algiz* rune in the air for protection, she whispered an incantation that called forth the magick of her ancestors and used it to the power of the minerals throughout the land underfoot. She found balance above the earth and her breath calmed as the energy of the water moved her, each hasty step guided by the wisdom of the trees.

Her need to get to Adriel drove her like the moon pulled the tides. The moment she hauled herself over the ledge, landing flat on her belly, she scented blood.

A dark shadow speared her with fear. "Dane!" She scrambled to his side, panic once again knifing through her as he lay unmoving, his eyes closed. She shook him roughly. "Dane, wake up."

He groaned and rolled to his back, his bloody face twisting in pain. "Save Ade."

Sucking back a sob, she traced the shape of

the *algiz* rune on his brow and ran toward the trees. A horrific scream cleaved through the air, sharp enough to cut the night in two.

Juniper scented her blood but couldn't find her. "Adriel?"

"Juniper, run!"

She spun and her blood turned to ice. Cerberus's claws were embedded in Adriel's body as he jerked her about like a ragdoll and she screamed in pain, her claws scraping down his face as she tried to wrestle him off.

Red filled his eyes, and his fangs were not that of a normal immortal's. They were long and curved, resembling the bite of a python.

"Let go of her!" Juniper raced forward.

He tore Adriel's clothes away, choking her into silence as he prepared to mount her. His head drew back on a hiss, and those viper-like fangs dripped with what Juniper feared was venom.

She staggered back in horror. "What the fuck are you?"

"Run!" Adriel choked. "Go—"

Her words silenced as he sank his fist into her stomach and laughed.

Those blood-red eyes locked on Juniper as he sneered and punched into the earth, but Juniper was prepared. She dropped to her knees and pulled the energy of the falls into her, then used the force of the gorges to ricochet the earthquake back at him.

His features twisted with malevolent intent as

he suffered the consequences of his own attack. Adriel tried to escape, but he dug his claws into her leg, wrenching her back to him. He snarled at Juniper with palpable wrath, and she only had a split second to protect herself.

"No!" She threw her arms upward, pulling the energy of the moon into her battered body. The lunar force ripped through her, surging into a vortex of energy that propelled Cerberus off of Adriel and slammed him into a tree.

Adriel disappeared in a blur of motion.

Juniper held the energy, plowing Cerberus's body deeper into the woods until her entire body vibrated as if being electrocuted. The air cracked, and time screeched as her body convulsed.

Her bones screamed as her weight crumbled, her muscles giving out as she hung suspended in the air, wavering in the centrifugal force radiating around her, and then she dropped. Her wasted body smashed into the earth with lethal force and pain exploded through her back and skull as all went black.

CHAPTER 22

*J*uniper gasped and jackknifed upward, her arms bunching into a defensive stance as she prepared to defend her life.

"You're safe! You're safe!"

Breath sawed in and out of her lungs as she scanned the bedroom. Dane stared wide-eyed, his hands held out in a calming gesture.

She was in bed, in her room, at Ruth's. Flecks of mud and debris still speckled her hands and arms. As memories rushed back, her panic spiked. "Where's Adriel?"

Regret flashed in his eyes.

"Dane, *where* is she?"

"She's in her room—wait."

She threw off the covers. When she tried to stand, her balance betrayed her. He caught her by the arm, saving her from falling to her face.

"You're hurt."

"I'm fine." That was a lie.

Her legs were barely stable, and her insides felt like they'd survived an exorcism. She gritted her teeth as she tried to find her bearings, gripping the bed and swatting Dane's hands away.

"Damn it, Juniper, let me help you." He caught her by the waist.

Resigned, she steadied herself on his shoulders and caught her breath.

"There you go," he said, voice low and eyes creased with concern. "Now, take it slow." His hands slid from her ribs to her arms, giving her space to move.

Sunlight filtered through the pea-green curtains. "How long have I been out?"

"Two days."

"T-two days?" How could that be? What happened in the woods? How did she get back to the house? And if she'd been resting for two full days, why did she still feel this shitty? "I have to check on Adriel."

"June, no."

"Why won't you let me see her?"

"She was adamant."

"I don't care. She almost died, Dane!"

"So did you!" His sharp response startled her and she stilled.

Dane paced to the window, his hands forking through his hair. Strands fell from the leather tie and hung around his face. Exhaustion showed around his eyes.

Seeing how stressed he was, she softly assured him, "I'm okay, Dane."

He shook his head and rubbed his face. "Can you just...stay in bed until you're a little stronger?"

Her body clearly needed rest and time to recover, but she couldn't stay there. "I need to see her, Dane, with my own eyes." The last time Juniper saw her... "He hurt her."

"He hurt all of us."

Dane didn't know about Adriel's stupid plan. He didn't understand how close they came to losing her last night. Cerberus had her pinned down, his claws embedded in her flesh. If Adriel had a way to end her life in that moment, she would have.

Juniper's head lowered. A mixture of relief and fear churned in her belly. "She almost died," she whispered, her voice constricted by heavy emotions she didn't want to name.

"But she didn't, June. They can't. Her body's healed, and she just wants to be left alone now."

That told her everything she needed to know. Cerberus had done more than claw at her.

"Just give her time. She'll come around."

She shook her head. "How could this happen to her? We were unprepared."

"No good comes out of blame like that."

She wasn't fishing for forgiveness. She was taking accountability. This was her fault. She should have been more aware of their surroundings. "I should have protected her better."

"Hey." He sat next to her on the bed and rubbed a hand down her back. "She'll be okay. She's alive. We all are. That's all that matters.

His words brought little comfort. *Some things are worse than death.* Rather than debate him on things he didn't understand, she nodded and dropped her gaze to the floor. They sat in silence for a heavy moment.

When she glanced at him again, she frowned. "Your arm's better."

He quickly covered where a large gash had been, and his expression turned guilty. "Yeah. She insisted."

Juniper gaped at him. "She was injured, Dane! You had no right to take her blood—"

"You took it too."

"What? Why would you let her do that?"

"Let her? She's a five-hundred-year-old immortal, June. No one *lets her* do anything. She does what she chooses."

"She shouldn't have done that."

"Well, you needed something. She made sure you swallowed a few drops while you were sleeping. I tried to talk her out of it, but she wouldn't take no for an answer."

Juniper stood and a wave of dizziness had her clutching the bedpost. "I need to talk to her."

"I don't think—"

"I don't care what anyone thinks right now. This is what I need to do."

Navigating the steps carefully, she sluggishly took them downstairs. When she reached

Adriel's room, the door was closed. She knocked softly. "Ade? It's me. Can I come in?"

The latch clicked as she turned the knob. Adriel lay on her side, her body turned toward the wall so Juniper couldn't see her face.

"Hey."

A soft sniff was her only reply.

She crossed the distance, unsure if her presence would be welcome. "Dane warned me to stay away, but I needed to see you."

Dried mud and blood still caked the crevices of Adriel's ankles and feet. Had she just been lying here for days in this filth?

"Baby?" When she rested a feather-light hand on her shoulder, her body trembled. "It's okay to cry." Climbing behind her, she gently curved her body close to hers and pulled her into her arms. "I'll cry with you."

A low whimper met her ears as Adriel's shoulders shook.

Juniper's heart broke. "It's okay," she whispered, stroking a gentle hand over her hair. Her tears made it hard to form words. "Whatever you're feeling right now is okay."

She knew too well the emptiness that followed an assault. That numbing void that turned a person inside out. There was no logical way through that sort of mind fuck. One could only suffer with it and hope living might become bearable again—despite the flashbacks, anger, and misplaced shame.

Her fingers gently untangled the knots in her

hair. "You didn't do anything wrong," she whispered, pressing a kiss to the back of her shoulder.

A jagged breath tore out of her. "I... can't do this. I can't go back to that."

"You won't. He caught us off guard this time. Next time, we'll be ready."

"There won't be a next time."

The undertones of her vow sent a shiver down Juniper's spine. She sat up and forced Adriel to look at her, but when she saw her battered face, she had to cover her own sob. Adriel had seen to their healing but not seen to her own.

That fucker was going to pay.

Shoving aside her hate, she drew in a galvanizing breath and focused on helping Adriel. "You listen to me, Ade. What happened up there does not change anything. You are not going back. No one is going to hurt you anymore. Do you understand?" She tried to speak firmly, but her voice trembled. "I mean it, Adriel. I will protect you, even if it means protecting you from yourself."

She turned to face her. A tear slid through the blood and grime on her cheek. "I'm so scared, Juniper."

She pulled her into a fierce hug. "I know. You would be crazy not to be. But, between the three of us, we can beat him. That's where I need you to put your faith right now. Okay?"

She squeezed her eyes shut and nodded tightly.

Juniper sighed and loosened her hold, but Adriel's hand still clutched her shirt. She liked the idea of comforting her, being the strong one, the protector. Adriel might be half a millennium old and immortal, but there was something utterly innocent about her. And no one was going to fuck with that.

She kissed her nose and combed the hair away from her shimmering eyes. "What do you say we get you cleaned up?"

When Adriel nodded and scooted forward. Juniper slowly stood and held out a hand to gently help her from the bed. In the face of Adriel's fear, her own pain somehow disappeared. "I'll take care of you."

"Thank you."

Small cuts marked her skin. She wasn't healing because she'd given her blood away. "After your bath, we'll see about getting you fed."

Adriel sat on the toilet while Juniper filled the tub. She kept her eyes on her task, but as she gathered a washcloth and towel from the closet, she noted how Adriel's shoulders hunched inward and how haunted she appeared as she stared blankly at the floor.

When she stripped away her nightgown, she winced at the purple marks covering her torso. "Jesus."

"It doesn't hurt."

Juniper glanced into her tired eyes, knowing that was a bald-faced lie. "You don't have to be proud or strong around me, Ade. I was there."

With gentle motions, she pulled away her clothing, knowing the worst injuries were never the outward ones anyway. She used a warm, soapy washcloth to sponge away most of the dirt before helping her into the tub.

"It will feel good to soak for a while."

Adriel's breath caught as she lowered into the water and breathed out a quiet thank you. The water sloshed and stilled, only the occasional drip from the spigot disrupting the over-whelming silence.

"While you're in there, I can call Danny—"

"No."

Juniper tried to understand her rejection. Was this it? Was she just going to starve herself? There was no way that was happening. Without feeding, her injuries would take forever to heal.

Juniper kneeled on a towel, deciding to face one obstacle at a time. "Let's start with your hair."

She filled a cup to rinse the grime from her copper waves. As she poured clean water over Adriel's head and down her shoulders, she lathered her fingers with shampoo.

"Just try to relax."

Juniper took great care to gently massage her scalp and wash behind her ears. This should have improved the situation, but the longer she gently washed her hair, the more Adriel wept.

Just as Juniper was about to ask if she wanted her to stop, Adriel stilled her hand and looked up at her with tear-filled eyes. "I'm sorry I didn't help you."

"What?"

"On the farm. I could have helped you. There would have been consequences, but I should have helped you anyway."

The blood rushed from Juniper's face. If she was going to stay strong, she couldn't entertain those memories of weakness right now. She wanted to be the rock, the one Adriel could lean on in her time of need.

"It's over. I'm free. And soon, you will be too." She couldn't go back there, mentally or otherwise. "Lean forward." But Adriel's apology struck a nerve that needed to sing. "Thank you for admitting that."

Adriel sat up, each vertebra of her spine slightly protruding beneath a spattering of bruises. Juniper washed her back. To an outsider, no one would ever assume this docile beauty was immortal. Her body might be battered at the moment, but once she fed, she'd heal, and then her beauty would be flawless again.

She dragged the washcloth over her shoulders and between her breasts. Soft peach flesh darkened with raspberry tips. As she carefully washed her delicate curves, her gaze followed the long length of her legs.

"You have adorable toes," she said, trying to lighten the mood.

She flushed, and her smile was worth everything.

"I want to bite them." Juniper teased, playfully snapping her jaw.

Adriel squeaked, pulling her foot underwater. When she looked up at Juniper, the laughter stopped. She felt it. They both did. It was there, heavy and impossible to ignore. Juniper closed her hand over hers and gently squeezed. Silently promising to take care of her once more.

As if hearing her unspoken vow, Adriel dropped her gaze.

"You need to feed, Ade." She couldn't bear to watch her wither away in pain. If she nourished her body and felt better, her optimism would return. She'd realize they still have a fighting chance. "Maybe I should clarify. I'm offering."

At that, Adriel looked up. "You're still weak—"

"I'm strong enough. Besides, the thought of you taking someone else's vein right now makes me want to break something." She wasn't taking no for an answer. Standing, she bent to pull the plug and refreshed the bath with warm water. "Soak a while longer. I'll find fresh sheets, and then I'll be back."

She needed a moment to clear her head. Adriel was confused and in pain. Getting her right was number one. But Juniper knew what feeding did. They would be close. It would be intimate. Her body would catch fire. She needed to keep a lock on her own personal desires. What Adriel needed right now was blood and a friend.

After making the bed, she returned to the bathroom. Adriel was wrapped in a towel, and facing the mirror.

"I would have helped you."

"I managed." She handed Juniper a folded towel and a fresh washcloth. "You're so worried about me that you forget to care for yourself."

When their hands touched, Adriel slowly dragged her fingers over Juniper's. She self-consciously glanced down at her dirty feet. "I should shower."

"I'll wait for you." Her stare hid promise and intent, enough to disarm Juniper's confidence. "Come to the bedroom when you're finished."

Her hand lifted to Juniper's face but paused to examine the feather hanging from her hair. Her lashes lowered, and she smiled.

"What you just did for me…" Adriel's dark emerald eyes lifted. "No one has ever shown me such kindness."

"The world's fucked up, Ade, not you."

Her smile turned sad and then thoughtful. "I don't know if this is the way you are with other females—"

"It's not."

She stilled, her smile once again stretching into something genuine. "Good. Because immortals can be quite territorial when they find something they want to claim."

Juniper's stomach tightened, and she nodded. "I feel that too."

"Do you?" Adriel asked, thumb tracing over her racing pulse as she studied her response. "Do you feel the traitorous way my blood pumps whenever I'm near you? Can you hear how fast my heart is beating right now? Because I can hear yours."

She could only hear her own unsteady breath. They couldn't do this in her filthy state. She was jittery as hell and needed to collect herself. "I need to rinse off first."

Adriel reached past her, and Juniper's breath hitched, her body momentarily pinned to the door as she reached for the knob. "Dirty wouldn't bother me." The door clicked open and she paused, her nose turning toward her neck and she whispered, "I have a confession."

Juniper's shoulders pressed into the wood, and her eyes closed, her soft spoken words a balm to her soul. Adriel could literally read a recipe at and it would be hot. The air was still warm with steam and Adriel smelled of soap and mint and something sultry that seemed to naturally cling to her skin. "W-what?"

"I've fantasized about…tasting you."

It was too much. Juniper caught her by the neck and spun them around so Adriel's back hit the door. Her mouth smashed to hers, hard and hungry, and Adriel growled.

Nipping and kissing, Juniper demanded entry, knocking her knee between her thighs and pressing her stomach flat to hers as she dragged a hand possessively to her chest.

Greedily, she kissed her in a way she had never kissed her before, showing just how much she wanted her. How much she needed to show her everything she'd been ignoring these past few days.

Desire blazed through her. She couldn't get close enough. She needed to slow down. But her touch was ravenous. Juniper gripped the damp towel and stilled at the sight of blood flecked across her knuckles and she stilled.

"Sorry." Her gaze turned away. Adriel deserved better.

"You don't have to apologize, or stop."

But she did. "Let me at least wash up."

She nodded then laughed softly. "You're the one caging me in."

"Oh. Right." Juniper stepped back and looked away. Her emotions were all over the place. "I was so afraid I'd lost you."

"Look at me, Juniper," Adriel gripped her nightgown, fisting the fabric as she stared at her with raw promise in her eyes. "You have me."

Her mouth was irresistible, and Juniper was kissing her again. "I want all of you," she whispered, drunk on desire and thirsty for more. "Every part."

"Do you sense opposition from me?"

Her eyes closed as she once again stayed her hand and tried to slow her racing heart. "I want you so much, I can hardly breathe."

"Juniper, love, you have me." She yanked the towel free, exposing her bare flesh.

"Fuck." She raked a hand through her knotted hair. "You're so beautiful."

Adriel bashfully mirrored the gesture, and

drops of water sprinkled her fingers. Her fiery hair spiked in haphazard clumps, making her look all the more adorable and sweet. "When you say that, I believe you mean it."

Juniper yanked her body close and squeezed her ass. "I wouldn't lie to you." She dragged her lips over her throat and licked the drops of water that fell from her hair. "I want to taste and know every sweet inch of you." She pressed her nose to her pulse and bit playfully at her shoulder.

Adriel gasped, her hands tugging at Juniper's clothes in frustration. "I want that too."

Juniper untangled Adriel's hands from her nightgown and pushed them to her sides. She was so clean and fresh, she didn't want to spoil her. "Let me just…" Leaning forward, she kissed the ruched tip of her nipple, and Adriel's head fell back on a moan.

Whimpering, she forked her fingers through Juniper's tangled hair. Juniper swirled her tongue lower, gripping her by the ribs and sucking her nipple into her mouth, never breaking eye contact.

Adriel's lips parted, and her knees softened. Delicate ivory skin trailed under her fingertips as she teased her fingers lower. Adriel gasped when she traced the seam of her dewy folds, warm and smooth, hot and inviting, but also delicate like a kiss. She nudged the tip of her finger inside, and Adriel's scent intensified then perfumed the air.

"Juniper…"

She heard the uncertainty in her voice and

stilled. Her finger withdrew, but she kept her hand over her heat, cupping her softly as she turned away to find some scrap of composure. "I'm sorry."

"It's not that. I just think we would be more comfortable in a bed."

Juniper smiled. "Definitely."

More than anything, she wanted Adriel to be comfortable. She kissed her one last time, briefly, and physically forced herself to step away.

"Go. Go now, before I attack you again. I mean it." The door clicked, and she was gone. Juniper shook her head at Adriel's inhuman speed. "And that's at her weakest."

She took the fastest shower of her life. Barely drying her body before going to Adriel's' bedroom.

Dark promises silently passed within their stare and the air charged with dizzying energy the moment she opened the door. "Do you still want—"

"Very much." She pulled back the covers and then flushed. "If you still do."

"I do." Her smile was nervous, which somehow made her even more tempting. Adriel might be the older one, but Juniper was definitely the more experienced of the two.

Adriel looked up at her nervously. "Do we—"

Juniper toppled her to the bed and kissed her deeply before she could ask any more questions. Her towel fell away. Flesh to flesh, their hands freely explored.

She greedily cupped her luscious curves as her mouth trailed hungry kisses to her chest, plumping her breasts and teasing her until her nipples were wet and hard. Adriel moaned and arched, granting her full access to her beautiful body.

She was a drug. Her surrender a rush. Her scent an addiction. Her soft little moans a spell in and of themselves. She couldn't choose just one place to explore. She wanted to lick and taste all of her, so much so that her gums started to hurt.

She sat up and gasped when a strange sensation stung her mouth.

"What is it?"

Covering her lips, she dragged a finger over her incisors. "I think…" She gasped again. "Is that a fucking fang? Did I just get my fangs?"

Adriel laughed and sat up, her hand lovingly caressing her jaw. "Let me see." She smiled the moment Juniper flashed her teeth. "Congratulations."

She supposed this would make things easier, but it was a little awkward to have it happen in the middle of a make-out session. She pressed her thumb to the tip, shocked by how sharp they were. "Sorry."

"Don't apologize." She leaned back, stretching out like an offering. "Use them."

Her eyes flared as Adriel's lush thighs called to her. Unable to resist, she rolled to her belly, and pushed her knees apart. She first kissed her hip, then trailed her touch lower until she found the sweet pearl hidden between her folds.

Adriel stiffened.

"It's okay." Juniper lowered her mouth, and placed a staying hand on her belly. "You'll like it. Just relax."

She dragged her fangs over soft inner flesh of her thigh, teasing her mouth upward. Adriel's head fell back with a whimper and her hands fisted nervously in the covers. Juniper recalled the first time a guy did this to her, he'd been all over the place, rushed, and sort of sloppy. Adriel's first time was going to be nothing like hers.

She pressed her thighs wider and placed a gentle kiss on her swollen flesh. Adriel whimpered and bashfully covered her face.

Juniper teased a finger inside of her. "Tell me if it's not what you want."

Hands still over her face, she murmured, "I don't know enough to know what I want."

"Then you'll have to tell me if it feels good. Or not."

"Every time you touch me it feels amazing."

She smiled and pressed another kiss on her clit. "Good. Then we're heading in the right direction." She sucked her little jewel between her lips, stroking slowly inside.

Soft moans keened from above as Adriel gently stretched and arched against her stroking touch. Curling her fingers, she delivered a rush of pleasure that had her breath quickening. She tasted of rain and mist.

Their moans grew louder, Adriel's peppering the air as Juniper's muffled against her slick heat. Arousal gathered at her fingers and she pressed deep, replacing her mouth with the heel of her palm to apply more pressure.

She climbed up her body and captured a nipple between her lips, sucking the tip hard enough to make her cry out. Adriel arched and dug her nails into Juniper's back as slick honey bathed her fingers.

"That's it, baby. I've got you." She pushed deeper, pumping her fingers slowly, not giving her time to come down before another wave of pleasure built.

"What's happening to me?"

"Nothing you need to fear. Trust me."

Her head tipped back as her channel clenched, gripping her fingers as they teased deeper.

"You can let go. I won't let you fall."

Her legs trembled as tiny spasms chased the aftershocks rushing through her muscles. Juniper lowered her mouth again, closing her lips around her sensitized flesh as she kissed her slowly. Adriel jerked and gasped at the mercy of her touch, drunk on pleasure.

The bed creaked with every shuddered moan. Juniper captured her tight fist, loosening her grip so she could lace her fingers with her. She held her like that, delivering open-mouthed kisses and stroking her through another release.

The way she gasped in gentle surprise and gripped her hand. The sensations of her body pulsing against her tongue. Every experience leading up to this moment paled in comparison. This was right. Perfect. Not simply because she was a female but because she was Adriel. Pure, selfless, and kind.

"What are you doing to me?" she rasped, her free hand resting over her pounding heart. Her breasts wore the rosy markings of Juniper's greedy kisses.

"Did you like it?"

She laughed. "What's not to like?" She abruptly sat up. "Show me how to do it."

She pulled her down to lay on top of her. "It's just like a kiss."

"It's better than a kiss."

Juniper tucked her short hair behind her ears and pulled her closer, dragging her mouth over Adriel's. "First, you tease until everything's nice and soft." Her lips dragged slowly back and forth as their breath mingled. "Then you get it wet." She licked slowly into her mouth. "You can use your fingers, but not too much too fast." She bit her lower lip and gently pulled, releasing it with a soft snap. "And when its time, you'll find that sweet little clit." Her hand pressed between her legs, and she gasped. "You can kiss softly or suck hard. It all feels good. You can even rub gently like this…"

Adriel's head fell back on a sigh. "It was supposed to be my turn."

Juniper caught her hand and shoved it between her legs. "Take whatever you want. I'm yours."

Adriel rolled her to her back and took the lead. Juniper gave her plenty of space to explore. Her kisses were tentative at first, but then they grew deeper and more intentional.

Their bodies aligned perfectly. Warmth and softness. Tender curiosity. It all added up to one of the most erotic experiences of her life. Carnal and new. Adventurous yet safe.

It was then Juniper realized why she could be so open with her. They would never intentionally hurt the other. That realization undid her more than any touch and she gasped, her chest tight with emotion as delicate kisses trailed over her.

Lighter than a butterfly wing, Adriel dragged her mouth against her sensitized skin. A low purr hummed from her throat and when she looked up at Juniper with elongated irises that seemed to glow under the shadows of her lashes, twin fangs poked past her lips, and she caught her chin.

Juniper traced her thumb along the razor-sharp edge of her teeth, no longer finding the sight frightening. On the contrary, she was stunning. "I'm ready," she whispered, with a curious smile.

"Are you sure?"

"Very. I want this."

Adriel pushed her fingers into her hair and yanked her head back, exposing her throat. The sharp pivot from gentle to possessive excited her in ways she couldn't explain.

"Don't forget to breathe."

Juniper gasped the moment her bite punctured the skin. There was no pain, only sharp pressure that expanded much like a puddle blooms. She drank deeply, with the precise purpose of feeding her natural hunger and that initial prick faded away to make room for something dark and heady

The more aggressive she drank, the harder Juniper wanted it. "Yes…"

Heat pooled low in Juniper's belly, and her breath quickened. She cradled the back of Adriel's head, holding her close as her body arched and stretched wildly beneath her. The purring grew louder like the slow rumble of thunder until Juniper's moans crested into desperate cries.

She needed more. Legs entangled, she rubbed her body against Adriel's, seeking friction wherever she could find it. Tremors zipped through her, as she clutched her shoulders and bucked her hips.

"Harder," she gasped. "You won't hurt me."

Adriel moaned, rocking her body over Juniper's as she fed. Her hands closed around her wrists, and she ground over her at a more aggressive angle, pinning her hands to the bed. But Juniper needed to touch her.

Pulling a hand free, she dragged it between them, adding pressure to her throbbing clit as she aligned her sex with Adriel's. Their bodies scissored and rubbed, driving the heat to an unbearable inferno she could hardly contain.

"I'm so close." She strummed her harder, wedging her fingers anywhere they would fit and grinding her body with seeking need. "I want you to finish with me."

Adriel cried out against her throat, gasping as Juniper thrust her fingers inside her heat.

"That's it, baby. Keep sucking my vein. Let me finish you while you take what you need."

Adriel moaned hungrily and rolled her hips, pulling hard at her vein as she moaned faster. The bed rocked and squeaked, but they were beyond caring about the noise as the sensations built and grew until every cell in her being burned with unparalleled pleasure. There was nowhere left for it to go. The more Adriel drank the closer Juniper came.

Then…bliss.

There was nothing delicate about that ecstasy-drenched moment. Neither of them were searching for whispers of refined femininity. They were lost in their baser instincts, primal and entitled to their own pleasure in a way she was certain neither of them had ever been before.

It was freeing to take what they wanted in such a raw, animalistic way. No shame. No guilt. No fear. Only pleasure.

It was easily the hottest experience of Juniper's entire life.

CHAPTER 23

*A*driel awoke to a cool bed, followed by a jolt of disappointment. Had she misinterpreted last night? Perhaps she was harboring unrealistic expectations. These emotions were unprecedented and the last thing she expected to feel, yet there seemed no drawing them back now—which led her right into regret.

What had she been thinking? She had no understanding of modern relationships and even less about relationships with females. A female hybrid witch, for that matter.

But she thought she knew Juniper. She felt so connected to her last night—truly understood for the first time in her existence. Juniper made her feel…

She inwardly cringed knowing there was no place in her life or heart for such a word, but she couldn't escape its inflated presence in her head.

She felt loved.

Her eyes shut and she winced. What was wrong with her? Juniper wasn't even there. What they did obviously didn't mean as much to her as it did to Adriel.

A bitter ache formed in her heart. Abandoned not even six hours later. She should have known better.

And why was she taking it so personally? It wasn't as though they were mated or married. There should be no ache in her chest or hurt in her belly. It was one night. Nothing. They only lived together out of necessity. They were friends. This must be what casual meant. Perfectly acceptable, no strings attached, don't ask, don't tell…

The logic continued, but the disappointment never eased. Last night had been iconic.

She covered her face with a pillow and groaned, hating the wishy-washy neediness ransacking her common sense. But the truth was, she didn't want it to end. She wanted to wake up beside her and—

"Morning."

Adriel's heart stilled. All debasing thoughts slammed to a halt as the weight in her stomach lifted like bubbles of air. Sliding the pillow from her face, she turned her gaze to the door and found Juniper staring at her.

"You okay?"

An embarrassed smile curved her mouth and her cheeks heated. She was losing her mind for this female—far from *okay*. "I'm great. How are you?"

Juniper closed the distance, her unique scent softening the air. A thousand butterflies took flight in Adriel's belly.

"I'm fantastic." She laughed, almost to herself. "Better even." Wrapped in only a towel, she bent to press a kiss to Adriel's mouth, lingering for a moment to caress her jaw before slowly pulling away. "You sure you're okay?"

Again, she blushed. "I…thought you left."

She chuckled and tossed the towel aside, sliding under the covers to pull Adriel close. Her body was warm and soft—safe and welcoming. "I'm not going anywhere, babe."

Adriel closed her eyes, breathing in the perfumed scent of the soap on Juniper's skin. Relief melted the knots of tension inside of her like butter left out on a hot day. Her entire being became soft and malleable just from having her arms around her.

Should she confess she was having such an extreme reaction to the intimacy they shared? Was this normal? She honestly didn't know if people discussed such things. She never knew anything could feel so incredibly…right.

Juniper's lips pressed to her shoulder. Time slowed as she simply held her like that. No one had ever—that Adriel could recall—nurtured her so affectionately. The more she thought about the absence of touch in her life the more her insides ached.

Her aimless touch teased lower, and tension

unraveled, swelling and waning like waves along the coast that built and then faded into softness. Her gentleness disarmed her as much as it unnerved her. Each little stroke was a lesson in trust and kindness. Like oxygen, Adriel breathed the comfort in, holding the intangible sensations for the briefest moment, then letting go and surrendering to the delicious pleasure.

"You have the softest skin," Juniper whispered, trailing her fingertips down Adriel's side. Tender caresses skated over her hip, swirling low on her stomach, and glided upward to trace her ribs.

Adriel laughed.

"Ticklish?"

Was she? No one had ever touched her so softly before, so she didn't know. "I suppose I am."

"Hmm, I wonder where else you're ticklish." She shifted between her legs, tugging Adriel closer as she grinned. "Let's find out."

A sharp, delightful whisp of pleasure chased up her spine as Juniper nuzzled her neck. Adriel's shoulders reflexively lifted as they both laughed. Soft lips teased the wing of her collarbone. Juniper watched her through thick lashes and violet eyes that hid dark promise in the depths.

Adriel stilled, the sole purpose of her entire existence now invested in seeing what she might do next.

"What about here?" Juniper whispered, kissing the slope of her shoulder. As she moved above her, the tips of her breasts dragged against Adriel's chest, teasing and titillating. "Or here?" Her fingers trailed low, past her hip, and lightly grazed her inner thigh. "Or maybe here."

She rolled her hips and their eyes met. Juniper held her stare, her knuckle dragging upward between her legs at a glacial pace. Time stood still.

The precipice of curiosity needled with excruciating wanting until she could take no more. "June..."

Juniper's mouth hooked into a playful grin, perfectly aware she was tormenting her. "Yes...?"

Adriel's throat tightened at her teasing tone. Emotion rolled through her like a landside, pushing words out of her mouth before she could call them back. "I never knew it could be like this. So soft and pleasant yet so...intense. I heard whispers, but I always assumed they were embellished."

Noting the tears in her eyes and the way her voice strained, Juniper sat up. "Hey, don't cry."

Embarrassed, Adriel wiped her eyes. "I'm sorry. I don't know what's come over me. It's as if you've loosened something that's been lodged in my chest for hundreds of years." She rubbed a hand over her heart where it hurt. "This is nothing like I imagined. Nothing like I remember."

"I'm as surprised as you are."

"Really?"

"Yeah. Before you... I mean, I was a kid.

Then..." Her stare skated away as if she didn't want to see those memories. "Last night wasn't planned, but it also wasn't a mistake. When I'm with you, I feel...safe, like everything is going to be all right." She laughed. "I sound like a Bob Marley song."

Adriel shook her head, not understanding the reference to modern music. "I never know what you mean when you reference music."

Juniper wiped away her tears and laid beside her, pulling her close and whispered, "Don't worry... about a thing... 'cause every little thing's gonna be all right."

Adriel turned to face her fully, her need growing as Juniper's soft breath fanned over her damp cheeks. Her confidence and self-assured autonomy was simply stunning. Combing a strand of hair away from her eyes, she smiled. "I think you're one of God's prettiest creations."

Her lashes lowered and she silently laughed. The spattering of freckles across her nose darkened as she blushed. "I've never been what anyone considers traditionally beautiful."

"You're not. That's what makes you so uniquely stunning, so...Juniper. You're strong yet fragile, brave yet cautious. When you want something, you go after it, and there's no telling you otherwi—"

Her words cut off as Juniper's mouth smashed to hers in a hard kiss. The pressure softened, and heat flooded her veins. It was such a passionate, life-affirming kiss, there was no mistaking her feelings and all of Adriel's were then validated.

The mind-melting kiss turned playful, awakening parts of Adriel that felt young and safe. That's what Juniper did when she touched her. She rewrote the cold, jaded parts with a sense of security that was new and delicate, bursting with hope.

There was no fear when Juniper pushed into her personal space. No pressure or demands. On the contrary, she seemed to bring a breath of fresh air and a burst of excitement. Adriel wanted to give her everything she asked for and more.

When Juniper kissed her, the world disappeared. It was only the two of them and loneliness seemed an impossible idea.

"I never want to leave this bed," Adriel confessed between long, drugging caresses.

Juniper's smile pressed against her skin. "Then we won't. We'll hire servants to bring us food and wait on our every need and never have to see anyone else ever again."

"Sounds perfect." She giggled—actually giggled as Juniper pressed a kiss to the sensitive curve of her neck. Adriel stretched out beneath her, surrendering to her desires.

She only ever touched her in ways that felt good. There was never any pain or adjustment. Just...decadence. Sometimes, the pleasure was so intense that her mind didn't know how to process all she felt.

Soft moans of delight whispered across her stomach as Juniper kissed lower. On a sigh, Adriel opened for her, still amazed that anything could feel so good.

"You're sweet, like a peach down here," Juniper said, stroking her finger slowly as she pressed an open-mouthed kiss between her thighs. "Warm on the inside, like you've been baking in the sun. Soft. Wet. Pink in the center." She licked. "Mmm. I could eat you forever and never get tired of the taste."

Adriel inhaled as her gentle touch slid slowly deeper. She closed her eyes as the pleasure carried her away. Every caress, every kiss, and every glance pulled her further under a potent spell only Juniper could weave.

Colors burst behind her eyes as emotion swirled inside of her. Waves of sensations spilled forward as muscles tightened and breathy cries broke the silence. When it ended and her body shivered, Juniper was there, holding her tight and kissing her once more.

A territorial thought crossed her mind, and possessiveness sharpened inside of her like a knife. "I don't want to share you."

Juniper laughed and kissed her shoulder. "I'm glad. I don't really like other people."

"I mean it, June. The thought of anyone else seeing you this way—"

"Hey." She caught her chin and made her look into her eyes. "This is only for you. Just you. Us."

Adriel grinned. *Us.* She liked the sound of

that. "What's going to happen to us when he comes back?"

Cerberus was always in the back of her mind and he wasn't going to go away. Juniper sighed and rolled onto her back. The intrusion shattering the beautiful moment so quickly Adriel regretted asking the question.

"When he comes back, we'll be prepared."

When, not if. At least they were on the same page. "He won't stay away for long, especially now that he's found us. I feel guilty lying here where there's so much we could be doing."

Juniper laced her fingers with hers and kissed her knuckle. "I think we needed this more."

Adriel agreed, but now the guilt and fear were seeping in. "What do you think our next move should be? We could keep moving—"

"I don't want to live a life in fear. And neither should you, Ade."

Cerberus had always been an indomitable force in her life. Mates were meant to be together. Escaping her fate was no easy task. She'd spent a lifetime evading him and avoiding punishment, but it wasn't natural for an immortal to fight their destiny. "I'm used to living in fear."

"Things are different now. You have me. I'll protect you."

Her devotion was sweet, but Juniper was still so young. She hadn't fully come into her powers. And she'd only just started feeding. Who knew what her immortal bloodlines would reveal?

"I could never live with myself if he hurt you."

"I feel the same."

If anything, life had taught Adriel just how resilient she could be. "He might hurt me, but he can't break me."

"We're all breakable, Ade, no matter how much we pretend or tell ourselves otherwise. There's only one way to ensure he doesn't hurt you again."

"We cannot try anything too dangerous. The thought of anything happening to you—"

"Hey." She caught her chin and forced her to meet her stare. "I'm strong. He might have gotten into my head for a moment, but as soon as I realized what he was doing, I forced him out. We got away."

"Hardly."

"So we got a few scratches. We're fine now. See?" She thumbed her chest and grinned. "Still here." She tapped a finger to her forehead. "Next time, I'll be more prepared. He has no idea how far I'd go to protect those I love. And love, is always more powerful than hate."

Her heart sputtered and she gasped. Did she realize what she said.

Juniper grinned. "What? You think we could get this close and stay dethatched? I can be just as territorial as you."

Adriel framed her face and pressed a kiss to her lips. "You know I love you too."

"I hope so. I nearly died for you."

They laughed, their new found happiness diluting the fear enough to forget that their lives were in danger for a moment. One kiss turned into another, and soon they found euphoria again.

The head and the heart were the holders of the soul and that was where Adriel felt Juniper's presence most when she touched her. She made her want things she never dreamed of having—made her believe happiness might be possible afterall.

CHAPTER 24

Ruth was having tea in the den and watching her morning shows while they gathered in the library to formulate a plan.

"We need to go after him before he comes after us," Dane insisted. "Now that we know exactly what we're dealing with, we can't hold anything back. Juniper, how's the research going? Have you made any headway."

"I'm no Gandalf yet, but I think I passed Disney fairy stage. Watch." She shoved her hands into the air and the table jerked three inches left.

Adriel pushed it back. "I don't want you or Juniper endangering yourselves on my account."

"We've been over this, Ade. If we try to handle him like a pack of pacifistic Amish, he's going to annihilate us. We have to fight."

"She's right," Dane agreed. "And we can't fight back. Defense starts at a disadvantage. We need to start on the offensive and go at him hard."

"Cerberus will not hesitate to kill both of you," she argued. "He knows we share a bond. He'll use it to hurt me."

"Can we die?" Dane asked, true curiosity in his eyes. "Seriously, what are the rules with half-breeds? And what about Juniper? Are witches mortal?"

"Juniper can burn herself with magic so I'd say she's far from invincible."

He pulled back his sleeve. "Well, my arm was mangled and I had cuts that should have taken weeks to heal, but a few drops of your blood and *boom*—I was good as new."

Juniper kept quiet, not wanting either of them to realize how much the magick actually drained her. There was still some lingering internal damage that Adriel's blood didn't heal. She wasn't sure if those internal scars would ever fully go away, but she also wasn't going to let such a mere concern work as an excuse to avoid Cerberus.

"I still think the wisest plan would be to relocate," Adriel argued.

"No," both she and Dane barked at once.

Dane stood and paced. "The other night, he had the element of surprise on his side. That's over now. I say we go after him like the buffalo rush the rain."

Both she and Adriel frowned. "I'm not sure I follow."

"Buffalo hate the rain," he explained. "When storms come, they have three choices: run away from it and keep running until it eventually wears them out and they get wet anyway, stand still and do nothing as they suffer through it, or run towards it. If they run toward the rain, they shorten their suffering. It's the fastest way to get through the unavoidable. And probably the least painful."

Juniper liked that plan, but could tell Adriel wasn't sold. "Cerberus is an inevitable conflict we'll eventually have to face, Ade. Why not confront him now and end this so you can have your life back?"

Adriel frowned. "Aren't buffalo extinct?"

"Endangered." Dane waved a hand at the stacks of books covering the table. "Juniper could do a locator spell so we know exactly where he is and then—"

"No. We are not delivering ourselves to him."

Juniper considered Dane's suggestion. Could she find Cerberus? She'd been able to locate Dane because she knew him. "I don't know if a locator spell will work."

"See," Adriel said with too much relief. "That plan won't work. It's too dangerous anyway."

"Then we need to find his weakness. What do you remember about him? There has to be something?"

Adriel shook her head. "No. He doesn't have a weakness."

"Everyone has a weakness, Ade."

"Not him. He's stronger than any immortal

I've ever come across. He's beyond vicious and he won't stop until he feels I've suffered for what we did to him centuries ago."

"Then he has to die—before he gets the chance to hurt you."

"He can't die."

"Everything can die."

Juniper shook her head. "She's right. As her mate, if we kill him, we risk also hurting Adriel. It's too dangerous."

Dane frowned. "You're saying your life is legitimately tied to his?"

Adriel nodded solemnly. "It's why they didn't kill him the first time. Mates often share pleasure and pain once they've bonded."

"Jesus," Dane cursed. "So, when they cut him up, you felt it?"

She frowned. "I was already in so much pain that I was in and out of consciousness. I can't fully recall the details of that night."

"Well, this complicates things."

Juniper pulled the oldest grimoire closer. "We're going to use magick. It's the only way to protect Adriel and see that he's disabled once and for all."

"June, that's too much pressure on you."

"No, it's not. I'm part immortal, remember? If I get a little banged up, we can fix it. Plus, I've got my witchy freak gene we've yet to identify. I'm a force to be reckoned with."

Dane rolled his eyes. "Let's not get too cocky."

"I'm not saying it to sound cocky. I feel more powerful than I've ever felt. There's something strong hiding inside of me."

"Yeah, it's called immortal blood. We all feel like that after we feed. Then it fades."

She shook her head. "No, this is something else."

Juniper hadn't told them about the presence of spirits she'd felt recently. Mostly because she wasn't sure if they'd believe her. Her aunts used to talk about ghosts, and it was the fastest way to clear a room. But now, Juniper believed they were telling the truth.

Spirits helped witches. They supercharged magical energy like no other element could. The more she welcomed their assistance, the easier it became to call upon them.

Some of the spirits were even developing personalities she recognized, sort of like auras that gave away secrets about their lives when they were living. Those secrets whispered to her through visions more than words, but Juniper was getting pretty good at reading the imagery they shared.

One spirit was burned. Another had indigenous roots that pre-dated the discovery of America. And one was a feisty Creole woman steeped in voodoo practices. Her name was Jacinta and she had been born and raised in Baton Rouge, Louisiana. She died hanging from a branch, and her last sight on Earth was the Mississippi River swaying under a sky full of stars.

They all had tragic endings, but none of them were evil spirits. If anything, they wanted to help her defend Adriel because they, too, had suffered unjustly in their lifetime.

"That may be true, but you would still be risking your life, June. It's too dangerous."

"We're already risking our lives by simply sitting here. Cerberus could strike at any moment, so the best plan is to be prepared. Dane's right. We need to consider his weaknesses and our personal strengths."

She understood Adriel was scared and did not want to jeopardize their safety, but their lives were already at stake. Juniper was not going to sit idly by while some deranged vampire fuck tormented her like this.

"Do I have a voice here?" Adriel asked, with notable irritation.

"Of course."

"Then why can't anyone hear me?"

"We hear you, Ade—"

"But you're not listening. I know him better than anyone. He has no weaknesses, and he won't stop until he has me. Then he'll hurt me. The fastest way to do that is by going after you two or my son."

"Adriel," Dane said calmly, "If that were true, you never would have escaped him the first time."

"It is true. He's done it before. He went back and slaughtered my siblings to punish me. We cannot underestimate his cruelty. And I only managed to get away the first time because I had the help of the elders. They're not helping anymore because they know there is no escaping an immortal's destined fate."

"Maybe they're just gone because they're a bunch of selfish assholes," Juniper mumbled. "And fuck them anyway. He's not your destiny."

Adriel sighed. "Your disdain for the elders can't alter my fate—"

"Because you won't let it! If you want a better life, Adriel, you have to fight for it. You can't just passively wish things will change."

"Okay, okay." Dane stepped between them. "Let's all take a breath. We're on the same side."

Adriel scowled, and she wouldn't meet her eyes. Juniper understood confrontation wasn't her forte, but doing nothing wasn't an option. She continued to brainstorm possible soft spots in Cerberus's defenses. Even Achilles had a heel that left him unprotected.

"What about his DNA?" she asked. "There was something different about his fangs."

"I saw that, too." Dane nodded. "They weren't like ours. They reminded me of a python."

Adriel frowned. "We all have different teeth. Dane's fangs are shorter than mine. And June's are thinner when they extend. What does it matter?"

"Ours are different because we're half-breeds."

Juniper frowned. "We're certain he's a pure-bred, right?"

"Only purebred immortals can be called."

She hated every reminder that this psycho was Adriel's mate and somehow part of her soul.

"We could test his blood," Dane suggested. "That's how the bishop found out what was in my DNA."

"What are we supposed to do, roll up with a Red Cross bus in the middle of a fucking war? Come on, Dane. You saw what he's like. We can't get near him."

"Gandalf could do it," Dane mumbled as he paced to the bookcase. Cocking his head, he examined the numerous spines.

"Are you looking for something?"

He grunted and moved to the small desk tucked in the corner, where he rifled through old bills and papers stashed in the drawers.

Juniper frowned and looked at Adriel. "I know you're scared, but I believe in us. We can do this."

Dane moved to the window.

Juniper ignored him and focused on convincing Adriel. "I'm working on some new spells with fire." The curtains opened, bathing the study in a distractingly bright light. "Dane, what are you doing?"

Rather than answer, he just stared out the window.

"Dane?" Juniper went to his side but saw nothing out of the ordinary. "Hey, earth to Dane." She snapped her fingers in his face, and he jolted. "Huh?"

"What are you doing? You were just staring like a zombie."

"I...I don't know. I was looking for something."

"Landmarks," Adriel whispered, and the hairs on Juniper's neck stood up. "That's how he must have found us before. He's getting into our heads."

A wave of panic rushed through Juniper. "There must be a tear in the protection spell."

Adriel rushed to the bow window and yanked the curtains shut. "I found myself doing the same thing the other day." She clutched her throat and paled. "He's going to find us."

Juniper mentally checked the spell and frowned. "It has to be something else. Everything's intact. There's no breach."

"He already did it once with me when you were unconscious," Adriel argued, her body tense and her voice high-pitched with panic. "He must have found a loophole."

"No, I checked. It's like Fort Knox up here." Juniper pointed to her skull.

"How do you hold the spell while you sleep?" Dane shaded his eyes and focused only on the floor.

Juniper shrugged. "I sort of set it like a watch. But I can tell when someone breaks through."

"Some immortals are travelers." Adriel's voice fell quiet. "They latch on to a host and can co-exist inside of their mind for decades undetected."

Dane curled his lip. "Like a parasite?"

"Exactly." Adriel shook her head. "He was always private about his disciplines. He could have hidden such a thing from me. I was young and knew very little back then."

A sense of paranoia drifted through the room like a draft of noxious gas. "Everyone stay away from the windows until we figure this out." Juniper paged through the grimoires, searching for any reference to such things.

"How do they get in?" Dane asked.

"I'm not sure. It's a very rare discipline."

"Ugh, I feel so…violated." Dane scrubbed his head as if it were infested with lice. "What if he's inside of me right now? How do I get him out?"

"I'm looking. Let me concentrate!" Juniper blocked out their questions and focused on finding some actual answers. "I found something."

She turned the book because the page had more hand-drawn illustrations than words. It depicted a physical body entering the mind of another.

"What's that say?" Dane pointed to the inscription at the top of the page.

"*Fantasi theid.* It means thief of imagination. They commandeer other people's visions and can even alter their thoughts. I think he was doing it to me on the mountain. I was completely paranoid with crippling anxiety, but it wasn't me thinking those things. As soon as I realized it was him, I pushed him out."

"How?"

Juniper shrugged. "I don't know. I just…did." She hunched over the book, her finger dragging down the inscription as she mumbled through the spell written in tongues. "Okay, both of you sit down and shut your eyes. Try to clear your minds."

They did as she said, with two very different results.

"Adriel, your aura's literally buzzing with cognitive activity. You need to push everything out so I can find any unwanted presence and block it."

"I'm picturing a black room," Dane said, eyes closed. "Do me first."

Juniper placed her hands on his head and whispered the words of the incantation. The spirits rushed toward her in a wave that let her know they were there and a low humming started in her ear, as if they were also whispering the spell from a different plane. Dane swayed and grunted. His body shook subtly then she found something—a shadow that seemed to cloak his frontal lobe.

He jerked as she latched onto the presence. Her voice grew louder, as did the buzzing in her ears. Invisible hands pressed into her back and shoulders, encouraging and lending strength.

Dane's body shook violently as if electricity were rushing through her.

"Are you hurting him?"

Juniper kept her focus, reciting the spell to completion and not taking her mental hold off of that shadow. Her eyes closed, and she imagined it shrinking away, much like a puddle dries up in the sun. The buzzing escalated into a roar, and then there was a strange *vip,* and all was silent.

Panting, she released Dane's head, and he collapsed to the floor. Adriel gasped and rushed to his side. "Dane! Look at me, Dane. Can you hear me?"

He groaned and rubbed his head, sounding as if he were about to be ill. Adriel helped him sit up and steadied him as he swayed. "That was… *Ugh.* I'd like to never do that again."

Adriel looked up at Juniper with wide eyes. "I don't want that."

The whispers hissed behind her like rushing water, muffling Adriel and Dane's words. She frowned at the strange tinnitus. "Would you rather have Cerberus in your mind?"

Adriel shrank a little. "No."

"I'll be as gentle as I can." She needed to finish this before she lost her strength and the chatter in her head got any louder. "Clear your mind so I can do it quickly."

Adriel nodded and sat in the chair, folding her hands in her lap. Her body was tense, and her eyes shut tight. "Do it."

Loathe to hurt her, Juniper reluctantly placed her hands on either side of her skull. Her energy slammed into a hard, sonar-like wall.

"What the…?"

"Is something wrong?"

"Your mind's completely blocked to me. I can't get past whatever barrier you're using." Perhaps they weren't ready for this level of trust. Some secrets should stay private. But this was the only way Juniper knew how to check if Cerberus was in Adriel's head. "Can you let me in?"

"I'm trying."

If she was trying, there should have been a crack or a slit of light—some sort of opening to push through, but it was all blocked.

"I'm only looking for signs of a trespasser. I'll be quick—just long enough to locate any unwanted presence and push it out."

Divots formed in Adriel's brow as she concentrated harder, her eyes still pinched shut.

Juniper adjusted her hands on her head. "You're still blocking me."

"I need time. I'm old. I've been blocking my thoughts for centuries. I'm not as malleable as I once was." Her face strained with concentration. "There."

Juniper located the slight crack and pressed into her mind. She expected similar traces of the shadow she saw in Dane's head, but that was not at all what she found.

There was no preparing for the savage reality she discovered in Adriel's mind, and as unbiased as she tried to be, it startled her into sharp judgment. Not the critical kind, but the terrified, survival kind. He was there. Everywhere. Scars of his presence ate up the terrain of her mind in ways Juniper didn't understand.

Was this what mating did when immortals shared a bond? He was embedded in her like a disease.

"Did you find anything?"

"Still looking." She concentrated on following the tattered thread of her psyche, ignoring everything else and dragging her touch back to the part of the brain that hid behind the left ear where the frayed edges of her memories began. The whispers in Juniper's mind went quiet and all she could hear were voices from another time.

A beautiful woman carried a basket and spoke in a language Juniper didn't recognize. There was a village. Huts freckled the land, constructed of mud, stone walls, and thatched roofs. A man with dark hair and piercing eyes took the basket from the female. She looked like Adriel.

Her parents. They were her parents.

Juniper repeated the incantation, pushing further into her mind. If she could find the first intrusion of his presence, she might also discover one of his weaknesses. Anything to help them better understand his motives would be in their favor.

She sensed the slightest incidence of him in Adriel's mind when she was only a young girl—thirteen, possibly fourteen years old. Then several long winters passed in waiting.

Her memories were tarnished by time but also blurred as if she intentionally tried to smudge them out. A dark murky haze disguised her girlish excitement as she waited through long bouts of anticipation for her mate to come.

Then, his physical presence pierced the time-line like an ice pick.

"Get up, girl."

That merciless voice sent shivers down Juniper's spine as she recognized his evil. Adriel's remembered fear added to her own as she watched the memory unfold. She'd been right-fully nervous but for all the wrong reasons. The young girl believed he was good and would love and protect her.

The hope and relief she experienced when he awoke her in her childhood bed contrasted harshly with the cruel reality that followed. Ripped from her home and plunged into the cold, dark night, he took her without a single show of affection. He denied her the chance to say goodbye to her family, and when she cried, her tears were met with harsh censure and threats.

Then came the truth of who he was, how he was, and the bottomless brutality that defined all he would ever be. Her innocence was shattered in every way possible and Juniper suffered through the memories as she searched for more traces of him. But Adriel's disappointment was the most unbearable of all, far worse than the memory of the pain.

She'd been so pure and full of hope. The little girl in her dreamed of bein a good partner, deserving of her mate's love. She'd done everything she could to please him, but all of her kindness was met with brutal cruelty and he slowly broke her down until the last of her hope fell away.

He truly was incapable of love. Love didn't lash out. Love didn't hit. Love didn't lie. Love didn't manipulate or harm.

He was a monster.

The mental lashes kept mounting, and the beatings never waned. The years they spent together were bleak. A barren wasteland of servitude and inescapable abuse. It wore on Juniper more than the actual use of magick did, and she wished she could pull out of the nightmare, but there seemed to be no escape in sight.

Speeding ahead, Juniper waited for the suffering to end, but it went on and on. Adriel's loss. Her infinite grief. It was incomprehensible how anyone could be so cold and cruel to someone so innocent.

Juniper couldn't stomach the full extent of his abuse, so she skimmed as much as possible. These were ugly little secrets, and Adriel deserved privacy. The physical abuses were gutting, but they were nothing compared to the mental scars.

Young Adriel tried to fight him, tried to stand up to him, but he taught her an unforgettable lesson about the cost of courage. The fucker went back and killed her siblings, bringing her trinkets of them for proof. She accepted defeat the day he gifted her with her youngest brother's severed head. After that, she lived a life of barren resignation and pain.

The fucker broke her every which way a female could be broken, leaving nothing but cold, hollow fear. Adriel existed in a state of crippling tension, never knowing what would trigger his fury.

Her needs meant nothing to him. He used her body like a slave in every possible way. He owned her so profoundly that she lost sight of herself.

And when her cycle was late and she learned a baby lived inside of her, she feared she'd done something wrong. She worried he'd cut it out of her or, worse, let it grow and fill her arms so he had one more thing to rip away.

Her protectiveness for her son sparked a willingness to survive. She hid her body and never told him she was with child. It was during that time that she met an accidental friend.

The Bishop. Juniper recognized him right away. Immortals were handy like that, other than their clothes and style of dress, they never changed.

Eleazar tried to help Adriel, but when Cerberus discovered another immortal male's presence in her life, he punished her dearly. The second time the Bishop tried to help her, he was better prepared.

As she said, she'd been badly injured and barely conscious. Only little glimpses of her rescue lived in her mind. The sounds of Cerberus's screams. The smashing of wood and shattering of glass. The feel of gentle arms scooping her off the ground and the startling sensation of safety after an eternity of vicious cruelty. She struggled, afraid and distrustful for good reason. But then she was on a boat in a bed, making a long voyage to a new world.

Juniper hardly recognized the undeveloped land as the farm The Order chose but saw the memories of barns and houses being built as they settled. Adriel's loneliness grew as her waistline expanded. The males of The Order rescued her, but they also condemned her.

Mates were locked at the soul. For her to anger Cerberus to such a degree... They all believed Cerberus's abuse was somehow caused by her actions, which it had never been.

When Christian was born, she pushed for him to have a seat on the council and as soon as he came of age, the Bishop took him under his wing. Then, she was left alone—for centuries.

Juniper's heart broke. How could anyone survive such endless isolation?

The despair was too much. The hopeless acceptance that this was all she deserved made Juniper want to hold her and convince her she was owed so much more.

When she reached the presence, she found only traces of Cerberus in her mind, but he was not there now. She looked again and again, but only found traces of pain in his wake. He existed in the scars. Her memories draped like torn lace and wilted cobwebs all throughout her mind, casting shadows like permanent tattoos that she would probably always wear.

Juniper lowered her hands, fighting hard not to shed a single tear.

Adriel's eyes opened, and she looked up at her with the same familiar innocence she had as a girl. "Is he gone?"

Feeling like a failure, she looked away. "I couldn't find him."

"Well, that's good, right?"

"I don't know." Unlike the fatigue she usually felt from magick, she now only felt discouraged, drained to the point of emotional bankruptcy. Depleted.

Sad.

Adriel read it in her eyes. "What's wrong? You saw something. Tell me."

She didn't know what to say. She could confess how much she initially downplayed the level of abuse she experienced. When Adriel told her how awful her mate was, Juniper had listened but she hadn't truly understood. Not by a long shot.

She'd been unprepared for such raw memories. No resolution. No knight in shining armor. No magic apples or fairy godmothers or any of that other bullshit kids are shown to believe good will always triumph over evil. It was just... bleak.

She cleared her throat. "Your mind is different from Dane's. He's been there several times, but…"

Perhaps it was the mating that made her psyche so complex. She wished she never saw those tender scars. She didn't want to pity her, yet she couldn't shut off her sympathy.

Adriel drew back in offense, likely smelling her emotions as immortals so annoyingly tended to do. "You said you were only looking for a presence."

"I was."

"Then why are you looking at me like that now, with regret?"

She was so worn out and tired, she didn't have the fortitude to argue or even the cognitive strength to explain what she saw—at least not gently.

"He's everywhere, Adriel. I was honestly only searching for his presence, but he's ingrained in you."

She stiffened and Juniper honestly didn't know if that level of entrenchment might also trigger some bizarre protectiveness. If that was how deeply mates rooted in each other's minds, maybe they really were fucked.

"What did you see?" Adriel's stare hardened as she waited for an explanation with unflinching stoicism.

Juniper shook her head, feeling small and far too attached to her. "It was a lot." She swallowed. "I…" A tear rolled down her cheek.

"Don't. Don't you dare shed a tear out of pity

for me." She shot to her feet. "You had no right to rifle through my memories."

Upset she'd unintentionally hurt her, another tear fell. "Ade, I didn't do it on purpose. I swear, I was only trying to sniff him out."

"And now you see how deeply embedded he is?" She scoffed and looked away. "What you must think of me."

"What? No." Juniper grabbed her arm. "None of that was your fault."

Adriel turned her face away, her eyes closing in shame as she pursed her lips. Her hands tightened into fists. "I had no one. I was young and foolish."

"You *survived*," Juniper explained. "That's all that matters now. You did whatever you could to survive and save your son. And here you are... living."

Adriel nodded tightly. "Yes."

Juniper slipped her hand into hers and squeezed. "Please forgive me. I didn't mean to violate your trust."

She dashed away her tears. "There's nothing to forgive. You were only trying to help. This is who am. Now you know."

That was not who she was. Those hideous memories were only part of her. Scars. She was a victim. That was it. An innocent child who was somehow mated to a monster.

The experience of seeing Adriel's memories bothered Juniper more than she could admit. Dane said mates were supposed to be two halves of one soul. Yet Cerberus's presence seemed very surface, up until he physically punctured her life, implanting himself in the whole of her new reality until he alone consumed her entire mind.

That felt very different from the romanticized crap she'd been told. But without seeing the topography of another mated immortal's mind, she had no basis for comparison and no real data to make sense of what she saw.

Which led her to only wanting to forget it. She needed to erase the visions of Cerberus attacking Adriel, hitting her, and holding her down. Just as Adriel had tried to snuff out the memories, Juniper now tried to do the same.

They needed a break.

"Dane why don't you make some food. Adriel, can you check on Ruth?"

"What are you going to do?" Dane asked.

"Rest. I'm tired from the spell and I need to shut my eyes for a few minutes." It wasn't the whole truth, but it was enough that they both backed off and left her alone.

Juniper laid on the sofa and covered her eyes, but that made the memories worse. She saw them no matter where she looked. No distraction seemed powerful enough to silence the past as it blared at her from all directions.

She remained in the library long after dark. Dane and Adriel had checked on her a few times but, for the most part, left her alone. She appreciated the privacy, needing time to process. Accepting the headache wasn't going to fade, she returned to her books, specifically searching for any information about fated mates.

"You're still working?"

She glanced up from her books and found Adriel standing in the doorway. "I haven't gotten very far."

"It's been hours."

She sat back, her body stiff and aching from staying in the same position too long. "There's a lot here. Sometimes I have to read an entry five times before it sinks in."

"Your mind needs a break, June."

She'd tried resting, but when she closed her eyes, she was haunted by visions of that psycho hurting Adriel. "I'll rest when he's dead."

"Don't say that." She stepped into the study and closed the door. "I've thought about what Dane suggested."

"And?"

"I'm putting my foot down."

"Ade—"

"No. You cannot ask this of me. I have lived through more than any person should, and I have a right to decide what I want for myself. I was helpless up on that cliff."

"We were under prepared."

"We will never be prepared, Juniper. You and Dane nearly died."

"But we didn't. That's won't happen again."

"You can't guarantee that."

"I can. See all this?" She shoved her hands toward the stacks of books. "This is me preparing.

I've set spells to help me absorb as much information as possible. My mind is open—"

"You just admitted that you were struggling."

"I'm tired. That's all. I haven't eaten. Maybe I need more blood. But those aren't reasons to give up." Didn't she realize she was more than enough reason to keep going. "I can't walk away, Adriel. Not now."

"This isn't your choice."

"It is. I'm choosing to fight for you and stand by your side. I'm sorry if that scares you, but that's… That's what love is. If it happens to one of us, it happens to both of us, and that sick fuck isn't getting near you again—not while I'm guarding you."

"You're young, Juniper. Arrogance is often the result of foolish youth."

"Don't patronize me. I'm not a fool, and I'm perfectly aware of what I'm risking."

"It took a band of male immortals to take him down the first time. I know your magick is getting stronger, but you have to think about this logically, up here." She pointed to her head. "You cannot let your heart lead. Not in this."

Juniper rejected such nonsense. "I love you. Maybe you don't get what that truly means, but I do. I'm not leaving you unprotected. We do that and he will *absolutely* win. I'm sorry if that's too much for you or too fast. But it's how I feel. Even if it ruins everything we have together, right now, I refuse to let you face him alone." Her hand splayed on her chest, where her heart still felt broken from the cruel visions she experienced earlier. "That's what real love does."

"I can't bear this!" Adriel snapped, turning away. "You're giving me no choice in the matter. Why do you get to protect me, but I cannot protect you?"

"I'm not trying to take your choice away. I'm trying to save your life."

She dropped her face into her hands and sat down. "What if I can't be saved?"

Juniper sat next to her, tucking her hair behind her ear as she pried her hands away from her face. "I hate seeing you cry." She dashed away a tear and kissed her damp cheek. "Maybe none of us can be saved, but I know without a doubt that you're worth saving."

"I just want to be someone else. I want a normal life that's peaceful and calm. I've been running and hiding for centuries, yet I've never truly escaped him or gotten away."

Juniper brushed away her tears and looked into her eyes, her fingers running softly through her copper hair. "I can take you away. Before you shake your head no, let me show you." She smiled, and slipped her hands into hers. "Don't let go." She closed her eyes and concentrated. *"Intuitum mentista et locum exoticum droc liberum deduc nos—fiat."*

The air buzzed and birds chortled in the distance. The gentle hiss of insects softened the air around them as the room transformed with lush green vines and sultry heat.

"Open your eyes."

Adriel lifted her lashes and gasped. "How…?"

Macaws screeched overhead as smaller birds chirped on lower limbs. A chimp caterwauled, and frogs croaked as other reptiles raced about the underbrush, hissing and striking prey from the ferns. Gone were the bookshelves and windows.

Adriel looked up at the canopy of trees. "Is this place real?"

"It's the Indo-Burma rainforest. Or at least what I remember of it. I did a school project on it in ninth grade."

"This lives in your memory?"

"I guess." Now understanding what lived in hers, she felt a sting of gratitude for having such a unique sanctuary on tap. "Now it can live in yours. Look." She sent a kaleidoscope of butterflies rushing past them, and Adriel laughed.

"It's stunning."

Juniper brushed her thumb over her hand. "It's just a parlor trick. But it shows you how much my magick's improved." The vision faded and the library gradually reappeared. The noise of the jungle vanished with the buffeted silence encompassing pages and pages of books.

Juniper met her stare. They were at a stalemate.

"We can beat him, Adriel. You have to have faith."

"Faith has done nothing to save me."

"I don't mean faith in a faceless god. I mean

faith in me—have faith in me, in our love. There is nothing you can do or say to make me stop protecting you, Adriel, so you might as well accept it and help me. We have enough obstacles to overcome. There's no reason for us to create more."

She sighed. "You're very stubborn when you want to be."

Juniper kissed her head. "So are you. It's why we get along so well."

Adriel's eyes creased with concern as she shook her head. "These past few weeks have changed me, Juniper. I need you to know that."

"Me too."

Adriel caressed her cheek and smiled, but sorrow remained banked in her eyes. "I never knew what it was to be loved—truly loved—by someone who only wanted the best for me. Nor did I understand what it was to want the same for them." She laughed. "You'd think it would feel more pleasant, but it's a relentless torment to care so deeply for someone dead set on endangering themselves."

"Love is a constant balance of putting other people's safety, comfort, and happiness before our own. But when we're in a relationship with someone who loves us equally and respects us, all of those drained areas are somehow refilled. I take care of you, and you take care of me, just as love should be."

Adriel placed a hand on her face and softly kissed her lips. "Thank you for teaching me what love is meant to be. If I hadn't met you… I never would have known."

"Adriel, this might be a messy start but this is not how it ends."

She smiled sadly. "I hope you're right."

"I am. Faith, remember?"

"I'm so tired of this life and what he's made me."

Juniper kissed her cheek. "Get some sleep. I'll be up in a little bit. I just want to finish reading and make a few notes."

It took longer than expected to actually pull herself away from her research. By the time she made it upstairs, the sky was a soft shade of grey with the glow of the approaching dawn. Apart from the muted haze drifting through curtains, Adriel's room was dark.

"*Ignisia.*" The candle on the dresser lit, and Juniper silently stripped out of her sweater, her eyes adapting to the shadows. Toeing off her shoes, she turned and—

"Adriel?"

Panic spiked her heart rate, and her stomach plummeted. The bed was empty, not a single pillow disturbed. "Fuck!"

She raced to the bathroom but it was also empty. Rushing upstairs, she prayed Adriel was in her bed sound asleep, but as soon as she opened the door, she knew. The air held no trace of her scent and the room was as silent as a tomb.

"Dane!" She sprinted down the steps and

burst into Dane's room, shaking him awake. "Dane, get up!"

"What?" He jackknifed out of bed. "What's wrong?"

"I can't find Adriel! She's gone!"

He scrambled to his feet. "What do you mean gone?"

"I don't know! She's not here!"

They tore the house apart, searching every room, but she was nowhere to be found. "There's no sign of a struggle. Are we sure she didn't just go somewhere?"

"She would have told us. She never leaves without saying something."

"Check the basement. I'll check her room again."

Juniper rushed to the cellar, checking every closet and crawlspace along the way. She was gone. She woke Ruth, but she hadn't seen her. There was no indication of where she might have gone.

"She's not here," Dane said when Juniper returned to Adriel's empty room.

"Someone doesn't just vanish into thin air—"

"She didn't." He held out a small piece of paper. "Here. I think this is for you. I found it on the pillow."

Her heart stopped. Nothing inside of her wanted to read what that letter said. Her head shook, refusing to take it from his hand.

"Read it, Juniper."

The way he said that made her fear it all the

more. That cold little letter could only mean one thing. She was leaving her.

"I don't want to."

He grabbed her hand and stuffed the note into her palm. "You have to."

Snatching her arm back, she growled at him. He was right, of course, but that didn't make this any easier.

Her fingers shook as she uncrumpled the paper. Sorrow morphed into anger, as the words blurred across the page.

June,

PLEASE DO NOT HATE ME. My heart simply could not bear the thought of anything happening to you or Dane.

YOU ASKED me to have faith in you, and I do. I have faith that you will recover from this and forget me. I have faith that you will one day love again. I have faith that you will find true happiness because that is everything you deserve.

YOU SHOWED me what love means, and I love you enough to let you go. It's my turn to protect you. My turn to love you the way you deserve. If you love me back, as you say, you must do the same and let me go.

Do not try to locate me. I do not wish to be found. You need to make a beautiful life for yourself. I'm sorry I could not give it to you. Do not waste your heart on someone like me.

WITH ALL OF MY LOVE,
   Adriel

THE LETTER FLUTTERED to the floor, and Juniper's heart crumbled with it. She was gone.

CHAPTER 25

*B*itter wind cut through the stone passageway as Darius pushed open the door. The night air smelled of snow. He predicted several inches by morning. If he wanted to leave, he had to go before his brothers could track him.

Adjusting his pack, he checked his gear one last time. Traveling in wolf form would be easier, but there could be no shape-shifting on this journey. When they were lupine, they were one, and if he shifted, his brothers would track him through their shared mental link. They might even find his mate first.

He couldn't let that happen.

Since the first ripple of awareness, he sensed her sorrow. She was alone and frightened. He tried to connect but something blocked his efforts. It was as if her mind was locked, not just from him, but the world. If he desired to speak to her, to fully understand what had weighed so heavily on her heart, he needed to do so face-to-face.

Looking back one last time, he sighed. His pack might never welcome him back after this. He was knowingly disobeying his alpha's orders to do what he, in his heart, felt was right. It was a choice he needed to make.

Was he compromising his loyalty to the pack? Probably. As brothers, they shared unbreakable vows, but what choice did they leave him?

Once Evander forbade Darius to look for her, he left no other option but to gamble the pack's trust. Darius would simply have to repent and prove his loyalty once he returned, which he had every intention of doing as soon as he claimed his mate.

Crossing the threshold, he entered the dark night and began his long journey. The Scandinavian forest stood still under the cold, piercing gaze of the moon. The branches of the ancient trees twisted like the fingers of forgotten gods, looming over the landscape and casting elongated shadows on the frost-covered ground.

The wind howled through the night, a mournful symphony that echoed the despair in Darius's heart. It had been several days since he'd caught a glimpse of his mate's mind. It was as if all the visions were deliberately cut off to purposely hide herself from him.

He tried not to lose his temper to assumptions that fed into distrust. She would explain her secrecy once he found her, and they would address her concerns together, as one.

He trudged through the dense forest, his senses sharp, his muscles taut with determination and desperation. After miles of trekking through the cold, damp night, he began to panic, never feeling any closer to his cause. His steps were aimless as he wandered like a lost drifter, unsure where to go.

Finding his mate was not just a matter of survival. It was a sacred duty, a bond that would ensure the continuation of their line. Yet, despite his efforts, she remained hidden, her mind blocked to him like a ghostly presence he could neither see nor touch.

Shadow-wolves had once thrived, their powerful bloodlines allowing them to live for millennia. But now, they were endangered, their numbers dwindling due to their mates' elusiveness.

As a member of the Lycaon tribe, his lineage was steeped in the legends. He opened his mind in hopes that his intuition and blessed bloodlines would guide him. Darius wasn't one to pray often, but moments of desperation called for desperate measures.

He stopped in a small clearing, the moonlight illuminating the frost blanketing the ground. Dropping to his knees, the weight of his responsibility to his kin pressed heavily into his shoulders. The expectations of his pack, his brother's lack of faith, and the fear of failure bore down on him with crippling pressure.

The icy wind bit into his skin as he opened his coat and shirt, but he welcomed the pain. It sharpened his resolve, fueling the ancient fire within him. With a steady hand, he drew an athame blade from his belt.

The blade was an heirloom, passed down through generations, its steel etched with runes of power and protection. The edge gleamed in the moonlight as he held it over his heart, the point pressing against his chest.

Taking a deep breath, he steeled himself and plunged the blade into his flesh, mimicking the lethal wound passed from father to son in the ancient history that defined his bloodline.

Grunting at the burning pain, he suffered through the blood sacrifice, knowing it was the only hope of righting his path. His sacred offering welled around the blade's tip, and his body shook. Gritting his teeth, he plunged the knife deeper, then pulled the athame free, cupping his hands to catch the blood as it trickled down his rigid abdomen, through his fingers, and onto the snow.

The stark contrast of his heated life source warmed his hands against the biting cold, a vivid reminder of his mortality. Holding out his hands, trickles of crimson followed the ropes of muscle twisting his arms, dripping onto the large leaf he plucked from a nearby tree.

The dry edges of the leaf were already

crimped with time. He hoped it held enough life to act as the offering he needed. It was a known truth that gods liked some sort of sacrifice for their favors, and he desperately needed their help now.

Drops of his sacred blood trickled from his cupped palms onto the leaf. "Hear my plea," he whispered, his voice raw with emotion, as he addressed the gods. "Guide me to my mate. Do not let our lineage fade into the shadows of history. I beg of you, show me the way. I sense great sorrow in her. Help me find her so that our union might honor you."

The wind pulled from the trees as if the branches inhaled to hold the forest's breath. He knelt in reverence to his prayer, eyes closed, blood spilling in sacrifice, and his heart seeking sanctions of the gods.

Minutes passed, or perhaps hours—it was impossible to tell. Then, as if in answer to his desperate prayer, the gurgling caw of a raven squawked overhead.

Eyes open, he looked to the sky as a vision shaped his mind. There she was. Her face remained blurry, but her presence was unmistakable.

She stood at the edge of a cliff, the sea crashing against the rocks far below, the wind whipping her hair around her face. The location was familiar, a place he had seen in dreams but never in waking life. It was a place tied to his lineage, a place of power.

He gasped, the vision fading but leaving behind a sense of purpose. The vision acted as a compass, guiding his heart in the direction he needed to go. She was out there. But there was no mistaking the ominous weight of what he saw. She was scared and in some sort of danger.

He needed to save her from whatever it was she feared. If her life was in danger, he needed to end whatever made it so.

His pack would not forgive him if he failed. They might not forgive him for hunting her alone. But his instincts had guided him correctly. She faced a great danger, and Darius could not risk another minute of waiting.

As her mate, he would lay down his life for hers if the gods willed it so. She was to be his, and he was therefore hers. One flesh, one heart, and one soul until the end of time.

CHAPTER 26

"Go away," Juniper groaned when Dane knocked for the twentieth time.

"I know you don't want to be bothered, but you didn't touch your breakfast or your lunch and it's now dinner."

"Not hungry." She pulled a pillow over her head.

"Juniper, there are a lot of things—I'm sensing—that you and Adriel didn't tell me. I can't force it out of you, but could you at least just…talk to me? I don't understand what happened?"

He wasn't going to leave her alone. Tossing her pillow aside, she huffed, "Come in."

The door creaked, and Dane's heavy footsteps ascended the narrow attic steps. "Can I turn on a light?"

She flicked her hand, and the candles lit. "I don't feel like talking."

"At least tell me what you're feeling."

Hurt. Angry. Sad. Betrayed. Scared. Alone. She could have said any of those words, but instead, she asked, "Do you hate Grace?"

"What? No. I mean, she pisses me off, and she's as stubborn as a mule, but I get it."

"You *get* it?" Juniper sat up, her eyes narrowing in disbelief. "You're just gonna accept that she doesn't love you."

"On some level, I think she does, even if it's just as a friend."

She scoffed. "That's worse."

"How is that worse?"

"Because it's unrequited love. You love her, she loves you, you've both decided to suffer." She flung out her hands in defeat and let them flop to her lap. "Neato."

He frowned. "What was going on between you two, June? I get that you're upset about Adriel leaving, but... Are you honestly that surprised? She's an immortal. Immortals are the most self-serving species on the planet."

"You read the letter—"

"No, I didn't."

She didn't believe him. "Oh, come on. You found it first and it wasn't sealed."

"So? It had your name on it."

"You aren't seriously that honest."

"Do I look dishonest?"

Her mouth twisted. "You robbed the tabernacle of a church."

"One time! And I was starving. Churches are supposed to help the needy." He shrugged.

"You guys found me and gave me a place to live. I'm not going to repay your kindness by betraying your trust or violating your privacy."

Her anger deflated in the face of his calm-headedness. "You're way nicer than me."

"Well, no offense, but you don't set the bar real high."

She gaped at him and shoved him off the bed. "Jerk."

He laughed and sat back down. "I'm just kidding. You can be sweet when you want to."

Her lip curled. Could she? Maybe her bitter attitude influenced Adriel's decision to leave. "You honestly think I'm sweet?"

"Not all the time, but I definitely think you pretend to be tougher than you are. It's a defense mechanism."

"Maybe."

He studied her for a long moment. "June, did you and Adriel have a fight?"

"Quite the opposite."

"What does that mean?"

She met his stare.

Too many emotions came to the surface. It was impossible to pick even one. She felt so much in regard to Adriel, explaining it seemed impossible. She wished there was a way to diminish her feelings. Maybe then she'd have better luck managing them.

Adriel thought leaving would fix everything. But Juniper still loved her. She still planned to protect her. It was just going to be way more complicated to do so now.

"I'm furious with her!"

He rubbed a hand down her back. "I'm sure she had her reasons for leaving."

That lump in her throat grew until she could barely breathe around it. What if *she* was the reason? She'd been trying so hard to protect her, she smothered her, and now she ran away. "I'm Lenny from *Of Mice and Men*." The sob came out of nowhere, as did the tears. "Why do I complicate everything? I should have just run away with her like she wanted. It wasn't a good plan, but at least we could have stayed together. Now, she's all by herself out there. How is that safer?"

He cautiously patted her back. "Maybe she'll come back."

She shook her head and wiped her nose. "She's not coming back."

"Well, she can't run forever. Don't forget, I wasn't on board with that plan either. You're being too hard on yourself."

"She knows that too. That's why she…" Oh, God, it was all clear. She was sacrificing herself to end this. Panic welled inside of Juniper. A sense of impotent urgency made her heart ache as if a knife twisted into her back. "How could she choose this?"

"I don't think she chose anything, June. I think she's just trying to—"

"Don't you get it, Dane? She'll run until he catches her. Then—" She choked on another sob.

"Then she plans to... She plans...." Her words would not come out. She couldn't say what she knew Adriel intended because then it would be real.

"What does she plan?"

Swallowing past the lump in her throat, she shook her head. "This isn't going to end well."

When she didn't say more, he frowned. Then he reached for the letter on the nightstand and opened it.

"Oh, shit." The paper folded, and he gaped at her. "You love her? Like...*that*?" He shook his head and scoffed. "I see it now. The way you two looked at each other. How protective you were of her. Not wanting her to take anyone else's vein. How long has this been going on?"

She sniffled and whipped her nose. "Not long. But it was the realest thing I've ever felt." She looked up at him with tearful eyes. "I wanted to protect her."

He reached for her hand, understanding reflecting in his gaze. "I get that."

She wiped her nose. "And now I can't."

"That's not true."

"I don't know where she is, Dane. And she doesn't want to be found."

"You don't have to know where she is. You just have to find him before he finds her."

Her tears stopped. He was right. Adriel might have run, but they could still proceed with their plan.

"She didn't run because of anything you did,

June. She ran because her entire life has left her powerless, and she's afraid."

She lowered her gaze, shame blanketing her. "I know." She believed she was doing what she thought was best by selflessly removing them from the entire situation, but Juniper's heart was still very much involved, and now her hands were tied. "She knows she can't beat him on her own."

"Adriel's incredibly strong. I've watched her stand up to immortals twice her size on the farm. Don't underestimate her."

"She doesn't intend to fight him, Dane. That's not what this is."

"Well, we've established she can't run forever, so eventually, she'll have to."

"No. She plans to end her life before he has the chance to hurt her. That's her solution. That's the only way she thinks she can make this go away."

"What?" His face contorted. "You're saying she's going to kill herself?"

Juniper pressed a fist to her mouth as the bile in her stomach rose. "That's her plan."

"Well…she can't." He was on his feet. "We have to do something."

"Tell me what and I'll do it, Dane. I'm out of ideas."

"Exactly what I said—we get to him before he can get to her."

She blinked at him in surprise. "We?"

"Yes, we. Did you think I would let you do this alone? We're a team."

She sprung off the bed and threw her arms around him. "Thank you for being such a good guy."

He hugged her. "I know what it's like to fear for the safety of someone you love. I worry about Gracie every day. I lost my parents, my grandparents, and my sister. I even had to give away my dog. I can't lose you guys too."

Her arms tightened. "When all this is over, I promise I'll do whatever I can to help you with Gracie."

He laughed awkwardly and pulled away. "I've accepted her choice. And I don't want her to love me because someone used magick on her. I deserve something real."

"You do," she agreed, wishing she could help him.

"But hey, maybe you could do some sort of spell that makes me fall out of love with her so it doesn't hurt so much."

She laughed. Love truly was a pain in the ass. "Deal."

CHAPTER 27

Adriel's attention jerked to the trees as a screech owl twittered and called. Her instincts were on high alert, as were her senses. Small predators often fled in her presence, but she was doing her best to mask her scent. The woodland creatures could warn her of other dangers creeping nearby.

It had been six nights since leaving. Six grueling days traveling by foot and keeping a paranoid watch over her shoulder.

She hadn't believed she'd make it this far. Her progress implied Cerberus might have been more injured at the gorges than they realized.

She didn't want to think about Juniper and Dane. By now, she had probably come to terms with her choice—or maybe she hadn't.

Adriel's guilt tugged at her resolve, and she went back and forth, never quite sure if she'd made the right decision. Her heart wanted to turn back, but who knew if Juniper would speak to her after the way she'd left?

She should have had the integrity to say goodbye to her face. She tried, several times, to reason with her, but Juniper refused to listen to reason. Cerberus was going to find her sooner or later. It was best if she was alone. That way, she was less vulnerable.

A bat passed overhead, and she tracked its silent flight. Once again, she scanned her surroundings. Aside from the occasional night critter scurrying about, everything seemed calm.

She'd made it past the Canadian border several nights ago. From there, she passed through Quebec and believed she was now in the Newfoundland mountains.

The high winds disguised her scent, but the cold made hunting and feeding difficult. She assumed she'd stop when she reached the coast. Or maybe she'd find passage east, toward Iceland, the UK, or perhaps Scandinavia—considering she lived long enough to get that far.

The moon hung heavy in the sky, its pale light casting eerie shadows over the rugged terrain. Fog drifted in, crawling over the ground and through the trees like long fingers. The relentless wind howled like the mournful cries of lost souls, and the biting cold burned her cheeks.

She kept moving, even when everything inside of her demanded she rest. The higher the altitude the more ragged her breathing. She needed blood, but hadn't passed anything worth hunting in some time.

A stick snapped, not far behind, and she stilled. Her heart pounded like a war drum in her chest, each beat a desperate plea for survival. Was this it? Had he found her?

She stilled and waited for the smaller animals of the mountains to scurry, but they appeared undisturbed. Yet, she sensed something out there.

Had it been Cerberus, he would have shaken her out and tormented her, using his power to rip open the earth and down trees in her path. The forest had been calm for hours, so why was she suddenly on edge?

When a branch fell, she bolted like frightened prey. Sprinting through the dense forest, her feet crunched over the frost-covered underbrush. The impenetrable darkness flashed whenever the occasional sliver of moonlight pierced the canopy above. Her senses were on high alert, every rustle of leaves and snap of twigs sending jolts of fear through her frazzled nerves.

No matter the distance between them, Cerberus's sinister presence loomed like a dark specter. Her mind played tricks on her, hearing sounds that were not there and seeing sights that did not exist.

Born of nightmares, she sometimes felt him most in that place between sleeping and awake. Once, she thought she saw his crimson eyes watching her in the dark, glowing like rubies on fire with malevolent intent.

He thrived in the darkness, a nocturnal predator who enjoyed toying with his prey. Perhaps her instincts were correct and he was close by, or maybe her mind was deceiving her, drunk on fear and her ever spiking adrenaline. The anticipation of the hunt wore her down mentally and physically, but it would further invigorate him.

Her steps slowed for only a moment so she could pause long enough to listen. Looking back, she sensed danger closing in. She was not alone.

It was either Cerberus or something just as threatening. The oppressive weight of a threatening presence bore down on her, and her mind raced, searching for an escape. She needed to outmaneuver whatever stalked her.

Varying her path, she leaped through trees, creating a labyrinth that would confuse whatever trailed her in the forests. When she reached an icy stream, she stepped into the water, covering her tracks in the brook's cold, unforgiving embrace.

She pushed herself harder, her legs burning with exertion, her lungs aching with every breath. The forest seemed to conspire against her, branches reaching out like skeletal hands to claw at her clothes and skin, roots rising from the ground to trip her. But these were merely natural pitfalls, not necessarily the evidence of Cerberus.

Still, she had to keep moving. Shivering, she struggled to regulate her temperature. In a moment of desperate fear, she wished Juniper was there to cocoon her in a protection spell. But most of all, she wished she could wrap herself in the sanctuary of her arms.

A sudden, sharp pain shot through her ankle as she stumbled over a jagged rock poking out of the stream. She cried out, the sound swallowed by the night, as she fell to the ground.

A low, guttural growl purred into a malicious laugh. Panic surged through her, adrenaline spurring her to scramble to her feet despite the agony that shot up her leg. He was there.

Desperation clawed at her insides as she limped in frantic flight. The forest thinned, and trees gave way to a steep, rocky incline. She scaled the walls, using her hands to steady herself, her fingers numb and trembling. The summit seemed an impossible distance away, each step a battle against the treacherous terrain and her weakening resolve.

The earth trembled, marking his nearness and taunting her. When she lost her footing again, it was too late. Her pack slipped from her hands, tumbling down the incline and hooking onto a branch. Her weapons were in there. She needed to get to them. This was it. She needed to end this before he got to her.

"You can't run forever, girl. We have a score to settle." His voice echoed through the canyons, sinking like a nearby whisper into her mind.

She frantically scrabbled the rock wall, backtracking to her pack, and then saw him. He moved with a preternatural grace, his dark form a blur as he closed the gap between them.

Her pulse thundered in her ears, and her vision blurred with tears of fear and frustration as she stretched desperately for her bag, only to knock it loose from the root and watch it fall down the mountainside.

Her breath turned to ice in her lungs. She spun and climbed upward, forgetting the pack to once again focus on escape.

His low laughter taunted her hopeless flight. He was nearing on her in unmarked strides, appearing closer and closer without ever seeming to move.

Chest heaving, her gasps turned to sobs as she scaled the wall. Her wet clothes froze under the relentless wind. She screamed as Cerberus emerged from the shadows ahead, his eyes locking onto hers with a predatory gleam.

He had her.

This was it.

She'd waited too long and there would be no escaping him now.

"It's time to have that long-awaited reunion you've been putting off, girl."

She spun to flee, but Cerberus was upon her instantly, his hand clamping around her wrist with a vice-like grip. She screamed, a sound of pure terror, as he jerked her to her feet.

"Did you honestly think you would get

away?" His breath washed over her face, and she whimpered. He laughed, the sound cruel and promising. "What's that now?"

Lips trembling, her words stammered out. "K-kill me. Please."

Another cold laugh cut through the air. "Oh, no. There will be none of that. At least not the way you're hoping. I have so much to show you."

He traced a razor-sharp claw down her cheek, slicing open her skin. She tried to pull away but he yanked her closer.

"I want to show you everything you missed while we've been apart. Namely, the insufferable misery of being quartered and buried alive for more than a century. Doesn't that sound fun, precious mate of mine?" His eyes burned with sadistic pleasure. "But first, I'm going to drain you dry."

She gasped, unable to draw a single breath into her lungs. He struck with the precision of a viper, his curved fangs sinking into her throat as he bit down and ripped open her flesh. Blood rushed into her mouth, choking her, as he ravaged her throat.

This was it. There was no escaping him now. He would leave her too weak to run, just as he'd done before. Her life was over, but her suffering would be endless.

She should have never left Juniper. She was her purest love. Her truest love. She would never look into her kind eyes again. She would never see Christian, her son, again. They were all lost to her now.

He drew back and hissed, slipping easily in and out of her mind now that he had her blood. "Tell me more about those you love. I look forward to such introductions."

Memories of her siblings flooded her with trauma as if he'd hurt them only yesterday. "Please. You have me. Don't—"

He slapped her so hard her head snapped back. "Don't you dare think to tell me what I should and should not do. For that, alone, I should eat your friends."

Rage, unlike anything she'd ever experienced before, tunneled through her and she screamed, bearing her fangs and unleashing her fury on him.

Clawing at his face, something primal came over her. She sank her teeth into his shoulder. But in the end, he was stronger.

When he yanked her off of him, her fang snapped loose, and she howled as blood sputtered past her lips. Something inside of her snapped and rage erupted from the darkest shadows of her soul.

She had nothing left to lose. After centuries of blocking her mind and making herself small, she let the fury seethe out of her, slashing her claws into his face, ripping at his eyes and growling like a feral animal. *I hate you!*

He jerked her off of him, slamming her down on the rock hard enough that white light burst behind her eyes, momentarily stealing her sight. Gripping her by the throat, he hoisted her overhead. Blood flooded her vision as capillaries burst in her head. She pushed her mind into his, embedding herself deep in his thoughts, frantically searching for any weakness she might use to end him.

She expected the dark, twisted thoughts and the deeply disturbed memories she found. She even flinched at the images of his time underground. But what she had not expected to find was visions of her mother.

"Get out of my head!" he snapped, slamming her into the rock wall.

She would not relent. So long as she was conscious, she needed to understand why her mother was in his memories.

Castles. Armor. Royalty. These were not visions from her time. Her mother was there. But not with her father. A malformed sense of affection stabbed into her.

Tenderness. Protectiveness. These were not sentiments Cerberus displayed. Then it occurred to her...

He loved her.

He had a life before becoming her mate, a life that involved Adriel's mother. How was that possible?

"Stay out of my memories!"

She refused to let go. She needed to understand.

In some way, he saw her as his. And she betrayed him when she accepted her calling to Adriel's father. Then she found the moment he decided to strike back.

"No…" He choked her, but she'd punctured his deepest memories and there was no prying her from his mind without killing her.

He lied. It was all a lie. That's what this was. Centuries of torture and vengeance all in the name of revenge. He was not her mate. He was a traveler who had used and abused her in a scheme to punish her mother.

His fist sank into her stomach. Her crushed windpipe wheezed as she desperately tried to breathe.

"You think it matters now? You're mine. You'll never be rid of me. And I plan to make you suffer for the rest of eternity.

He struck again, burying his fangs deep in her ransacked throat, determined to finish her. In a desperate grasp of hope, she blew open her mind and reached for Juniper, hoping she still had enough of her blood in her system to hear her call.

My parents. Go to my parents. Lilias and Lazarus Schrock. Find them. Tell them he has me. Please. Juniper, he's not my mate—

He drained her veins until her heart had nothing left to pump. She looked up at him, unable to wheeze in a single breath, devoid of any essence of life. Then he threw her body down the rocky mountainside until she landed in a broken heap on the bedrock far below.

CHAPTER 28

"*D*ane!" Juniper raced out the backdoor, heart pounding franticly in her chest. "Dane! Where are you?"

"I'm right here." He stepped out of the shed with a set of hedge trimmers in his hand.

"He found her! We have to go! Now!"

"Who?"

"Adriel! Cerberus has her and she's in trouble. We need to leave, *now*." She rushed inside, stuffing her books into an old leather carryon she found in the closet. "Pack whatever you want to bring. I don't know if we'll be back."

"Wait. What about Ruth?"

"Ruth will be fine."

"How did this happen? Did you do a locator spell?"

"I didn't find her. She found me." She hurled a bag at his chest. "Pack!"

"Tell me what happened!"

"I don't exactly know. I can't explain it. I've never felt anything like it. She was just there, in my head, telling me to find her parents."

"Her parents?" His face pinched with a mixture of surprise and confusion. "They must be older than dirt."

"Really fucking old." She couldn't deal with the added pressure of in-law stress right now. "Please start packing."

"Why now, all of a sudden? Are you sure it was her? What if it's him doing that traveler shit again?"

Her heart hammered against her ribs, her fingers trembling as she clutched the ancient leather-bound grimoire to her chest. "It was her." Doubt wheedled in. "Shit. No. It was definitely her. I could hear her voice."

Her body shook with worry. What if they didn't get there in time? What had Cerberus already done to Adriel in the time he had her? Such questions led her to a dark and dangerous place, one she feared could destroy her.

He caught her arm. "June?"

She looked up at him, fear choking her. "We have to find her, Dane. I can't—" Her words cut off as she sucked back a sob. "I can't lose her like this. Not to him. I can't bear the thought of her suffering."

"Hey, hey, hey." He quickly pulled her into a hug. "Don't get worked up. If we're going to help her, we have to stay calm and focused. We'll find her, June. I promise." He lifted the bag. "I'll go pack what I need."

They had a harrowing journey ahead of them, one Juniper wasn't sure they would survive. She couldn't stand the thought of her sweet, innocent Adriel in the clutches of a monster like Cerberus, whose cruelty knew no bounds.

She could still hear the fear in Adriel's voice when she contacted her. Hints of abuse were there, beneath the sound of desperation. If Adriel wasn't already hurt, she was absolutely terrified. It was the only reason she would have reached out the way she had in such puncturing haste.

The good news was that she was still alive. But they needed to hurry.

Juniper's hands shook as she packed the last of the grimoires. The urgency of their mission was palpable, every second ticking away like a countdown to doom. Juniper loved Adriel with an intensity that transcended lifetimes. She would stop at nothing to save her, even if it meant delving into the deepest, darkest corners of witchcraft.

Why was she sending them to her parents? She quickly jotted down the message verbatim so she wouldn't forget Adriel's exact words. She said she their names were Lilias and Lazarus Schrock. Was that enough to find them?

If they were out there, they would be ancient immortals. Juniper hoped they were friendly and willing to help rescue their daughter, but she honestly had no idea what to expect or how to prepare for such a task. Her own immortal father wanted nothing to do with her, so it wasn't like blood was necessarily thicker than water when it was also on the menu with these bloodsuckers.

Her mind raced as they quickly gathered helpful items throughout the house. Ruth watched her shows undisturbed in the den. When Juniper opened the window to let nature in, the scent of herbs and candles mingled with the bite of winter in the air. She concocted a few spells to help them on their journey—things they could grab on the go in an emergency. She stashed the ingredients in small jars throughout both her and Dane's bags.

The link she briefly felt to Adriel had severed. It felt like she was truly gone. No matter how often Juniper tried to reconnect, nothing was there but cold, empty oblivion.

She feared they were already too late. What if Adriel was wrong, and Cerberus planned to kill her? Her hand rushed to her chest as the unbearable thought created a physical pain in her heart.

"How can I help? Give me something to do," Dane insisted, his deep voice steady but urgent. His eyes scanned the room, taking in the counters lined with jars of mystical ingredients Juniper had collected for weeks. "We can't possibly take all of this. TSA would never let us through."

Juniper waved away his words, her resolve hardening. "I'm not worried about customs. It's a simple sleight of hand that shifts a person's perception. I can make them see whatever I want on their little computer screens and X-ray machines."

He chuckled. "I like this cocky side of you."

"I'm not being cocky. I'm confident. There's a difference."

"Yes, ma'am. What else?"

"I need some personal items of Adriel's. Something with her DNA. Her hair brush. I might be able to use that to find Lilias and Lazarus."

"That'll work?"

She bit her lip as worry climbed into her throat. "I don't know. But I'm confident we can try."

Dane ran upstairs as Juniper set up the spell with practiced precision. Her strategy rested in the belief that anything was possible. She told Adriel to have faith, and that was the plan. As long as Juniper believed she could do this, the spirits and elements would all come together to assist her.

"I'm counting on you guys," she whispered under her breath, praying they wouldn't abandon her now. "How do you feel about airports?"

She tried not to panic when she felt nothing.

"Got it!" Dane yelled, returning to the kitchen with Adriel's hairbrush in hand.

Needing all the help she could get, Juniper took the necessary tools out back. With chalk, she drew a large, intricate circle on the brick patio, inscribing ancient runes around its perimeter. At the center, she placed a map of the world, a lock of Adriel's hair, spelled ink made of berries and herbs, and a moonstone that shimmered with an ethereal light.

"Let's hope this works," she whispered as she knelt beside the circle, her hands hovering over the map.

Closing her eyes, she channeled the spirits and grounded into the earth. Her breathing slowed as she chanted in a language older than time itself. The air around them crackled with energy, the temperature dropping as the spell took hold, and the comforting sensation of phantom hands pressing power into her shoulders.

They were there, by her side, offering their assistance. *Thank the goddess.*

Juniper's voice grew louder, more insistent, as she poured her will into the incantation.

"Adriel, filia Lilias et Lazarus, revela mihi sanctuarium tuum progenitum..." Her voice resonated with power. The crystal casted an eerie glow outward. *"By blood and by bond, ostende mihi ubi sint."*

The map shifted, rotating slowly beneath her hands as if alive. She poured a puddle of ink onto the center. It spread into fingers, the lines morphing and twisting to converge on a single point.

Juniper's imagination blurred and sharpened as she was transported to another place, another time. She found herself in an ancient town. The vision was vivid, every detail etched in her mind with stunning clarity. She searched for carved signs etched in the granite walls.

It wasn't the words that told her where she was. It was the letters. They were ancient and curved the way they often were over the American doorways of fraternities and sororities. But this was no college campus. This place was old. Very, very old.

"They're in Greece!"

"Where?"

Ἄργος. "I don't know. Everything's written in the Greek alphabet."

She closed her eyes, focusing on the foreign letters, regretting all the years wasted in Señor Jimenez's Spanish class. The city's name looked to start with an A, but she didn't have a clue how to translate or pronounce the rest of the name into English.

Her mind pressed into the word, and she pulled from the support of the spirits, mentally requesting anyone of Greek descent come forward to help her. That was when the city's name whispered through her mind.

Argos.

The city was a tapestry of history, its cobblestone streets winding through clusters of whitewashed houses with terracotta roofs. Juniper's gaze was drawn to a secluded cottage on the outskirts of town, nestled among olive trees and vibrant blooms of the bougainvillea flower.

Ivy crawled up the walls, weaving in and out of the wrought iron balcony that overlooked the town. Lanterns hung in large, arched windows, spilling a warm, golden light from the shadows.

The scent of salt from the nearby Aegean Sea mingled with the aroma of blooming jasmine, creating an intoxicating perfume that hung in the warm air.

Her body jerked as a woman with long auburn hair appeared. She carried a basket of linens. Her eyes were green as emeralds, and her skin as pale as a fresh lily bloom. There was no doubt in Juniper's mind that this beauty was Lilias, Adriel's mom. Their loveliness appeared almost identical, save the length of her hair and the fullness of her hips.

The vision faded and Juniper gasped as her body jolted back to the present. Her eyes snapped open. "They're in city called Argos in Greece. I saw their house—it's beautiful, secluded, surrounded by olive trees and flowers. We need to get there right away."

"What about passports?"

"Leave that to me. You load the car while I finish packing and say goodbye to Ruth. We're leaving in ten minutes."

"June, they aren't going to let us past the first gate without the proper documentation."

"Dane, I'm working on it," she said, plucking a strand of hair from his head.

"Ouch!"

"You want a passport?"

He scoffed. "You're so bitchy when you're witchy."

She smiled, hearing the affection masked in his voice and trusting him to have her back through whatever came next. Grabbing his arm, she said, "You know I'd still be in the cell if it wasn't for you. Whatever happens next, Dane, I want you to know that I love you like a brother. We might not be family, but—"

His chest slammed into her as he gripped her up in a bear hug. "I'll be your pseudo-brother, June. Right now, you're the only family I've got."

"Same."

He let her go and rubbed his head where she'd yanked out his hair. "Let's go save our girl."

As soon as Dane went to gather the bags, Juniper's fingers flew over the pages of the old grimoire. It was a simple masking spell that started with a carbon base that would act as a carrier. She used tree bark since it held the energy of the elements and the vitality of the sun.

Once she had the needed tools set on the altar, she muttered incantations. Her hands wove through the air as if conducting an orchestra, and the sky filled with a faint, shimmering light as particles gathered around the bark, transforming it into a rather convincing document.

She placed a piece of her own hair next to Dane's. Moments later, the passports were complete, photos and personal details authentically printed inside.

Juniper stuffed the grimoire and documents into a worn leather satchel alongside the vials of potions and bundles of some powerful herbs.

"That's it," she said, her voice tight with urgency. "I feel completely unprepared, and we need to be ready for anything."

"We've got this." Dane slung the heavy satchel over his shoulder, his expression resolute. "We'll save her, June. He doesn't get to win this time."

She thought of all the others. Her evening visitor. The monster that took Dane's sister. Jonas. All of her vengeance pulled from those past atrocities and worked into one clear target. Save Adriel. Kill Cerberus.

She met Dane's stare. Their bond had been forged through shared traumas of very different battles that somehow formed a sense of unwavering loyalty in both of them. "If we actually do this, it will be our first kill. Are you ready for that?"

He hoisted the last of their bags over his shoulders. "The world needs less monsters. If I get to kill one, good. I couldn't pick a better primal kill."

As they stepped into the cold night, the weight of their mission shrouded them from distraction. The journey ahead would be perilous, fraught with danger, uncertainty, and the stress of getting through customs with a shit-ton of witch paraphernalia. Two half-breed hybrids off into the great wild yonder to confront two ancient vampires and kill a monster. What could go wrong?

Everything.

But together, they would face whatever horrors awaited in the shadows. And they would risk all that they owned in this world, including their lives. For Adriel, for love, for family, and for the promise of a brighter future.

The doors of their little stolen rental car slammed, and they both drew in a deep breath and let it out in slowly. Juniper smiled nervously. "Let's rock and roll."

Dane turned the key, and the engine purred to life. "Let's go fuck some shit up."

There was not a spell in the world that could get her onto the back of that mule. "No." Juniper stood, stubbornly holding her bags and wearing twenty-four hours of collective travel dirt from weird taxi cabs, train stations, airports, and public restrooms. Donkeys were where she drew the line.

Dane looked at the stack of their luggage. "Do you see that hill? I'm not carrying this shit anymore."

His patience ended at the Kalamata airport. "It's not necessarily *up*hill."

"It's a hill all the same. Get on the mule, June." They were both tired, hungry, and devoid of wanderlust.

"I'm not riding a mule."

He dropped the bags he was holding. "I'm done lugging books. Did you notice how everyone at the airport had wheels on their suitcases? Not us, though. Nope. We went one hundred percent hand held carryon because—" He pitched his voice high to mimic her. "Ruth's vintage bag collection's so cool," he mocked her earlier enthusiasm. "I've been carrying this crap for five thousand miles!"

She rolled her eyes and picked up the bags. "Put the bags on the mule, jackass. *We* can walk."

Dane mumbled something under his breath and loaded up the mule. "Not a single part of me envisioned this as part of my life."

Ignoring his grumpy protests, she adjusted the satchel over her shoulder and climbed the decaying steps. They still had miles to go and only a few hours of daylight left.

"You're a miserable traveler. And I'd like to point out that it took no physical effort for you to carry our bags once we were on the plane, drama queen."

"I don't want to talk about that tin can that got us here. That wasn't a plane."

"Then what was it?"

"People aren't supposed to fly with caged chickens on their laps!"

"I didn't realize you were so bougie. Next time, I'll spring for first class."

With little certainty of the welcome they would receive once they reached their destination, Juniper hoped Adriel's parents were the warm, hospitable sort. If not, she was going to have to sedate Dane.

As the crumbling stone paths darkened with

shadows, the earthy aroma of wet stone mingled subtly with the faint scent of olive groves surrounding the city. A chill hung in the air as the sun went down. The soreness in her feet was a constant reminder of the miles they had traveled.

The flight hadn't been as miserable as Dane claimed, but it had been long. Juniper's back ached, her clothes were dirty, and she just wanted to shut her eyes—but there wasn't time to rest. Adriel was in danger and they needed to keep moving.

Thankfully, as they trekked into the old city, they fell into agreeable silence—for most of the journey at least. "How old is this place?"

"Ancient." No wonder immortals flocked here. Like the Amish farm, this place also seemed untouched by time and modernization.

The stone columns stood like relics steeped in history. Juniper felt traces of magick in the air. History had its uses with witchcraft, and she was eager to test her skills in this place.

The cobblestone roads were worn smooth by centuries of time. Back roads and passages echoed with the footsteps of ghosts. She opened her heart so the spirits would recognize her as a friend and hopefully lend their energies like the spirits back home did.

The solemn cadence of their tired steps moved at a steady pace with the clip-clopping hoof beats of the mule. Juniper looked ahead, her eyes tired with awe and exhaustion. She hoped they hadn't come all this way for nothing.

Unlike the iconic cerulean blue buildings people typically envisioned when thinking of Greece, the architecture here was constructed from pale limestone. Intricate carvings, worn and weathered by time, adorned many surfaces. Ivy clung to the walls and wove through cracks and crevices in a way that made the structures feel alive. Secrets of great tragedies and victories lingered in the wind, whispering through the streets as they traveled deeper into the crumbling city.

"It's getting dark. Maybe we should find a place to crash for the night," Dane suggested, leading the mule. His head turned toward the distant lights where more modernized buildings dotted the horizon. "I bet there's a hotel with room service that way."

"That's not the direction we need to go. The location spell is pulling us north-east."

"Aren't you hungry?"

"We can eat when we get there."

"If we're not on the menu," he grumbled.

He was right. They had no idea what they were walking into. Not all immortals followed a peaceful code. Not that being Amish was any sort of guarantee against cruelty and corruption. But it at least set a standard.

These guys could be cold-hearted killers. What if they were evil, like Cerberus? Adriel never spoke about her upbringing. If her parents were nice, wouldn't she have mentioned them?

It didn't matter. Without Adriel, Juniper had

little to live for. She would do whatever was necessary to save her. If her mother and father could somehow help their crusade, she would get down on her hands and knees and beg them for assistance. She could not lose Adriel.

Her love had become inarguably clear. They might not be mates, but something brought them together. Adriel was a part of her destiny.

The scent of the sea thickened the air. Juniper's skin wore a layer of sweat under her clothing despite the cold, and she welcomed the gentle breeze that whispered through the narrow streets. Sometimes she caught the fragrant bouquet of blooming jasmine nearby, but this place mostly smelled of salt and sea—two powerful elements that could help her if needed.

As they made their way deeper into the ancient city, the temperature dropped with the sun. Juniper shivered, pulling her jacket tighter around her neck.

"How much longer?"

"We're close. I can feel it." Or was that more weariness creeping in?

Magick guided them through the labyrinth of streets and passageways, but the use of her powers also exhausted her. Each turn revealed a sense of comfort that they were nearing their goal, but she honestly had little evidence that they were any closer. What if they got there and no one was home? They could be anywhere. Did immortals vacation like humans?

They passed beneath an arched gateway, the surfaces etched with faded inscriptions she recognized from the visions. "It's this way."

Statues of gods guarded sealed doorways, their marble eyes watching them. Dane stared at the figures as if waiting for them to come alive. "Is it just me or is this place getting a little creepy?"

"There are definitely old souls here."

"Old souls? You mean ghosts?"

"Spirits."

"Good spirits?"

"Some. Some not so much."

"Great." Dane pushed the mule harder, picking up pace.

The soreness in her feet grew with each step, and a dull ache spread from her legs into her back. Cobblestone, though beautiful, was an unforgiving bitch to walk on, and she had not packed proper shoes.

She paused, the hair on the back of her neck lifting.

"What is it?"

She looked around. "I'm not sure. I thought I felt something."

"Something like a ghost?"

"Don't be a baby. If you don't bother the spirits, they won't bother you." That was mostly true. "But this isn't a spirit." Something flashed in the corner of her eye—fast and silent.

Her heart raced. They were not alone. Something or someone was following them. "This way."

They rounded the corner into an open square that looked like the ruins of an ancient temple. Massive columns, some still standing, others toppled and broken, ringed the perimeter. In the center of the square stood a large olive tree, its gnarled branches reaching skyward as if in supplication to the gods.

"Is this it?"

She scanned the area and frowned, not seeing the home she saw in the vision, but her instincts telling her this was where she needed to be. The crumbling façade boasted an air of majesty and power but also wore the scars of battles lost.

"I'm not sure." Wind whipped through the square. A carpet of dry fallen leaves covering the ground twirled skyward as if disrupted by something. "Somethings here."

Dane gripped the reins of the mule and scanned the area. "I don't see anyone."

That didn't mean anything. It could be a spirit, but she wasn't getting that vibe. This was something living. Something fast. "Stay still. Look."

The leaves shifted again, parting as a current of wind cut through the piles, then drifting back to earth slowly. Whoever was there was not merely air disrupting the stillness, they were taunting them.

"Show yourself."

Another burst of wind, this one close enough

to lift the hair from her shoulders. Her gaze snapped to every shadow.

"Are you sure this is—Shit!" Dane ducked and covered his head. "Did you feel that?"

Now she was pissed. "Whoever you are, we're not scare—"

Her words cut off as a thick arm wrapped about her throat, choking her, as her feet lifted off the ground. "Perhaps you should be, witch."

"Juniper!" Dane charged then stilled when the man holding her growled.

"I wouldn't do that." The masculine voice spoke with thickly accented authority.

Dane's eyes widened with worry as he held her stare. Her vision blurred as she squirmed for air. "Let her go!"

Juniper's feet kicked, and her shoe fell to the ground. She couldn't see him, but his immortal strength was unmistakable.

"You're choking her!"

The immortal sniffed close to her ear. "Not just a witch. *Kitsune.* What is your purpose here?"

She debated telling the truth over a lie, but the choice wasn't hers. As long as he held her by the throat, she couldn't say a word.

"Let go of her, and I'll tell you."

"Tell me and I'll consider letting her go." He jerked her higher into the air. "I'll smell any trace of deceit."

Her heart thundered. Her magick was useless in this state.

"Fine!" Dane snapped. "We're looking for a

couple that goes by the names Lazarus and Lilias."

He loosened his grip, and Juniper wheezed in a painful breath. As soon as she started to cough, he cut off her airway again. "What do you want with them?"

"You're killing her!"

"And I will if you don't tell me what you want with Lazarus and Lilias!"

"We have news about their daughter!"

The immortal stiffened and Juniper slipped out of his grip, her knees slamming down on the cobblestone road as she dropped to the ground and coughed.

"That's impossible."

Dane rushed forward, dragging her up before she could draw in a full breath. Her vision dotted with white spots as she gasped for air. "You could have killed her!"

The man turned, his expression haunted and showing no concern for either of them. "Lazarus and Lilias have no children."

"We're telling the truth," Dane snarled. "We have a message from their daughter, asshole. She's in trouble—"

"Dane," Juniper rasped, clutching her throat. "Shut up—"

The immortal growled and snatched Dane off the ground, pinning him to a crumbling pillar. "What did you say?"

"*Scintilla!*" Juniper sent a spark of fire to his hand.

He dropped Dane and flashed his fangs at her, his eyes glowing with predatory intent.

Juniper scrambled to her feet and lifted her chin. "Do you know them or not?" She'd come too far to get scared off now.

"Witch!" He drew back to lash out and she held up a staying hand.

"Stop!" Dane yelled. "Adriel's in grave danger!"

The massive male stilled, not due to magick but something much more powerful.

Love.

Was this who they were looking for? Perhaps he was a close friend of Adriel's parents.

Juniper pleaded their case. "She needs help. Please, if you know them, we have a message for them and we don't have a lot of time."

"A message from their daughter?" His eyes narrowed.

"Yes, their daughter sent us. It's urgent we reach them. Please. If you know them, we need to talk to them about Adriel—"

"A—Adriel?" The immortal's face notably paled as he staggard back.

"Do you know her?"

"I..." He looked away, his broad shoulders heaving as he grasped for composure.

"I give you my word. We mean no harm. But we're in a rush. It's life or death."

His gaze snapped to her and fierce hostility glimmered in his glowing eyes. "Adriel is in danger?"

"Her life's at stake. If you know Lazarus or Lilias, we must speak to them."

The immortal nodded. "I will take you to Lilias."

CHAPTER 30

The moon cast long shadows as they followed the immortal male through the streets of Argos. The towering male said nothing after agreeing to take them to Lilias, but that did little to bolster their trust.

In the distance, Juniper spotted a house similar to her vision. The night sky slightly altered the appearance, dousing the home in shadows and an eerie blue glow. A figure appeared on the balcony, slender and petite as the wind caught her hair. Juniper knew right away that it was Lilias.

"She knows you're coming and she knows why you're here. One sign of disrespect and I'll end both of you without hesitation. Understood?"

Both she and Dane nodded.

The weathered iron gate hardly protected the home, a clear sign that the inhabitants were immortal. Its stone cornerstones showed signs of decay, and the windows were all open.

The gate creaked as their immortal escort pulled it open. Juniper looked back at Dane, communicating her worries silently. She hoped this wasn't a mistake.

They stepped inside the yard, and the female from the balcony appeared in the shadows of the doorway, her face drawn with worry and her arms crossed protectively over her chest.

Her stare went directly to Juniper. "You're a witch."

"Kitsune." That was the second time the male immortal used that unfamiliar word, and Juniper didn't know what it meant. "Half witch, half immortal."

Well, wasn't he astute?

The female appeared unmoved by this information. "You have news of my daughter?"

The immortal escort watched them closely, obviously protective of the female. Juniper stepped closer to the house, hopefully appealing to the female's good nature if she had any. "Your daughter, Adriel, is alive but she's in great danger."

The female's hand rushed to her mouth, her brow pinching tight and her eyes flooding with tears. "She's alive?"

"For now."

Relief surged through the air like a wave. "Did you hear that, Lazarus? Our daughter lives."

Both Juniper and Dane did a double take. The big bastard was Adriel's dad?

Juniper pushed her objective to the forefront of the conversation. "Your daughter's in danger."

"Where is her mate?" Adriel's father snapped.

"He's the problem."

"I don't understand. Her mate should protect her at all costs."

"He's not her real mate. He's a traveler who's spent centuries manipulating and controlling her."

Both immortals rushed forward, speaking in a language she couldn't translate. Their confusion morphed into frantic concern as Lazarus tried to calm Lilias down, but there was no reasoning with the female. She swiped a hand through the air and snapped at him, then turned back to Juniper.

"You must tell us everything. We assumed our daughter was lost."

"She may be soon if we don't help her."

Lazarus stepped forward, his energy completely different from what he displayed in the square. "You will come inside and tell us everything."

They followed the couple into the house, where they sat at a plain table. Lilias offered them water but urged Lazarus to pour. Distraught by the news, she sat in shock and explained, "My daughter was called more than half a millennia ago. We never had the chance to meet her mate. The night he claimed her, they left without a goodbye." Lilias covered her mouth as a soft sob escaped, then gathered her composure. "This is quite a surprise for us."

"As much as I'd like to be delicate, time is of the essence, and we need your help. The immortal that has her intends to torture her. He wants to punish her for evading him. I believe he already has."

"Who is this immortal?" Lazarus stood, his hulking body seething with uncontainable rage. "Where is he?"

"I'm not sure. We've been traveling nonstop, and my magick's lagging. I can try another locator spell, but my power's weak right now."

"You must regain your strength." Lilias grabbed the glass of water and flung the contents into a basin on the floor. She sliced open her wrist and filled the cup with her blood. "You will drink and nourish yourself."

Juniper glanced at Dane. He nodded.

She pulled the cup closer but hesitated. She'd only ever shared Adriel's vein and didn't fully understand the laws of blood exchanges. What if this somehow endangered her? They didn't know these immortals.

"I will pay you the respect of not using compulsion," Lilias said. "But if what you say is true, my only child is in danger. Please, drink the blood. It is good and strong, and it will help you."

She looked at the female and recognized love

in her eyes. Nodding, Juniper brought the glass to her mouth. The warm, life-renewing blood was dark and rich, spiced with ancient flavors, and aged like a potent wine. She swallowed every drop and immediately felt its regenerative power working through her system.

"Thank you."

Dane cleared his throat and pushed his glass toward Lazarus. The old immortal glared at him.

"I'm Juniper. This is Dane." She glanced at the glass. "We both plan to save Adriel."

The male immortal snatched the glass and dumped the contents, adding blood for Dane, but only half as much as Lilias offered. "You are a strange pairing. How do you know our daughter."

"She's our close friend. We're risking our lives for her—if that means anything to you."

"It does," Lilias said, shooting Lazarus a look of censure.

"Holy shit." Dane set down the empty glass. "I feel like I just drank lightning."

"Who has our daughter?" Lazarus snapped, his fist rattling the table.

Juniper swallowed. "His name is Cerberus Maddox XI—"

Lilias was on her feet. "*Impossible!*"

Oh shit. She hadn't expected that reaction. "I'm guessing you know him."

Adriel's mother looked up at Lazarus, pure panic in her eyes. "He wouldn't... After all this time… How…?" She covered her mouth, unable to comprehend.

"Are you claiming that *he* is the immortal posing as our daughter's mate?"

Juniper and Dane nodded. "It's been five hundred years of hell for her."

Lilias whimpered. "Oh, Lazarus!" Her eyes flooded with tears. "He vowed to punish me!"

When Lazarus tried to comfort her, she shoved him away. "Tears will not help matters." He bundled her in his thickly muscled arms and she punched his chest.

"He's had her all this time, Lazarus! We've failed her!"

"Actually," Dane chimed in. "She got away from him for most of it."

Both parents looked at them, and Dane explained what happened. He didn't go into much detail about the quartering, but he made it clear that Adriel was no helpless victim, which made Juniper want to get to her that much more.

"Your daughter's stronger than she realizes," Juniper said, hoping to add some relief, but Lilias collapsed.

Lazarus caught her in his arms as she fell into a state of inconsolable grief. He carried her to a different room, whispering soft-spoken words in an unfamiliar language Juniper didn't recognize.

"What do you think?" Dane asked, voice low.

The blood had hit her system, and she found sitting still challenging. "I think her parents are older than the ancient guardian trees of Vouves."

"No kidding. His blood's buzzing through my veins like rocket fuel." He glanced at the door where Lazarus carried Lilias. "Do you think they're going to help us?"

Following his stare, she nodded, then smiled back at him. "Cerberus is going to die."

CHAPTER 31

Dane and Juniper waited at the table for over an hour, drifting in and out of sleep but never fully resting. This news was clearly deeply disturbing to both Lilias and Lazarus.

"Should we do something? I feel like we're just wasting time."

"I don't know what else to do. If they're going to help, we need to work together."

The floor creaked and Lazarus appeared, his expression resolute. "We're going to help you."

Juniper sagged with relief, glad to hear they were fully devoted to their cause. "Thank you. If I do a locator spell, I can probably—"

"Fire magick will not work on a *draugr*."

She glanced at Dane to see if he understood what Lazarus was saying, but Dane only shrugged. "I'm sorry, a what?"

"Cerberus is not of our species. He's a *walker*.

A *draugr.* They are of dragon ancestry and immune to fire-born incantations or death by flame."

That must be why she was having so much trouble locating him. "I can use other magick."

"Depending on other elements would be best, but magick can only detain him. It cannot destroy him. The only way to ensure a *draugr* doesn't come back is to sever the head from the neck, burn the body, and dump the ashes into the sea—a Norse warrior's burial. Otherwise, the body could be purified by sunlight and eventually return. The ashes must be scattered far enough apart to ensure that doesn't happen. The sea will carry him to his ultimate end. But first, I intend to do my part."

It looked like they were going to a Viking funeral. "Okay. Any clue how we disarm him?"

"Aconite." Lilias appeared in the doorway. Her eyes were devoid of light as she stared blankly at them. "It's what we used to sedate him the last time."

Juniper's brows shot up. "So, you know him?"

A tear slipped past her lashes. "He was my guard, long ago, when I was married to the mortal King."

Juniper's eyes again widened. Adriel's mom's history was sick. "If he was your protector, why would he do this to your daughter?"

"Not just my daughter. All of our children were taken from us. I had suspicions, but… Now,

I'm almost positive our cruel fate has been by Cerberus's design."

"He was in love with Lilias when I claimed her as my mate," Lazarus explained. "She'd been ordered to court and forced to serve the King for bloodletting purposes."

"I married the King to enhance my station."

"He was a measly little whelp." Lazarus curled his lip. "Cerberus guarded her like a hound as part of his service to the crown. He did not take it well when she was called."

"I warned him that I would not stay in the kingdom once my mate found me, but he did not believe in such things. *Draugr* are said to be soulless, so they cannot be called."

Juniper's heart hurt for Adriel. To think, all this time she believed this monster was her destiny. The courage it took to walk away from her faith and choose herself became that much more astounding, but this also explained how Cerberus had been able to hurt her and how Adriel could tolerate being apart from him for so long.

"This is starting to make a lot of sense."

Lilias's hand rested on her arm. "I can sense your emotions. You care very much for my daughter."

Juniper tried to keep her reactions in check, but it was a lot to process. She wiped her eyes and cleared her throat. "He was not kind to her."

The solid table cracked as Lazarus gripped the slab of wood. "Perhaps you should tell us what you know."

Juniper's stare went to the crack in the surface and she swallowed. "He beat her. Broke her down. Left her starved."

Lilias's eyes closed as she turned her face away. "This is my fault."

"It's mine," Lazarus argued. "I should have killed him when I had the chance."

"She was so young. I knew better." Lilias dashed away more tears. "Immortals are rarely called so early. Her body had only just flowered. I should have cautioned her, but I feared questioning the gods."

Juniper found it interesting that all the faiths among their species generally followed the same rules when it came to fated mates, but cultural differences linked their belief systems to different deities. Yet the stories were all the same, just as mortal religions tended to be when one looked deep enough. Father, son, Allah, Mother Earth, Spirit, they were all merely humanized messengers of the universe's plan.

"Tell us how to kill him," Dane said, looking Adriel's mother in the eye.

It seemed that the only acceptable plan of action to any of them was one that ended in Cerberus's death. "The challenge with any *draugr*," Lazarus explained, "is in the absolute certainty that it is, in fact, dead before you are killed."

Over the next several hours, they were given a crash course in historical lore. Aconite was a powerful plant, poisonous to *draugen,* and they planned to use it to bring Cerberus down. Only this time, when they ended him, it would be final.

"We will rest tonight and leave at dawn." The day had been long and they were all exhausted. They needed to recharge if they were going to stand a chance.

Juniper organized their packs, ensuring everything was where she needed it to be. Tomorrow morning's locator spell would be the final one to lead them to Adriel.

"Can't sleep?"

She glanced up from her supplies. "I've been up for so long, my body's fighting it." Lazarus moved through the house with the feline grace of a giant predator that demanded a person's full attention. "When we arrived, you used a word I didn't recognize. Kitsy or—"

"*Kitsune.*"

"What does that mean?"

He raised a brow. "Are you not aware of what you are?"

Heat tinged her cheeks. "My immortal father didn't raise me. Adriel said because my mom was a witch and my dad was a vam—immortal, that my blood would create a genetic mutation. Is that what that means?"

"A *kitsune* is a powerful shifter of fox decent. One of your parents must have been sired in Asia. *Kitsunes* are extremely rare in these parts."

There must be some mistake. "But I'm American. And not a shifter."

"That you know of," he explained. "I had a

close childhood friend who was *kitsune.* I know the smell. There's no mistaking the breed."

She scrunched her face. "Are you saying I stink?"

"No," he chuckled. "The scent isn't unpleasant. But it is unique."

"Wouldn't I know if I was part fox?"

"Not necessarily. There are more than a dozen different kinds of kitsune, each kind corresponding with a different element. As a witch, you're probably familiar with the four basics—water, earth—"

"Air and fire—yes, I think I've heard of them."

He smirked at her sarcasm. "Well, the celestial faiths take it a bit deeper. There is darkness, river, ocean, thunder, forest, time, sound, mountain, and many more elements to be honored. A specific one calls to *kitsune* more than the others."

"Fire," she breathed, settling back in her chair, no longer making jokes. "That's where my magick started. I was in the woods. My friends and I were sitting around a bonfire when it started to rain. They went back to the car, but I stayed a little longer. Something happened to me that night. I took control of the fire. It moved with my breath. I could make it rage or make it flicker smaller than a birthday candle."

"That's exactly right." When Lazarus shared his knowledge, he became less intimidating. He encouraged others the way a patient teacher might, further deepening their alliance. "Did it ever happen again?"

Fire often helped her feel the spirits, but strange things had happened before then. She nodded. "Something happened to me the night I escaped The Order."

"The Order?"

"It's an Amish sanctuary for immortals. They hate witches, so it wasn't a sanctuary for me. More of a prison."

"But you escaped."

She flashed a cocky grin. "I'm here, aren't I?"

"Tell me about your escape and how fire aided you."

Juniper told him about how she awoke in a field, confused and smelling like an animal. She explained the incredible power she channeled from Adriel's burning house and how she used it against the immortals.

"I stopped when I realized the females felt whatever pain I inflicted on the males."

"Because they were mated," Lazarus explained. "Called mates also share pleasure. The longer the partnership, the deeper the link. It's why we rarely survive the death of a mate."

"That explains why the elders never killed Cerberus."

"But he would not share such a link with Adriel. True mates are the other half of each other's soul."

"And exactly why Cerberus should have never been able to hurt her," she said angrily.

But if Cerberus wasn't Adriel's true mate, that meant someone could be. What if some dude was out there, waiting to get called to her? What did that mean for them?

Saving her was a given, but what if they found her, killed Cerberus, and the moment they started their life together, some new immortal showed up to claim her.

She scoffed. That was not happening.

"You are distressed," Lazarus observed.

"I'm just thinking."

Why were there so many complications? Was mating like menopause? After a certain time did the chances of a calling get smaller? Maybe Adriel was at an age where that immortal clock stopped ticking.

Aware that Lazarus was watching her, she squirmed uncomfortably, the heaviness of these new worries weighing on her. "Do you know how long half-breeds live?"

Lazarus glanced at the fading sky. "They're all different. Like mortals, it typically comes down to genetics. *Kitsunes,* however, are said to live more than a thousand years."

Relief flooded her. "That's good."

The front door slammed, and Juniper sensed Dane was the cause. She looked at Lazarus in concern, unsure what upset her friend. "Do you mind if I—"

"Go ahead," Lazarus waved a hand and she followed Dane outside.

The night was silent, as all the birds were now asleep in their nests and the residents were tucked safely into their beds. "Hey, what was that about?"

He stood at the gate, with his back toward her and his face angled up at the moon, hands stuffed deep in his pockets. Unease radiated from his broad shoulders.

She approached slowly. "Dane—"

"Don't," he snapped, bunching his shoulders when she touched his back.

"What's the matter?"

"Didn't you hear Lazarus? He's a *draugr*."

She hadn't realized anyone was listening. She also didn't understand why he was so upset. "Yes, but there are ways to end a *draugr*. Lazarus is super smart and—"

"He's my father, Juniper."

She took a step back fearful he was suddenly suffering a change of heart. "But you said you didn't feel anything for him."

"I don't. That's not my point." His voice broke, and his eyes shimmered. "What if I'm like him?"

Her heart hurdled into her throat. "Oh, Dane—"

"I don't want your pity."

"Empathy is not pity." All of this talk about how awful Cerberus was, and she hadn't once considered that he was a part of Dane's DNA. Her heart broke for him. "We are more than genetic pieces of our parents. Our experiences matter."

He looked away, his jaw tight with tension and his body vibrating with the effort to keep his anger contained. "All this time, I was lying to myself—lying to all of you. I thought if I gave Gracie space, something would change, and we could end up together. It was me against one faceless guy. Turns out, I'm a soulless monster—"

"Hey," she snapped, yanking his arm and forcing him to look at her. "You have a soul, Dane Foster. All of those religious constructs, they're just desperate ways to rationalize coincidence. That's what religion does, it puts a pretty story over nature. It's just nature. Just like instinct, hunger, and love. Having a little competition does not mean you drop out of the race."

"You don't honestly believe that."

Her jaw twitched. "I have to. I love Adriel, but I'll never be her called mate."

"Oh, shit." Realization and understanding flashed in his eyes.

"Yeah. There could be someone else out there, someone way more capable of stealing her heart."

"I'm sorry. I didn't think of that."

She shook her head. "It's fine. It's not like I'm going to give up. I don't care what her destiny is. She's mine. Even if I only get a handful of moments with her, I refuse to give up a single one."

He finally pulled his hands out of his pockets and hugged her. "We'll save her, June. You guys will have your chance." He pressed a kiss to her head.

"The hour's getting late."

They turned to find Lazarus standing in the doorway. He held a tattered book in his hand.

"I'll uh…get our stuff together." Dane shot a thumb over his shoulder and slipped past Lazarus into the house.

Her gaze dropped to the book in Lazarus's hand. "What do you have there?"

He stepped past the doorway and held it out to her. "The pages are delicate, and the ink's mostly faded, but I figured you might want to read it."

Juniper took the offering and frowned at the cover.

"It's written in Akkadian, but there are several sections about the *kitsune*. It will help you understand."

"Thank you." Looked like she had a date scheduled with Google Translate. "I can't wait to read it." She wasn't ready to go inside, so she sat on the step.

Lazarus joined her. "Something is weighing on you?"

She sighed as she stared out at the black night, the horizon slowly shifting into shadows as the dawn approached. "I just keep thinking we could all die today."

"That, little one, is a truth you could tell yourself every morning."

She thought about the other children Lazarus and Lilias lost and how they all perished at the hands of one monster. She didn't understand how anyone could tame such rage. Lazarus was one of the chillest immortals she'd ever met. But he was also scary as fuck when he needed to be.

"Do you think we can kill him?"

"Yes. Some animals simply need to die, no matter the cost. I'm willing to do whatever it takes to see to my family's safety."

Was he saying he was willing to die? "What about Lilias?"

"Lilias is willing to risk the same. Adriel's our daughter." He cleared his throat. "But I find myself wondering… What is she to you?"

"Oh." Juniper dropped her gaze. "You know… We're friends."

"Foxes are a member of the canine lupus family. Like wolves, we cannot hear their thoughts."

She frowned. "Are you telling me I'm part dog?"

He chuckled. "I'm trying to delicately explain that after nine hundred years, I've learned to lean on my disciplines to communicate. Your thoughts are blocked to me, so that puts me at a bit of a disadvantage."

"How so?"

"I don't like it."

"Oh."

"Care to enlighten me about your and my daughter's *friendship*?"

Her lips pressed tight as she tipped her face to hide a blush behind the curtain of her hair. "I'm relieved you can't see into my head."

"So it appears."

That also explained why Adriel and the others could never pass her defenses. She glanced nervously at him.

"What if we were more than friends?"

"Who am I to judge how she lives her life? She's made it this far on her own. I'm a stranger to my only surviving child."

Her heart pinched when his voice turned to gravel. "It won't always be that way."

A smile ghosted over his lips. "I hope not." He stretched out his long legs like two tree trunks. "I would like to know her. And you."

She smiled at his acceptance. "And Dane. He's sort of ours. Like a stray dog that goes wherever we go."

Lazarus chuckled. "And Dane."

She fidgeted, nervous about the upcoming hours. "Once we're on our way, I can implement a protection spell."

"That will be helpful." He glanced back at the house. "After losing the children, Lilias lost part of herself. She entered what I refer to as her endless winter. If it comes down to it, I'll ask that you protect her before me."

His love for his mate had never been more evident. "If that's what you want."

"Her safety is always paramount."

"I won't let anything happen to her."

"Thank you." He glanced at the book he'd given her. "As you get older, your powers will become more defined. *Kitsune* are of fox and Asian descent. Once they reach their full maturity, they become *tenko*—celestial beings able to commune with the heavens. They're patron thieves, so they have a reputation for stealing."

"Swiper no swiping," she muttered under her breath. Her fox knowledge was limited to cartoon characters. "How do I do it?"

"Shift?"

"Yeah."

"That's one area where I have very little insight."

"Well, this helps." She patted the book. The weight of his grief shrouded the home. She looked up at him with concern. "Are you okay?"

"I regret that I've lost my sons. They would have fought for their sister."

"You're afraid we can't beat him?"

"I'm also concerned with the cost of victory."

He meant they weren't going to walk away unscathed. If a big old bastard like Lazarus was concerned, the rest of them should be shitting their pants. "There is someone who might be able to help." When he met her stare, she explained. "Adriel had a son."

"A son?" His eyes lit with wonder. "We have a grandchild?"

"A very *old* grandchild."

"Who is his father?"

"Cerberus, but—"

"Then no."

His rejection of Adriel's son brought instant relief, but logic set in. Damn her for opening her mouth. But Adriel was in trouble, and the only thing that mattered was getting her out safely.

Putting her personal feelings aside, she said, "Christian is a Schrock. Adriel raised him with *her* values, and I'm sure he would do anything in his power to help his mother."

"How are we to know his loyalties don't lie with his sire."

"Because Cerberus already tried to kill him and his mate to get to Adriel." She thought about Dane and how he feared others would judge him. "We can't hold sons and daughters accountable for the sins of their father."

"You're very wise, little witch."

She grinned. "It must be my *kitsune* showing."

Lazarus chuckled. "Lilias will be happy to meet our grandson."

Juniper's heart jolted. Contacting Christian meant returning to the farm and facing The Order again, something she vowed never to do, but as she'd already decided, for Adriel, she would do anything.

CHAPTER 32

Flying with vampires as old as Lilias and Lazarus was wild. They did not belong to a cult or society that rationed their use of power, so once they were going, it was a balls-to-the-wall compulsion for all.

If there was a chance for an upgrade, they got it. If they wanted silence, it happened. There were no primitive limitations, religious rules, or forced modesty cramping their style. And it was something to behold.

Once on the plane, Juniper wrapped them in a protective spell that gave them privacy to speak freely without the worry of others overhearing.

"How is it you didn't know about The Order when you seem to know so much about everything else?" Dane asked.

"Just as mortals break off into religious sects and small societies, there are countless covens around the world," Lilias explained. "Lazarus and

I never wanted to give anyone that sort of authority over our lives."

"Why should we, when we were born superior?" He spoke factually rather than arrogantly, and Juniper hoped that once this was over, their way of thinking would have a positive influence on Adriel.

Adriel should've trusted her own instincts more than her Bishop's, but she had been indoctrinated for centuries, and meek pacifism was the result. Now, after meeting her parents, Juniper realized just how strong Adriel could be. She wanted her to step into her power and grow her confidence as high as possible.

The elder Schrocks weren't afraid of the modern world. Lazarus didn't hesitate to feed when it came to meeting his and his mate's needs. This would have deeply troubled Juniper a few months ago, but now it only helped her cause. They needed all the strength they could muster.

Lazarus fed off the vein of the Uber driver, not explaining his choices, just as mortals offered no apology to a fish hanging from a line. He acted with respect and civility, taking great care of the donor and even displaying gratitude for his service.

The driver was fine, just slightly lightheaded and dazed, but fully able to continue his day. Taking pity on him, Juniper doused him with a quick abundance spell.

Lilias then drank from Lazarus's vein in the

back of the SUV, which reminded Juniper of how much she missed Adriel. She closed her eyes, quelling the anxiety pumping through her veins and focusing on the happy outcome. They would collect Christian, find Adriel, and then kill Cerberus.

That seemed straightforward enough.

The closer they drove to the farm the more anxious Juniper felt. After vowing never to return, she wasn't sure she had the strength to visit again. Her eyes found Dane's, and they exchanged a nervous glance.

He reached for her hand and squeezed. "You don't have to come."

Was that the coward's way out? Adriel needed her. They needed her son.

Dane squeezed her hand again. "We can do this part without you, June. We'll be fine."

She hated any sign of fragility.

The couple in the back shifted as Lazarus leaned forward. "What has you worried?"

Juniper glanced over her shoulder, but quickly averted her eyes as Lilias continued to feed from his neck. "Sorry, I don't mean to disrupt."

He frowned and whispered something in a different language to his mate. Lilias pulled her fangs from his vein and licked the wound shut. Her pupils dilated, and her lashes lowered as she sat back.

She knew that warm daze that came from

feeding from a partner and missed Adriel even more.

"Juniper's sitting this next part out," Dane said before she could decide.

"Hey—"

"It is what it is, June. There's no reason for you to get upset. We need you calm and focused."

"Why would she get upset?" Lilias asked, joining the conversation.

"She was a prisoner there."

"Dane!"

"What? It's true."

The energy of the car shifted. "I thought this was a place of decency."

"Juniper attacked an immortal and cast a spell on him, so they imprisoned her."

"Why?" There was no accusation in Lazarus's tone, only curiosity. "I'm sure you had a valid reason."

She didn't like talking about her time at The Order or what happened with Jonas. "He killed my aunt."

Lazarus nodded and sat back. "The females will stay at a hotel while Dane and I retrieve my grandson."

Juniper looked at Dane. She wasn't the only one who promised not to go back there. "Do you think you'll see her?" There was no need to specify she was asking about Grace.

He shrugged. "I'd rather not. She wouldn't approve of what we're doing."

Juniper sat back in her seat. "Well, she doesn't get a say."

He folded his hand in his lap and stared out the window as the landscape opened to a patchwork of fields and farmland. "Be nice."

"I'm always nice."

Dane chuckled. "Sure you are."

Juniper liked that Lazarus and Lilias had taken them under their wing. Unlike the Amish, they weren't afraid of violence and understood that sometimes life got messy.

Lilias told her that Lazarus was once a great warrior. It seemed his greatest weapons, however, were patience and knowledge. Lazarus never got worked up, and that helped Juniper stay calm.

But her mood shifted the moment they reached the motel. She wasn't sure separating was wise. On edge and anxious, she pulled Dane aside. "Maybe I should go."

"June, we'll be fine," he assured her.

She paced nervously. "They exiled you. What if they don't let you in?"

"The Bishop is one of Adriel's closest friends. He'll hear me out."

She rubbed the back of her neck, feeling foggy and unfocused like an addict going through some sort of withdrawal. "My heart's racing."

"Lazarus," Lilias snapped. "What did you do?"

Juniper looked up at the immortals, startled. "What do you mean?"

Lilias shook her head. "He has a habit of calming others when they're nervous. It can have a few side effects if you're not used to it."

"Such as?"

"Jitters and hyper-awareness when it wears off. Lazarus, you shouldn't do such things without permission."

"Apologies. I was merely trying to help. She was upset in the car."

Juniper paced. "I thought you couldn't get into my head?"

"It's not compulsion."

She frowned and Lilias explained, "It works like a pheromone. Very subtle and undetectable. The effects should wear off in a few minutes."

Thank God.

"Feeding might help."

The scent of manure and country air spoiled her appetite. "You're probably right, but I can't right now." She hated this place. "The guys should get going. The sooner they leave, the sooner we can get out of this hell hole." Every moment that passed was another chance for Cerberus to hurt Adriel.

Dane returned from the front desk with a room key. "We're in room six."

Perfect. Juniper hoisted her bag onto her shoulder and headed that way. Her nerves were starting to regulate, but a little blood might speed things along so she could feel normal again.

"Speaking of blood, I think there's something else we should do."

Lilias glanced at her in question. "Such as?"

"Your blood shares DNA with Adriel. We can use yours to find your daughter's exact location."

Once inside the motel room, she pulled out the grimoire and shut the curtains.

"Take whatever you need," Lilias said, already rolling up her sleeve.

Dane carried in the last of their bags, and another whiff of farmland wafted through the air. Lilias placed a calming hand on her shoulder. "You have nothing to fear of this place, child. Lazarus and I will protect you."

As much as she appreciated her words, they did not stave off the memories flooding her mind. She could smell the musty floor of her cell, hear the howls of Cybil, and the grunts and growls of Isaiah. The heavy footsteps of company approaching. The clink of keys and the creak of the bars opening.

"Juniper, look at me." Lilias held her by the shoulders, her green eyes creased with worry. She looked so much like Adriel. "You will get through this. *She* will get through this."

Light swept across the room as the door opened again and Lazarus stepped in. "We need to get moving. Is she—"

"She's fine. We're just having a moment, but it's nothing we can't manage on our own, dear. Juniper's tough. Isn't that right?"

Juniper nodded.

Lilias released her so she could say goodbye to Lazarus. Dane came to Juniper's side and frowned. "We won't be long." When he placed a hand on her shoulder, she flinched but then closed her hand over his.

"Be careful."

"I will."

It helped knowing Lazarus was going with him.

She closed her eyes and faced the panic welling inside of her. Calming her breathing, she pictured Adriel. Air reached her lungs as a placid vision filled her mind. She recalled the sweet scent of her skin and the gentle way she laughed. How warm and safe she felt when she was wrapped in her arms. The whole world quieted and all the ugly parts faded away.

Juniper's eyes opened and Lilias smiled. "Were you thinking of my daughter?"

"How did you know?"

She tapped her nose. "Your love has a scent, soft, like the inside of a rosebud. It's very young and pure."

Juniper pressed her lips tight and tipped her face down to hide her smile and blush. "Yeah, I was thinking of her."

Lilias brushed a hand down her arm. "We should try that locator spell now."

CHAPTER 33

Dane should have anticipated someone stopping them before they even set foot on the farm. Immortals had noses for scenting other immortals, and the males were extremely predatory when it came to protecting their females.

"Who's your friend, Dane?" Cain stepped out of the woods and eyed Lazarus with territorial challenge.

"Easy, son," Lazarus said, not at all threatened.

Cain raised a brow. "I'm not your son. And you're on my land."

"Cain, this is Lazarus Schrock. Lazarus, this is Cain Hartzler."

"Schrock?"

"He's Adriel's father. We came to speak to Christian."

"First, you'll need to ask the Bishop for permission."

"Seriously?"

Cain shrugged. "I'm not worried about you. But your friend here… I don't know him."

"Fine."

They walked to the safe house where the Bishop lived. Though only a few months had passed since he left, everything wore the foreign unfamiliarity of a dream. It was then he realized, the farm hadn't changed, but Dane had.

Lazarus was quiet along the journey, his sharp eyes taking in every detail as if mentally recording the property and noting any security pitfalls. Dane only wanted to get Christian and go. He hoped his half-brother could put their differences aside for once. This was about Adriel. If he couldn't see that, he truly was the bastard the rumors claimed him to be.

As they crested the knoll, the safe house came into view. Cain led them away from the houses and took a detour, eventually leading them to the steps of their destination.

"Stay here. I'll get Eleazar." He left them in the public lobby of Council Hall.

Dane wondered if there had been any sightings of Isaiah or his sister, but he didn't feel welcome to ask especially since Cain wasn't being his usual chatty self in front of outsiders.

Lazarus scanned the farm from a window, his eyes narrowing at the sight of three females walking in the distance. He was no doubt drawing comparisons about their Amish lifestyle.

"He won't be long."

Lazarus nodded, taking in the sign over the entrance to the main chamber where meetings were held. He frowned.

"Can you read Swiss German?"

"I cannot, but the message is implied."

Dane didn't know what the sign said, but he imagined it had to do with religion or submission.

Lazarus crossed the corridor, stopping just in front of the double doors. His stare dropped to the bench and his hand trembled as he reached out to touch the wood, exactly where Adriel used to sit.

"My daughter has been here in this exact place."

"Many times." It was her bench. The Bishop had put it there upon her insistence. "She liked to listen to the meetings. Females weren't allowed inside unless summoned by the elders."

Lazarus appeared confused by such a rule. "Why?"

Dane shrugged. "They have primitive beliefs."

His frown deepened. "And my daughter accepted this?"

"Not really." He chuckled. "She challenged them every chance she got." He looked at the bench. "She was also good at psychometry."

Adriel had a gift for tracing the ephemeral passing of living things, which was likely how Lazarus knew she'd been there.

He smiled. "She did?"

"Yeah. Guess she inherited that from you."

A wave of pride radiated from him just as the doors to the private offices opened. "Dane," the Bishop greeted with guarded curiosity. Cain followed silently. The Bishop extended a hand to Lazarus. "Good afternoon. I'm Eleazar King."

"Lazarus Schrock."

"So it's true. You're Adriel's father?"

"Yes."

Eleazar looked at Dane. "Is she—"

"Cerberus found her."

The Bishop's expression shuttered. "I'm sorry to hear that. I had hoped…"

"I appreciate your sympathy, but we haven't much time," Lazarus said, getting right to business. "My daughter's in danger, and we require all the help we can get. I'm told she has a son."

"Christian will certainly assist you. But if you're enlisting help, I'd like to also offer myself. I've faced Cerberus before. Three won't be enough."

"We also have my mate and a *kitsune* witch."

Eleazar frowned. "You're working with a witch?"

"We are."

"Is that wise?"

"Juniper is under my protection. As is Dane."

"I see." The Bishop studied Dane, but when he tried to probe into his memories, Lazarus stepped in front of him.

"Like I said, they're under my protection."

"Fair enough. I'll escort you to Christian's house."

Dane followed Lazarus and the Bishop only to get yanked back by Cain. "Who is that guy?"

Dane frowned. "You heard him. He's Adriel's father."

Cain stared after the two elders. "He's rogue."

"That doesn't make him bad."

"I didn't say it did." Cain looked after them with a spark of awe in his eyes. "You don't see many like that."

"Not here. He says there are lots of free covens in Europe." He smirked and plucked his suspenders. "No dress codes either."

Cain scowled at him and then grinned. "You look like you're doing all right on the outside."

"I'm managing."

"Good. I'm glad to hear it." He glanced at the large clock in the corner. "I have to get going. I told Destiny I'd be right back and that was a while ago."

"Tell her I said hi."

"I will." He was gone in a blink. So were any signs of the Bishop and Lazarus. Dane sighed and headed toward Christian's house only to pause when a soft female voice called his name.

"Dane." Her voice shot through him like a bolt of lightning.

Grace appeared leaving the private estate connected to Council Hall and words failed him. She must have been visiting her sister.

Her expression hardened and she scowled. "Are you back?"

"No."

Her lips formed a fine line, and her jaw trembled. "Then why are you here?"

"We're only passing through."

"We?"

He debated how much to share, knowing Gracie often worried more than necessary about his safety. It was sweet, but also an emasculating reminder that she viewed him as weak. "I'm traveling with an immortal couple named Lazarus and Lilias Schrock."

"Schrock? As in Christian and Adriel?"

"Her parents. We found them in Greece."

"*Greece?* Is that where you've been living?"

"Well, no, not exactly. I was in New York for a while. Ithaca. But then we left."

"We?"

He inwardly cursed. "I was staying with Adriel, but also Juniper—"

"The witch?"

"It's not like that, Grace. We're friends."

"Of course. Why wouldn't you befriend the one person who destroyed my family."

"She's sorry for that."

"Does she plan to fix my father?"

"She can't. Not yet, at least, but she's getting stronger. Her magick's improving. You should see what she can—"

"Spare me your gushing praise. That witch is dangerous and you shouldn't trust her."

"You don't know her."

"I know you."

"What does that mean?"

She looked away, but not before he caught the sheen of tears in her eyes. Was she jealous?

"We're only friends, Grace."

"Don't you have enough *friends*?" A tear slipped past her lashes.

"Hey." He caught her hand. "Don't cry."

"I'll survive." She wiped her eyes and straightened her shoulders, but she wouldn't meet his stare.

"Have you been…okay?"

She shrugged. "It's been quiet here since you left."

He tried to smile, but failed. "Bet you're not getting as many headaches with me gone."

She laughed, the sound watery and adorable. "Sometimes I miss them."

"No you don't."

She finally met his stare, and a million secrets passed between them. "As much as a literal pain blocking you from my mind was, I got used to it. Without the headaches, I always feel like I'm forgetting something."

She would eventually forget him. He released her hand and rubbed his chest. "Has there been any sighting of…"

"No." Genuine remorse flashed in her crystal blue eyes. "No one has seen Isaiah or Cybil since the night you left."

Dane thought about Lazarus. The immortal had so much knowledge about so many things. "The family I'm staying with is teaching me things they don't teach you here. There's a whole world of immortals out there, Grace. Covens that make their own rules. The females are treated as equals and have so much freedom."

"I like my home. I feel protected here."

"I'm just saying you have options if you ever want to leave."

"I don't."

"Well…" Some things never changed. There was no point spiraling toward the same old arguments. "I should get going."

"Why are you here, Dane?"

"Adriel's in trouble. We're picking up Christian."

"Why?"

He didn't want to worry her, but he also didn't want to lie. "Our father abducted Adriel. He's hurting her, and we have to save her."

"You mean her mate."

"He's not her mate. He's been lying to her. It's a long story, but we need all the help we can get. The Bishop's also joining us."

"Eleazar's going with you? Does Larissa know?"

"I'm sure he told her by now." Mates typically communicated through a live mental link from what he understood.

Grace looked back at the house. "I should check on her."

"Okay."

She hesitated, her stare pulling between her sister's house and him. "This is dangerous."

"I'll be careful."

Her breathing quickened as she prepared to argue, but there was no chance he was sitting this one out.

"I love you, Gracie."

"Dane, don't. We've been through this."

"I don't know if I'll have the chance to say this again, so let me just get this out. I love you. I'm not mad anymore. I just want you to be happy, so whatever it takes for that to happen, do it."

Twin tears chased down her cheek as she nodded at the ground. "Do you have to go?"

"You and I both know I can't stay."

"If you ask the Bishop to forgive your transgressions—"

"That's not why I can't stay here, Grace."

She sniffled and looked away. "Promise you won't put yourself in danger."

"I can't."

"Then promise me you'll survive."

Even that might be a tall order. "How about you make a promise to me."

"What do you want?"

He closed the distance, unable to stand the sight of her tears. "Promise not to waste anymore tears on me."

She turned her face away, unable to meet his stare. "I don't want you to get hurt." She wiped her eyes. "You're only half-immortal."

And just like that, she cut him down to size. He'd never be more than half a man to her. It was best she viewed him that way than realize what he really was, some mixed mortal *draugr* that hailed from an abusive psychopath.

"I know what I am. I also know I have to do this." Leaving her was never easy, which was why he'd avoided the goodbye the first time. "No more tears, okay?" He wiped away the last of them, forced himself to turn away but her thoughts flooded his mind in a wave of soft images, each one tightened his chest like a vise around his heart.

"Dane, wait!"

He turned, and she threw her arms around him, her lips sealing to his. Heart thundering, he caught her waist, lifting her feet off the ground, and kissing her hard enough that the bonnet covering her hair fell to the grass.

"Grace…" The heady perfume of her desire sweetened the air like a soft rain.

"I don't want you to go," she said, her lips damp with tears as they pressed into his. "I know you have to, and this is for the best, but I hate it." Her fist thumped over his heart, and a storm of emotion crashed over him.

"Shh-shh-shh." He sank into the kiss, not strong enough to deny himself the final pleasure that would most certainly end in agony.

The heat of her palm on his skin sent his heart hammering. Knowing this would be the last time, his last chance to show her what she did to him, he held nothing back.

He pulled her closer, and she pushed into him as if trying to embed herself there. It didn't matter that her kisses were untrained or inexperienced. Her desire ravaged him in ways that would haunt him for the rest of his life. No other female could ever compare.

She was perfect. In all of her charming imperfections, she was somehow flawless. Everything he wanted. Everything he needed. And the one thing he'd never truly have.

Breathless, he broke the kiss and stared into her eyes. Dark, damp lashes spiked around those stunning pools of crystal blue. His thumb brushed softly over her lower lip, and he smiled at the sight of her fangs.

For once, she didn't hide her feelings from him. Her mind was open, but he read all he needed to know -- the truth in her stare. "You shouldn't look at me like that, Grace. Not when there will inevitably be someone else."

Her gaze turned away. "Eventually, yes, my mate will come. But you will always be my first love, Dane Foster."

She was killing him. How was he supposed to let her go now, knowing some other man would eventually touch her like this?

With aching slowness, he lowered his mouth to hers one last time and whispered, "I may be your first love, Gracie Hartzler, but you will always be my greatest."

The agony spread from his chest to his legs as he gently stepped away, caressing her cheek until his hand could no longer reach her. He bent to retrieve her bonnet and placed it over her hair. "Take care of yourself."

She nodded, already breaking her promise about the tears. "Stay safe, Dane."

His mouth formed an ingenuine smile. Guess they both planned to break their vows. "I will," he lied then finally turned away.

CHAPTER 34

The cave perched high above the sea, far removed from the world. There was no life here, nor hope. And when Adriel prayed for a merciful end, there was no relief in death either. There was only desolate, hopeless suffering.

The crippling atrophy of her legs, hands, fingers, and arms left her gnarled. She lay on the cold floor, naked in a heap of torn flesh and broken bones, shivering as the bitter winds screamed through the rocky cliffs, while Cerberus ate meat off the bone of some kill.

She didn't remember entering the cave or much that happened after her fall. She only knew she wanted to die. By this point, she gave up hoping that Juniper had heard her cry, and she was certain her future would only get worse.

Bite marks left dark patches all over her battered body. He drained her of blood, ensuring her cells would not heal. The tissue around her organs had withered and tightened to a brittle husk, so even the shallowest breaths strangled parts of her.

He tossed a bone into the pile by the entrance of the cave. Flames licked at the shadows of the stone ceiling, but she was too far from the fire to feel its warmth.

It hurt too much to cry or shiver, so she simply retreated to a numb part of her soul. Her body might still be whole, but her mind had fractured some time ago. Inside, she was screaming through the gaping void of time with no relief in sight. Her eternity belonged to him now, and she would live in agony, under the command of a monster.

Clouds rolled overhead marking time. Darkness flickered in the distance as a storm approached. At this altitude, one might think they could touch the heavens, but she was in hell. Only evil existed here.

Thunder rumbled over the sea and wind howled through the moors like a chorus of tormented souls. She wished it were the voices of angels coming to take her away.

The jagged walls sparkled where water dripped. The crystal sediment reminded her of Juniper, and the pain in her heart formed a steady throb that never dulled.

Starved, weak, and broken, her mind teetered on the edge of collapse. But her heart shattered days ago, when she accepted she would never see Juniper again.

I'm sorry... she wished she could tell her how much she wanted a life with her, a new beginning, and a chance at happiness. But those things were never meant for her.

"You think someone could love you?" Cerberus taunted, tossing away another bone. He easily penetrated her mind once she was injured and weak . Once he embedded himself there, he could see everything she saw and hear every private thought. "Perhaps I'll find your little friend. We can have her for dinner one night—the two of us."

Her eyes closed but the horrific image lingered. She tried her best not to think. Like a fire without oxygen, she tried to starve him out of her mind.

His low chuckle challenged the howling wind as he walked to the entrance. "You're not getting rid of me that easily, girl."

Looking out over the black sea, his silhouette loomed like specter against the blustery night sky. Nothing was out there. Time was losing meaning. No one was coming to save her.

His crimson eyes gleamed with malevolent satisfaction as he glared at her, his foot sinking hard into her stomach. He enjoyed her suffering too much, and it would only get worse.

"I own you now, girl." He stepped on her wrist, applying pressure until the bone snapped, and she whimpered. The cruel lines of his face twisted with sadistic gratification as he watched her struggle to breathe. "Your will, your mind, your very existence. All of it belongs to me."

He laughed, and Adriel's gaze flickered with a spark of defiance.

"You have something you want to say to me?" he bent closer, mocking her as if he cared about what she wanted to say. "Of course not, because *you're weak!* You've always been a contemptible cunt." He spit on the ground.

She closed her eyes and breathed, "You…"

He stilled and grinned. "What was that?"

She panted through the pain, forcing her mouth to form the words. "Will never… have all of me." He would never have her heart.

Cerberus cackled darkly, the chilling sound echoing through the cavern. "Your heart? If I wanted your heart, I'd cut it out of you." He sneered, wrenching her head back by her hair as he stabbed his claw into her flesh. "I could eat right from your chest while your arteries are still beating—but I'd never let you fully die." He dropped her head, letting it smack on the stone floor. "What fun would that be?"

He faced the entrance again. "Keep your heart." He dragged his razor-sharp claws down the cave wall. "I prefer you alive. Although…" He glanced back at her, his fangs gleaming. A small bite wouldn't kill you."

Her breath hitched as he was once again slicing into her chest. "I could cut you open here." His claw scraped down her breast with scalpel-like precision. "Steal a hunk. Not enough to kill you, but enough to make you suffer."

Her vision blurred with fresh tears.

"Tedious tears. Like that ever worked on me."

He yanked her to her back and settled his weight over her. He loved her surrender most when it wasn't voluntary, so she refused to fight him as it would only excite him more.

"Shall we begin?"

Her head lifted with a breathless gasp as his claw stabbed deep, embedding in her chest and scraping the tissue of her heart. She prayed he'd go too far and kill her once and for all. The plunging pull and pressure of his fist tightening around the organ gave her hope. If he yanked it out of her, this torture would finally be over. She welcomed the thought and closed her eyes.

"You think—" His words cut off, and his hand yanked away, leaving her racing heart intact.

A sudden crash, louder than thunder, barreled into the cave as lightning struck the entrance, igniting the earth with flames. Blinding light filled the cavern, and she shut her eyes.

Perhaps her brain was having some sort of attack. The flashes of light were so intense they lanced through her skin, and her vision strobed behind her lashes.

A vicious growl pierced the air and her eyes shot open. Cerberus bolted to his feet, crouching in a defensive pose. Wind surged through the cave, throwing him against the wall, and he hissed angrily as something moved too fast for Adriel to fully see, but Cerberus snarled and she enjoyed watching him struggle against the unseen enemy.

Another boom, and he crashed down again. The flames of the fire roared to life as the rock walls trembled and crumbled. Cerberus roared and rushed forward, throwing her into the wall and out of his way as he tried to evade the intruder. His blood-red eyes flashed as he bared his fangs, hungry for battle.

Another blast threw him back.

Was she imagining it? Had she hit her head too hard? What was doing this?

Light radiated from below, bright enough to carry a hum. Cerberus covered his ears as the frequency grew to a sharp whistle. The glowing white aura screamed so loud the wind became a whisper.

From the blinding light emerged a hulking figure, tall and imposing. A halo of white light defined every limb of the massive figure. It was no one she recognized.

Cerberus growled and lunged, but he was thrown back. Rocks fell onto Adriel, one heavy bolder landing directly on her skull.

Winking in and out of consciousness, she watched the imposing figure close in on Cerberus, never giving him a chance to fully recover. He displayed unearthly power and the authority of an all-powerful god as his eyes blazed with righteous fury. The air tinged with the sharp oxidized scent of magick.

Then the hair on the back of Adriel's neck rose as her blood tingled with the sense that others were near. *Juniper!* It was too late. She shouldn't come here. The damage was done and if Cerberus saw her he would recognize her from Adriel's mind and hurt her just to punish Adriel.

No, no, no, no!

She couldn't come now. Escape was hopeless. She needed to leave her and save herself.

Cerberus hissed, bared his fangs, and clawed at the avenging immortal. He jumped and pounced, slamming his fists into the ground and shaking the cave hard enough to rattle Adriel further into the wall. The massive newcomer only growled and stepped closer, unmoved by the tremors racing through the cave.

Something was protecting him. Adriel squinted through the cloud of dust at the entrance of the cave. Fear siphoned the breath from her crushed lungs as Juniper's familiar form revealed in the smokey light.

Adriel choked on a sob of relief and worry. It was too late. She shouldn't be here.

Go back! Run! She internally screamed, too weak and devoid of blood to communicate any other way.

Juniper couldn't hear her. Her eyes were locked on Cerberus, her hands crackling with magical energy, and her face a mask of fierce determination. The sorcery she conjured went beyond her skill and Adriel wondered who was helping her.

Relentless, energy balled like fire between her fingers, tinged with dark purpose and glowing light as it blasted from her palms, hurling Cerberus into the back wall. Was she working with the hulking angel?

Adriel didn't trust the vision. It had been days of torment, and hope had abandoned her long ago. This had to be a hallucination from the pain.

For a moment, it seemed they were truly there. The formidable duo of her greatest love and whatever god fought by her side. They were a beacon of hope, too surreal to believe. Yet, the cruel fantasy briefly masked the pain.

Cerberus hissed and charged, lunging for the god-like male.

"No!" Juniper heaved a blazing ball of white light at him.

He slammed into the shadows.

"Protect Adriel!" the male yelled.

Adriel shrieked as hands lifted her broken body from the ground. The slightest movement caused her excruciating pain. Gravity pulled at her broken limbs like anvils.

"It's okay. It's me."

Her eyes opened, but she couldn't see through the smoke and tears. A white light flashed over the cave's crevices, and the familiar silhouette of Dane took form. He was armed and dressed all in black. His mission was clear.

"I've got you, Ade. We've come to take you home."

"Careful," another voice called as Dane laid her on a blanket by the cave's opening. "Put her here."

"She's as fragile as a broken bird and needs blood." The slightest touch brought agony. "We can't move you any further until you feed. I'm sorry if I hurt you."

The other figure drew closer, and she gasped, praying this was a dream and she wasn't actually seeing her son emerge from the shadows of smoke and flashing light as a battle broke out behind them. "You're safe now, Mother."

No! She wanted to argue, but panic choked her. Christian had a mate. She needed him. It was too dangerous! They must leave this place.

"Mother, be still."

When she tried to stop him from helping her, Dane restrained her. "Adriel, let us help you."

Her heart jolted as she tried to speak, but her jaw was broken, and she was far too weak to fight them.

"She needs blood. Now. We cannot wait." Her son rolled back his sleeve, blocking her view of the cave.

Cerberus roared as Juniper chanted in ancient tongues. A whirlwind of energy erupted and twirled through the cave, lifting debris and pebbles that whipped around with hurricane force.

They needed to leave this place before Cerberus went too far. She could bear the physical pain, but seeing her greatest loves harmed would destroy her in ways she couldn't bear.

Her voice scraped against her crushed throat. "Do not strain yourself, Mother."

Christian draped a light cloth over her withered body. The weight of the material burned her flesh but shielded her from the wind.

When she couldn't escape the hallucination, she shook violently. Were they truly there? Chills wracked her battered limbs. She could feel the blanket on her skin and smell her son's hair.

"Drink, Mother." He pressed his wrist to her mouth.

Warm, life-giving blood coated her tongue, but her throat was too ravaged to swallow. She coughed and sputtered, choking violently.

Dane cradled her head in his lap. "Try to relax, Ade."

How could she relax when there was a nightmare unfolding behind him?

She coaxed a few drops down but then violent growls spewed from the dust clouds. A blast of wind swirled with ghostly howls into the cave and someone's body slammed into the wall.

Juniper screamed, and Adriel's heart stopped.

"You must keep drinking, Mother."

She weakly pushed Christian's wrist away and rasped, "Help... June."

"The witch knows what to do."

What did that mean? Cerberus would kill her.

Adriel's throat was a ravaged open wound, and her voice no more than a scratch of sound, but she refused to let Juniper die for her sake. "Hel—p her…Chris… Plea…" Her body convulsed with a hacking cough, and she could speak no more.

"*Adriel,*" the sharp command cut through the chaos as Eleazar's tall figure appeared, his dark eyes as familiar as his authoritative tone.

"We aren't leaving without you or the witch. But you must listen to your son and drink."

Are you truly here?

He pressed into her mind. *We are here, my friend.* He crouched before her and carefully cupped her cheek. *And we're taking you home, but you must feed.*

Juniper—

Is helping us. No one will harm her.

Her eyes fluttered shut as her strength depleted.

"I've got her." Dane gently cradled her hand, curling his fingers loosely around hers. "We need you to drink now, Adriel. Please."

The few drops of blood she managed to swallow hit her insides like cannon fire. There was too much damage to repair. Bile rose and her body rejected the offering, pain knifing through her intestines where Cerberus had injured her.

"Mother, please…" Christian held his wrist to her lips, but she couldn't do it. "Eleazar, you'll have to compel her. She's resisting me."

The sharp intrusion of the bishop's compulsion came without anesthetics. Her broken jaw opened as life-giving blood flooded her ravaged throat. The agony in her belly locked into knots like barbed wire, and she screamed, but they kept feeding her.

"You're doing great," Dane whispered, gently cradling her head in his lap. The comfort broke her more than the pain, and she wept inconsolably as they forced the blood down.

Cerberus broke free of the scuffle with a feral roar. *"You dare to touch my mate?"*

He lunged at them, his claws outstretched and his face dripping blood. Something came from the darkness with supernatural speed and crashed into him head-on, plowing him back into the shadows and smoke.

The clash reverberated through the cave. Fists flew, claws raked, and blood spilled as violent hisses spattered the earth as it spewed through the wind-swept air. Whoever they were, they fought with primal ferocity. They fought without rest. They fought to kill.

The longer Juniper wove her magick, the more dark energy spiced the air, far more potent than anything Adriel witnessed her conjure before. It was too much. There would be a steep cost. She shouldn't do this. Her strength would eventually wane, and then he would punish her.

A sharp female cry split through the chaos as the smallest immortal went down. A guttural roar ripped through the air, and the hulking immortal slammed Cerberus into the wall, violently scoring his claws through his flesh and choking the breath from his lungs.

He repeatedly slammed him into the rocks with the force of a meteor. Enraged beyond reason, the giant immortal roared as cracks webbed at Cerberus's back, fracturing the stone.

Cerberus bit into the immortal's throat, but he countered by plunging his fist into Cerberus's chest. Slate crumbled from the ceiling, showering the cave in blinding dust and debris.

Eleazar dove into the melee, and more growls spewed from the cloud of smoke and grime. The walls deteriorated, and it became harder to breathe.

Bolts of energy shot into the brawl, taking Cerberus down, but he continuously broke free of the magick. His rage was bottomless, but Juniper always drove him back. Eleazar and the hulking immortal fought with terrifying resilience.

Adriel could not look away. A spark of hope ignited, and then Cerberus turned his fury on Juniper, his eyes promising death.

"*No!*" Adriel screamed, fighting out of Dane's arms.

Cerberus sprung with lethal intent.

Adriel lunged forward, but Christian caught her, forcing her back. "Help her!"

"We're trying to help *you!* You need more blood." Her son struggled to calm her, but she would not give in. "Mother, you're hurt!"

Defeated, her vision blurred. She couldn't help Juniper. She was at their mercy and helpless. "Please…"

"Look at me," her son commanded with sharp authority. "Let us help you, and I will then help her. But you are my first priority."

His *first* priority, but not his last.

Tears burned her eyes as she searched the clouds of smoke, her gaze always seeking Juniper. The dust cleared, and Cerberus spiked his fist into the ground.

A brilliant flash gathered between Juniper's fingers, and she projected a shield of light around herself before the tremors reached her, deflecting his attack. His rage doubled.

He growled in frustration. The hulking immortal delivered a devastating blow to his chest, crushing bone and caving in muscle. Cerberus howled in pain but retaliated, lunging at the petite female figure on the cave floor.

He yanked her up by the hair, lifting her face from the ground, and Adriel gasped, realizing who these avenging angels were. They were not angels at all. They were her parents.

Chills wracked her body as emotion clogged her throat. Juniper heard her plea after all. She found them.

What she must have gone through to accomplish such a task…

All this time, Adriel thought they were dead and gone because Cerberus told her they were. One more lie. One more betrayal. It was no wonder she was without hope. He destroyed her faith in not just her god but also those she loved. But they were actually here, fighting to save her, because they loved her.

Juniper unleashed another blast of energy, but Cerberus used Adriel's mother as a shield.

"Stop!" Adriel's father roared, a look of horror in his eyes.

Juniper froze. Fury banked in her eyes, deferring to Adriel's father's command. Eleazar crept slowly along the wall.

"Let her go, Cerberus," her father ordered.

Cerberus seethed, holding her mother by the throat, his other fist twisted in her hair as he rose to his full height. "Now, you will truly know what loss is." His claws lengthened, and the air crackled as a storm raged over the sea, blowing gusts of salty wind and rain into the cave.

The air charged with electricity, and Juniper siphoned it all. Her fingers spread wide as she prepared to strike, only needing a safe opening and a signal from the others.

Adriel's father hesitated, reading the dangerous situation for what it was. Cerberus jerked her mother's body higher, shielding himself in a way that left the others at his mercy.

"Lazarus, just say the word," Juniper growled.

Her father raised a staying hand. But there was no reasoning with Cerberus.

If Juniper released her magick and missed her target, Adriel's mother might not survive.

Memories flooded her mind as a damn broke

inside of her. She remembered their unfathomable love and the possessive way her father adored and guarded her mother. He would do anything to protect her, including lay down his own life.

Adriel couldn't look away. This might be the last time she saw her parents alive. As deep as that ache burrowed inside of her, it was nothing compared to the thought of losing Juniper.

Cerberus roared, his fangs dripping with blood and venom as his wild glare bounced from each enemy.

Sniffing her mother's hair, he slowly hissed, "Lilias…"

"*Cerberus!*" her father growled, but it wasn't enough to stop him from dragging his slick nose down her mother's cheek.

Her mother's body hung limply in his arms, but then her head slowly lifted, her stare directed to Adriel's father's. Something private whispered between them, spoken through the sacred link shared only by mates. Adriel feared it was a goodbye.

Eleazar watched cautiously, waiting for a signal to strike. Wind tunneled through the cave, and the scent of their fear overpowered the sea air. Dane fumbled with a small leather pack, his hands trembling violently as a vile of crushed herbs slipped out of his grip and rolled across the cave floor.

"The aconite," he hissed, lunging forward to

catch the tiny jar. He passed the vile to Christian. "Go. It will sedate him."

Adriel caught her son's arm. She couldn't let him risk getting that close. "He's won. Save yourself. Go home to your mate."

"He hasn't won," Christian snapped, evading her grasp.

"Christian, I cannot lose you too."

"You won't." Dane shoved her back into Christian's arms and snatched the vile, running directly toward Cerberus.

Chaos exploded. Cerberus bit into her mother's throat, and her father went ballistic, exploding with uncontainable rage. Eleazar ripped her mother out of Cerberus's arms the moment his grip loosened.

"Now, Juniper, strike now!" Adriel's father yelled the moment Eleazar and Lilias were out of the cave.

Cerberus sprung, but her father tackled him to the ground. A landslide of stone crumbled from the far wall.

Juniper hesitated when Cerberus threw Adriel's father backward with bone-shattering force.

"*Papai!*" Adriel's voice cut above the noise, and Juniper turned, her eyes wide as Lazarus's body lay heaving for breath as blood pooled beneath his hulking form on the floor.

Juniper raised her glowing hands and shouted, "*Vi maris, vim lunae—*"

Cerberus rammed through her forcefield,

slamming Juniper into the wall. Adriel screamed in horror as she collapsed to the ground, a puddle of blood forming beneath her head.

"You bastard!" Dane leapt over Juniper's fallen body and time stilled.

Adriel screamed as Christian restrained her, forcing her to watch helplessly as Cerberus raked his claws down Dane's chest. Blood sprayed, and he gripped his throat, but it was too late.

A vicious growl ripped through the cave, territorial and female. A new, tiny form bolted into the cave and caught Dane before his body hit the ground. A sharp cry of distress pierced the air as his limp body fell into the female's arms, and Adriel's eyes widened at the sight of Grace Hartzler.

What was she doing there?

"We must go." Christian lifted her into his arms.

"We can't leave them."

"This is our only chance."

Adriel looked back at the chaos. Juniper wasn't moving, and Gracie cradled Dane's limp body in her lap. She begged him to open his eyes and look at her, but he only gasped for breath as blood choked him and spilled down his pillaged chest.

Cerberus straightened, his eyes locking with Adriel's as his body heaved and his shoulders puffed with rage. He smiled slowly, his eyes scanning from Gracie to her parents and settling on Juniper.

Adriel fought her son. "I can't leave her." She broke free of his hold, but her legs were still too weak to carry her.

"Mother, we must leave. Now!" Christian hauled her toward the opening.

"*No!* I won't leave her like this!" The wind howled at their back as he dragged her.

Gracie sobbed over Dane. Juniper still wasn't moving. Adriel's father crawled to her, his arm slashed open and outstretched. He struggled to reach her. Cerberus kicked him to his back. He slammed his fists into him, lifting his hulking body over his head and hurling him toward the cliffs. Her father's body slammed down, sliding dangerously close to the ledge.

It was over. He won.

Throwing back his head, Cerberus cackled, blood dripping in black rivulets from his jaw, his evil glare settling on Dane. Gracie set his body down carefully and stood, her dress drenched with Dane's blood and her eyes lit with uncontained fury.

Christian tugged Adriel to keep moving. "Mother, you will die if we stay here!"

"Then I will die!" She ripped her arm free and lurched toward Juniper. Her body gave out when something feral lanced through the air, knocking her off balance.

Adriel slammed onto her knees. Cerberus raised his claws and leapt through the air, prepared to strike Gracie down, when a roar ripped through the cave. A hulking animal-like form collided with him mid-flight. The clash was a horrific explosion of growls and feral intent.

A clawed fist—that of a man but with tufts of fur and dark grey talons—swept violently down Cerberus's body just as her son threw himself protectively over her. "Don't look!"

Time silenced and she heard the exact moment his scream cut off. Life flashed before her eyes. Childhood. Joy. Sorrow. Grief. Pain. Longing. Loss. Escape. Her son. Love. Juniper.

She jerked her son's hand away from her eyes as Cerberus's body collapsed, his head rolling toward her, his eyes blindly staring.

The furred creature landed in a hunched pose, his body that of a man, but his back and shoulders heaving under ropes of muscles and sinew where pelts of hair grew. A low growl purred through the cave as he turned his green eyes on Adriel.

Cerberus's fingers twitched, and the warrior spun, punching his clawed fist through Cerberus's chest and ripping out his black heart. Adriel flinched and screamed, as did Gracie. The creature, unbothered by his display of savagery, tossed the heart into the flames where it sizzled.

Juniper lifted a trembling hand and pointed a finger at Cerberus's headless body. *"In....s-s-sig....nia."* A blaze lit the cave, engulfing the corpse.

The green-eyed creature reached for the head, grabbed it by the hair, then lobbed it into the fire beside the burning heart. He turned, towering over them as he growled and flashed a mouthful of fangs that were unmistakably canine.

"I wish you no harm," he said in a thickly accented voice with a Nordic lilt. Holding up his palms, he displayed dark pads beneath tufts of fur, then his claws retracted and his flesh lightened from dark grey to tan. He glanced back at the burning body and to Adriel. "That thing was a *draugr*."

Weary and depleted, the last of her strength gave out. Juniper dragged herself closer, her fingers weakly stretching toward Adriel's. Dane coughed, and Adriel's father grunted as he tried to crawl to them.

The beastly warrior growled and stepped between them, withdrawing a vicious dagger. "Do not come any closer to my mate."

Mate?

Adriel looked up at him in horror. His was neither wolf nor man. He had no mate here.

"They need…blood." Her father swayed to his side, hardly able to crawl.

The armed wolf warrior growled, aiming his blade at the males. "Move any closer to her, and I'll end you."

"There must be some mistake—"

"There's no mistake. I'll collect my mate. Then, you may carry on as you wish."

Cold dread settled in Adriel's stomach as she turned her sorrowful gaze to the others. There was no joy in this moment. Only desolation, shock, and a sense of permanence that could not be undone.

As she looked at Juniper, her heart drowned in empathy. But the warrior spoke with absolute certainty. There had been no mistake. He was not here to fight. Only to claim what was irrevocably his.

CHAPTER 35

*P*ain radiated from Dane's skull through his spine when he coughed, blood spilling from the deep grooves scored across his chest as his throat pulsed and burned. His eyes could hardly open. Fear sparred with feebleness as a blade angled toward him in the misshapen hand of the stranger glaring possessively at Gracie.

Lazarus lurched closer only to still when threatened by the heavily armed man. "Move any closer to her, and I'll end you."

Lazarus stilled his intent to offer Dane his vein. "There must be some mistake—"

"There is no mistake. I'll collect my mate. Then, you may carry on as you wish."

Dane's blood chilled to ice. The gash at the back of his head was deep and in need of attention. Words were jumbled, and he must have misunderstood what was being said.

Lashes heavy with blood, he scanned the cave. Juniper lay in a puddle of carnage on the floor. Adriel panted in a heap only a few feet away, her arm outstretched to reach her. Lazarus huddled before him, and Gracie stood between him and this dog-like creature.

What are you doing here, Grace?

Fury bubbled up inside of him, but a brutal cough seized his lungs the moment he tried to speak. Gracie stood in front of the man as he bared a wicked blade, her shoulders heaving as she caught her breath and stared at the dagger.

Gracie! Dane couldn't get into her head.

Her dress was covered in blood. Was she hurt?

"Grace..." Dane sputtered through the gurgling coughs choking him. His damp shirt clung to his body, soaked through with his own sweat and blood. Weakness slowed him as much as pain, but he had to pull her back. "Gracie."

A growl snapped from the man's throat as his glowing green stare locked with Dane's.

What was he? Part wolf, part man? Dane had never seen such a creature. And why was he looking at Gracie in such a possessive way.

"Grace, are you hurt?"

She glanced back at Dane as if she'd forgotten he was there. Uncertainty flashed in her eyes, and she glanced back to the rugged man holding the knife. She appeared unharmed. Was the blood on her his?

Looking down at his ravaged chest, Dane

noted how much had spilled. He glanced back at Lazarus, who struggled to crawl to him. They needed to heal.

Adriel crept slowly toward June, but neither was capable of walking. Eleazar stood against the wall near Christian. They were all watching the stranger with the blade.

"Do you not recognize me?" the man asked, his eyes locked with Gracie's.

She took a step back, her hand fluttering to her chest. The smoke cleared as the dust settled, and only Cerberus's charred remains burned in the back of the cave. Adriel pulled herself closer to Juniper, the blanket dragging behind her. Regret flashed in her stare when she looked at Dane, and his addled brain slowly caught up.

No.

He looked back at Grace, who stared at the man.

"Who are you?" she finally asked, and Dane's heart sank.

By the possessive way the creature watched her, he knew this was his enemy.

He was a maker of nightmares, a stealer of souls.

He was the reason she was called to this very place in time.

He came for one purpose only—to take her away from him.

The pain in Dane's chest became unbearable. "No!"

She wasn't meant to be here! She never left

the farm, and yet, here she was. This had to be a horrific dream. He didn't trust his blurred vision as his pounding head tried to process. There seemed a lethal wound tunneling through his heart, but he found no opening there.

"My name is Darius Størm. I am of the shadow-wolves, and I've come a long way to find you."

"*Me?*" Gracie took another step back.

"Yes. You're the female from my visions."

She shook her head. "That's impossible. I'm immortal."

"That is an unexpected complication but not one that will change our circumstances. You are my mate."

"The hell she is!" Dane dragged himself up, only to slip and lose his balance in the puddles of blood.

Gracie instinctively reached out an arm to help him but froze when the stranger growled. "I wouldn't."

She scowled and turned her glare on him. "I haven't had a calling—"

"You keep your mind blocked. The gods guided me here." He frowned at the burning body behind him. "Do you typically engage in dangerous crusades with lethal predators? Are you some sort of vigilante?"

Gracie nearly choked on a laugh. "I've never even left the farm…" Her words faded as her frown deepened. "I've had no symptoms."

"I said stay back." The shadow-wolf's glare cut

to Dane as he struggled to his feet, gripping his side and wavering from blood loss.

Fuck this guy. "Only true immortals can be called."

The corner of his mouth curled in a half smile, a sharp canine fang flashing as he scoffed. "Who told you that?"

"It's true," Gracie argued. As someone who let faith mold her entire life, she would know.

The shadow-wolf frowned. "No, it's not." He looked at the others. "Someone has lied to you."

"Bullshit." Dane lurched forward and staggered back when a sharp dagger plunged into the cave floor, a mere inch from his boot.

"One more step, and you're in the fire."

Dane's stare found Gracie's. *What the hell is going on? Grace? Gracie!* But her mind remained locked to him.

Lazarus shifted with a grunt and pushed off the ground. His arms and legs were drenched with blood, making it impossible to see where his injuries began. The shadow-wolf growled, but Lazarus held up his palms. "I must check on my mate."

They held their collective breaths as he lurched to the cave entrance. Lilias threw herself at him, coming out of nowhere and speaking frantically in their ancient language, already pushing her wrist at her mate, insisting he feed.

Lazarus stilled her hand and met the Bishop's stare. "Thank you for protecting her and providing blood when I was unable to meet my duty and she was in need. I am forever in your debt."

"There is no debt, friend." Eleazar's gaze returned to the shadow-wolf. "It is unusual to see your kind this far east."

"I do not plan to stay long."

Lazarus and Lilias stood back, hands locked and their longing stares protectively pinned on their daughter. He drew his mate's arm closer and casually started to feed.

Did no one care that this stranger was planning to steal Gracie away?

"Eleazar, did you hear what he wants?" Dane snapped. "Is anyone going to say something?"

"We heard, Dane." The Bishop looked at Grace, then at the shadow-wolf. "May I?"

The shadow-wolf considered Eleazar for a long moment, then nodded. The Bishop approached her slowly, never attempting to touch her or stand too close. "Grace, do you recognize him?"

Jaw trembling, she looked up at the Bishop with shimmering, trusting eyes, desperately seeking council. She shook her head.

"Have you opened your mind?"

"There's nothing to search!" This was ridiculous. "He's not like us," Dane snapped.

The shadow-wolf scoffed. "Not like *you*, half-breed." His attention returned to Grace. "I had a vision of you standing where you're standing now. I come with only honor and integrity in my heart."

Eleazar frowned. "Why are you here, Grace? You did not have permission to leave the farm."

Fear filled her eyes, and her chin trembled. "I was worried. Dane said there would be great danger. I know it was reckless, but I felt compelled to follow you. It was only out of concern."

"Compelled or called?"

Darius held up his hands. "There has been no compulsion on my part. My visions started months ago."

"How is this possible?" Her whole body shook like a leaf. "I've not had any symptoms, and he's… not like us."

"There are always exceptions to the rules, child—"

"This is horse shit!" Dane snapped. "Since when are there fucking exceptions?"

"Easy," Lazarus warned with a staying hand. "This shadow-wolf does not want trouble, Dane."

"Fuck him! Grace, you do not have to go with him."

"Grace," the Bishop said in a much calmer voice, which she responded to. "An unexpected calling is no less righteous. If it is God's will, it is your sacred duty."

She looked down, tears shimmering in her eyes. "I know my purpose."

"Then you must honor it."

Dane's body vibrated with uncontainable rage. "Gracie! Don't listen to them! Eleazar, what the fuck are you telling her? This is not your goddamn purpose, Grace. You don't even recognize him!"

He might not be a full-bread immortal capable of a calling, but he'd dreaded this outcome long enough to learn how these things work. This jacked-up, dog-looking mother fucker was not part of her destiny.

"You have a family waiting for you at home."

"Now, she has a pack. That's all she needs."

"A pack? Fuck your pack!"

The wolf growled, and Lazarus clasped a hand on Dane's shoulder before he could take another step. "Excuse my friend."

The wolf curled his lips, then sniffed the air and smirked.

"What the fuck are you grinning at?"

His fanged sneer stretched wider. "They don't know, do they?"

Dane jerked his arm, but Lazarus's grip was unbreakable. "Know what?"

"What you are. They think your immortal half is like their bloodline."

The blood rushed from his face. Gracie looked at him with deep concern. Dane couldn't speak. He wouldn't lie, but he also couldn't bring himself to say it.

"Should I tell them?"

He looked to Lazarus, who had protected and accepted him. And the Bishop, who—despite their differences—gave him a safe place to live and advocated to keep his sister alive. Was this the last time they'd look at him like a normal person? The moment they pieced to-gether his *draugr* roots, they would view him as a parasite.

His stare returned to Grace. He didn't want her to know. It was bad enough he was already a half-breed. He couldn't bear to become anything less in her eyes.

The wolf's stare followed his, and under-standing dawned. "I see." He closed the distance, softening his stare as he looked into her confused eyes. "It's Grace then?"

"G-Grace. Or G-Gracie," she stammered.

His smile gentled. "Gracie."

The wolf looked back at Dane triumphantly, challenge in his cold green eyes. One wrong move, and he had the power to ruin him with only words. Turning back to Grace, he held her stare.

"I want you to open your mind, Grace. You'll find me there."

She looked nervously at Dane, then the Bishop. Eleazar nodded. Gracie shut her eyes and swayed. The wolf steadied her.

"Tell me what you see, *min pärla*?"

Her breath hitched and her lashes fluttered open. Tears filled her eyes as breath rushed past her trembling lips. "I don't understand."

"What has you confused?"

"I...saw you, but I can't read you."

His smile fell and his brow creased. "Try again."

She closed her eyes in concentration. Lifting

her hand, he pressed her palm to his chest. "I'm here. My mind is open to you."

Her frown deepened, then she blinked and shook her head. "There's nothing."

"Because he's a shadow-wolf," Lazarus explained. "They're unreadable to immortals."

Darius frowned. "My pack brothers will explain it to us. Perhaps there is something to be done."

"No way," Dane argued. "If she can't read you, there's no calling."

"Dane." The Bishop's tone carried heavy warning. "What did you see, Grace?"

"I…" Gracie glanced at the Bishop then back to the wolf. "Us. It was hazy, but he was there. We both were."

"Where, child?"

"A castle hidden deep in the Alps, buried by long winters and protected by cold winds. I saw stone walls and lavish tapestries. The scent of fire and fur."

"Yes," the shadow-wolf agreed. "Winters are long, but the privacy is cherished and our blood runs warm. There are plenty of acres for hunting, and the locals rarely bother us."

Was anyone really buying this?

"What about my family?" she asked and Dane gaped at her. "My possessions…"

When the shadow-wolf closed his hand around hers and she didn't immediately pull away, Dane knew they were in trouble.

"My family will become yours, *min pärla.*"

"Your family will be happy for you, Grace" the Bishop assured. "And your belongings can be shipped."

Any doubts she might harbor hid beneath a mask of duty and submission. She lowered her stare and nodded. "I trust that God has chosen this for me."

"Has everyone lost their fucking minds?" Dane snapped. "Dude shows up, kills without question, and we're just going to stand here and let him kidnap Grace?"

"He killed Cerberus, Dane. This man is not our enemy," Lazarus reminded.

Lazarus's acceptance was the hardest to swallow. He was not like the others. He was modern and a free thinker. The moment Dane lost his support, he knew he was on his own.

"Grace, you do not need to go with this guy."

Regret flashed in her eyes. "I'm sorry, Dane, but it's true. I cannot read him, but I sense that I've seen him before. Something pulled me here. At first, I needed to protect *you.* But now... Perhaps it was the calling guiding me all along." Her eyes welled as she looked up at the shadow-wolf towering over her. "My soul recognizes yours, Darius Størm."

"And mine recognizes yours, *min pärla.*"

Seething, Dane glared at the two of them. "He's a stranger to you!"

"Not for long." The promise in those cold

green eyes would haunt him forever. He'd barely touched her, yet his claim was clear.

"This is what you choose?" he turned his anger on Grace. "Say it! Tell me you choose this dog over everything else, Grace. Your family. Your life. You don't realize what you're saying!"

"I choose him." Her whisper cleaved through him so fast he staggered back, sure he'd never feel whole again.

"Dane," Lazarus's call was lost behind the ringing in his skull.

"Fuck all of you!" He shoved past the others, turning his back on the lot of them.

The Bishop caught up to him the moment he made it outside. "Dane." He caught his shoulders, stilling his escape. "This is her calling. You always knew it would be this way."

"I never knew it would be *this* way. And neither did you, so I'd appreciate it if everyone stopped acting so goddamn calm like this is fucking normal!"

"I understand you're angry and disappointed. But that doesn't negate the fact that this is how it was always meant to be."

He shook his head, emotion clogging his ravaged throat. "I'm so sick of this."

The Bishop's brow furrowed. "Let me help you. Take my blood—"

"I don't want your fucking blood!" He shouldered out of his grip. "It's just one more way to control the situation, so you can track me."

"I only want to help you, Dane. You're injured."

"I don't want your fucking help." His jaw locked as he glared at Eleazar, no longer able to believe this man was a trustworthy friend. "You all have an agenda. You instill your bullshit rules on the females to keep them obedient to the men, so they trust you to protect them." He pointed angrily at the cave. "Do you honestly feel like she'll be safe with him?"

"He's her mate, Dane."

"He's a fucking wolf, Eleazar! A wolf who cut a *draugr* in half with one swipe of his claw and ripped out his heart with the other!"

"And you should be grateful he did. Cerberus would have killed all of us—including Gracie, who should not have been here! Do not be so naive to think she followed you all this way. Grace has never ventured far from home. *Something* pulled her here. Only a calling could compel an immortal so strongly."

"You don't know that!"

"I do. Because I lived it. He will kill you as quickly as he ended Cerberus if you interfere in his destiny. We are alive because of him—because he saved us and because he permits us to live."

"What if it was Larissa?"

A low growl vibrated from the Bishop's chest. "You're upset, so I'll forgive you this one time for posing questions about my bonded mate, but if you ever suggest such a thing again, my kindness will end and you will meet a side of me you do not want to know. Gracie is going to leave with that shadow-wolf and you are going to let her. This is her calling, Dane. Your obsession with her has no basis for comparison. She has chosen to abide God's will, and I will not let you stand in the way of her destiny."

Seething with uncontainable rage, his eyes narrowed. "There is no fucking God." He shoved past Eleazar with no intention of ever looking back.

Drifting toward the coast, he slipped on a muddy slope and winced as his injured body twisted painfully. He'd rinse the blood away in the frigid sea, then see what see to his own damn injuries. If he needed blood to heal, he'd hunt a fucking rabbit because nothing was getting him back up that hill.

Dabbing the back of his pounding head, disturbed by the warmth, Dane pulled his hand away and scowled at his blood-drenched his fingers. "Damn it."

Dawn cast a golden glow over the water and birds started to sing. He was in the middle of fucking nowhere with no clue where the nearest hospital was. A gaping wound in his head, a severely bruised larynx, and probably a concussion—yeah, he was screwed.

"Dane."

He spun, startled to find Lilias and Lazarus approaching. "Go away."

"We want to help you." Great empathy filled Lillias's green eyes.

"I don't want help."

"You're bleeding. Why suffer?"

He scoffed. Like his suffering would stop with the bleeding. "It doesn't matter."

Lazarus crouched at the banks and rinsed the blood from his arms. "The shadow-wolf said something interesting up there, something I hadn't considered." He glanced over his shoulder then returned his attention to washing out his wounds. "Cerberus was your father. That makes you half *draugr*."

Ice formed in his veins. They offered help a moment ago, but maybe that was a ruse to get close to him, so they could kill him.

Dane took a step back and then wondered why he was fighting it. Death would be a peaceful change. He was exhausted by more than this day and he welcomed an end to his pain. Any sense of survival abandoned him.

Lilias placed a gentle hand on his shoulder, and he flinched. "We won't hurt you, Dane. We've vowed our protection, and our word is our bond."

He didn't feel relief the way a normal person should. "It doesn't matter. Nothing matters anymore."

"It's clear she was someone special to you."

"*Was*, yes. That's over now." His anger with Gracie burrowed deeper than he could follow. He didn't want to think about her anymore. He wished he never met her. "She's nothing to me."

Lazarus rose from the banks. "It's known that

draugen can become obsessive about the past. It's why Cerberus would not let Lilias go. He spent centuries torturing her and rejected the natural order of things. You don't want a life of torment like that for yourself."

Was that why he couldn't move on? Dane assumed it was natural grief, but perhaps it was some sort of genetic defect. First, his obsession began with his mother's death at the hands of Isaiah. Then, his grandmother's life mysteriously ended when she left with Jonas. After that, he lost Cybil. Gored by the bull, and transitioned into something heinous. She was there but gone. Lost.

They were all lost. Yet he couldn't let them go.

And now Grace… It was more than he could take.

He crossed to the banks and pulled off his blood-soaked shirt, welcoming the frigid cold. "I'm done with the past." He plunged his shirt into the water and it clouded like mud. "I don't care anymore—about any of them."

Let her run off with some fucking dog. He hoped they were happy. She deserved everything she got.

"Dane, no one judges a broken heart."

His heart broke long before today. She just finished it off. Wringing out his shirt, he stood. "They're not my family. I'll get over it."

"What about Juniper? She needs you. She told us so."

"Look, Juniper has Adriel now, and Adriel has

you guys. I'll be fine. I'll figure out a place to live and start a new life. It'll be good."

"What if that new life was in Greece?" Lazarus asked, glancing at his mate.

Dane stilled and Lilias stepped forward. "Juniper will not go back to the farm where Adriel lived. We plan on helping them start over. In Argos. We would like it if you joined them."

He blinked, unable to process what they were offering. "You want me to live there?"

"We own plenty of land. You could have your own place and the freedom to live your life as you please," Lazarus explained.

Lilias smiled and took her mate's hand. "Adriel is our family. We want to be close to her."

"Not just Adriel, all of you. Families should stay together."

"What about all the *draugr*—"

"We don't care that Cerberus was your father. There's good in you, Dane. We only see the good."

He lowered his stare, unsure what to do. In one breath, he wanted to reject them, but when he looked up and saw nothing but sincerity in their eyes, his resolve shattered. They didn't care that he was different or half-mortal. They accepted all of him. Saw him as family.

Throat tight, he nodded, as the pain in his chest slightly retreated. Unable to voice his acceptance, Lazarus read it in his mind thanks to their earlier blood exchange.

"Then it's settled, son." Lazarus held out his arm. "I offer you my blood and protection."

The boulder in his throat crushed his words, but he managed to force his gratitude out. "Thank you."

A shaky smile crossed Lilias's lips. "Thank *you* for finding us and giving us a family again."

CHAPTER 36

*A*driel awoke to the sound of cracking trees and the low buzz of insects chirruping. Her brow pinched at the unfamiliar scent of jasmine in the air.

She wiggled her fingers. No pain.

Opening her eyes, her vision was crisp, but her location was completely foreign. A four-poster bed draped in white gossamer. White walls. A mirror. Juniper.

Her heart instantly settled at the sight of her love sleeping peacefully by her side. What was this place?

A vase of pink flowers sat on the bedside table next to a glass of water. "June?" She touched her beautiful face, and her heart fluttered with joy. This wasn't a dream. "Juniper, wake up."

Dark lashes twitched, then revealed violet eyes. She smiled and sighed. "Hi."

"Are you well?"

She shifted, drawing her arm under her head and reaching for Adriel. "I feel good. How do you feel?"

"I feel…perfect." She glanced over her shoulder and whispered, "I don't know where we are."

Juniper hitched herself up on her elbows and chuckled. "We're at your parents' house."

A strange emotion surged through her veins. "We are?"

Juniper nodded. "In Greece. They probably brought us here."

"My parents?" A flash of memories strobed through Adriel's mind and her breath hitched. The cave, Cerberus, an avenging angel, Juniper. "They were there."

She nodded. "You told me to find them. Remember?"

It was all coming back to her, even the bad parts. She shivered and reached for June. "You heard me?"

"I did. Your father said that can happen when a couple shares enough blood." Juniper grinned and pulled her fingers to her cheek, turning her face to kiss her palm. "Let's just say I won't be touching anyone else's veins."

Adriel laughed, stunned that she was actually there with her. She caressed her beautiful face and smiled. "I never thought I'd see you again."

"I was never going to let that happen. One way or another, I was coming to save you."

Her heart grew heavy with shame. "I'm so sorry I left you."

"I know you are. You were scared and only trying to protect me."

"It was foolish and cruel." Tears rushed to her eyes. "You asked me to believe in you and I couldn't see past my fear. I only wanted to protect you the way you wanted to protect me."

"Hey." She caught her chin and forced her to meet her stare. "I forgive you. We're both here—alive—and he can't hurt you anymore. It's finally over."

Her vision blurred. The surreal concept of a life without Cerberus felt unfathomable and it wasn't easy for her to trust such a permanent assumption of safety. "It's going to take some time for me to get used to that."

"Take all the time you need. I'm not going anywhere." She kissed her softly, and Adriel closed her eyes.

The gentle affection drew a shaky breath from her lungs. "I love you, Juniper."

"I love you too." Juniper pressed her forehead to hers and hummed happily. "Do you want to meet your mother and father?"

A hand fluttered to her chest. "I... Are they kind?"

"Very. Lilias is so sweet and nurturing. And Lazarus is incredibly wise and brave. He used to be a warrior." She gripped Adriel's hand. "They love you."

Uncertainty needled. "They don't know me."

"That doesn't matter. They want to get to know you, and no matter what they find, they will love and accept all of you, because you're part of them. They're your family, Ade."

She considered how lucky such a gift was, especially in the eyes of Juniper who had lost all of her loved ones tragically. "They know about us?"

"Yes. I told them."

"And?"

"And what?" She laughed. "They live in the modern world. Baby, they just want you to be happy. That's all that matters to them." She wiped a tear from Adriel's cheek. "Don't cry. Today's a new and beautiful day."

"This is unbelievable. I'm...overwhelmed." She tried to piece together her memories, but there seemed huge gaps in her timeline. "Is Christian here?"

"No, he had to go home to his mate. But he promised to visit soon."

She smiled. "They met him?"

Juniper nodded. "Kind of crazy seeing three generations of immortals. Collectively, you guys are older than the Roman Empire."

Adriel scowled. "I'll have you know I'm still in my heyday."

Juniper lunged forward, pinning her to the bed and kissing her deeply. "I'm just teasing."

"I missed your kisses." She leaned up to steal another.

"I missed yours. Oh! I have to tell you something. Remember how you said two supernatural genes can form a third?"

"Yes."

"Well, I know what I am!"

"You do?"

"I'm *kitsune*—part fox-shifter, part witch, with a dash of vampire."

"Immortal."

She waved away her need to correct her terminology. "Lazarus is teaching me all about the different supernatural cultures. He has tons of books. Some are even written in languages that don't exist anymore."

"And he knows about this race—*kitsune*?"

"Your father knows about everything! He's fascinating. They're nothing like the immortals you lived with in The Order. They're open-minded and curious, not at all afraid of people who are a little different. As soon as they knew who we were, they accepted us."

"You and Dane?" She recalled the creature in the cave and what that meant for Gracie. "How is he?"

The light in Juniper's eyes dimmed. "He's… processing. That creature took her away before we even scattered Cerberus's ashes into the sea. Dane left, but Lazarus said he'd meet us later. I think it was just too much for him. To think, all this time, he was told a half-breed could not get called only to watch her go with that wolf-creature… My heart breaks for him."

Adriel rested her head on the pillow, trying to

take it all in. There was so much to absorb. Life here would be very different from The Order, but knowing how Juniper suffered, she would never ask her to return to the farm.

Tucking a strand of hair behind her ear, she confessed, "I've never dreamed of such independence. To think, I can do anything I want, be whatever kind of female I wish to be."

"Imagine that." She raised a brow, her eyes teasing. "No bonnets or bossy men deciding what's best for you. Every choice from here on out is yours."

A sense of power rushed through her. "I choose you. You're my future, June."

She kissed her and whispered, "And I choose you. We're going to build a life together, Ade, you and me."

"And my family."

"And your family."

A cool breeze swept through the windows, carrying the scent of herbs and jasmine with it. Clothing had been set out for them.

"Your mother," Juniper explained, following her gaze. "She insisted on taking care of everything."

"No one's taken care of my needs in centuries."

"Well, that's going to change now." She pulled her fingers to her lips and kissed her knuckles. "What do you say we get dressed and I reintroduce you to your parents?"

"I'd say I must be dreaming."

"You're not. Come on." She flung back the covers and tossed her a sweater. "You can put this over your nightgown."

Adriel donned the cardigan and fussed with her hair. It had grown a great deal since leaving the farm, and she no longer knew what to do with it, but she no longer felt the rebellious need to cut it.

"Soon, you'll be able to pull it into a ponytail —if you wanted."

She considered her reflection. It had been a long time since she wore her hair long, and back then, she'd only styled it with braids, bonnets, and pins.

"A ponytail might be nice." Turning to face Juniper, she glanced down at her bare feet. "Do I look all right?"

"You look beautiful." She took her hand. "Let's go meet your parents."

Juniper seemed to know her way around the old home as they walked the silent halls. Terracotta pots clustered in corners, and hand-woven baskets hung on the stone walls. Shadows pooled on the tile floor where natural light spilled in. The house was strangely quiet.

"No one is here."

"They're probably out back."

Curtains blew in the wind, and laughter carried on the breeze. "Go fish," a female voice called.

Drifting past the flowing linens, Juniper pulled the curtains aside, and Adriel stilled. Her father noticed them first. Then her mother turned, a smile frozen on her face.

Nostalgia washed through Adriel as she took in her mother's familiar, timeless beauty. Those painful memories she'd tucked away spilled into the forefront of her mind.

Dane stood, holding a handful of playing cards. "You're awake. How do you feel?"

Adriel couldn't move. She felt safe and cherished. Loved and accepted. It was so much to process when, only days ago, she believed she'd never have reason to smile again.

She laughed, the sound coming out like a stunned sob.

Her mother slowly stood, and her father followed. Her voice was soft and her eyes watchful. "We're so glad to see you, Adriel." Lilias crossed the yard with cautious steps. "I can't begin to express how much I've missed you. How I feared…"

Her father took her mother's hand when emotion got the better of her. "Welcome home, *filha*."

Filha. Adriel remembered that word. She was *Filha.* Daughter.

They did not spoke a mixture of heavily accented English with various Portuguese words sprinkled throughout. She hadn't spoken the language in centuries, but it was there, in the deepest part of her memories.

She held out her hands to them. *"Eu também senti sua falta, Mamãe e Papai."*

They rushed forward and gathered her into

their arms. Laughing and crying, they pressed kisses to her hair and face.

"I'm so sorry for all the pain I've caused—"

"No, we're the ones who must apologize. We never would have accepted your calling if we knew Cerberus was behind it. We assumed, once mated, you wanted your own life, so we tried to respect that."

"I never would have intentionally left you without a goodbye!"

"Those troubles are behind us now," her father said, grasping her shoulders affectionately. "Let us not waste another moment on the past. From here, we only look forward."

"Agreed," Dane said, closing this distance.

Adriel rushed to hug him. "I was so afraid when I saw you get hurt."

"I'm fine. Solid as a rock." He pounded a fist on his chest.

Her father clapped Dane on the shoulder. "Your friend here has been teaching us American card games, but I think he cheats."

"Yeah right." Dane cupped a hand at the side of his mouth and mumbled, "Your dad sucks."

They were so comfortable with each other, so accepting. Juniper's hand slipped into hers and squeezed. Their eyes met and she could so easily picture them living a happy life here.

She looked at her parents and smiled. "You met Christian?"

Her mother beamed. "What a fine son you've

raised! He says he will come for a visit as soon as his mate delivers."

Adriel's eyes widened. "Delilah's pregnant?"

"Oh, I thought you knew."

"I'm going to be a grandmother?" She looked at Juniper and Dane. "Did you know about this?"

They both shook their heads.

Her father wore a proud grin. "The Schrock line is strong."

Adriel remembered how hard she'd been challenged when she chose to give her son her family name. Now it all made sense. This was how it was always meant to be. "Yes, it is. Our line is very, very strong."

Juniper smiled, her eyes twinkling with shared pride. She'd always claimed Adriel was stronger than she realized. Now, she believed she was right.

"Is it true, *filha*? Christian is, in fact, Cerberus's son?"

A cold wave pushed into her chest as she met her father's questioning eyes. There had never been anyone else until Juniper. Would this truth change things?

Her gaze lowered. "He is of his line, yes, but he has always been *my* son." Deciding to no longer live in fear, she met her father's stare. "My son Christian is an honorable—"

"I have no question about his honor, my dear. I was only asking because I think this is helpful information for Dane."

Adriel frowned. "Why?"

"Delilah is Christian's called mate, correct?"

"Yes."

"If Cerberus was Christian's father, he is half *draugr*. Your son's calling further proves that crossbred immortals can be called."

"Crossbred, but not half-bred," Dane clarified. "Christian is fully immortal where as my birth mother was mortal."

"It's still worth investigating," her father argued. "I have a theory that the cross-pollination of species is altering our evolution."

"Wait," Juniper cut in. "If Christian is a combination of two supernatural races, doesn't that make him a hybrid like me? Shouldn't he have some additional mutated gene that makes him something else?"

"Technically, yes. But we will have to spend more time with him to know for sure."

Juniper glanced back at Adriel, a look of worry in her eyes. "If Christian's a hybrid and he was called, does that mean I face the same possibility?"

"No," Adriel said, disregarding all science in favor of love. "I won't have it."

"Fuck callings," Dane snapped. It was an easy position for someone who didn't face such possibilities. But for Adriel and Juniper, the threat of being called was a very real concern.

"Why would The Order keep this from us?" she wondered. "They teach that only purebred immortals can be called to other immortals."

Both Dane and Juniper rolled their eyes.

"They lie, Ade. They like their neat little world as simple as possible. People like Dane and I mess that up. That's why they despise outsiders."

Her father frowned. "It's my understanding that they kept a great deal from the females. Is it possible the males knew, but the females were kept ignorant for a reason?"

Adriel clutched her throat as a sense of betrayal choked her. Was that true? Did Christian know? He was an elder on the council.

She couldn't imagine such deliberate deceit. "I listened. I've never heard whispers of such things or sensed any desire to interfere with destiny. The Order views any calling as sacred."

Her father rubbed his jaw contemplatively. "Many creatures with supernatural bloodlines have destined mates. Some callings have even been known to skip generations, traveling through time and the cosmos in order to find the other half of the soul. These are the mysteries philosophers have tried to solve since the dawn of immortal man."

"Hold up," Juniper interjected. "Are you talking about reincarnation?"

"Indeed."

Adriel's faith did not recognize reincarnation, so she had difficulty aligning with such claims.

Dane sank into the bench, his face as white as a sheet.

Adriel released Juniper's hand to go to him. "Dane, are you all right?"

He rubbed his head. "My grandmother… She

was called to Jonas, but died before the claim. Does this mean she'll come back?"

"Possibly. But such things take time," her father explained. "No one knows how fast a lost soul can be reborn."

"Did you say lost soul?"

"Oh, no." Adriel sensed where this was going and tried to intervene, but her father spoke too fast.

"That's the traditional term."

"They called my sister a lost soul."

"That's different, Dane. Cybil died."

"Then why is she still breathing?"

"Who is Cybil?" Lilias asked.

"She's my sister."

"Dane, I could possibly understand such theories in cases like Isaiah's, but Cybil's situation was a tragedy." Adriel hated to see him lost to false hope when the chances of his sister ever recovering were completely unlikely.

"Whoa." Juniper dropped into the seat beside Dane. "Is no one else thinking…" She looked at them one by one. "You all didn't immediately think…" Her mouth snapped shut. "Never mind. Ignore me."

"No, say it." Adriel wanted to know what she was thinking.

"She means Isaiah," Dane said, a look of horror on his face. "There's a reason he was in our area. A reason why he never left."

"Perhaps his mate died."

That seemed obvious to Adriel. "You never considered that possibility?"

Juniper scoffed, her eyes shifting to awe. "It makes sense why he was so protective of her."

"Who?"

"Cybil," Dane said and chills raced up Adriel's legs, her head already shaking in denial.

Cybil was a lost tragedy. Dane needed to accept that and move on.

"He drank from her," Juniper whispered as she stared into the distance as if recalling a different time and place. "I heard them at night, growling and slurping."

"I saw it too," Dane confessed. "I even reported it to the council."

"Maybe that's why she went ballistic when you tried to kill him." Juniper looked at Adriel. "How long ago was he called?"

"It's been nearly a century."

"A hundred years seems like a nice round number." She shrugged. "Your sister would be of age by then."

"It doesn't work like that," Adriel argued.

"Do we honestly know anything about how it works?" Juniper challenged. "Gracie was just called to a wolf-man."

"He's a shadow-wolf," Lazarus corrected, sounding very much like Adriel.

"Whatever. I'm just saying, those two were in that basement with me for months. I heard them attack anyone who came within reach, but they never hurt each other."

"She's right," Dane breathed. "He protected her. And she protected him. They were both feral but not nearly as deranged as everyone believed. They trusted each other. If their humanity were truly gone, that wouldn't be possible."

"Be careful, Dane," Adriel warned. "Some answers only complicate matters."

"No offense, Adriel, but I'd rather know the truth than hide behind ignorance."

There would be no arguing with him. No matter what the outcome, she was certain neither Isaiah nor Cybil could be saved and that was going to be another painful lesson Dane would eventually learn.

CHAPTER 37

*J*uniper slipped a book from the shelf in Lazarus's library and drifted out back toward the greenhouse. Adriel was reconnecting with her family and she didn't want to rush them. It was still sinking in that they had a lifetime to get to know each other and the three of them were buzzing with questions and curiosity.

They weren't the only ones wrestling with this new kind of normal. Juniper had to constantly remind herself the battle was over. The grueling existence they survived had finally shifted like a dancer swiftly changing directions on a stage, and the wind now blew in a new direction.

It was a strange awareness, and Juniper couldn't easily accept a life of ease after years of confined torment and life-or-death battles with a monster. Survival had been so hard for so long, that peace made her uneasy.

She sometimes caught herself laughing, and a spike of nervous energy would shoot through her. Her eyes would meet Dane's or Adriel's as if they felt the same stab of guilt, and then a shaky smile would appear. Who knew letting go of anger to create room for joy could be so challenging and feel so unnatural?

Happiness was definitely a process. Together, they would get there.

Adriel's laughter coasted on the breeze. Juniper smiled at the illuminated house, warmth spreading through her chest at the perfect sound. Yes, they were getting there.

Opening the stiff pages of the book brought about the scent of time and wisdom. This one had a spine sewn of thread so rotted, the pages slipped loose from the binding. She righted the loose pages and dragged her finger down the crease.

"Sarciri glutino ventoque ad tempus." The scent of ash filled the greenhouse, and the spine's filament cinched tight.

The corner of Juniper's mouth curled into a half grin. Damn, she was good.

Settling into the hammock chair, she turned her back to the moon and flipped to page one. The ink was faded but at least this one was written in English. Lazarus had the most extensive library on paranormal lore she'd ever seen, and she planned to read every single book on his shelf as well as every personal entry of his and Lilias's journals—with their permission of course.

The elder Schrocks were an open book. They believed knowledge needed to be shared for the sake of survival and that censorship led to corruption in more than mortal governments, and the history of supernatural species was an essential part of avoiding extinctions.

Juniper understood why Lazarus was so passionate about preserving the truth, especially when his own family had been so ravaged by lies. Even witches, nowadays, were commercialized into cutesy Hallmark card beings. There was an entire subculture of crystal pushing, tchotchke selling, tarot reading phonies out there dressed in gypsy clothing while wearing goth eyeliner pretending to be witches. It normalized the literature, but also buried the real magick in a slush pile of self-published bullshit that balanced between herbalist secrets and manifesting coincidence.

Lazarus's library was the real deal. He had books on all types of immortal creatures and those who lived far beyond mortal possibility—*draugrs,* shadow-wolves, spirits, fairies, banshees, demons, and more. Lazarus had information on all of them.

She peeked over the tattered pages of the book and spied Lilias and Adriel walking the gardens, their distant laughter rolling out like a

Harry Styles song, the kind that promised by the first note it would be a banger. Another jolt of happiness followed. She was growing used to those little spikes and learning not to fear them.

Sighing, she let the warm wave of contentment unlock the tension in her back. They looked more like sisters than mother and daughter, but the pride in Lilias's eyes gave her away. Only a mother's interest could transcend to awe the way Lilias's did whenever Adriel had something to say.

Juniper's hand rubbed over her chest where a bolt of joy stabbed. It was a good love, the pure kind a mother should hold for her child, the kind Juniper's birth mother had never given her.

Things would be different now. The Schrocks invited them to stay and they were going to be a family. She and Dane would always be a little more outside of that definition than Adriel, but trust would grow with time.

As a guardian, Lazarus's watch would never truly end, especially where his mate and family were concerned. Juniper felt safe here. She believed him to be more honorable than all the elders of The Order combined, and her gratitude for what he'd done to help rescue Adriel went beyond words.

This new life would take time, especially for Adriel, who had been sheltered by primitive beliefs for centuries. Gender stereotypes suppressed her gifts, and there was so much potential inside of her that was yet to be dis-covered.

Juniper couldn't wait to see her explore her innate gifts without the fear of consequences. She wanted Adriel to proudly embrace who she was so they could live, play, laugh together, make love together, and grow.

She smiled, grateful she was hidden like a flower in the shadows of the greenhouse while experiencing such a deluge of soft and squishy emotions. Her vision blurred as she continued to think of the life they could make for themselves in Argos. It seemed almost too good to be true, but it was true.

They were safe and they could finally be happy.

The moon illuminated the sky overhead, shining through the glass ceiling and casting shadows on a variety of exotic plants. They were so removed from modern light pollution, the stars shined twice as bright. They would be at peace here, now that the tides had shifted, but she worried about Dane who still remained restless.

He skulked about the house, so tense he put others on edge. He refused to talk about Grace and what happened with the shadow-wolf. In-stead, he renewed his interest in rescuing his sister.

It was an obvious distraction and a vendetta without end, so if his goal was to avoid the Gracie thing forever, he'd found the perfect place to divert his attention. Juniper expected him gone by the end of the week. He was too unsettled to stay in one place for long—no matter how peaceful.

His restless pacing and pensive reflection displayed an undying eagerness to ignore the wreckage of his broken heart. Juniper would respect whatever he chose to do, because had she lost Adriel, she would have been in the same desolate place.

Love could be such a bitch.

Gracie's claim had come faster than expected, but it was the shadow-wolf that gutted Dane most. All of this time, he'd been told he wasn't enough because of his tainted bloodlines, but it turned out bloodlines had very little to do with callings. This changed everything, but Dane's sense of inadequacy remained the same, if not worse.

She truly hoped he found the happiness he deserved. Like her, he'd lost everyone he loved. That was a scary state of mind to live in, one where a person can afford to be reckless because they have nothing left to lose.

Dane was a good man, but there was no guarantee he would stay that way if he dwelled too profoundly in the past. His best chance at finding happiness rested in embracing the future.

The door creaked and Juniper's gaze jumped to the entrance of the greenhouse where Lilias stood. "You've been hiding out here all night."

"Not hiding. I was giving you two privacy."

She drifted inside the conservatory with the grace of a goddess. "My daughter has quite a story." She examined the dark, waxy leaf of a palm and grinned.

Juniper smiled. "This is just the beginning."

"Since you've agreed to stay, I hope to be a part of the happy ending."

"You will be."

Lilias's hand rubbed over her flat stomach as she grinned. "To think, I went from believing I had lost all of my children to discovering I still had a daughter. And then I met you." Her green eyes flashed in the moonlight, the corners creasing ever so slightly. "I now have two daughters."

"You have a grandson too."

"Yes," she said with a look of awe. "And a mated daughter-in-law with a great-grandbaby on the way."

She was obviously thrilled about such news. Juniper shut the book and sat up. "If there's anything we can do—"

"No, no. It's my pleasure to take care of you. Please just enjoy this time and let me mother all of you. I've grieved for so long. I'm ready to come out of mourning now."

Fair enough, Juniper thought, eager to find those feelings of safety again. No one had taken care of her in years. "If I haven't said it enough, thank you."

Lilias laughed. She must have heard those words more than a hundred times today. "Thank you for finding us and giving me a family again." She looked through the glass where the valley sloped and moonlight danced on the placid sea. "Adriel took a walk to the grotto. You should visit with her. It's beautiful at night when the moon is full."

While the thought of a full moon and all of that charged water was enticing in itself, the image of Adriel wading into the grotto under that blue glow was pure carnal temptation.

"I think I'll check it out." Unable to resist such a tantalizing vision, she slipped off the hammock seat and set the book aside.

Lilias chuckled. "Goodnight, Juniper."

"Goodnight, Lilias." As soon as Adriel's mother left the greenhouse, Juniper headed for the grotto.

The scent of tropical blooms perfumed the air. She followed a stone path through the valley toward the caves. The moon hung low in the sapphire sky, casting its silvery glow across the rugged landscape as it rippled majestically over the sea.

She spotted the hidden grotto within the ancient rocks. Secrets from a forgotten time whispered in the gentle wind. She approached slowly, her gaze searching for Adriel.

Her senses prickled the moment she saw her. The delicate line of her back caught the moonlight as she turned, slowly stepping into the calm waters. Juniper disguised her presence with soft magick so as not to disturb her.

She was lovely. Her natural beauty stole Juniper's breath and made her feel and want things she never believed she would desire.

When she looked back nervously, her arm loosely draped across her naked breasts, she frowned, likely sensing her presence but unable to see her through the cloaking spell. A smirk pinched in the corner of Juniper's mouth as she removed her clothes.

Adriel slipped silently into the crystalline waters, dropping low so the water covered her. She stared back at the rocks where Juniper stood and grinned. "You know I can scent your presence. And your arousal."

Juniper released the spell, and her nude body flickered into view. "You're no fun."

"Being fun is something I'm still figuring out. Come in. The water's lovely, and you can help me practice being fun." The currents cradled her as she glided away from the stone edge. Ripples lapped at her skin as she stroked slowly toward the cave's opening, where the moon reflected on the surface.

As the cool, midnight sea touched Juniper's toes, goosebumps rose over her body. "It's freezing."

Adriel laughed. "Regulate your body temperature."

Her head cocked in confusion. "We can do that?"

Her soft, melodic laughter danced across the breeze. "Yes, silly."

"How?"

"Concentrate on your blood flow. Feel it beating through your heart. Then send a mental command outward to your skin."

Juniper did as she said and gasped as a warm surge of heat pushed through her body from her chest to her limbs. "Whoa." She waded into the water and laughed. This hybrid vampire thing definitely had its perks.

The air was thick with the intoxicating scent of salt and jasmine, mingling with the earthy musk of the surrounding olive groves. Adriel swam toward her, a goddess under the moon's ethereal glow. Her green eyes shimmered as she pulled her into her arms. The luminescent backdrop cast sparkles like diamonds floating on every ripple against her skin.

It was hard to believe she was hers. "You're stunning."

A soft blush darkened Adriel's ivory cheeks. "Can you believe we're here?"

"No." Juniper scoffed. "But I'll take it."

Adriel's hands closed about her hips and tugged her closer so their legs could entwine underwater. Engulfed in her warmth, she no longer needed to escape the night chill.

Slick fingers danced over heated flesh as they caressed each other under the surface. "Did you have a nice time with Lilias?"

"Mm-hmm." Adriel's fingers gently traced up her arm. "As grateful as I am to have my parents back, I'm more interested in this right now." Her touch trailed lower.

Juniper tightened her legs around her waist. "I see." She kissed her slowly, the sensation of Adriel's mouth on hers a pleasure she'd never tire of. "I've missed this." Arms wreathed around her neck, she glanced down at their entwined bodies.

Adriel caressed her throat. "You have me now —forever, if you want."

"I want all of it. All of you," she rasped, scraping her teeth along her throat. "This moment and a thousand more. I want your mind, your body, and your heart, Ade. I want forever with you."

She drew back and studied her in the silence. The gentle lap of waves against the rocks contrasted with the steady beat of her racing pulse. Crystals clung to the alcove ceiling in a canopy of sparkles that glistened in the reflection of the water and the world outside ceased to exist.

"I can't imagine what that looks like," Adriel confessed. "I want forever too. But it's been so long since I've allowed myself to dream, I can hardly picture that sort of happiness."

"We'll figure it out together."

There were no rules here like the ones of The Order. They were free to live as they wanted and love who they wanted. Juniper loved Adriel. She'd do anything to show her how much. "We could…marry."

She looked startled by the suggestion, but

then her mouth curved with the most genuine smile. "Is that possible?"

"There are others out there like us—well, sort of. There are other female couples."

"I didn't know." She looked away but couldn't stop smiling. "The elders say—"

"Who cares what the elders say? Are we really going to give those guys any more authority than they've already taken? The elders aren't living in the modern world, baby. But we are."

Adriel looked up, her grin impossible to hide. "The modern world. Imagine that—*I* am becoming a modern female!"

"That's you. You get to decide how you want to live, dress, act… It's all you, baby."

She surged forward and pressed her lips to Juniper's, the velvet water lapping around them.

Juniper forked her fingers through her hair and took command of the kiss. As her touch traveled over her thighs and between her legs, Adriel's soft, erotic cries were swallowed by the night breeze.

Carnal need coursed through her veins. She wanted her on a primal level, deeper than ever before. She needed to possess every inch of her being. Drawing from the ancient energy hidden in the grotto, she charged her touch to enhance the sensation, and Adriel gasped.

"What are you doing?"

"Do you feel that?"

"Yes. I feel—*Ah!*" Her head angled back as she sucked in another sharp breath.

Juniper teased every erogenous zone at once, and Adriel's body pulsed under her touch as she came apart in her arms—so graceful yet unrefined, a true natural beauty.

Pulling her toward a low rock step, she lifted her out of the water and kissed a trail down her belly. She licked away the salty droplets and playfully bit at her ticklish curves. When she reached heaven, she tasted her like a holy offering.

Adriel moaned as Juniper dispensed a relentless wave of pleasure, driving Adriel to the brink of madness only to ease her back and start again. When she begged for release, Juniper delivered.

Juniper crawled over Adriel's tempting body as she lay panting on the rock bed. Their bodies pressed together, rocking, thrusting, deriving pressure from friction as fingers teased and mouths kissed. The magic added pressure where it was needed most, and when they peaked together, a wash of calm blanketed them both.

Such sweet ecstasy.

"You taste like a winter morning," she whispered against her thigh, licking over the fluttering artery there.

"My blood feels hotter than a summer day."

"Mmm, I want a taste."

"Yes..." she begged and Juniper's fangs sank deep.

Hot, delicious blood filled her mouth as Adriel writhed under her touch. She fed from her vein as she fucked her fingers into her heat, driving her to another climax.

The tension of the last few weeks dissolved, replaced by a burgeoning sense of freedom and rightness. It would take longer for older wounds to heal, but for now, hope had at least been restored.

"I feel like all the pieces finally fit," Juniper said, kissing her way back up her body.

A sense of weightlessness settled in as Adriel pulled her closer. Still trembling with the aftershocks of release. She whimpered hungrily as Juniper lovingly caressed her breasts.

"I've never felt anything so pleasant in all my life. If this is what it's always like, how does anyone get anything done."

She smothered a laugh against Adriel's shoulder. "Sometimes it's okay to be lazy and indulgent, Ade."

"I wouldn't even know where to begin."

"We could start here." She kissed her nipple. "Or here." She licked her stomach. "Or maybe here." When she nipped her throat, Adriel arched.

"Yes... More..."

Juniper sank her fangs into her flesh and pulled hungrily at her vein. It was easier now that her fangs had formed. Nails scraped down her back as Adriel held her close, wrapping her legs tightly about hers and rolling her hips.

When her fingers boldly traced lower, Juniper parted her thighs. Adriel's touch delved into her heat, gently exploring and teasing all the right places. Her over-sensitized body became a riot of pleasure. Every ripple of water and whispered breeze a caress against her skin.

Drawing back, she moaned through her release. Adriel rolled her to her back, scooting lower and lower as Juniper arched and edged her on. When she bit into her thigh, pleasure ignited in her veins. Her fingers forked through her hair, fisting tightly as she rocked her hips. Adriel kept her touch where it needed to be, pushing her closer and closer to that carnal edge, and then… she was free.

Falling into an abyss of ecstasy.

Juniper had never felt anything so exquisite. When Adriel licked the bite closed, she looked up at her with kiss-swollen lips. "Was that okay?"

"That was…" Juniper panted. "I don't even have a word to describe how good that was."

She laughed and blushed, modestly dropping her face on Juniper's thigh as she stared up at her. "I love you, June."

She laced her fingers with hers. "I love you too."

They swam out of the grotto, where the moonlight poured beyond the cave's opening. Wading into the liquid silver pool, they floated, safe in each other's arms as the gentle current allowed them to be.

"June?"

"Mm?"

"How long can we stay here?"

"In the water? I imagine until our fingers and toes are pruned."

"No." Adriel laughed, pinching her playfully. "In Greece."

"I knew what you meant." She kissed her nose. "We can stay as long as you want. Forever, if it pleases you."

She sighed and rested her head on Juniper's shoulder. "Dane will eventually leave."

"I expect it." Juniper didn't know if that goodbye would come tomorrow or a year from now, but she sensed he was already growing restless. The moment he found a new purpose, he'd move full speed in that direction. Anything to take his mind off the reality he didn't want to face. "I wish there were some way we could help him."

"He's broken hearted. Mourning takes time."

"I just don't want him to feel alone. We're his family now."

"And while family is wonderful, some of life's hardest moments are best passed alone. Grief can make a person quite ugly at times." Her fingers trailed slowly up and down her spine. "The bonding's probably already happened."

Juniper's head tilted. "How does that work?"

"I thought I knew, but..." Rather than dwell on past deceptions, she shared only what she understood. "The bonding is said to be very powerful between immortals. There's a blood exchange and then the mating takes place, at which point two souls are reunited and become one again. Once it's done, it cannot be undone."

"What about with shadow-wolves? Do they drink blood?"

"I don't know. The elders implied it was impossible to be called by another species."

"The elders are not to be trusted. Christian's one thing. As your son, he has earned your trust. And the Bishop—I guess he's okay. But the others…"

"Perhaps my father will have some insight."

"Now, Lazarus I trust."

Adriel smirked. "You're cute with my father."

Juniper paused. She hadn't thought much about her interactions with Lazarus, but when she did think about him, she felt a wave of security. He somehow earned her trust when she didn't easily give trust to anyone. In only a short time, she learned to look to him for advice and input as if it were something she'd always done.

"I've never known anyone like him. He's so knowledgeable and encouraging. He's like…" Words failed her.

"A father," Adriel supplied.

"Yes. I guess that's it. He's a *good* father. I've never known anyone like that. At least not in my personal life."

"Well, now you do. We're in this together."

"A family," Juniper confirmed, finally letting that sense of belonging settle in. "You're sure you're okay with staying here? It's going to be very different from The Order, Ade."

"I would never ask you to return to a place that holds such bad memories for you."

Knowing that the farm had been her home for centuries, that level of sacrifice seemed unfathomable. "What about Christian?"

"He'll visit. This is exactly where I want to be."

"Thank you for considering my feelings. I know you loved the farm."

"You don't have to thank me. I did love the farm, but that doesn't compare to how much I love you. We're in this together. We're going to make a new home that's ours."

"Together." She liked the way that sounded.

Adriel tucked a strand of hair behind her ear. "I know you hate discussing The Order, but there's one more matter of business we must address."

Juniper drew back at her serious tone. "What is it?"

"I plan to send a letter to Eleazar. He needs to know what happened to you, Juniper. The Council must be questioned, and whoever committed those despicable acts against you must be held accountable. I will not let their conduct go unpunished."

"What happened to passivity and forgiveness?"

"Some wars are worth fighting. If they can do such vile things to you, no female is safe. Predators, like any storm, must be confronted head-on."

She grinned. "Like the buffalo face the rain."

Adriel nodded. "I'll fight this battle for you because I am yours and you are mine. I claim you, Juniper Tempest, and offer protection to you in all things."."

When Juniper pressed a kiss to her mouth, lips were wet with droplets, her heart felt whole again. Adriel pulled her tight, and the current drifted them out to the sea where they lost themselves in the pleasure and tranquility of this magical place. There was no fear, only hope. And as foreign as that concept might seem to both of them, they surrendered to it easily, like a warm, overdue welcome home.

CHAPTER 38

"Can't sleep?"

Dane's eyes jolted from the book to the door. "You startled me."

"Sorry. Immortal habit." Lazarus crossed the study and looked down at the desk where Dane had been hunched for hours. Pulling the old book across the leather surface, he turned the cover to read the spine. "You're looking for information on the shadow-wolf?"

Dane sat back with a huff. "Unsuccessfully."

"Their lore is very guarded. Even seasoned immortals cannot enter the mind of a shadow-wolf unless welcomed in. And there is no hope for reading them once in wolf form."

"All these rules," Dane grumbled, picking at his fingernail. "Everything's so absolute until it's not."

"Life is full of exceptions, son."

He sagged in defeat. "And never good ones."

Lazarus lowered into the wingback chair across from the desk. "Don't shortchange yourself. You're still young. Others would be foolish to underestimate you."

"Because I'm *draugr*?" He turned his face in shame. "I hate that *he's* still a part of me."

"We all come from something, Dane. No one gets to choose. But understanding our genealogy can unlock many secrets."

"Like what a monster I am—"

"Enough," Lazarus snapped, surprising Dane. "We're all capable of becoming monsters. It's our self-control that determines the outcome more than anything else—including whatever our DNA claims. You've only just become a man. Give yourself time to unravel what that means."

"It means nothing."

"Doesn't it? You have a half-brother."

"So?"

"Christian is also part *draugr*."

"Yeah, and he's a total asshole. Now, I see why."

Lazarus cocked a brow, looking unimpressed. "Trust me when I tell you, Dane, the *draugen* are often haunted by the past. They get lost in it and miss lifetimes of everything the present world offers. You can either dwell on the unchangeable or put your energy elsewhere. If you don't like the destiny you've been dealt, why don't you work on designing a better future for yourself. No one is stopping you."

"I know you're right." He couldn't work

through the anger pumping inside of him. He felt like there was a hurricane under his skin.

Lazarus moved to the wall covered in bookshelves and searched the spines. "There is one story you might want to read."

Sliding an old book free, he blew the dust off the cover. The spine creaked when he opened it and the pages ruffled like dry leaves in an autumn breeze.

"We don't know much about the shadowwolves, but we do know how they came to be." Lazarus set the book onto the desk.

The aged parchment made the tome especially thick, but there was very little to it. The cover was black and oiled with strange engravings burned into the leather. "What language is this?"

"Old Norse. It was once the language of Europe."

Dane pulled it closer. A painting of a bright red leaf filled the first page. "What does this say?"

Lazarus glanced at the inscription and read, "When the gods created man, they also created war."

Dane turned the page. Another crude, glyphlike illustration. This one in brown ink and depicting men fighting with spears and bows. He didn't have to read the words for Dane to follow the story.

Men were apparently fighting in many wars, which angered the gods. A great light resembling biblical depictions of the Holy Spirit approached an older man and a young boy and gifted them magical fur pelts, which they donned as cloaks. They were then transformed into enormous wolves. The gods wanted the wars to end. The wolves defeated the armies as the book illustrated in great carnage.

Dane turned the page. "Is this his son?"

"Yes."

Red ink bled across the parchment. The boy lay amongst the forest trees, wounded, as the father stole the pelts.

"He killed his son?"

"Lupine comes from the Latin word *lupus,* which means wolf. Shadow-wolves are a rare primordial breed, but at their core, they're dogs —loyal to the hand that feeds them but hounds at the heart. They possess a wild magick, very different from the sort witches and sorcerers practice. It comes from the ancient gods rather than nature. Sacrifice is at the core."

Dane turned the page. A black bird gifted the boy with a red leaf pinched between his beak. "I don't understand."

"The raven is offering an exchange—the boy's life for that of another."

"The father's?"

Lazarus nodded. "The gods bestowed power in exchange for peace. The father abused that power and created havoc."

The next page showed the boy healed and the father deceased. "This doesn't make sense. The Order believed in one God. The shadow-wolves believe in many. So how are they divinely called if they worship separate deities?"

"The shadow-wolves are very careful not to anger the gods since they exist at their mercy. Faith is only a story we tell ourselves. It changes like secrets stretched over generations. But the bones are all the same. Immortals—even the atheists—will eventually be called. It has absolutely nothing to do with how they pray and everything to do with what the universe decides."

The Universe, Gods, The Bible… It was all colliding into chaos. "How long do lycan live?"

"Close to two thousand years. They're said to feed off the essence of mortals."

"They drink blood?"

"I believe their feeding habits are slightly different than ours." He tapped his temple. "Remember, sacrifice. Everything they do must somehow serve the gods."

Tension clamped down on his shoulders and neck as he thought about Grace. "Are they cruel?"

"Cruelty exists in every species. It's an individual trait, not a predisposed one." He removed the book from the desk and closed it. "Regardless, we cannot change destiny. It's clear you care for the female who followed us to the cave, and I'm sorry for that. Chances are, the mating is done. There's nothing anyone can do to sever such a bond."

Dane couldn't catch his breath. Seething, he got up and paced. The thought of that thing putting his hands on Grace…

He stared out the window at the black night. Had it happened already? Was Gracie's innocence gone? Was she okay?

"I should have stayed." Regret weighed him down like iron chains.

"There was nothing you could do."

"She's innocent."

"They all are, at some point."

"Why are you telling me this?"

"Because lies are what monsters are made of. Real men face the truth. They own it, overcome it, and certainly do not fear it."

Dane wanted to be stronger than he felt, but life had a way of cutting him down five feet every time he grew an inch. "I'm working on acceptance."

"You have time. It's my understanding that, once the bonding is done, she'll go through a pack orientation with the others. *If* you hear from her, it won't be for some time."

He stilled. "Pack orientation? What does that mean?" When he purposely didn't answer, Dane scowled. "Lazarus, tell me."

"They are dogs, Dane. Their loyalty is to the gods and their pack, nothing else. They'll do whatever is necessary to keep their bloodlines alive. Unlike immortals, they only have a small window to mate."

"But Gracie *is* immortal. She's not a wolf."

"But they are, and she now belongs to their pack. They are one. What belongs to one brother belongs to all of them. They'll expect a litter. It's how they diversify their species and outlive extinction."

"What?" He couldn't breathe. He couldn't see past the blinding rage clouding his mind. "Why are you saying *they*? Mates don't share."

"Immortal mates don't."

There was no escaping the volcanic rage building inside of him. He was going to explode. "I have to save her."

"You can't."

"She's not like them! You don't understand! She's innocent! Litters? Packs? None of this is right!"

"Except it is. She accepted her fate, Dane. There was no compulsion in that cave when she left with him."

"She doesn't know what she's consenting to!"

"He protected her the way a mate should. They will work out their differences in time, like all mates. Do not think to interfere, Dane. They will kill to protect their own, and Gracie is now one of theirs."

But she wasn't. She was his. His Gracie. "I need to…" He shook his head, certain there was no place he could go to outrun the sick feeling inside of him.

Lazarus clamped a heavy hand on his shoulder. "Self-control, Dane. Steer your energy where it's most useful. Do not waste it on that which you cannot change."

His fist closed around a small shell set on the windowsill. He squeezed it until it shattered into dust. He thought about Abilene, Gracie's mother.

"What if she can't get pregnant?"

"She's immortal. Of course she can. Our females are in impeccable health."

He shook his head. "Her mother had miscarriages. A lot of them."

Lazarus frowned. "With her mate?"

His gaze dropped. "No. Her father was called to another."

"There's your answer. That's not the case for Gracie."

Was it that simple? It couldn't be. "They have five other kids together."

"Five children in how many years? Our females are eternally fertile, Dane. My wife is far from finished bearing young. When her grief passes, we will try again. And our next will be our twelfth."

How sad it was that they had twelve kids and only one survived. "How do you do it? How do you manage not to lose your mind after what he took from you?"

"Like I said, we're all capable of becoming monsters. Humanity comes down to self-control."

Nodding his understanding, he tried to control his anger. With shaky breath, Dane tried to face the truth. "This is going to destroy her."

"She is immortal. We aren't destroyed easily. With time on her side, she'll eventually adapt to their culture."

"And what of her offspring? If two supernatural genes create a wild gene, her children won't be like either of them, so will it really do anything to save them from extinction?"

"Perhaps that's why she was chosen. Evolution works without the interference of man."

She was more than a womb. More than a vessel to save their fucking bloodline.

"I can smell your outrage, son. You mustn't do anything foolish. He's a purebred shadow-wolf. His brethren will defend him and his mate to the death."

"I'm not an idiot. I know I can't interfere. But I don't have to like it, and I'll never accept that her fate comes down to being a breeder for a pack of dogs." He shoved past him and headed for the door.

"Dane."

"What?" He couldn't face any more truth tonight.

"I'm truly sorry for your pain."

"So am I."

CHAPTER 39

Warmth.
Heat.
Gracie's mind stirred, and she frowned.
"I've got you…"
The gentle voice rumbled like low, non-threatening thunder rolling in. Calloused fingers traced down her cheek, delicately awakening her conscious mind. Gracie turned her face into the soft touch and moaned. Then, her senses came alive, and she bolted upright, body tense, eyes wide, instincts on full alert.
"Easy."
Her back pressed into a wall, and her palms flattened to the wooden headboard as her eyes skipped about the unfamiliar room. "Where are we?"
Amber light sparred with dark shadows as a small, open fire burned in the hearth at his back.
Him.

Her heart raced.

She knew him from the cave but also recognized him as her mate. The sentiment that word carried her entire life evaded her now. She did not know this creature and while part of her subconscious accepted him, her mind did not. She'd always assumed the heart would be the first to sway, but all of those sentiments abandoned her in the face of the unknown.

"You fainted." He held up his palms in a gesture of peace.

The pads of his fingertips and hands showed roughened prints, the kind her father used to get from working in the field that quickly healed thanks to their immortal blood.

More evidence that he was different.

A stranger.

He studied her in the dim lighting, shadowed by the flickering flames that danced from the hearth. He likely sensed she was scared and she suspected he didn't want to further startle her.

Her gaze never left him for more than a split second as she noted the windows and doors of the primitive cabin. She could leave if she wanted. Immortals were the fastest species on earth and said to be the strongest.

Or where they? She knew nothing of his breed or the fact that such creatures even existed.

"Is this your home?"

"No." He took a slow step but nothing more. "We've been traveling for some time, *min pärla*."

"My name is Grace."

"Grace," he amended.

She flinched, her hand rushing to her chest as her heart quickened at the sound of her name on his tongue.

"You are safe with me, Grace." He spoke slowly, placing a heavily accented R in her name that rolled seductively into the soft hissing C.

The fire crackled in the stone hearth where clothes draped over a chair. She gasped and covered her body, dressed only in her underclothes.

"You removed my clothes!" She bunched the thin chemise, pulling it away from her defined curves as she crossed an arm over her chest like a shield. Her cheeks burned as she considered his audacity. Had he acted honorably while she'd slept? She didn't know him well enough to trust his words.

"There was rain. I had limited supplies to cover you. As soon as I found shelter, I wanted to get you warm. Your clothing was drenched."

The musty trace of rain on her skin confirmed his story. He possibly told the truth. "If not your home, what is this place?"

"It's a rental." When she looked confused, he said, "An Air BnB."

Her frown deepened. "Air BnB?"

He laughed at her ignorance. "It's ours for the night—or longer if we need. I live quite far from here." He took a step closer and her back pressed firmly into the wall. "You needn't be shy with me, Grace. Now that you're rested and we have privacy, we should … get to know one another. Before we return to the others."

"The others?"

"My pack brothers. They're very eager to meet you."

He was a family man. That comforted her. Family was important.

"My family will also want to meet you." She needed to get a letter off to her sister. The Bishop would inform Larissa and the rest of her family, but Grace wanted to prepare them for the unexpected details of her calling.

Her stare drifted to the rumpled bed, then darted to the floor. Aside from a small wooden table, a few simple chairs, and the hearth, the bed dominated the room.

Her chest tightened as her mediocre understanding of matings formed a deformed picture in her mind. Flashes of hidden secrets she'd unintentionally lifted from others flickered rapidly through her memory.

Mouths, moans, flesh, lips, teeth, legs… The erotic onslaught of all she knew collided into a knot of unknowns that choked the air from her lungs. "What will happen here?"

He took another step and her ribs cinched tighter making it near impossible to breathe. "We'll talk. Get to know one another."

Her gaze skated to the bed and back to him. He traced her path with his own eyes.

"You needn't be afraid. I won't hurt you, Grace."

It wasn't supposed to be like this. There was supposed to be time for her to consult with her mother and sister. Conversations had been put off because she'd had no symptoms. No warning.

"Perhaps if you tell me what you're thinking, I can help you make sense of things."

He couldn't read her. How was that possible?

She reached for his mind and found utter silence. Another unexpected outcome, though a peaceful one. She let down her guard and the steady tension that always left her neck in knots loosened.

She knew what happened between mates. Her extrasensory gifts cursed her with an extremely sensitive telepathic mind. She'd suffered countless unwanted images whenever in the presence of newly mated couples. They were always the most distracted and obsessive in their carnal ruminations. Whenever they failed to properly block their minds, Gracie got an unwanted show of things she'd prefer to never see.

But he was not like them. When she looked into his mind, she saw nothing but grey silence. "Our mates can read each other. They share emotions such as pleasure and pain."

"Things will be different for us, but that is not to say those privileges will not develop with time."

She could not smell his emotions so she could not detect his intentions. Some men reeked of arousal while others carried the dull stench of boredom. He smelled like the earth. The organic fibers of his clothes carried traces of rain, but his skin wore a unique musk she didn't recognize. Clean and appealing, but also woodsy and masculine.

The laces of her underclothes settled over her chest as she lowered her arms. Her throat worked hard to swallow as her situation caught up with her and she realized this surreal moment was her actual reality.

Air stopped moving through her lungs, and her shoulders started to quake as she mouthed a cry for help that never formed into sound. Her hand fluttered to her throat.

"Grace?"

"I can't…" She looked at him in utter panic and he rushed to her side. "Breathe."

"Let me help you." He took her hand and placed it on his chest. Heat rushed up her arm, and she tried to pull away. "Leave it."

Holding her stare, he unhooked his belt, intentionally stripping away his weapons. The leather and metal clattered to the floor and her shoulders jumped to her ears.

"Feel my heartbeat. Breathe with me."

Shallow gasps were all she could manage.

"You're fine. There's nothing to fear."

Her stare dropped to the blade on the floor. The scent of fresh blood clung to the metal.

"Eyes up here."

When she looked at him again, her lungs opened, and refreshing oxygen filled her chest.

"There. That's it. Follow my breathing. Deep breath in…"

His heart beat steadily against her palm, his chest expanding as he demonstrated how he wanted her to breathe. She mimicked him, and her nerves slightly settled.

"Good girl," he spoke softly. "Now let it out slowly."

Together, they exhaled, their breath mingling into a delicate breeze that teased across her skin. Feeling calmer, she studied the sharp angles of his face. Unlike the smooth skin of immortal males, his chiseled jaw wore a dark layer of stubble. His eyes were dark pools of moss and his skin a flawless olive tone. The flesh of his full lips was tanned and plump, a strangely delicate feature on such a masculine face.

"Another deep breath in."

She held his stare, matching his breathing until her racing heart slowed. A sense of safety enveloped her, and the tension in her arm relaxed.

His thumb dragged softly over the back of her hand where he held it to his broadly muscled chest. "That's it, *min pärla.*" His other hand reached for her face. Calloused fingers trailed over her cheek, tucking a loose hair behind her ear.

Her hand reached for her head, only to find her braids undone. "You took down my hair." No one, save her mother, had ever touched her hair.

His full lips firmed. "For your comfort. I took

no other liberties. I only removed the pins when I removed your wet clothes."

Her gaze dropped as heat rushed to her face. He caught her chin, forcing her to keep her eyes on him.

In that moment, he saw not only her fear but her ignorance. Shame for being so utterly unprepared sent tears rushing to her eyes. Did he expect her to do something?

Humiliation burned her face. "I don't know what you want."

"Isn't it clear? I've come all this way to find you. I merely want what is *mine*."

His claim settled around her like an invisible harness. He was taking her in. Gentling her. Building a foundation of trust and safety.

Her body shook, but she did not fight his closeness.

"I've come a long way to find you, Grace. I want to be patient with you, but..." The soft touch of his fingers trailed along her jaw. "There is the matter of..." His touch dropped away. "Business."

She frowned and pulled her hand away. "Business? Do you mean the bonding?"

"Yes. Now that I've found you, I find there to be..." He cleared his throat. "An urgent need inside of me that demands I claim you."

He moved quickly when she sprung to the corner, caging her in with his hulking body, casting shadows that further emphasized the differences in their size.

Too many emotions tumbled through her at once. All mates needed to consummate their calling with a bonding, and she knew what that meant. A blood exchange, intercourse, and then the mating was complete. But he was not like her or the other males she knew, so she had no idea what the expectations were.

"I don't know what you want."

He frowned, his long, hard body a distraction every time it brushed against hers. "Must I spell it out?"

"Must you stand so close?"

He chuckled. "No, but I want to." If it were possible, he shifted even closer and her breath hitched when the long length of his arousal pressed into her, hard like the hilt of a tool.

Woefully ignorant, her hands flattened on the wall at her back. "I've never done this before."

A slow grin curved his mouth as he shut his eyes and breathed in her scent. "Well..." He couldn't hide his male satisfaction. "I'm going to assume you were saving yourself for me."

The patch of smooth flesh showing from the open collar of his shirt bore a fresh scar, barely healed. She averted her gaze, looking lower where the long bulge formed in his pants. "You're hurt."

"It's nothing."

It wasn't *nothing*. She could scent the dried blood and his sweat from battle. "How did you know how to kill that thing in that cave?"

"I know many things. For instance, I know

you're nervous, maybe a little afraid, but you have nothing to fear, *min pärla.* Your mate is finally here and the long wait ends tonight." He lowered his mouth and she escaped his hold, darting to the other side of the room.

"Wait!"

He turned and laughed. "You're quite fast. And skittish?"

She was not skittish. She simply saw no need to rush. Breathing heavily again, she glanced at the table. "We should talk first."

"What would you like to know?" he navigated the furniture without ever taking his stare off of her as he closed in.

She mirrored his steps by circling the table, always keeping a furnishing between them. "You said you have brothers. What are their names?"

"Emmerich." He dragged a wooden chair over the planked floor, moving it out of his way. "Atticus." The shadow of his large body fell over her, and she danced backward, walking herself right into a corner. "Evander." He planted his hands on either side of her and pressed his nose to her neck, drawing in a deep, audible breath. "My gods, you smell incredible."

Her eyes widened when the bulge at his crotch intentionally pressed into her. "D-Darius..."

"Mmm, I like the way you say my name." His fingers went to the laces of her chemise, pulling the ribbon free. "Your shyness is more tempting than I expected."

The ribbon slipped free of her collar and fell to the floor. The fabric gaped open.

"So supple." He dragged a knuckle over the swell of her breast, touching her like no male had ever dared to touch her before. "The pleasure will please you, Grace. You must trust me on that."

She gasped as he cupped her possessively. "You're very forward."

"Certain things are inevitable, *min pärla.*" With his other hand, he reached for her hip, his palm sliding behind her possessively. "The sooner we complete the bond, the less you will have to fear."

She caught his wrist, her grip firm and unbreakable.

The corner of his mouth kicked up as the dark moss of his eyes was swallowed by black. "Are you denying me?"

Was she?

She wasn't a defenseless weakling. She could fight him off and outrun him. But he was her mate. Her gaze turned away in confusion. She felt her soul reaching for his as much as his physical body gravitated toward hers. The instinct was there, but her knowledge was lacking.

"I know what happens," she said. "But I do not know how it begins."

"I'll show you."

He traced her collarbone toward her shoulder, nudging the collar of her chemise down her arm. She grabbed her chest before he fully exposed her.

"For this to happen, I'll need to see all of you."

She wasn't used to being this exposed, but when he pulled her hand away from her chest, she didn't defy him.

Her chemise dragged down her shoulders and gathered at her arms, exposing her breasts to the cool air. Her nipples puckered and darkened under his intense stare.

"Once I've seen all of you, I'll kiss you. Here." His thumb dragged over her plump lower lip. "And here." His other hand cupped her breast possessively, plumping her flesh and massaging softly. "And here."

She whimpered as he cupped her sex.

He added pressure, wedging his hand between her clamped thighs where the material of her underclothes gathered. "There isn't any part of you that will be hidden from me, Grace. So there is no need for modesty between us. As mates, we are one. My body will act as your shield, my word as my pledge to protect you in all things."

Her body was made to glorify God's holy plan, in modesty and obedience. She had been taught to act in good stewardship to her mate, and surrender herself, trusting him to lead and protect her always.

According to The Order, the female body was a vessel created to redeem her mate's soul. She now had a duty to uphold. And once done, it could never be undone.

"I will not deny you." Her words shook.

She always imagined this intimate moment to be intense, but she'd assumed the wanting would guide her. There was no wanting now, only apprehension.

"That pleases me." He moved quickly, tugging her chemise lower and letting it fall to the floor. He glanced down at her body and exhaled. "Yes, I'm *very* pleased."

A sense of caution spiked inside of her as his earthy musk intensified. He reached for his pants but she caught his wrist. "Wait."

His eyes met hers in question and she swallowed.

"Will it hurt?"

His expression softened and he used his free hand to cup her cheek. "I'll always do everything in my power to save you pain, *min pärla*." His hand released the button of his pants, but then stopped, showing her he was in no rush. "I'm only making myself more comfortable."

She glanced down and quickly away. His clothing had certainly become more restrictive than it had been a moment ago. She didn't understand how something so hard and swollen could fit inside of her without pain.

Her brow pinched when she realized he hadn't exactly answered her question. He only said if there was any way to protect her from pain that he would.

This was discomforting news.

"There's no need to worry, Grace. I'll prepare your body, so there is little discomfort. But you have to let me touch you in order for that to happen."

She loosened her grip and he turned his hand, palm open in a show of gentleness. She didn't want it to hurt, so she had no choice but to trust him. When she released his wrist, he smiled.

"Very good, *min pärla*. You're very brave, and I appreciate your trust."

She closed her eyes and forced her hands to her side, presenting herself to him. First, he grazed her hips, sending chills over her belly and down her spine. Then he cupped her breasts as if measuring their weight in his large, calloused hands. Her nipples puckered as he dragged his thumb over the beaded tip and pinched.

"Ah," she gasped as pleasure and a strange awareness shot through her. It was not painful, but it also wasn't gentle. His touch traced down her spine, along the crease of her backside and she whimpered.

"Soften your knees." His voice whispered against her ear, gentle yet confident, making it easy to obey.

The moment her stance loosened, his hand pressed between her bare thighs, dragging up, upward until he cupped her possessively. This time there was no barrier of clothing between them.

"You're already preparing for me." His finger

parted her delicate folds, pressing inside her slick heat. Her breath hitched at the strange intrusion. She caught his shoulder for balance as he gently explored.

Her knees trembled. "Perhaps the bed..."

He paused and glanced over his shoulder. His touch disappeared. "You're right."

Taking her by the hand, he towed her toward the bed. She trembled like a leaf, but wanted to push past her fear.

There was no greater sacrament than the union of souls expressed between mates. She wanted to please him more than she desired any personal pleasure from the act. As the male, he would be the head of the household, and as the female, it was her duty to act as the heart.

Together, their hands would lift each other's sorrows. Her body would welcome his seed. And if God was pleased, He would bless them with many children. She found comfort and strength in such teachings, trusting God's plan to guide her so that she may fulfill her true purpose.

Glancing down at the bed, fully aware of her naked body as he watched her—still clothed—she took a deep breath. Lifting her chin, she faced him.

"I offer my body and full compliance so that your duty may be done."

He chuckled, the sound hitting like a wave of self-conscious doubt . "Grace, it is my duty but also my pleasure."

Was he mocking her? Her guard went up, but he caught her hand before she could turn away.

"My pleasure *and* yours."

"I don't like when you laugh at me," she told him. "I've never done this before."

"I'm sorry. Your words took me off guard." He smiled, but resisted the urge to laugh again. "I want a mate who thinks for herself and comes to my bed out of desire, not merely a sense of duty."

She scowled. "I'm quite capable of forming my own opinions, and I happen to have a lot of them."

"Good. I look forward to hearing them."

Her eyes narrowed at the hint of amusement in his eyes. "Why are you smirking?"

"I'm happy. I've waited a long time for this. What happens in this bed tonight... Don't cheapen it by labeling it like some burden. It is a blessing. Yes, we were called here by destiny, but I stand here by choice, not because of duty." He pulled her closer. "You're breathtaking."

Vanity was a form of pride she knew little about. "While your sentiment is flattering, it's also distracting."

This time his laughter escaped. "Sorry. Sorry." He glanced away and composed himself. "Sometimes distraction is good. What am I distracting you from? Your nerves? Your shyness? Your sense of obligation? If that's the case, then bring on the distractions."

"*I* have a duty to serve you, do I not? I do not

want to cloud my judgement with unnecessary emotions. This is a special night."

"Yes, it is a special night, which is exactly why I don't care about anything anyone else has told you. Here, in this cabin, it's only you and me that matter. I want to learn you, Grace, not control you."

"I have nothing to teach in this department. I'm ignorant."

He withdrew his touch and she swayed in confusion, bereft of his nearness the moment he stepped away. Could he not understand how difficult this might be for a female?

When he paced to the hearth and gripped the mantle, she asked, "Did I say something to disappoint you?"

He forked his fingers through his hair. "You did not disappoint me, no."

"But I've upset you?" She was making a mess of things.

"No, you did not upset me either."

"Then what? I told you I have no experience with these things. I've only been kissed—"

"Who kissed you?" His sharp stare pinned her in place, a dark, predatory gleam swirling in the black of his eyes.

Her voice abandoned her under the weight of fear. She backed up, but there was nowhere to go. When the bed hit her knees, she steadied herself but he was there, moving faster than she realized he could.

"Is there something you need to tell me?" He

towered over her, forcing her to arch backward until her shoulders touched the pillows. Their mouths were a mere inch apart.

She shook her head nervously, not trusting the territorial glare in his eyes. "N-no."

"I assumed you were innocent. Was I wrong?"

"No. You were correct." He didn't move, but the weight of his penetrating stare bore so heavily into her that she eased back until she lie stiffly beneath him on the bed.

His calloused fingers traced her lips. "Who kissed you, Grace?"

"It was nothing. A childish whim."

"When?"

"A long time ago," she lied.

His green eyes narrowed. "You're sure?"

Nodding, she blocked her mind for safe measure. "It meant nothing." Desperate to undo whatever she'd done, she reached for his hand with trembling fingers. "You're the only one who matters... D-Darius."

He studied her through a veil of suspicion that wasn't between them moments ago. A crease formed between his brows. "I find it inconvenient that we cannot see into each other's minds."

She found it relieving. "We will learn to trust each other."

He backed off and the chill of the room made her painfully aware that she was naked. Sitting up, she pulled her dark hair over her shoulders like a thin shelter. Though he didn't appear agitated, he did seem less sure of himself.

"You can trust me, Darius. I am yours."

"Mine…" he said the word with slow consideration, then his stare snapped to hers. "Show me how you were kissed."

Her heart plummeted. "What do you mean?"

She couldn't. She didn't want to deceive him, and she wanted to please him, but some part of her needed to protect her memories. They were all she had left of Dane. All there would ever be.

He closed the distance and pulled her to her feet. "Show me."

With labored breath, he stared down at her with pure determination. If she challenged him now, it would demean something later. She was sure of it. He needed to feel powerful. Denying him would cause the opposite.

Licking her lips, she said, "You will have to lean down."

He did, but kept his hands locked at his side. "Go ahead."

Rising on her toes, she pressed her mouth to the corner of his, brushing her lips softly over his, then pulling away. The spark of electricity that snapped between them was unexpected, but he seemed to feel it, too. She'd downplayed the kiss on purpose, but even for such a prudent gesture, there seemed an incredible amount of heat between them.

She lowered her gaze and looked away. "It was something like that."

He chuckled, the easy sound now welcomed after having a glimpse of his temper. "It seems I lost my temper for nothing. That was hardly a kiss." He cupped her cheeks, angling her face upward so she could see his smile. "You're very innocent," he whispered, voice once again pleased. His thumb traced her lower lip. "I wasn't expecting that, but I am glad it was nothing more."

"I told you I was inexperienced."

His grin stretched as promise danced in his green eyes. "Tomorrow, you won't be able to make such a claim."

Heat tugged low in her belly. He stirred a mixture of desire and fear in her that left no room for much else.

His hands lowered, loosely framing her neck. The contrast of his great strength and her delicate build was abundantly clear. Understanding passed between them. She might be faster, but he was bigger and could snap her like a twig.

"Let me show you what a real kiss is." His mouth lowered to hers before she could respond and her eyes widened.

She had no time to prepare as his tongue swept past her lips and he swallowed her startled moan. It was an unmistakable claim. He yanked her hips forward, slamming her body against his hard length, forcing her to feel the steel press of his arousal.

The kiss rapidly changed, taking over her senses and far surpassing anything she'd ever experienced with Dane. His hands were everywhere. Gripping her breasts and pinching in ways that sent little gasps from her mouth into his. He grabbed her backside, handling her with absolute entitlement as his hands pulled her flesh and his fingers explored private parts of her no one had dared to touch.

He swept her into his arms before she knew what was happening and deposited her back on the bed. "That's one."

"One?"

"One way I will kiss you."

The mattress dipped under his weight as he climbed over her. His nose dragged slowly along the side of her throat as he breathed her in. His teeth scraped below her jaw, and she gasped when his tongue licked a sensitive spot.

"I can also kiss you here." His breath teased the shell of her ear as he bit the lobe and tugged the fleshy edge. "Or here."

Startled by how much pleasure that little nibble caused, she gasped in surprise.

"And here." He cupped her breast, dragging his thumb over the turgid tip as his chin scraped past her collarbone. The stubble at his jaw abraded her delicate skin and sent chills through her body. She instinctively arched into his warmth and his touch turned even more possessive. "Is that what you want, *min pärla*?"

"I...I don't know."

"Sweet, innocent Grace, let's remedy that."

His head lowered, his hair falling forward and teasing her flesh as wet heat engulfed her nipple. Pressure tightened in her belly as he suckled the tip and groaned. That sound overwhelmed her senses and loosened a thousand knots of tension. Instinct took over and she reached for his shoulders, her hands sliding over his muscled back.

"Ah," she gasped as he plumped her breasts and moved to the other nipple. She'd seen mothers nursing and animals feeding, but never knew females could feel such pleasure from a male this way.

Warm breath shifted to wet heat. He moved to the other and cool air increased her sensitivity. The pressure inside of her built, bordering on pain, as he continued to suckle and pull. When he finally released her, the sensitive tips of her breasts were hard and swollen. Her breasts rosy from the chafe of his stubble.

He looked at her, his dark lashes low and his grin full of masculine pride, then he lowered his head and licked her, never taking his stare off her face. His knee nudged her legs apart and the heavy weight of his arousal pressed against her. He was still clothed, but she sensed he wished he wasn't. He ground his body against hers, pressing into her in a way that rocked her into the bed and forced her legs to open.

Although his pants formed a barrier between them, the strain of his cock was pronounced enough that there was little mystery to what he wanted next. She squirmed beneath him, a sense of need building, which she had no idea how to relieve.

He caught her hand and pressed it to the bulge. "Feel what you do to me."

Her eyes widened. Her fingers could hardly close around his girth, regardless of the way he was compressed in his clothes. "Does it hurt you?"

"No, but it makes it more difficult to take my time. And I want to take my time with you, Grace."

"I want that too." Or at least she thought she did. "What can I do to make things less difficult?"

He laughed. "If you touch me, it will only speed things up."

"Oh." She let go of him. "Then why did you put my hand on you?"

"To show you where you will kiss me." He thrust his hips and groaned. "But first, I want to be inside of you. I want that more than I want to live past dawn."

She could feel his wanting as much as she felt his struggle with restraint. He seemed to be more pained than in any sort of pleasure. "We don't have to wait—"

He kissed her mouth, his tongue gliding over hers possessively as his hand tangled in her hair, silencing her words. She surrendered to his lead as he crushed his body against her, grinding his hard length against her sex with enough promise to make the bed creak.

When he broke away, he was panting. His hungry stare traveled down her body as if he wanted to devour every inch of her. She fought the urge to cover herself, unsure what he intended.

"You're gorgeous."

His fingers trailed over her breasts, caressing the gentle slopes and teasing lower around her belly button. She instinctively sucked in a breath when his hand closed over hers.

"No." He pulled her fingers away. "Don't ever hide yourself from me." He trailed his touch between her legs, gliding back and forth until he parted her folds. "Open yourself to me."

Heaviness gathered at her core as she slowly forced her knees to widen.

"More."

Her face heated as he pressed his finger deeper. The intrusive pressure wasn't painful but it certainly wasn't anything she'd experienced before. Gentle strokes probed in and out as arousal slickened his knuckles. He penetrated her with careful progress, never pushing too hard or too fast. Although he was deep, his touch was incredibly gentle and controlled.

"This is where my body will connect with yours." He sank his touch deeper and held, the bone of his knuckle kissing her pelvis. "My cock will be much thicker, so I'll stretch you first to assure there is little pain. You want me to show you pleasure, right?"

With a shaky breath, she nodded, her deepest desire not to disappoint him in any way.

"Good." The pressure between her legs expanded as he fit another finger inside of her. "Does that hurt you?"

"No. I just feel…pressure. Heaviness. And hot."

He grinned. "Hot is good."

His touch withdrew only to surge forward again. He created a slow rhythm that built the way a bellows feeds a flame. Heat burned her skin the longer he touched, teasing a sensitive spot that caused her to stiffen.

He chuckled. "Did you feel something you liked?"

He grazed the spot again, and she gasped.

"There's one more kiss I want to show you." He trail his mouth down her stomach, and his mouth opened over that sensitive spot, and the pressure inside of her released like a cloud letting go of rain.

His finger continued to stroke and tease, nudging deeper but never sharply. A gentle haze softened the air around them as he kissed and nibbled her, every slow lick causing her to blush fiercely, but the pleasure was too great to ask him to stop. His lips closed over her and moaned as if she tasted sweeter than honeyed wine.

She sensed he'd reached a sort of barrier. "A bit of pain is a small price for the pleasure we'll experience tonight when we bond."

"I'm sorry?"

"So am I. This part will sting."

"What?" She gasped as the gentle teasing sharpened into something unpleasant, that thin barrier she'd sensed tearing away.

"Drink." His wrist was at her mouth the moment she tried to scoot away, and her fangs instinctively punctured the skin. Rich, earthy blood flooded her mouth and the pain subsided as her body rapidly healed from the slight injury.

He groaned and pressed his wrist tighter as his body caressing her everywhere they touched. "Keep drinking."

His head lowered and his mouth returned to kissing her intimately between her legs. The pain was now only a memory and when he thrust his fingers inside of her, her body was open to him in ways it wasn't before.

She drank hungrily, swallowing down his blood as she became accustomed to its robust flavor. The wet slide of his tongue skating over her flesh, teasing until she eagerly stretched and arched into him. She greedily cradled his wrist to her mouth, taking everything he offered as if drunk on lust and gluttony.

"That's it, *min pärla,* take all that you need from me." He pushed her thighs wider, making room for his broad shoulders.

Of all the kisses he'd shown her, this one was by far her favorite. He was very skilled and knew what touches felt nice and where she sensed the most pleasure.

A divot formed between her brow as she considered *how* he knew such things, but before she could dwell on such curiosities, he altered his touch and she moaned deeply, his tongue gently laving in a way that made her entire body tremble. He groaned against her, the masculine sound rich with satisfaction that made her preen with pride.

Faster, firmer, the friction built until another cloud of pleasure burst over her. She licked the bite at his wrist, and gasped, her breath panting as wave after wave of pleasure rushed over her.

"I think you're ready now."

"How can you tell?"

"Feel," he said, pulling her fingers between her legs. He slipped his finger inside of her effortlessly. Then another. Their entwined touch wet with arousal.

"*Ah,*" she gasped as he stretched her channel, to distracted by the pleasure to mind the pressure. Her hand fell away as he pressed his fingers deeper, folding his hand to fit all four.

A low chuckle escaped his throat. "Deep breath, *min pärla.*"

She held his stare, breathing in. The pressure became more than she could bear. "I can't."

"You can. Think of everything your body can do, Grace. It was designed to bear children. I promise you can tolerate so much more than this."

She gripped the bedding. There was no pain, only pressure, but it was a lot to bear. Her desire to please him made it tolerable, and slowly, she found the pleasure again.

"Almost there." He stretched her some more, until she could hardly move under the intrusion. "That's it, *min pärla.* Show me what you're capable of. Make me proud."

His words bathed her in a sense of encouragement. Her body opened under his praise.

"Ahhh," she cried out as his hand sank into her. She couldn't move, couldn't breathe. She feared she might split in two, but then she looked into his eyes and saw his absolute possession of her, his pride and satisfaction, and tears rushed to her eyes as she gasped out a sigh of relief.

"Beautiful."

The pressure disappeared as he withdrew his touch and turned away. She shivered in shock, her body still adapting to so many shifts. Her eyes closed as she caught her breath, flinching when the mattress dipped and he was above her once more.

"Easy, love. Now I show you how it's done."

He tugged her lower, arranging her body beneath his. The velvet-smooth weight of his cock glided over her. Gone were the barriers of clothing as the mating was about to happen.

"I promise there will be no more pain." He aligned his body with hers, gliding his length through her folds and then nudging slowly forward. This time it was not his fingers trying to breach her. Her breath hitched at his startling girth.

"Breathe, Grace."

She inhaled, and he nudged deeper. Pulling back, then sliding closer and closer.

"There are some things you should know, things your mother might not have prepared you for." He caught her hand, first lacing his fingers with hers, then raising it over her head and pressing it into the pillows.

Dragging back his hips with slow, precision, he nudged deeper still. He placed her second hand above her head, beside the first, then crossed her wrists and pinned them there. He thrust forward and groaned, burying himself to the hilt, and she quickly became accustomed to the strange intrusion only to have him draw back and thrust forward again.

Each time he slowly pulled back, she feared their bodies would disconnect, but then he'd slam into her, deep and possessive, as if he wanted to mark her from the inside. Every hard advance wrenched a cry of pleasure from her throat. It gradually built as she became accustomed to the rhythm, eagerly awaiting his dominant possession.

"Shadow-wolves are different from immortals. When we mate, our bodies do something called knotting. Has anyone told you about this?"

She shook her head, finding it difficult to concentrate on his words. The weight of his body pressed into her wrists where he still held her down.

"You have to trust me, Grace. Can you do that?"

In her current predicament, she didn't have much of a choice. "Yes."

"Good girl." He bent forward and rewarded her with a loving kiss that soothed her nerves. When his mouth left her lips, it traveled right to her breasts. He suckled the tips of her nipples harder than before, releasing each one with a wet pop. "You're body's very responsive to my touch. That pleases me."

She preened under his praise. "I want to please you. Very much."

"You are, *min pärla*. You are." He thrust hard, his pelvis grinding into hers as he held himself deep inside of her. "Here it comes," he warned.

His length noticeably swelled inside of her. She inhaled sharply. She was full, pinned beneath his weight, impaled by his length, and something was locking them together. "What's happening?"

"It's as I told you. The knotting. Breathe through it, and your body will adjust."

She couldn't move. They were one. He held her completely at his mercy.

Leaning forward, he kissed her gently, breaking away as a guttural groan escaped his throat and his head tipped back. His muscular body shivered as his rigid cock pulsed inside of her.

His grip tightened on her arms as his seed filling her. He tried to thrust, but there was little give with their bodies knotted as they were so they merely rocked as one. When he pinched her nipple, all the pressure inside of her burst outward in a wash of white light.

She gasped as waves of pleasure spilled over her. He jerked her forward, claiming her mouth with a possessive kiss. She felt small and cherished, cradled in his arms and protected by his strength. Then he sagged into her, his face nuzzling into the curve of her shoulder with a satisfied sigh.

She tried to move but he stilled her efforts.

"You can't," he said, trailing a hand down her arm. "The knotting will last for some time, so my seed can take root."

"We're stuck like this?"

He chuckled. "It's not a bad way to pass time." His nuzzled her ear and whispered, "We're far from finished, Grace. Maybe immortals are done in an hour, but wolves are not." He rolled to his back and took her with him.

Every movement caused a response inside of her. They were locked together, his body swollen to the point that she felt his absolute, undeniable possession of her.

He adjusted her knees, positioning her the way one might mount a horse. His hand flattened over her soft belly just beneath her ribs. "Do you feel me here?"

She shivered, her breath slightly unsteady. "I feel you everywhere."

"What about here?" He dragged his touch lower, strumming his thumb over the tiny bud of her sex and she gasped. He smirked. "You like when I touch you here."

"Yes..."

He pulled her hips forward then pushed her back, so that she rocked over him. "Move like this, Grace. Can you do that for me?"

She concentrated on repeating the motion as

his fingers teased her, rubbing and pressing until she was eagerly rocking into him.

"That's it." He bucked his hips, lifting them slightly off the bed.

She lurched forward, clutching his chest for balance.

"Yes, lean into me. I've got you."

Reminded of how deeply he was embedded inside of her body, she believed he was right.

"We're truly one, now, Grace. No one else will ever know you as intimately as I." He continued to tease that pleasant little bud and pleasure built like a combustible flame inside of her. She closed her eyes, rocking as the building pressure consumed her.

"Let it out." He rubbed faster, applying more pressure and she practically screamed at the sweet release.

He bucked his hips. Pulling her onto his chest and holding her tightly as he pounded upward. She surrendered to his hold, allowing him this moment to use her body as he liked so that she could process the aftershocks of pleasure. Little tingles of sensation teased her everywhere. Her knees, her spine, and even her skull. There was no single place on her body that she did not feel him.

His wild bucking eventually slowed and they simply lay together in the aftermath of so many new feelings. He brushed her tangled hair away from her face.

"You okay in there?" he teased, trying to work

his way through her messy waves. She was going to have a vicious time combing through such knots.

"I'm lovely," she purred.

The pressure had turned into decadent pain and then—nothing. Though the knotting subsided, she was at ease with him buried inside of her. Weightless and hollow, floating in the ether of some unknown plane far above the clouds but still safely in his arms.

His chuckle was expected. "Good. Then we can do it again."

Awareness slammed into her as he toppled her onto her back, his hips rutting hard and fast as he pumped into her with relentless speed. The pleasure returned and would not abate as he pushed her higher and higher.

She was a raindrop far above the earth falling into infinity. She never wanted to land. She only wanted this…this…this endless nothingness of euphoric bliss.

Her mind went blank until only her subconscious existed amongst the rainbow of pleasant sensations beaming through her. No pain. No worry. Only pleasure and a sense of true belonging.

She was a passenger. Free of thought and clear of any pressure to make decisions. He had total control.

She smiled against his lips as he softly kissed her. It was as if they'd kissed this way a thousand times before.

She reveled in his possessive hold, comforted by his unbending claim. Her mate had finally come for her. She was his and he was hers. Together, they were all either of them would ever need. She eagerly looked forward to becoming his everything.

Body relaxed, she welcomed the sense of completeness and sighed.

My Dane...

Her eyes snapped open, and she stiffened. *Darius.* Her mate was Darius.

He slowly pulled his mouth away and looked down at her with dark, lustful eyes. "You're beyond my expectations, *min pärla.*"

Her heart thumped hard, and her mouth formed a hollow hole around empty words. She failed to think of *anything* to say back to him, fearful the wrong words might come out.

He tucked a strand of hair behind her ear. "How do you feel?"

Deceitful... Disloyal... Confused...

Any one of those answers would have been true, but instead of giving her mate the truth, she forced an artificial smile on her numb face and said, "I feel like I'm finally where I was always meant to be."

"Me too." He kissed her again, briefly, and smiled, but it didn't reach his eyes. His gaze skated away as though he had more to tell her, but he said nothing.

She had the strangest suspicion that he hid something, something he didn't want her to know. As someone who had always been able to overhear others' darkest thoughts, it seemed odd to have a mate who was a closed book to her. But secrets were slippery little things, and the truth always slid out eventually.

Curiosity sparred with exhaustion as Grace debated how much she wanted to know what he was hiding. Their mutual withholdings formed and invisible wall between them. Or was that hers? Her mind once again returned to Dane and guilt soured her stomach. She should not be thinking of him now, especially here, in this intimate moment with her mate.

The weight of her deceit curled around her divided heart like barbed wire, tightening with every silent breath. Guilt seeded the secrets, growing into a terrible pressure that internally pushed and pulled her heart in opposing directions. The ache of division became so all-consuming, she found it hard to swallow or breathe.

"Grace?" Noticing something was wrong, Darius framed her face and studied her, concern tightening his brow.

It was then that the finality of this moment settled in, and she knew it would always be him and never Dane. She'd said it all along but never truly felt it until right now.

Those barbed roots tightened another degree, forming a shell around her heart. She wasn't simply keeping a secret—she was withholding her heart from the one person meant to have it.

She knew, with bone-deep certainty, there

could be no going back. She could never see Dane, out of respect to her mate. It was her duty to banish him from her mind and force him out of her heart.

"I'm sorry," she whispered, faking composure she did not feel. "I was just overwhelmed by the moment."

"That's understandable."

She forced a smile, but her jaw trembled. "Did you have something you wanted to tell me?"

His gaze skittered away, looking anywhere but in her eyes. She thought he would lie and say nothing. She thought this wall of secrets between them would remain two-sided. But, instead, his brow hardened, and he looked at her with hard determination.

"Actually, I do have something I need to tell you. It's probably best I prepare you now, regarding my expectations and the pack's."

The End
For now...

ALSO BY LYDIA MICHAELS

BOOKS BY SERIES

Many First in series books are FREE

Grab them here!

MCCULLOUGH MOUNTAIN

Almost Priest

Beautiful Distraction

Irish Rogue

British Professor

Broken Man

Controlled Chaos

Hard Fix

Intentional Risk

JASPER FALLS

Wake My Heart

The Best Man

Love Me Nots

Pining For You

My Funny Valentine

Side Squeeze

CALAMITY RAYNE

Calamity Rayne Gets a Life

Calamity Rayne Back Again

Calamity Rayne Gets Hitched

BONUS: Calamity Rayne Veiled & Railed

Calamity Rayne Over the Moon

Calamity Rayne Knocked Up

THE SURRENDER TRILOGY

Falling In

BreakingOut

Coming Home

Ruthless Billionaires

One Billion Secrets

Two Billion Enemies

MASTERMIND

Blind

Untied

NEW CASTLE

First Comes Love

If I Fall

Shattered Vows

ADDICTED TO YOU

Crush

Bang

Throb

THE ORDER OF VAMPIRES

Original Sin

Dark Exodus

Prodigal Son

Immortal Bastard

Primal Kill

Blood Moon

STAND ALONES

La Vie en Rose

Simple Man

Sugar

Breaking Perfect

Hurt

Protege

ABOUT THE AUTHOR

To receive Lydia's Newsletter and receive a FREE Book CLICK HERE!

Lydia Michaels is the bestselling and award-winning author of more than forty novels. She writes heart-clenching, unpredictable romance with dark elements and high heat. Her work is character-driven and bursting with broken heroes and badass females. With a sweet spot for overbearing, territorial types, her deeply emotional books are spicy, emotionally satisfying, and guaranteed to leave readers with many book hangovers.

Lydia is the consecutive winner of the *2018 & 2019 Author of the Year Award* from *Happenings Media* and the recipient of the *2014 Best Author Award* from the Courier Times. She has been featured by *USA Today, Romantic Times Magazine,* the *Women in Publishing Summit,* and more.

Michaels started her author career in 2007 and has become a recognized presence and advocate within the publishing industry. She is the CEO of LMC Consulting, a certified author coach specializing in character and plot development, and the founder of the *East Coast Author Convention*, the *Behind the Keys Author Retreat*, and <u>www.LydiaMichaelsBooks.com</u>.

She is happily married to her childhood sweetheart. Her favorite things include cooking Italian cuisine, hosting extravagant dinner parties, sipping espresso martinis, listening to her husband play piano, and escaping to her coastal home on the Jersey Shore. She's an LGBTQ ally, a BLM supporter, a firm believer that the patriarchy must end (women's rights are human rights), and an advocate for pediatric cancer research.

L Y D I A

Follow Lydia Michaels on social media!
Facebook | Instagram | TikTok

THANK YOU FOR YOUR REVIEW!

Reviews help authors so much! If you left a review for this book, I greatly appreciate it!
Thank you,
Lydia

Click HERE to return to Amazon.

www.ingramcontent.com/pod-product-compliance
Lightning Source LLC
Chambersburg PA
CBHW061529190726
48289CB00004B/985